MINDBOUND

A Starstruck Novel

BRENDA HIATT

dolphin star
PRESS

Mindbound

A Starstruck Novel

Copyright 2023 by Brenda Hiatt
Cover art by Ravven Kitsune

All rights reserved
This is a work of fiction. Any resemblance between actual events or persons, living or dead, are purely coincidental.

License Notes
This ebook is licensed for your personal enjoyment only. This ebook may not be re-sold or given away to other people. If you would like to share this book with another person, please purchase an additional copy for each recipient. Thank you for respecting the hard work of this author.

Dolphin Star Press

ISBN: 978-1-947205-39-0

Dedication

For everyone making their way back to a better place.

Preface

AN INTRODUCTION TO NUATHAN
HISTORY, 86TH EDITION

(BASIC CURRICULUM TEXT—USE IN PLACE OF PREVIOUS
EDITIONS)

Overview

Nuath's true origins have been lost in the mists of time. However, it is generally believed that nearly three thousand years ago, a technologically advanced alien race created the underground cavern on Mars with its Earth-like environment. The aliens then transplanted the inhabitants of a small Earth village to this cavern, in order to conduct genetic and social experiments on their captives. As the human population increased from a few hundred to many thousands, the habitat was gradually expanded to its present size. Then, approximately one thousand years after establishing this underground Martian laboratory, the aliens departed for reasons unknown, leaving no record of their nature or their future plans.

Without their alien overlords, the abandoned community, by then known as Nuath, continued to evolve on its own. By necessity, a system of government emerged, the earliest leaders chosen from among the most gifted colonists. This led to the formation of the first documented *fine*, or bloodline, which diverged a few generations later into the Royal and Science *fines*. Most of Nuath's governing body is still drawn from those two bloodlines. Meanwhile, increasing specialization of various skill-sets led to the rise of numerous other *fines*. There are currently no fewer than ten major *fines*, most now containing multiple sub-*fines*.

As the colonists learned to use and adapt technology left behind by their alien abductors, they were able to advance scientifically to the point of building and launching spacecraft of their own. 524 years ago, under Sovereign Arturo, Nuathans first visited their nearest neighbor, Earth, and discovered it was their planet of origin. More expeditions followed, with small groups of Nuathans occasionally emigrating to Earth despite the harsher conditions found there. Those earliest *Echtrans*, or expatriate Martians, are believed to have sparked Earth's Renaissance period. To facilitate communication, Nuath eventually adopted the calendar and measurement system of Earth's Ireland, home of the first real *Echtran* outpost. Because the planet remained socially and technologically backward by Nuathan standards, it was early decided to keep emigrants' origins and abilities secret from their Earth (or *Duchas*) neighbors.

Safely concealed on Mars, Nuath remained peaceful and prosperous, if not perfect, until approximately twenty years ago, when the ambitious upstart Faxon began sowing discord, stirring up resentment in the less-prestigious *fines* against the Royals and Scientists. In time, Faxon gathered enough support to stage a coup, deposing and then assassinating Sovereign Leontine and his wife. A general purge of the Royal bloodline followed, though some survived Faxon's depredations by fleeing to Earth. Among those were Leontine's son, Mikal, with his wife and infant daughter.

The majority of Nuathans, even those who had helped Faxon rise to power, were horrified by his excesses. As his support waned, Faxon resorted to intimidation and repression to maintain control. Fearing Mikal and his family could become a rallying point for the fledgling Resistance movement, Faxon sent a few loyal adherents to Earth with orders to eliminate them. When word came back that the last of the Sovereign line had been killed, most Nuathans were thrown into despair. Rebellion having been largely bred out of the early colonists, the Resistance faltered and would have failed but for the efforts of a few Royals, most notably the O'Gara family, who obscured their origins to remain on Mars and rally their people's spirits, restoring to them a measure of hope.

This hope was greatly bolstered when Nuathans learned that the last of Sovereign Leontine's line had not, in fact, perished. The news that his granddaughter, Princess Emileia, had been discovered alive on Earth galvanized the Resistance, allowing them to finally cast off the yoke of Faxon's oppression and remove him from power.

Afterward, Nuathan society began to rebuild itself, striving for an eventual return to its former prosperity and security. This was helped along by the return of the Princess, soon to be Acclaimed Sovereign Emileia. Nuath's recovery now continues under Regent Shim, only slightly hampered by the recent discovery of the colony's near-depleted power reserves.

Though Nuath's Scientists are currently working to extend the power supply, the situation has necessitated accelerated emigration of the colony's populace to Earth, to conserve resources. To encourage voluntary emigration, Sovereign Emileia herself has returned to Earth, where she and the *Echtran* Council have overseen the resettlement of the first wave of those who heeded the call to relocate for the good of Nuath.

Shortly after the Sovereign's return to Earth, our original alien founders returned to this solar system with the apparent intent of disabling all of Earth's technology. Thankfully, that catastrophe was averted by a heroic collaboration between *Echtran* Scientists and Sovereign Emileia. It is hoped no further interference by those aliens, now known as the Grentl, will hamper the progress Nuath's people are now making, both on Mars and on Earth.

The most recent development as of this writing has been the discovery of a second heir to the Sovereign line. An apparent Agricultural *fine* foundling, adopted as an infant by the aforementioned O'Gara family, was proven to in fact be Princess Malena, fraternal twin to Sovereign Emileia, hidden before birth to safeguard her from Faxon's depredations. Her role in Nuath's future is yet to be determined.

Stress factors

"TRY to really relax this evening if you can," Rigel says, turning into the long driveway of his family's big yellow farmhouse. "You've been under a lot of stress lately, with so much Sovereign stuff to deal with. You're allowed to take a break for your birthday party."

I smile over at him, struck yet again by how lucky I am to have such a great—and impossibly gorgeous—guy as my bonded soulmate.

"I'm sorry, Rigel. I know you pick up on everything I feel, and that stresses *you* out. There are just so many more balls I have to keep in the air these days. I'm getting a little better at juggling them, but I'm scared if I fumble one I'll bring everything crashing down."

He pulls to a stop in front of the house and puts a hand over mine. "You won't, but I get why you worry, you always have so much going on at once. I wish I could help more."

"You help just by being here." I put a grateful hand on his cheek. "At least I only have the Earth elections to deal with, now that the ones on Mars are over—and Shim did most of the work on those. Among other things, that means they can finally start Faxon's trial back in Nuath."

The usurper Faxon was ousted from power and imprisoned more than a year ago, but they couldn't try him for his crimes until a full judicial panel was seated after the recent elections.

"About time! Though it's just a formality, right?" Rigel asks. "If anyone deserves the full mind-wipe, he does."

I can't disagree, since Faxon's the reason I don't have parents or grandparents. "Definitely, but they still have to follow the steps laid out in Martian law."

"You won't have to testify, will you?" Rigel frowns in sudden concern. "Like you did for Allister's and Lennox's trials?"

"No, I was way too young to remember any of the awful things he did before I left Mars. Seriously, Rigel, I'm doing okay. Anyway, you have enough to worry about without adding my stuff to it."

He shoots me an incredulous glance. "Me? I don't have a fraction as much to worry about as you do. You can totally unload on me whenever you want."

"Thanks, but I was thinking about Shim," I clarify. "Has your dad heard anything yet?"

Shim, Rigel's grandfather and my Regent back on Mars, was scheduled to have a minor medical procedure early this morning. Supposedly routine, but because Shim is one of the oldest Martians alive at nearly three hundred years old, we can't help being concerned.

"Not as of when I left," Rigel admits, some of the anxiety he'd been suppressing leaking out enough for me to feel it. "Dad insists it's a simple surgery, though, so I'm sure everything is fine."

"I'm sure it is. Anyway, there's no point borrowing trouble, as you constantly remind me."

"Does that mean it's finally sinking in, I hope?" he asks with a grin. "Good. Because today's all about you having fun, birthday girl!"

Unbuckling his seatbelt, he turns toward me, that special light in his hazel eyes. "Looks like none of our friends are here yet. Nice. Let's take advantage—" he begins when two more cars turn into the driveway behind us.

"Oops," I mutter, as disappointed as he is to be cheated of a chance to make out. Again. We get *way* too few opportunities these days, between all my duties and everyone harping about "appearances."

We have to settle for a quick kiss before stepping out into the chilly evening air. There's still a dusting of snow on the ground from last week. I hope that'll be the last of it, now that it's March.

I turn to greet my longtime *Duchas* friends Bri and Deb, their *Echtran* boyfriends Liam and Lucas, then my sister Molly and her boyfriend Tristan. As we all start toward the house, Sean and Kira drive up, so we wait for them before going up the porch steps.

"Looks like the gang's all here," Rigel says lightly, hiding his lingering frustration at the interruption.

"Yep," Molly cheerfully agrees, hugging me. "Happy birthday, M!"

She and I only learned we're sisters a few months ago, and Bri and Deb are the only non-Martians at school I've told. The other *Duchas* only know Molly as the O'Garas' adopted daughter and Sean's sister.

Of course, I've only known who *I* really am for a year and a half. Up till the start of my sophomore year of high school, I thought of myself as a misfit orphan loser, being reluctantly raised by my equally clueless "aunt" and "uncle." It was quite a shock to learn I was actually a princess, heir to the Martian throne.

The others echo Molly's birthday greeting as we follow Rigel into the house. I thank them all, determined to forget my pesky Sovereign duties for a few hours and pretend I'm just a regular high school girl celebrating her seventeenth birthday with friends.

Unfortunately, that resolve is tested the moment I walk into the Stuarts' big living room. Rigel's parents are here, of course, but so are Mr. and Mrs. O'Gara and Tristan's mom, Teara Roark—almost half the *Echtran* Council. I didn't expect that, after last night's lengthy Council meeting—one reason my party got pushed to Sunday evening.

"Happy birthday, Excellency." Mr. O'Gara bows deeply with his right fist over his heart. He's not technically on the Council, but attends most meetings with his wife, who is. "May the coming year be your best yet, both personally and for our people."

I sigh inwardly. I've repeatedly asked him *not* to be so formal during social occasions, but he apparently can't help himself. At least the other adults refrain from bowing as they repeat his birthday wishes.

"Thanks, everyone," I reply after an almost-awkward pause. "And thanks for letting Rigel host my party here, Dr. and Mr. Stuart."

At that, Mrs. O'Gara clears her throat. "Perhaps this isn't the best time, Excellency, but we were just discussing an item from last night's meeting, and—"

"How about we give M a break from the business stuff today, so she can enjoy her party," Rigel breaks in firmly.

I give Rigel a grateful smile as Mrs. O and the other adults sheepishly agree. He really does try to take good care of me. I should let him do it more often.

After that, the grownups retreat to the kitchen, where they'll probably talk about stuff I'd rather not think about right now. At least I won't hear them. Once they're gone, it feels more like a party. Molly pours out lemonade and sodas for everyone, Rigel puts on music and the couples start to disperse around the spacious living room.

"Your house is so perfect for entertaining, Rigel," my longtime best friend Bri comments. "Remember what a mob scene your last birthday party was, M? I said then you should've had it here—though I guess that would have been awkward at the time."

True. A year ago everyone, both *Duchas* and Martian, thought I was dating Sean O'Gara, thanks to a deal I made with the *Echtran* Council. Definitely an awkward situation. Especially for Rigel, since most people assumed I'd dumped him for Sean.

You know I don't hold that against you, he sends telepathically, picking up on my thought. *How could I, when that deal saved my life?*

He's right, it did, but I hated putting him through that.

"All this space is almost wasted with so few of us here," Bri continues, "though I guess if you invited everyone from school they'd want to know why you're having your party today instead of next weekend."

Also true. The birthday I grew up celebrating—the one on my fake birth certificate and my new driver's license—is a week later than my actual birth date.

"Not to mention all the stuff we couldn't talk about, with a bunch of people here who don't know about…you know," I remind Bri. In other words, about all of us genetically enhanced humans from a super-secret, technologically advanced underground colony on Mars.

"Yeah, good point," Bri concedes. "Though you could have invited some other Martians, er, *Echtrans*. Like Alan."

Liam, Bri's boyfriend, throws an arm around her shoulders. "I did invite him. He claimed he had something else going on, but I think he mostly didn't want to come solo when the rest of us are couples."

"He also still gets embarrassed around Molly because of the way he treated her before anyone knew she was my sister." I glance over to where she and Tristan are chatting with Deb and Lucas, Liam's identical twin brother.

"Yeah, that makes sense," Bri says. "It would've sucked if Alan brought Trina as a date!"

Rigel and Liam laugh, but I give an exaggerated shudder. "No kidding!" I agree. "Talk about someone guaranteed to spoil a party."

Trina, head cheerleader and all-around mean girl, has always hated me. Since second grade, I've been her favorite target for all kinds of petty nastiness. She's had a crush on Alan since he took her to Winter

Formal—my fault, for foolishly suggesting Molly and Tristan nudge him her way, to test their newly-enhanced persuasive power. It worked a little *too* well, but Alan fortunately came to his senses and broke up with her before things went too far.

"One reason I wanted this party to be just us," I continue, "was so we could talk about, y'know, bond stuff."

Bri and Liam suck in a startled breath and look at each other. "Did you—?" they simultaneously say, then break off with nervous laughs.

"No, neither of you told me," I assure them. "Neither did Deb or Lucas. But I've noticed things these past several weeks since you started dating and figured it was time to bring it out into the open. Well, not *open*, open—just with the other six of us here. We've all learned sort of a lot about bonds by now."

Bri giggles nervously. "I guess that wouldn't include Alan, then—much less Trina."

"Um, no." I don't even want to *think* about Trina developing super powers! If anyone would use them for evil, it would be her.

Turning, I motion to the others to join us. Clearly curious, they all move our way.

"What's up?" Sean asks. "News?"

"Not news, just something I've been wanting to talk about with you all. Especially Bri and Deb and Liam and Lucas."

Those four suddenly radiate nervousness I can pick up without trying.

"Did we do something we shouldn't have?" Lucas asks.

"No, not at all," I quickly reassure him. "It's nothing you could have helped anyway. I'm right, aren't I, that the four of you have started noticing certain…changes since you got together?"

Cautiously, they all nod.

"I have to work a lot harder now to hold back during basketball games," Liam volunteers. "Like being with Bri has sort of amped me up or something."

I grin. "I'm sure it has. Bri and Deb also seem more confident and, well, prettier since you all started dating."

"My hair's the best it's ever been," Deb agrees.

Bri nods. "Mine, too! I also seem to learn Chorus stuff a lot quicker than I used to. I read faster, too."

"Same," Deb says. "The Chorus director's actually talking about moving me to the front row, my dancing has improved so much."

Lucas looks thoughtful. "I made two pretty big breakthroughs on my energy project at NuAgra last week. It's like I can see the whole picture better than I could before. Do you really think it means—?"

"That you've developed—or are developing—*graell* bonds?" I finish for him. "I think maybe you are, even though Bri and Deb aren't *Echtran*. That would sure surprise our Scientists...if we tell them. Which is totally up to you guys, of course."

Deb tilts her head to one side, her brow furrowed. "Do you think we should?"

"Not if it'll put Deb—or Bri—at risk." Lucas puts a protective arm around Deb. "Remember what happened a few weeks back?"

We all nod. A few rogue *Echtrans* were so upset to learn my *Duchas* friends had been told about us Martians that they kidnapped Bri and Deb from a basketball game. If the Walsh twins, with some help from Rigel and me, hadn't found them in time, they might have been killed.

"I didn't mean I'd announce it in our weekly broadcast or anything," I quickly clarify. "The only bond *all* our people know about is Rigel's and mine—and not everything about that. Nobody knows about Molly and Tristan's, or Sean and Kira's, except the *Echtran* Council and a few Scientists."

My non-Martian friends stare at the other two couples.

"Wait. You guys have *graell* bonds, too?" Bri demands, then turns an accusing look on me. "You never told us that."

I shrug. "It wasn't my secret to tell. Especially since school is practically the only place we see each other these days."

Until Rigel arrived in Jewel at the start of our sophomore year, Bri and Deb and I did everything together. Now that we all have boyfriends...not so much.

"Our bonds won't be secret long, if Gwendolyn Gannett finds out about Nara's research and blabs on her show," Molly comments sourly. "I'm glad we agreed in advance to only let the Scientists test the more obvious stuff, not our, um, *special* abilities."

"We had to let them test our telekinesis." Sean's still not happy about that. "Since you and Molly told the Council about it."

I wince. "Yeah, sorry. We kind of had to, after they started remembering how we got rid of that Ossian Sphere. But you held back during those tests, right?"

"We just levitated some ping pong balls for them," Kira confirms.

"Nothing big or heavy. And I never even mentioned how my Ag abilities have improved."

"Or that I finally developed Royal 'push,'" Sean adds with a grin. That persuasive power is relatively common, though definitely not universal, among those in the Royal *fine*. "Of course it's nowhere near as strong as Molly's. Or yours."

Supposedly the more closely someone's related to the Sovereign line, the more powerful their "push." But since Molly and Tristan bonded, their combined power to convince people to go along with whatever they suggest has become almost scary. We all agreed they should keep *that* particular talent secret, even from the Council.

"Anyway," I say to the Walsh brothers, "it's completely up to you guys whether you want to let *any* other *Echtrans*, including your parents, know you've—"

I break off at the strains of "Happy Birthday" coming from the hallway. A moment later Dr. Stuart walks in, bearing a cake with lit candles. Rigel's dad and the other adults come in behind her. As Rigel's mom sets the cake on the coffee table, Molly and Rigel nudge me forward and I suddenly flash back to my sixteenth birthday party again.

Then, it was Sean urging me to blow out my candles—because we had to play along with the fiction that he was my boyfriend. All Rigel and I could do was send yearning thoughts to each other. Now, I smile over at Kira, hand in hand with Sean.

Their happiness together finally absolved me of the helpless guilt I felt during all those months when Sean made it clear he wanted our pretend relationship to become a real one. Which of course was impossible, since I was irrevocably in love with—and bonded to—Rigel. Still, because I had to play along in public, it sometimes felt like I was leading Sean on, even though I had no choice.

Picking up on my uncomfortable memory, Rigel puts an arm around me, bringing me back to the much-better present. I give him a quick smile, then take a deep breath and blow out the candles. *My wish is that we'll never have to go through anything like that again*, I silently tell him.

We won't, Rigel thinks back. *Even the traditionalists are starting to accept that we're together. For good.*

For good. I like the sound of that. Not just the idea of being together permanently, but that our love commitment, our bond, will always be for the good of both our people and ourselves.

I've barely started handing out slices of lemon cake when Mr. Stuart's omni pings.

"Ah, finally!" he exclaims, glancing at the screen. "I expected—" He breaks off with a frown.

"What is it?" I feel a trickle of foreboding. "Is it from Shim?"

He shakes his head. "Not from him, about him. The message is from the head Healer on Nuath. Apparently there was a...complication during Shim's surgery."

My trickle of foreboding becomes a rivulet. "Complication?"

"Is he okay?" Rigel asks at the same time. "He's not—?"

"He's alive, and expected to fully recover," his father quickly reassures us. "But he's still unconscious, and will need to stay in the Healing facility for at least several more days. Perhaps longer."

Council member Teara Roark, Tristan's mother, speaks up. "Unconscious? That makes Ewan Lloyd the Acting Regent, correct?"

"For the moment." Mr. Stuart looks back at his omni screen. "They're still trying to work out exactly what went wrong. All of the instruments are undergoing diagnostics to determine whether there was some sort of mechanical failure."

"Is that likely?" I ask. "I thought Shim was in Nuath's premier Healing facility, attended by the best Healer in the colony."

"He is," Mr. Stuart confirms. "So no, I wouldn't think it likely. But it makes sense to explore every possibility." Tucking his omni back in his pocket, he gives me an apologetic smile. "I'm sorry if this has put a damper on your party, Excellency."

I shake my head. "Hardly your fault. I've been nearly as anxious to hear about Shim as you have." My glance encompasses Rigel and his mom, too. "I'm just glad to hear he's expected to recover. You'll let me know if anything changes?"

"Of course. Meanwhile, let's all have some of that delicious-looking cake, shall we?"

The party resumes after that, but the news about Shim has cast a definite pall over the previously festive mood. People are starting to make noises about going home when Mr. Stuart gets another call.

"It's from Kyna," he tells us all in surprise. "Just a moment."

He sets the omni on the table and an instant later a holographic image of Council leader Kyna appears in the room with us. Her expression is grave.

"Excellency, I must apologize for being the bearer of bad news, on this of all days," she tells me with a bow. "But I've just received information I must pass along without delay. I understand you've already been told about the Regent's condition?"

We all nod.

"I'm afraid there is now reason to believe the complication with Shim's surgery was not an accident," Kyna continues. "At least, I cannot believe it is coincidence that at the very same hour Regent Shim was incapacitated, the deposed dictator Faxon unexpectedly—and inexplicably—escaped."

2

Reaction formation

I STARE DISBELIEVINGLY at Kyna's image. "Escaped?" I echo. "How? Wasn't he being held in the most secure prison in Nuath?"

"Yes. Until yesterday, when he was transferred, sedated and under guard, to Nuath's main Mind Healing facility. They were to perform a memory extraction in advance of his long-delayed trial, which was to begin next week. As of yet," Kyna continues, "I've been provided no theories as to how his escape was effected, but I would imagine he had help from someone. Possibly several someones."

"I assume you've been in touch with Acting Regent Ewan?" Mr. O'Gara asks from behind me.

Kyna nods, her expression now showing a trace of distaste. "He seems to be in rather a dither at the moment. Though he insisted Faxon will be recaptured within hours, he failed to mention what steps he's taking to ensure that. Clearly he did not expect this level of responsibility to be thrust upon him so suddenly, nor for as long as he's likely to have it now."

I recall Ewan Lloyd as pleasant and well-spoken, but he didn't strike me as particularly bright or decisive. He was appointed to the position of Deputy Regent primarily to appease the traditionalists who objected to a non-Royal Regent—and because I sensed that of the many Royals I interviewed, he was the most sincerely loyal to me as Sovereign.

Unfortunately, being pleasant and loyal doesn't exactly qualify him for leadership of an entire colony of a quarter million people, particularly during a crisis. It won't surprise me if it turns out he's not up to the job.

"I guess we'd all better hope Shim recovers quickly." I exchange a worried glance with Rigel.

"Indeed," Kyna dryly agrees.

If anyone on Mars can get to the bottom of the why and how of Faxon's escape, it'll be Shim. After nearly three hundred years of existence on both Mars and Earth, he has an almost preternatural insight into how people think, so almost nothing gets past him.

"How much of this is public knowledge?" I ask Kyna then.

"I strongly recommended keeping Faxon's escape from the public until he's caught," Kyna replies. "News of Regent Shim's incapacitation will be troubling enough for our people. That cannot be hidden, as the Acting Regent must announce his temporary assumption of Shim's duties. I'm afraid this is all the information I have at present, though I will of course notify you at once when I hear more. Oh, and happy birthday, Excellency." With a concluding bow, she signs off.

There's a long moment of silence as everyone absorbs what we just heard. Then several people start talking at once.

"Weren't the Mind Healers supposed to keep him sedated until the memory extraction took place?" Teara Roark asks.

"Yes. They certainly were." Mrs. O'Gara looks outraged.

Mr. O'Gara frowns. "Between that and what happened with Regent Shim, it seems likely at least one Healer was in on this." He darts an apologetic look at Rigel's mom, the only Healer in the room.

"We must be careful not to jump to conclusions," Mr. Stuart cautions. "As nothing concrete is known yet about either situation, it's still possible they are unrelated. Though, like Kyna, I doubt it." The worry I sense from him is understandable —Shim is his father.

I feel a touch on my arm and turn to see Bri and Deb anxiously regarding me.

"Should we be here?" Deb whispers.

"She means, is this the sort of thing we shouldn't be hearing about?" Bri quietly clarifies. "Faxon's the guy who killed your parents, right?"

I nod. "And my grandfather, who was Sovereign at the time. But Faxon shouldn't have enough supporters left now to become a threat again." I hope. My smile feels forced even to me. "As for you guys being here, if I say it's okay, it's okay. Still, don't mention this to anyone else— not even the other *Echtrans* at school."

"We won't," Deb assures me. "We're not really friends with any of the others anyway."

It's barely been a month since I told my two best *Duchas* friends who I really am, explaining about the Martian colony and the other *Echtrans* here in Jewel. I didn't have much choice, once they noticed so many anomalies they started spinning wild theories —though none *quite* as wild as the truth.

Since then, their *Echtran* boyfriends and I have filled them in on more details, but they're still sometimes boggled by the idea of a bunch of genetically and technologically advanced humans from Mars living and working right here in their little home town.

"So much for avoiding Martian politics at your party," Molly mutters as the parents continue talking about the news.

I manage a sour laugh.

Rigel gives my shoulder a sympathetic squeeze, then calls out, "More cake, anyone?"

That draws a stilted chuckle from the adults, though most of the teens are quick to take seconds—or thirds, in the case of Sean and Liam. Both boys are on Jewel High's basketball team and with the season in full swing, they're bottomless pits these days.

Once the cake is gone, the party breaks up. Today's double dose of bad news took most of the fun out of things, plus it's getting late for a school night.

"Bummer that your party ended on such a downer," Molly remarks as people start leaving. "Rigel really wanted to make it a fun little break for you."

"I know. It's not his fault it didn't turn out that way. But hey, by the time your birthday rolls around in June, I'm sure all these current issues will be long resolved. Then we can both celebrate properly at your party."

Molly grins. "Darned right we will. By then Shim will be all better, Faxon will be history, and *Echtran* elections will be over."

Even though we're twins, Molly and I have different birthdays because we were secretly separated while in utero, to safeguard the Sovereign line from Faxon. I was born normally, but Molly's embryo was kept in stasis until a non-Royal surrogate mother could be found. Until our momentous discovery this past fall, everyone, including Molly and the O'Garas, assumed she was an Ag foundling.

"Maybe by June you'll even have appointed an Earth Regent," Molly concludes—in a whisper, since it's a bit of a sore spot with the O'Garas that I haven't done that yet.

Though he's never said so, I know Mr. O'Gara hopes to get far enough back into my good graces that I'll consider him for that role. I don't see that happening, though, after the way he betrayed Rigel and me last summer.

"Here's hoping," I reply with forced lightness, glad Molly can't sense my emotions the way I can sense hers. I give her a hug and she and Tristan follow their parents out.

When I'm the only guest left, I turn to Rigel's parents. "Do you really think there could be a conspiracy in Nuath to bring Faxon back to power?"

Instead of the quick denial I'm hoping for, Mr. Stuart sighs. "I'd like to think not, but Kyna is right that the timing of Shim's surgical complication and Faxon's escape would seem to imply it. Of course, until we know more, that's just speculation. Coincidences do happen," he concludes, though without conviction.

"I wish I could be there to help question people," I say, frowning. "Mrs. O'Gara, too." Both her lie-detector power and my ability to sense people's emotions would be super useful in figuring out who was involved in Faxon's escape.

"I wish you could, too," Mr. Stuart agrees, "but the next launch window won't open for more than a year. I'm afraid the Nuathan investigators are on their own."

Unable to think of any possible way to help from two hundred million miles away, all I can do is hope Shim won't be incapacitated too long.

Rigel drives me home after that, but stops a block from my house so we can finally indulge in the makeout session we didn't get earlier. As always, Rigel's touch, and especially his kiss, give me a welcome boost of strength and clarity. Pleasure, too, of course, though I'm so distracted by tonight's news I can't enjoy it quite as much as usual.

Unfortunately, we don't dare park for long. After repeated urging by certain Council members —mainly Mrs. O—my adult Bodyguard Cormac sometimes shadows me even when I'm with Rigel, which he rarely used to do. After just five mostly-blissful minutes, I *very* regretfully sit up and refasten my seatbelt, so Rigel can drive me the rest of the way home.

Sometimes being Sovereign sucks.

"Did you have a nice time at your little party?" Aunt Theresa asks when I walk in.

"Um, mostly." I try not to lie to my aunt now that she knows the truth, but there's no point freaking her out. "Dr. Stuart made me a yummy lemon birthday cake, and the music was great. We did get some bad news about Rigel's grandfather during the party, though— unexpected complications from a medical procedure."

Aunt Theresa regards me warily. "Rigel's grandfather? Is he the one that's…that's on…"

"Mars, yes. He's my Regent there—but it sounds like he's going to be okay. He'll just have to stay in the hospital longer than they thought. I'll stay in touch with his deputy, who'll be Acting Regent until Shim is better."

She swallows. "In touch. With—" She breaks off shaking her head, clearly still weirded out by the idea that I actually communicate with people on Mars.

"I should go finish my homework before bed," I say, tactfully changing the subject before Uncle Louie comes in and asks questions.

Unlike Aunt Theresa, he's fascinated by everything to do with the colony on Mars, the transplanted Martians on Earth and the fact that I'm their Sovereign. A little *too* fascinated. I'm constantly having to remind him how important secrecy is, because he's just dying to tell everyone he knows. I'd much rather he not find out about the whole Faxon thing.

Once upstairs, I send a quick omni message to Acting Regent Ewan asking for a more complete update on the situation. Unfortunately, with Mars currently on the opposite side of the Sun from Earth, I can't expect a response for at least an hour. Or at all tonight, since Nuath's on Ireland time and it's well past midnight there. Ewan probably won't even see my message before morning. Just in case, I keep my omni handy while I draft my next *Echtran Enquirer* column and get ready for bed, but he doesn't answer.

As soon as I'm under the covers, I reach out mentally for Rigel for our nightly "chat." *Are you still awake?*

Of course. Is something wrong? You sound stressed. Again.

I'm fine, I reply. *Just frustrated that we know so little about what's happening on Mars right now.*

Even from five miles away, I can sense the calm he's trying to project my way.

There's nothing you can do tonight anyway, M. Try to relax and get a good night's sleep if you can. For me?

The love and concern that come through with his thought make me smile…and wish more than ever he was really right here with me. *I'll do my best*, I promise. *G'night, Rigel. I love you!*

I love you, too, M. See you in the morning.

✦

To my relief, Ewan's response is waiting when I wake up the next morning. I tap it and a lit screen appears in midair above my nightstand.

"Greetings, Excellency." The recorded video image bows deeply. "Acting Regent Ewan Lloyd, reporting as requested. I regret to inform you that the traitor Faxon is still at large, though our security forces hope to have him in custody by the end of the day. He cannot have gone far. It unfortunately seems clear now that the unexpected complication with Regent Shim's surgery was indeed timed to coincide with Faxon's escape. The instrument that malfunctioned had been serviced only two days prior, and records show the Maintenance worker who serviced it visited the maximum-security facility where Faxon was housed earlier that same day.

"The investigation into how his escape was engineered is still ongoing, but early indications suggest he had help from at least one person in the Maintenance *fine*, as a Mech assigned to the Healing center failed to report for his duty shift last night. He has not yet been located, but his friends and family will be brought in for questioning.

"I'm also sorry to report that while *Echtran* Council leader Kyna recommended keeping news of Faxon's escape quiet, that was not entirely possible. In the confusion surrounding his disappearance, most of the staff at the Mind Healing facility became aware of it. Many had already left before I thought to insist on secrecy, though I doubt the news has had time to spread far. In hindsight, I realize I should have done more to prevent the information from leaving the facility.

"In better news, Regent Shim's Healers believe he may be able to resume his full duties in as little as two weeks, as his recovery is progressing nicely. He could regain consciousness as early as tomorrow.

"I will message you again, Excellency, the moment I have additional information to pass along. *Faoda byo Thiarna Emileia* (long live Sovereign Emileia)." Again bowing deeply, he ends the message.

Though Shim's prognosis is encouraging, I'm more worried than relieved. The very fact that Faxon is still at large suggests more people were involved in planning his escape than Ewan is willing to admit. Yet.

I forward the message to Kyna in case she didn't get it, then start getting ready for school.

As always, Rigel picks me up in his spiffy Audi with the extra security features his father added, since he's my main chauffer as well as my Bodyguard. On the way to school, I tell him about Ewan's message.

"Kyna did warn us we probably couldn't keep Faxon's escape a secret for long, but now it'll probably be all over the Nuathan newsfeeds by tonight. A lot of *Ecthrans* keep in regular touch with friends and family back home, so it won't take long to spread to Earth after that. Crap."

My omni pings just as we reach the school. It's Kyna.

"Excellency," she begins without preamble, "given this information, I believe we should send out a MARSTAR Bulletin as soon as possible. I would have preferred to wait until we could also assure our people of Faxon's capture, but apparently there is now no guarantee that will be imminent."

"I agree." If anything, Ewan's message gives me even less confidence in him than before. "The longer we wait to tell people, the more time we give someone like Gwendolyn Gannett to put out their own version of the story."

Kyna gives a little cough. "Indeed. I'll message the Council at once."

.•*•.

The other four members of our "Bond Squad" are waiting in the school parking lot, so I play Ewan's message for them—audio only—and tell them Kyna and I agreed a MARSTAR needs to go out ASAP.

"They've *got* to catch him soon, though," I insist. "I mean, Nuath isn't that big, just twenty by twenty miles—and there are cameras and tracking devices everywhere."

"No, not everywhere," Kira corrects me. "In city and village centers, sure, but not in rural areas or even the poorer sections of cities, like the Cogs in Monaru. I'm sure the Mind Healing center Faxon escaped from had them, though, and I have no idea how he could have evaded them all. He must have had plenty of help."

She's giving off waves of anxiety. I sense Molly and Sean are also super stressed. Concerned, I look closely at all three of them.

"Are you guys actually worried he could mount some kind of comeback?"

They all frown at each other, then Sean says, "You'd be more worried too, M, if you knew what it was like while he was in power. I mean, I know he murdered your parents and grandparents, but you didn't *live* it. You three—" He nods toward me, Rigel and Tristan— "grew up on Earth, so you never experienced it like we did."

"No, I guess that's true," I admit. "It's even been hard to research very thoroughly, because so many records of his rise in popularity and his years in power were destroyed. But he was incredibly unpopular by the time he was ousted, wasn't he? Even if people were afraid to say so?"

"Sure," Kira agrees. "Probably less than twenty percent of Nuathans actively supported him by then. But that's still a lot of people."

Doing some quick mental math, I realize she's right. Twenty percent of a quarter million people would mean fifty thousand supporters—ten times the population of Jewel, and more than three times the number of *Echtrans* currently living on Earth.

"It must be a lot less now, though, right?" Rigel asks. "Nearly ninety percent of Nuathans voted for M's Acclamation."

"True," Kira says, "but by then a lot of Faxon supporters had been arrested, so couldn't vote. Those arrests spooked most of the rest into either changing their loyalties or pretending they had. Still, I'd guess close to ten percent of Nuathans still secretly support him. Maybe twice that among the *Echtrans* who moved here this last launch window, after M became Sovereign. There were definitely some on the ship my family took to Earth."

I remember her telling me that. "It's not surprising a lot of Faxon supporters decided they'd rather leave Nuath than stay and be ostracized. And nearly all the new arrivals who disappeared off-grid after getting here had a history of supporting him. Mostly Maintenance *fine*, I think, plus a few from Mining and Agricultural. Once they hear he's escaped—"

"It could spark a movement." Sean finishes my thought. "Mum and Dad think it should be kept secret as long as possible."

I grimace. "Sounds like it's already too late for that."

The warning bell rings and we start heading toward the school building.

"Hey, it's not like he can sneak off to Earth with the next launch window more than a year off," Tristan comments, throwing an arm around Molly's shoulders and giving her a reassuring squeeze. "Nobody *here* needs to worry yet."

He's probably right. So why do I have a sinking feeling things will get worse before they get better?

3

Conditioned response

AT LUNCH, Bri, Deb, Liam and Lucas all hurry to our usual table, where I just sat down with Rigel, Molly and Tristan.

"Hey, we wanted to catch you guys before anybody sits here we can't talk in front of," Bri whispers. "We're all dying to know more about what you started to tell us last night. You know, about us maybe having —" She scans the cafeteria with exaggerated caution— "bonds."

Deb nods. "We were also wondering if you have any more news about Rigel's grandfather, or that guy Faxon who escaped?"

"Not much," I admit. "On the good side, Rigel's grandfather is improving. But on the bad side, they haven't caught Faxon yet. About your bonds, I want to hear more about the changes you've all noticed since you started dating." Glancing up, I see a couple of *Duchas* basketball players coming our way. "Not now, but as soon as we have a chance."

I've decided not to say anything about potential new abilities. I don't want them to be disappointed if it turns out they don't have any—which is totally likely considering Bri and Deb are *Duchas*.

All afternoon and evening I keep checking my omni for the MARSTAR Bulletin Kyna mentioned, wondering what the delay is. Finally, about an hour before bedtime, it shows up.

For Immediate Release

The *Echtran* Council regrets to inform you that late yesterday, the deposed dictator Faxon escaped from custody shortly after being transferred from prison to a Mind Healing facility pending his trial. His escape coincided with complications that arose during Regent Shim's scheduled surgery and there is suspicion the two incidents are linked. Be assured that Regent Shim is expected to recover fully. While Faxon remains at large as of this writing, Nuathan authorities are confident he will be apprehended in short order. Another update will be sent when that occurs.

And that's it. Short as it is, I wonder why it didn't go out sooner. A few minutes later, Kyna calls to answer that question.

"Excellency, I assume by now you have seen the Bulletin?"

"Just a few minutes ago, yes," I reply. "What took so long?"

I hear a tiny snort from her end. "Some on the Council were opposed to sending it at all until we could include news of Faxon's capture. They feared doing otherwise would needlessly alarm people…and make the Council look bad. I finally agreed to wait until the end of the day. No update from Nuath is likely before morning now."

"Did the Bulletin at least go out before the news started spreading here on Earth?"

"I hope so. In any event, we've done all we can for the moment. I'm sure some will demand more details, but we cannot provide what we don't yet have. Perhaps Acting Regent Ewan will have a more comprehensive report for us tomorrow." She sounds doubtful.

So am I. "Thanks, Kyna. I'll forward you anything he sends me."

"I'll do the same, Excellency. Good night."

I'd message my Acting Regent right now to request a more complete update, but not only is it the middle of the night in Nuath—again —it might make him think I lack confidence in him. Which I do, but I probably shouldn't undermine *his* confidence while he's navigating his very first crisis.

Who knows? Maybe he'll prove me wrong.

Unfortunately, the next morning's update from my Acting Regent is even less informative than yesterday's. The text-only message merely reports they've confirmed Faxon's not still hiding anywhere in the Healing facility, so they're widening the search.

As news of his escape has already spread throughout Nuath, we're in the process of launching a colony-wide manhunt, Ewan concludes.

That MARSTAR definitely didn't go out in time, then.

When we get to school, I read Ewan's brief message to Rigel and the other Bond Squad members, who all share my irritation at the man's apparent incompetence.

"What, it took them this long to check all the hospital closets?" Molly exclaims indignantly. "They must have all kinds of high-tech scanners that should have located him minutes after he disappeared!"

"Maybe whoever helped him disabled them?" Tristan suggests. "They've got to catch him soon, though. Where could he go?"

"If Shim were in charge, they'd have caught him already," I grumble. "Every message I get from Ewan Lloyd makes me sorrier I appointed him Deputy Regent."

Molly shakes her head in disgust. "Not that the Council's much better, waiting till last night to send that Bulletin. Mum said it was mostly Malcolm and Breann who insisted on the delay. I'll bet Gwendolyn Gannett has something snarky to say about that."

Sure enough, when Rigel and I leave the building at the end of the school day, Molly waylays us on her way to cheer practice.

"Have you seen it?" she asks. "At least you and Kyna can say 'I told you so' to those idiots on the Council who insisted on waiting."

"Does Gwendolyn Gannett claim it's part of some big conspiracy?" I tighten my grip on Rigel's hand, resisting an urge to scream. "We should have known that would happen."

In answer, Molly hands me her omni, open to this week's *Echtran Enquirer* and an article titled, *"Yet another coverup by the Echtran Council?"*

With a groan, I start reading.

Many of you are no doubt wondering, as I am, why our *Echtran* Council chose to wait until nearly every *Echtran* on Earth was already aware of Faxon's escape to put out an official acknowledgment of that fact. Did they feel the news was not important enough for a more timely statement, or are they engaged in yet another deliberate coverup? That such an escape was possible certainly calls into question the competence of

Nuath's security forces. Perhaps our Council chose to delay notifying our people in hopes of taking credit for his eventual capture—though how such ineffective leaders could manage such a thing from here on Earth, I cannot imagine. In any event, my sources in Nuath confirm that as of this writing, Faxon remains uncaptured.

Much as I hate to cast aspersions on Sovereign Emileia, one must wonder why she appointed such an obviously incompetent Deputy Regent. Or, for that matter, why she named such an elderly Regent for Nuath, given his current health challenges. At any rate, I believe it is safe to say that such a thing could never have happened under her grandfather, Sovereign Leontine.

With Faxon still at large, we can only hope that those who previously rallied to his banner have by now had their eyes sufficiently opened to resist any attempt to reconstitute his support. Unfortunately, certain rumblings I have heard from some in Faxon's own Maintenance *fine* make me less than confident that is the case. Join me tonight on the *Echtran* News Network for more.

"Gah!" I exclaim. "For someone who hates to cast aspersions on me, she sure does it a lot. Faxon's original rise to power happened under Sovereign Leontine! Why she has to—"

"Shh!" Rigel cautions, giving my hand a shake.

I *am* getting a little strident. Clamping my mouth shut, I glance around the parking lot, relieved no *Duchas* students are close enough to hear—not that they'd understand what I was talking about.

"Sorry. Now I have to watch her stupid show tonight, to hear what else she has to say. Ugh."

I usually avoid watching Gwendolyn's weekly broadcast, but if she's going to talk more about Faxon's escape and keep ragging on me and the Council, I should hear it.

"Why don't you guys come over to our house to watch?" Molly suggests. "Once they read this, Mum and Dad will want to see it, too."

I thoughtfully reread the next to last sentence in the article. "What do you think Gwendolyn meant by 'Faxon's own Maintenance *fine*'? Is that really where he's from?"

"That's what I always heard," Molly says with a shrug. "Does it matter?"

"Not sure." It sounds wrong to me somehow, though I'm not sure why.

I keep frowning at the article until Molly clears her throat.

"Um, can I have my phone back? I need to get to practice if I don't want Trina reaming me."

"Oh, sure, sorry." I hand it to her. "See you tonight."

As she trots off, Rigel puts his arm around my shoulders. "Don't let that article get to you. You know most of what she says is just to stir up controversy. Come on, I'll take you home."

I nod, already looking forward to the end of the drive. Because Cormac is also Jewel High's vice principal, he generally stays late at school, giving us some extra alone time. Jewel's little arboretum, one of our favorite places to make out, is surprisingly crowded today, considering the early-March chill, so we park instead. Rigel is just gathering me into his arms… when my omni pings.

"Oops, I meant to put that on silent," I apologize. Then I glance at it and groan. "Oh, crap. I forgot I have another stupid holo meeting today. It's not for another twenty minutes, though." Now I do silence my omni before turning back to Rigel with a smile. "Now, where were we?"

Though we only get ten minutes of kissing instead of the half hour I was hoping for, it's way better than nothing. When Rigel drops me off, my ever-growing mountain of problems seems a little less insurmountable

"You're coming to Molly's after dinner, too, right?" I ask as I get out.

He nods. "That show always sucks, but it's a chance to spend another hour together."

I lean in for one last kiss before going inside. Grabbing a snack from the kitchen, I go up to my room for my meeting —this one to finalize timelines for our upcoming *Echtran* elections. It's boring, but mercifully brief—though I still have to deal with a bunch of other Sovereign stuff that's been piling up.

The oldest item involves a dispute between two groups of *Echtrans* in a new settlement in New Zealand. Until we can elect a proper *Echtran* judiciary, it's on me to mediate any disagreements that can't be resolved by local magistrates. With roughly fifteen thousand *Echtrans* now scattered around the planet, that can take a while. I did the same back in Nuath when I was first Acclaimed, a task I was more than happy to hand over to Shim.

I render decisions on half a dozen such disputes, then sift through several relocation petitions from newer *Echtran* immigrants unhappy with where they've been settled. There are more of them waiting than

I realized—yet another duty an Earth Regent could handle, if I had one.

I feel like I've barely made a dent in the backlog before I have to turn my attention to my homework assignments that are due tomorrow. I've fallen behind on a couple of class projects, too, but those will just have to wait. At six o'clock, I finally stand up and stretch, then go downstairs to set the table for dinner.

Aunt Theresa has no objection to me going over to Molly's after dinner —she rarely does these days—but does remind me it's a school night.

"I know. I shouldn't be back too late." I hurry outside just as Rigel pulls up and greet him with a kiss when he gets out. "Mmm. I know it's only been a few hours, but—"

He enthusiastically kisses me back. "You sure you want to go to the O'Garas' instead of somewhere more private?"

"I don't *want* to, but I need to know what other garbage Gwendolyn's spouting so Molly and I can counter it in our Thursday broadcast."

Resigned, he takes my hand. "We have a few minutes. I'll leave my car here so we can walk."

We make the most of the half-block walk to the O'Garas' house, sneaking another quick kiss on the front porch before ringing the doorbell.

Mrs. O greets us cordially, though she's clearly tense. "Come in, Excellency, do. We all may as well hear what else that woman has to say."

Molly and Tristan are already sitting together at one end of the couch, so we go to the other end. At first I wonder where Sean is, then remember he has a basketball game tonight.

On the coffee table, next to a pot of tea and a plate of cookies, Mr. O's omni is already displaying a large holographic screen filled by the red and blue *Echtran* News Network logo. As we sit down, the logo is replaced by Gwendolyn Gannett's overly made-up face smiling brightly at the camera.

"Hello, everyone! I have an exciting show for you tonight, as you no doubt expected after the explosive news of Faxon's escape."

She goes on to repeat several conspiracy theories about the Council and Nuath's leadership that have already been debunked, then shows a few clips from earlier today, of her interviewing random *Echtrans*, some of them panicked by the news. After that, she motions to someone off-camera.

"And now we have a live interview with Donnal Murragh, who is familiar with NuAgra's security systems." A man in a NuAgra uniform steps nervously into view to sit gingerly on the edge of an overstuffed floral chair. "Donnal," she continues, "what sort of blunders could have allowed Faxon to escape what was supposed to be a completely secure facility?"

Mr. O'Gara swears aloud. "No one at NuAgra is supposed to speak to the press without authorization! Nor is Donnal connected to security, other than occasionally maintaining the equipment."

"I don't know what precautions are in place at Nuath's Mind Healing Center," Donnal replies, looking uncomfortable in the extreme, "but I expect there are cameras. Maybe they saw what happened?"

Gwendolyn looks less than pleased by his answer. "I haven't been able to discover that yet. Have you overheard anything from your superiors?"

"No, I already told you I'm not, er, particularly high in the command chain."

"Yes, yes, I know. But Maintenance people often hear things others don't."

He looks even more uncomfortable now. "No, sorry, I haven't."

"What about from others in your *fine*, then?" Gwendolyn persists. "I imagine many of them are following this news closely, given Faxon's history."

Donnal scowls. "Faxon gave us all a bad name—he's a stain on our *fine*. Most of us hope he's either caught or killed, and the sooner the better."

Gwendolyn flicks a hand and the camera zooms in on her, cutting the man out of the picture. "As you can see, the coverup is still ongoing. The truth is bound to reveal itself eventually, and I promise to report it the instant it does. Meanwhile, I'll conclude with an interview I recorded this afternoon with Fallon Blaine in Dun Cloch. Fallon, also from the Maintenance *fine*, has a rather different view."

A dark-haired woman appears on-screen in an inset, her expression alight with excitement. "Yes, Gwendolyn, some of us do feel vindicated by this news. We may not have supported everything Faxon did, but he sure was right about *one* thing. You can't keep a good Mech down!"

Beside me, Molly gasps and out of the corner of my eye I see Mr. and Mrs. O'Gara flinch violently.

"What?" I look back and forth between them as the broadcast ends.

"That…that slogan." Mrs. O'Gara's voice is shaky. "I hoped we'd never hear it again."

"It was the rallying cry used by Faxon and his followers," Mr. O explains, "though some substituted their own *fines* for 'Mech.' Ag, Miner, et cetera. He used that chant to inspire his supporters to violence. Repeatedly."

I must still look confused, because Mrs. O clarifies, "For us, it's on the order of someone here saying, 'Heil Hitler.' An abomination."

"I never knew that." Tristan puts a comforting arm around Molly, who's clearly still distressed. "No wonder you're all upset."

"Mech," I repeat. "That's a nickname for people in the Maintenance *fine*, right?" All three O'Garas nod. "Do they find the term insulting?"

Molly shakes her head. "They refer to themselves that way all the time, probably because it's easier to say than Maintenance. Like saying Ag instead of Agricultural."

"That makes sense. But I'm curious." I turn to Mr. O'Gara. "Do you think Faxon's speeches would have had the same effect if he weren't a Mech?"

His eyebrows go up. "Possibly not, though it's rather a moot point now."

Unless he starts building support again—and my gut feeling about his story is right.

"Are his former followers likely to use his escape as an excuse to bring up their old grievances?" I ask then.

"Surely not," Mrs. O replies, though I sense her sudden alarm. "By now everyone must realize Faxon's claims of so-called inequalities were based on lies. Nuathans won't forget how rapidly their economy went downhill after he took power, nor the brutal tactics he used to maintain that power. Our people are not fools."

"No, they're not," I agree. "But he still convinced a whole lot of them to support him. What was his original appeal? I've tried to research that, but there's almost nothing in the records, so much was erased."

Mr. O'Gara frowns. "That's because false information was almost all that remain in the databases, after Faxon ruthlessly eliminated anything or anyone critical of him."

"Yes, that was explained to me before," I remind him. He was there when I antagonized a roomful of Royals with that question while aboard the *Quintessence* a year ago, on my first and only trip to Mars. I got very few answers.

"His appeal was based entirely on falsehoods," Mrs. O repeats. "He claimed the Royal *fine*, and particularly the Sovereigns, had always oppressed various groups, when of course they hadn't."

"*Some* people in those groups must have felt marginalized," I insist. "Enough to help him stage a violent coup. Since our people aren't fools, they must have had reasons to believe what he told them."

The uncomfortable silence that greets my words reminds me again of that awkward formal dinner on the *Quintessence*.

"I don't know why so many chose to believe Faxon's lies, Excellency," Mrs. O finally says. "Once we began our secret Resistance, those people tended to avoid us—and we them. During our last several years in Nuath it became…unsafe to have such conversations unless everyone present was in political agreement. As was proven when we were betrayed by a new member of our cell. Shall…shall we all have a spot of tea?"

Sean and Molly told me how their meeting place was raided and their older sister seized, along with records revealing that the O'Garas were Royal, not members of the Agricultural *fine*, as they'd pretended. As Resistance leaders, they'd have been executed if they hadn't been smuggled to Earth by a sympathetic ship captain.

The O'Garas are clearly eager to change the subject, so I take a cup and a cookie without protest, though I'm still thinking hard. It's frustrating that there's virtually nothing I can do from here, especially without knowing how Faxon swayed people to his cause in the first place.

Then it hits me that I *do* have another tool to research Faxon's rise to power—one that's lived in Molly's bedroom closet since our return to Earth late last summer.

Molly and I and our boyfriends are the only people on Earth who know my Royal Scepter is a whole lot more than a pretty, jeweled staff. It's also a sophisticated technological device that can access Archives containing the stored images and memories of previous Sovereigns… and Molly's and my deceased parents. Both Sovereign Leontine and our parents lived through Faxon's rise to power, so they probably have exactly the kind of info that was wiped from the regular databases.

When Rigel walks me home, I mention my idea to consult the Scepter Archives for more info on Faxon. "Maybe I can learn enough from the Archives to undercut any renewal of support for him. It's all I can think to do, and I've got to do *something*. I'm the Sovereign, after all."

"You do plenty, even without that," he assures me. "Too much, if you ask me. Anyway, it's not like anyone here on Earth is in any immediate danger. I doubt anyone on Mars is, either. Faxon's obviously lying low somewhere, so he won't be actively drumming up support anytime soon."

I hope he's right.

$$\rule{6cm}{0.4pt}$$

4

Implicit memory

RIGEL and I are just getting out of his car in the school parking lot the next morning when Kira and Sean hurry over to us.

"You two saw Gwendolyn Gannett's show last night, right?" Sean says. "Mum and Dad said you came over to watch it."

We both nod.

"Then you heard that…slogan thing?" Kira asks. "My parents were so upset when I got home from the game last night, I watched the replay. This could get bad."

I don't even have to focus to feel the strong emotions she's giving off —a combination of fear and disgust.

"How bad?" I exchange a glance with Rigel. "The O'Garas were upset by it, too, but not really worried. Do you think it could actually sway people Faxon's way again?"

"I don't know," Kira admits. "I hope not."

Before I can ask more questions, Molly and Tristan join us and shift the conversation.

"Hey, bummer about last night's game," Tristan says to Sean. "Molly told me. I guess you had no choice, huh?"

"No," Sean replies. "It still sucked."

"What—?" I start to ask, then realization dawns. "Oh, was this the game you agreed to lose?"

Sean nods glumly. "Yeah. Liam and Alan were great about it, played their parts so well it didn't look at all deliberate, but none of us liked it much."

"I'm sure the fans didn't, either," Molly commiserates. "I'm kind of glad I wasn't there to hear whatever Trina had to say."

"Exactly what you'd expect, since she had no idea we could hear her. If Alan *was* starting to soften toward her again, he's not now. Two-faced little—" He breaks off as a few *Duchas* students pass close to us.

As we head into the school, I ask Molly if I can come over this afternoon. "We should plan for our program tomorrow night."

"Sure. I have cheer practice, but we can get together after that."

"Cool. Thanks." I'll explain my real reason later.

✦

I'm able to work off some of my anxiety in Taekwondo class that afternoon, when Master Parker pairs me with Kira for sparring practice.

"That was fun," Kira comments as we're taking off our padded gear afterward.

I agree. We both enjoy sparring more when we don't have to hold back. After we pack up our gear, I follow her outside.

"This morning you said that Mech slogan could still be dangerous," I say quietly as we start walking. "Why?"

She hesitates for a second. "There's still a fairly rigid class system in Nuath, despite what its Constitution says about equality…and we Ags are only about a half-step above the Mechs. My parents were always staunch Royalists, but some in our *fine* totally bought into Faxon's propaganda."

"When I've asked any Royals what led to Faxon's rise to power, they get prickly about it, claim it was all just lies," I tell her.

Kira snorts. "I'll bet. Sure, most of his claims and promises *were* lies, but people in the lowest *fines* still flocked to him because he made them feel special."

"Because he claimed to be from the Maintenance *fine*?" I guess.

"Yep. You can imagine the appeal of a leader who understood what it was like to be looked down on—even if those in other *fines* pretended they didn't. Regent Shim is doing more to change that than Faxon ever did, but…old ways of thinking die hard."

I ponder that for a minute. "Did Faxon ever *prove* he was a member of the Maintenance *fine*?"

"I doubt it. Why would anyone claim to be a Mech if they weren't?" Then she blinks. "Oh. Right. To get their support."

"Exactly. So what was his story? Where did he claim he grew up?"

"In The Cogs, in Monaru. I doubt you ever visited it—it's probably the poorest sector in Nuath. Even that struck people as admirable, since not many who live there ever escape."

The word startles me. "Escape? Were they prisoners?"

"Not technically," she says, "but it probably feels that way to the poorest of the poor. Especially the ones with…problems. Even with no *sochar* at all, they could get food, and some would rather live in squalor than work. Or get help from the Healers."

Disturbed, I frown. "I had no idea." Definitely something I'll ask Shim about once he's better. "Was there any proof Faxon grew up there?"

"No idea, but it would have been hard to *dis*prove. The Cogs isn't known for keeping good records—and Faxon could have wiped any they did have."

I wonder if that's why he claimed to be from that neighborhood—so his real background couldn't be traced.

"If that's where he's hiding," Kira continues, "he'd be awfully hard to find. The Cogs are a maze of alleys and tunnels."

It's probably been searched already, but I'll mention it to Acting Regent Ewan. "How many people do you think only supported Faxon because of his *fine*?" I ask. That's what matters most.

"A lot," she replies. "According to my parents, anyway. I was only a toddler when his coup happened, and they cut ties early on with anyone who supported him. My dad's still not on speaking terms with his own father, because he took Faxon's side. He supposedly regrets that now, but Dad hasn't forgiven him for it."

"Then you never had much contact with anyone who truly supported Faxon while he was in power?"

She shakes her head. "It wasn't safe. Especially since I tended to be pretty, um, outspoken about my own feelings."

"Not just about Faxon, as I recall," I remind her with a grin. When Kira first came to Earth, she was nearly as opposed to me as Sovereign as she'd been to Faxon before his ouster.

"Yeah, well, I came around on that one, didn't I?" She grins back. "Anyway, I'd better go or I'll be late to basketball practice. Give me a call later if you think of more questions I can answer."

She sprints off then, her Taekwondo gear bag hitched over one shoulder.

I need to hurry, too. Molly should be back from school by now, and I want to spend as much time as possible with my Scepter.

Aunt Theresa's in the kitchen when I get home, mixing up yet another batch of cookies.

"Sorry I'm a little late," I tell her. "Is it okay if I don't help with tonight's dinner? I told Molly I'd stop over to discuss our show for tomorrow as soon as I grab a shower." It's a plausible excuse, since we often do that.

"That's fine," she says. "Louie's picking up a pizza on his way home from work. I hoped you might use the extra time to catch up on your homework, as you've mentioned being too busy to keep up with it."

I didn't realize she'd paid attention. I guess Rigel and Molly aren't the only ones who've noticed how thin I've been spreading myself lately.

"Thanks. I'll spend some time on homework later this evening." With a parting smile, I hurry upstairs.

It's nice to be on good terms with my aunt after a lifetime of…not. Even if she still prefers to avoid all mention of anything Mars-related.

Less than half an hour later, I ring Molly's doorbell.

"Hey, M," she greets me. "Glad you're here. I was just thinking we probably don't want to use the recording we made Saturday, huh?"

"After the stuff Gwendolyn Gannett's been saying? Definitely not. But that's not the real reason I wanted to come over. I'd like to spend some time with my Scepter."

Her brows go up. "Oh? Cool. Mum and Dad are still at NuAgra, so we should have the house to ourselves for a while."

She makes a quick detour to the kitchen for glasses of milk and some cookies left over from last night, then we go up to her room.

"I can't believe it's been nearly a month since we've done this," she says, locking her bedroom door. "I thought we'd be talking to our parents almost every day, once we found out we could."

"So did I, but it's tricky to find time without letting anyone know what we're doing. Especially lately, with both of us so busy."

Going into her closet, I retrieve the heavy, gem-encrusted staff tucked away in the back corner. As always, it warms to my touch, imparting a distinct sense of "mine-ness." The pink crystal containing the Archive of previous Sovereigns is still embedded at the top of the Scepter from the last time I accessed it.

"Don't you ever sneak in here to talk to our parents on your own?" I ask Molly.

She lifts a shoulder. "I thought about it once or twice, but it doesn't seem quite…fair to do it without you, just because I have easier access to the Scepter. Which isn't your fault."

"Aww." Touched, I give her a hug. "Thanks. But I wouldn't be mad if you did."

Molly hugs me back, hard. "I know. So, should we talk to our parents first, or was there something else you wanted to use the Archive for?"

"I'm actually hoping it'll have information about Faxon's original appeal. That could give us a better idea of whether anyone's likely to support him again, and how to push back if they do. Leontine was there right up until—" I swallow. "The coup." When he was murdered by Faxon.

Pressing her lips into a tight line, Molly nods, her expression echoing my own anguish at what I left unsaid.

Ignoring the lump in my throat, I place my palm over the pink crystal at the top of the Scepter. "*Chartlann rochtana.*"

The opening command makes the whole staff vibrate in my hand, then a lifelike image of Sovereign Leontine appears. "Hello, my dears," he says with a grandfatherly smile for both of us. "I hope you are well?"

"We are," I tell him, "but our people may be facing yet another crisis. A couple of days ago, Faxon escaped somehow and hasn't been caught yet. I wanted to ask you a few questions about him. Maybe you'll have some answers I haven't been able to get out of other Royals."

At mention of Faxon's name his eyebrows go up, but then he nods. "I'll be happy to help if I can, of course."

"Thanks. Can you tell me what made people follow him in the first place? There's almost nothing about that in any of the databases."

"Yes, you included that fact in one of your early reports. Fortunately, no one had opportunity to delete anything from this Archive, so what was known at the time of my final update is still intact. I rather hoped it would not be needed, however."

I'm again struck by how very human his stored image is, since of course it can't really "hope" anything. But my real grandfather would have, and this image is programmed to react as he would, based on his stored personality profile.

"So did I," I admit. "But now that info might help us counter any renewed support his escape might inspire. I know he promised lower *fine* people a better life without Sovereigns in charge, but what convinced them he was telling the truth? Were their lives really that bad?"

With a sigh, Leontine shakes his head. "I never thought so, but as his support grew, I made more of an effort to research the matter. I discovered there were more inequities between the *fines* than I'd realized, though no evidence of actual hardship. Still, Faxon used those inequities to play upon the people's emotions, stoking what had been only minor resentments into major ones. At least one is no longer pertinent now, based on what you've reported. The Nuathan government is more representative now than it was in my time, is it not?"

"Yes, since the recent election, there's at least one member of each major *fine* in the Legislature, which wasn't true before."

For more than a century prior to Faxon's coup, the Nuathan Legislature only included people from the Royal and Science *fines*—still considered the most prestigious.

"I'm afraid that's correct," he agrees. "One of Faxon's promises was to balance that inequality. Did he?"

"No," I reply. "Once he took power, he dissolved the Legislature completely, then made vague promises of future elections that somehow never took place. But equal representation wasn't the only thing Faxon agitated about, right?"

Leontine shakes his head. "He also claimed the Royal *fine* had been hoarding Nuath's wealth for generations rather than sharing it with those who produced it. That was totally false, of course. He also repeatedly insinuated that the Royals and Scientists used genetic manipulation to keep the lower *fines* in their places. That making them less intelligent and more compliant allowed Royals to dominate public discourse and decision-making. Unfortunately, there was a grain of truth to that claim, though it was our colony's alien founders who created that ancestral disparity, not Royals. Genetic manipulation was indeed something they practiced on the earliest colonists before disappearing a few centuries later."

I know better than to probe too deeply into that, since any direct questions about the Grentl always make this version of Leontine clam up. The truth about those aliens was kept so secret that for over a century almost everything to do with them was stored in a whole separate Archive and apparently never the twain shall meet.

"I've heard the Maintenance *fine* was one of the first to support Faxon because he claimed to be one of them," I say, rather than pursue the other subject. "He wasn't, was he?"

"As far as I know, he was," Leontine replies, "but you look troubled. Do you have reason to believe his claim was false?"

"Yes. I mean, no. I mean, I don't think I ever asked anyone about his *fine* or where he grew up, but it sounds wrong to me." In fact, I'm nearly *positive* it's wrong, though I still don't know why.

Leontine regards me thoughtfully. "My dear Emileia, I've learned from your reports that your intuition has often proven correct. If you believe Faxon falsified his background, you likely have a reason. Based on one of your earliest reports, I could suggest a way you might attempt to verify your belief if my, ah, programming did not preclude my mentioning it here."

"A way to—? Oh. Oh!" His meaning sinks in and I grin. "Thank you, Grandfather. I'll try that other way right now. *Chartlann fionragh.*"

Sovereign Leontine's image disappears.

Still smiling, I turn to Molly, who looks confused.

"What was that last bit about?" she asks. "What are you going to try?"

"The Grentl Archive. I think that's what Leontine meant when he said he couldn't explain. The main Archive version of him can't talk about anything Grentl-related. Which gets inconvenient sometimes."

Molly blinks. "Huh. I'll bet."

"I'd love to merge the two Archives now that the secret is out," I say, ducking back into her closet, "but even asking if that's possible made this Leontine go silent. I should ask the other one."

I come out with the genetically-locked case containing the other two crystals and set it on Molly's bed. Pressing my palm lightly on the lid makes it spring open. "Leontine must think there's something in this Archive—" I hold up the purple stone— "that can tell me if I'm right about Faxon. Let's find out."

Molly still looks baffled, but rather than try to explain further, I put my palm over the pink crystal at the top of the Scepter and rotate it to the left, popping it out. Then I insert the purple crystal and rotate it to the right before again giving the command, *"Chartlann rochtana."*

Like before, the Scepter vibrates and Leontine reappears. He looks exactly like the one we were just talking to, except he doesn't smile.

"Greetings, Sovereign Emileia," he says with a formal nod. "May I be of assistance?"

"I hope so. I want to know whether the usurper Faxon is really from the Maintenance *fine.* Your image in the main Archive hinted this one might be able to tell me."

There's a long pause, which means he's searching all the Grentl records. Finally, he says, "I find no mention of such a person in this Archive."

"Really?"

That seems weird. Then I realize that while I've uploaded regular reports to the main Archive, I've only ever asked this one questions. So of course it won't include anything that happened after the last time Leontine updated it, when he was still alive.

"Um, Faxon was a dictator who overthrew the Nuathan government soon after I was born and, um, killed you and a lot of other Royals," I explain. "Years later, he tried to access the Grentl communication device and it knocked him unconscious. That's how he was finally deposed. I guess I should've added that information to this Archive?"

"Yes. Any updates pertaining to the Grentl should be stored here," he agrees, with no change in expression. "Would you like to do that now?"

It's my first time using this Archive since getting back to Earth last summer and I'd nearly forgotten how disconcerting it is to talk to these personality-less images.

"Er, not right now, but I will. Soon. So I guess you can't give me any information about Faxon at all?"

"I cannot," he confirms. "However, if you interfaced with the Grentl communication device after he did, you may already have access to the information you seek."

Startled, I frown. "Huh? How?"

He answers without hesitation. "When I first interfaced with the device, I received my mother Aerleas's memories. If the same was true for you, you likely also received her memories, as well as mine and Faxon's."

"Ohhh," I breathe. "Yes. Yes, I did! I only remember flashes, but— Do you mean I might have *all* of those memories somewhere in my brain?"

"That is certainly possible. I never attempted to retrieve all of my mother's memories, though more surfaced over time. You likely absorbed more than you initially realized."

An interesting, if disturbing idea.

"Thank you. You've been very helpful." I don't know why I bother with pleasantries, when images in this Archive never respond to them, but it seems rude to omit them. "I promise to return later to update this Archive with everything I can add about the Grentl. *Chartlann fionragh.*"

His image disappears.

"Whoa!" Molly exclaims. "That's… Was that really Sovereign Leontine, too?"

"Sort of, but without his personality. This Archive is strictly limited to all things Grentl, so it's kind of stripped down compared to the other one. But useful. Without it, I never would have known to send that report to the Grentl that stopped them from destroying Nuath."

Still clearly boggled, she shakes her head. "I guess I never thought about the Grentl Archive much, once they weren't a threat anymore."

"Neither did I," I admit. "I wouldn't have thought to use it just now if our *real* grandfather hadn't given me that hint."

She grins. "Real grandfather?"

"You know what I mean. He seems way more real in the main Archive. Speaking of which, if we're going to talk with our parents, we should do it before your, um, parents get home."

Nodding, Molly reaches into the case holding the crystals. "It must seem strange that I think of them both that way, but until we opened this Archive—" She hands me the blue stone— "the only parents I ever knew were the O'Garas. I can't just *un*think of them that way because we've met our real ones."

"No, that makes sense. Ready?" I put my palm over the purple Grentl Archive stone and remove it from the Scepter, then replace it with the blue crystal containing our parents' Archive. "*Chartlann rochtana.*"

An instant later, Mikal and Galena stand before us—the parents Molly and I never knew, since they were murdered by Faxon's thugs when we were babies.

"Hello, Malena, Emileia." Galena's warm smile is echoed by Mikal.

"I trust our daughters are well?" he adds.

We both nod.

"We're sorry we haven't had a chance to talk to you for a while," Molly tells them. "We've both been really busy."

Mikal's smile is now amused. "No apologies are necessary, as we were unaware. How long has it been?"

"Oh, um, I guess almost a month?" Molly replies.

"But kind of a lot has happened," I say. "The biggest one is that Faxon has escaped, back in Nuath. They're still trying to figure out how."

Between us, Molly and I quickly bring them up to speed on that and everything else of note since we last opened this Archive, including the conversation we just had with Leontine about Faxon.

"Do you remember anything else about how Faxon built up support, especially early on?" I ask then. "What was his appeal? All the Council and Sovereign Leontine could tell me was that he stirred up resentment against Royals and Scientists."

"And the *Duchas*," Mikal says. "He urged conquering Earth for both the *Duchas*'s own good and Nuath's benefit, pointing out Earth had more resources than they could use, while ours were dwindling. He claimed he'd spent two years on Earth and found them savage, depraved and bent on self-destruction."

That sparks a fragment of memory. Faxon's? "Yes, I think he did spend some time here. And he definitely planned to invade—I over-heard one of his Earth co-conspirators talking about it while he was still in power."

"Good thing he was overthrown when he was," Molly says. "But how—?" She breaks off at the sound of the O'Garas' car in the driveway. "Oops! Mum and Dad are back. We'll try to talk again soon."

I deactivate the Archive and stow the Scepter back in Molly's closet while she opens her bedroom door. By the time her parents come upstairs, we have notebooks out like we've been working on tomorrow night's broadcast all this time.

"So I guess we'd better reschedule that interview we recorded with the candidates for Fiarway's mayor," Molly says as her mother walks past.

"Definitely," I reply. "We'll sound as out of touch as Gwendolyn Gannett claims if we don't tackle this Faxon thing head-on."

Mrs. O'Gara pauses in the doorway. "Excellency, I can't help thinking this current situation underscores the importance of your having a competent and trustworthy person to take over most of your Terran responsibilities. You're having to take on more duties than most adult Sovereigns ever had to manage, and I'd hate to see your school work suffer."

"My grades are fine," I reply, forcing a smile, "but thanks for your concern."

Though clearly not satisfied, Mrs. O nods and moves on. I turn back to Molly with a sigh.

"Anyway, back to our broadcast. I wish we could count on Faxon being captured by then, but based on Ewan Lloyd's update this morning we'd better not. I did send a message to Shim for whenever he's alert enough to respond, but that could still be days."

"How about we just come up with a few talking points, then wing it live?" Molly suggests. "Why pre-record something we'd just have to scrap?"

I nod, cringing a little. I'm not nearly as good at 'winging it' as Molly is. "You're probably right. I'll jot down some notes when I get home," I tell her. "Which should be soon. It's getting close to dinner time."

At that, Molly goes to the door, listens for a second, then softly closes it. "So…do you really think you might have all of Faxon's memories?" she asks me.

I hesitate. "I don't know. Probably? If I can access them, they'd definitely show whether Faxon's really a Mech or not. If not, it might undercut his support from that *fine.*"

"I think it would…if you could prove it. Even if you get those memories and your hunch turns out true, how do you convince everyone else?"

"Hm. Good point. The truth would sound totally crazy, plus it's classified. I'd need other evidence. But the first step is finding out if I *am* right."

Molly grimaces. "Combing through Faxon's memories sounds pretty gross, M. Are you sure you want to?"

"No, I definitely don't *want* to," I admit. "But if I can, I probably should."

No matter how much the thought scares me.

5

Reinforcing stimulus

AS SOON AS I LEAVE, I telepathically update Rigel on everything I learned.

You really think you have all of Faxon's memories? He sounds skeptical.

Maybe? I think back. *Remember how I sort of unzipped the whole Grentl plan for disabling Earth last fall? Maybe I also absorbed more memories from their device than I first realized.*

Now I sense concern, too. *Even if you did, do you really want to unzip them?* he asks, just like Molly did. *There could be some pretty nasty stuff in there. Let's at least talk face to face before you try.*

Though our long-distance communication is a whole lot easier these days, it still takes more effort than talking in person.

Okay. Maybe after school tomorrow?

Still, I can't resist pausing on the porch when I get home and concentrating briefly, to see if I can pull up more details of Faxon's life than the tiny flashes I remember from the Grentl device. I can't. In fact, I barely recall what those flashes were. A street fight, maybe? Equal parts frustrated and relieved, I go inside.

I try not to dwell on the Faxon issue while we eat dinner, though Uncle Louie's stories don't offer much distraction, since I've heard them all before. I'm debating whether I want a third slice of pizza when the phone rings.

Aunt Theresa answers, then looks at me. "Yes, she's here. Marsha?"

Surprised, I get up and take the receiver. Hardly anyone ever calls me on our landline now that I have a cellphone, so I'm startled to hear Rigel's voice.

"Hey, M, do you think you can come over tonight so we can work on that Government project? It's due in less than two weeks and we still have a lot to do on it."

"Why—? Oh, um, sure, I guess." Still baffled why he'd call like this instead of just reaching out mentally, or at least on my omni, I turn to my aunt and uncle. "Is it okay if I go over to Rigel's to work on a school project?"

Unlike last year, Aunt Theresa rarely questions me going out on school nights, much less forbids it. She does, however, ask, "Will his parents be home?"

"I'm sure they will. They're as strict as you are about us being alone in the house. Right, Rigel?" I ask into the phone.

"Yep, they're home. I'll pick you up in a few minutes, okay?"

"Okay. Bye." I hang up and take my plate to the sink. *What is this really about?* I silently send to Rigel as I turn on the faucet.

Homework. Mostly. I figured asking this way would make you less likely to beg off because of Sovereign stuff.

He's right. I'd already planned to put off that project for yet another day to go over the list of *Echtran* judicial candidates Kyna sent me today.

See? he sends. *Meanwhile, you're still mediating disputes yourself. I'm just trying to inject a little balance into your life. See you soon.*

I go upstairs to brush my hair and grab my Government notes—and my omni, which has that list of candidates on it. A few minutes later, Rigel arrives and we head to his house.

"Working on our project might not be fun, but at least it'll let you shift gears, take a break from your other duties," he says when we're on the way. "Do you still have to meet with the elections board this week?"

"Friday afternoon," I admit. "But only by hologram. I don't have to go to Montana or anything."

He slides an exasperated glance my way. "Still, you have way too much on your plate, you know you do. I don't get why the Council can't take on more of it until you appoint an Earth Regent. Even someone who's not one hundred percent ideal could—"

"Don't you start, too," I interrupt. "The *only* people I trust enough for that job are your dad and Kyna. I can't afford to lose Kyna as head of the Council, and you can imagine the flak I'd get if I named your dad, when his father is already my Nuathan Regent. Nepotism, much?"

"I know, I know. I just…worry about you, M."

I reach over and put a hand on his cheek. "I know you do, Rigel, and I love you for it. Once this Faxon thing is behind us, I'll get serious about finding myself an Earth Regent, I promise."

"Good. You had enough stuff to stress about even before this."

"Like this Government project. If we can knock that out tonight, at least *that* won't be hanging over my head anymore."

To my relief, that gets a chuckle out of him.

When we get to his house, he leans over to give me a quick—but wonderful—kiss. "C'mon. Let's subtract an item from your agenda."

We go inside and Rigel leads me to the kitchen, where his mom is just pushing the button on their ionic sanitizer cabinet that doubles as a dishwasher. I really do need to convince Aunt Theresa to let me have one of those installed.

Dr. Stuart turns with a smile. "I left out some dessert to help you study," she says, nodding toward half a pie on the kitchen table. "There's also ice cream in the freezer."

"Thanks, Mom," Rigel says, pulling out a chair for me as she leaves the kitchen.

Rigel immediately gets out his notes for our Government project, so I follow his example and do the same. For this grading period, we're supposed to be putting together a complete report comparing the U.S. system of government to that of another country. Rigel and I chose France, since I take French and no one else had claimed it yet.

Looking down at my notes, I realize they're awfully sketchy. I really have let my Sovereign duties crowd out my schoolwork lately.

"You've done way more research on this than I have," I admit to Rigel. "Who has more power in France, the President or the Prime Minister?"

"I'd say the President." He hands me a couple of sheets he printed from a website. "He's democratically elected, then appoints the PM. France's government is kind of a hybrid between the UK's and what we have here, but with a whole lot more political parties." He shoves more notes my way.

With a smile of thanks, I read over them, grateful—again—that our bond has easily doubled or tripled my reading speed beyond the already-superior rate most *Echtrans* can claim. In less than fifteen minutes, I'm massively better informed than I was when I sat down. I also have a few new ideas for how we might structure the new *Echtran* government.

We really do get to work then, even sketching out comparison charts that Rigel promises to duplicate more legibly on his computer, complete with color coding.

After an hour and a half, Rigel closes his notebook and stretches. "Glad I suggested this. We've made a lot of progress. How about some pie as a reward?" *And if we leave soon, maybe we can get in a bit of alone time for an even better reward?* he adds silently.

"Sounds great," I respond. *Especially that second part.*

With a grin, he gets up for plates, forks and a knife. "You want ice cream?"

The apple-cranberry pie is delicious, the tartness perfectly complemented by creamy vanilla ice cream. Swallowing my last bite, I sigh contentedly.

"It's good, isn't it? Mom got the recipe from Ms. Donner, at Donner's Farm, Dad likes it so much. Ready to go?"

"Yep."

As I tuck all my Government notes into my backpack, I think of something else I can do while I'm here—though Rigel may not like it.

"I should thank your mom for the pie before we go," I say lightly when I stand up, motioning to my empty plate.

Rigel's not fooled for a second. "You're blocking, M." His tone is accusatory. "What are you plotting?"

With a shrug, I drop my mental shields. "Not plotting. I just thought since your mom's a Healer, she might know how to access buried memories."

"She's not a Mind Healer," he reminds me, frowning.

"I know, but it can't hurt to ask."

He just sighs and shakes his head.

Mr. Stuart is in his office when we walk past, so Rigel pauses in the doorway. "Any more news?"

"Not about Faxon," his dad answers, "but I had a brief note from Shim earlier, which was encouraging. Hopefully he'll feel up to sending a longer one soon."

"Oh, he's awake?" I say, relieved. "That's great to hear." I won't pester him with questions any time soon, though.

We move on and find Dr. Stuart's in the living room watching some show that was obviously recorded in Nuath. She pauses it when we come in.

"Did you get a lot done?" she asks.

We both nod. "I feel a lot more caught up now," I tell her.

"Yes, I imagine it's hard to balance your schoolwork with your other responsibilities, especially right now. I sometimes worry you take on more than is healthy for a girl your age."

"You too, huh?" Rigel's voice holds a sour edge. *Go ahead. Ask her,* he adds silently.

"Thanks, Dr. Stuart," I say. "I hope I can cut back soon. Meanwhile, I have kind of a weird question. Do you happen to know a good way to retrieve memories? My own, I mean, not an extraction."

Her eyebrows go up. "Most of us—*Echtrans*, I mean—have such good recall, I've never needed to look into it. Is there something specific you need to remember?"

"Maybe. Did you ever read my report to the Council about my first experience with the Grentl communication device?"

She nods. "Van let me read that and other reports once it was decided to allow spouses and significant others—" she glances at Rigel — "to be privy to Council business."

"Then you know when I first, um, interfaced with the device, I was bombarded by the memories of everyone who'd previously used it—Sovereign Aerleas, my grandfather Leontine, and…Faxon. I only caught flashes at the time, they came at me so quickly, and then there was so much else going on, I didn't think much more about them. But now, with Faxon still on the loose, I thought if I could remember more of his memories, I might learn something useful."

After a startled moment, she regretfully shakes her head. "I'm sorry, but that sort of thing is completely outside my area of expertise. It's possible Ava, NuAgra's Mind Healer, can help."

"She won't have a high enough security clearance, will she?" Rigel clearly hopes the answer will be no.

"I imagine not," his mother admits. "Though perhaps M can ask her advice in more general terms, without revealing any, ah, classified information?"

I think for a moment. "I can just say I want to dredge up details from my earliest childhood for the autobiography I'm writing."

"What autobiography?" Rigel asks suspiciously. "This is the first I've heard of it."

"That's because I just made it up." I wink at him. "It's not a bad idea, though. For someday, when I'm older. Thanks, Dr. Stuart. I'll contact Healer Ava tomorrow. Oh, and thanks for the pie, it was delicious."

Rigel takes my hand then, his worry and disapproval coming through loud and clear as we go outside.

"Are you still in the mood for some alone time?" I ask as he starts the engine.

"Always." He gives me a reluctant smile, his disapproval fading. "How about we swing by the arboretum before I take you home? It should definitely be deserted now, and it's a good place to talk."

I grin, waggling my eyebrows. "Just talk?"

That gets a chuckle from him. "Well, no. But I want to talk, too." He pulls out of the driveway. "M, I don't like the idea of you trying to access Faxon's memories."

"I'm not a big fan of doing it either, but I'd like to at least find out if it's possible," I tell him. "From what the O'Garas, Kira and Sovereign Leontine said, a lot of Faxon's original appeal was because he claimed to be a Mech—and I don't think he is."

"Why?" Rigel turns toward downtown Jewel. "Have you already remembered more of the memories you got from the Grentl device?"

I bite my lip. "Not consciously," I admit, "but when Gwendolyn Gannet referred to Maintenance as Faxon's own *fine*, it felt wrong to me. Call it a hunch. A gut feeling. But I don't think he's really a Mech."

"Even if you're right, does it really matter?"

"You heard that woman Gwendolyn interviewed, who repeated that slogan of his. According to the O'Garas, it's what energized and radical-ized Faxon's supporters."

Rigel snorts. "Gannett probably searched all over for someone who'd say that, just so she could put it on her show for shock effect."

"Maybe, but proving he was never a Mech at all could still lessen the chance of a new Faxist uprising."

For a minute or two he drives in silence before suddenly saying, "Honestly, M, I think you're making Faxon out to be a way bigger threat than he is."

I shoot him a questioning look. "Really?"

"Really. Think about it. There's no way he can build up support while he's in hiding. And the moment he comes *out* of hiding, they'll arrest him again, so where's the danger? Exposing yourself to that psychopath's memories seems a lot more dangerous than anything he can do without getting caught."

The formless dread that's haunted me since I first heard Faxon escaped, and which the O'Garas' and Kira's reactions only made stronger, recedes a little.

"And even if Faxon does still have supporters in Nuath," he continues, "they'd be rounded up in a hurry if they staged any kind of uprising. I just don't see a huge risk there."

I let out a breath. "Maybe you're right. Especially since hardly anyone in Nuath has weapons, they're so tightly controlled there. I can at least find out what Shim thinks before I try this. From what your dad said, I should hear from him in a day or two."

I have no trouble sensing Rigel's relief as he pulls into the little arboretum parking lot and cuts the engine—a relief I cautiously share.

He gets out, then comes around to open my door. "I'll bet once Shim's brought up to speed, he'll figure a way to have Faxon dragged back to prison without any casualties," he says. "Then the Mind Healers can pull out whatever memories they need, without you risking yourself."

The last of my earlier dread dissipates. "Thanks, Rigel. You always talk sense into me when I need it."

"I try. You're under too much strain as it is, without attempting this. Though I do know one thing that always makes you stronger..." Taking me by the hand, he leads me through the archway into the arboretum, then pulls me into his arms.

I eagerly tip my face up to him. As always, the touch of his lips on mine sends an electric thrill through me, infusing me with vitality and a sense of well-being. For the next twenty minutes, nothing matters but Rigel and how much I love him. How much I love our bond.

Finally, I draw back with a happy sigh. "You don't know how much I needed that."

"Wanna bet?" his hazel eyes twinkle at me in the faint light from a nearby streetlamp.

I laugh. "You're right. You know exactly how much. You also must know by now that together, we can handle anything—so try not to worry about me so much, okay? As long as I have you around to shore me up like this, I'll be fine."

"Always happy to oblige." He smiles down at me, though a trace of his earlier concern still remains. "C'mon. I'd better get you home."

The next morning I wake up feeling better rested than I have since my birthday, thanks to finally getting some alone time with Rigel—plus him convincing me I'm *not* obligated to dig into Faxon's memories.

I stretch, roll over, and pluck my omni off my nightstand to check it, like I always do first thing. To my surprise and relief, a voice message from Shim is waiting, a full day before I expected one.

Yet another weight of responsibility lifts from my shoulders as I touch play.

"Excellency, I trust this finds you well," Shim's recording begins. "Given the extraordinary circumstances facing us, the Healers have cleared me to resume a measure of my duties, though they insist I remain under observation at the Healing Center for another week. I've now been fully briefed on everything that has occurred since I went in for surgery. I imagine those events have caused a stir on Earth, though perhaps not so great a one as Nuath has experienced.

"I wish I could tell you that Faxon's capture is imminent. Unfortunately, the situation here has unexpectedly worsened and Acting Regent Ewan has expressed himself unequal to taking on this new challenge. Thus, my involvement rather earlier than the Healers would like. Aware as I am of your many responsibilities on Earth, I am sorry to burden you with another, possibly greater one. However, as you yourself may soon be in danger, I see little choice.

"Two hours ago, the video I have attached to this message was broadcast over every network in Nuath, the signal somehow overriding all other programming. By now nearly everyone in Nuath will have seen it, as well as many on Earth, as it was no doubt forwarded to numerous *Echtrans* by friends and family here. Given that, I felt it best to share the video with *Echtran* Council leader Kyna, as well. Once you have viewed it, I would appreciate your thoughts as well as hers on how best to move forward.

"Meanwhile, our efforts are focused on tracing the source of the video. If we are successful, it may allow us to locate Faxon himself and minimize the danger he claims to pose. I remain, as always, your faithful servant."

Curious, but with a distinct sense of foreboding, I sit up and click to the video Shim attached. A holo screen appears above the foot of my bed and I have no difficulty recognizing Faxon from the archived pictures

I've seen. Black-haired and flashily handsome, his dark eyes are almost hypnotic in their fanatical intensity.

"Greetings, fellow Martians! Are you surprised to see me after my long incarceration by your oppressors? You should not be, for as I've always said, you can't keep a good Mech down!

"I'm told the media has spread false rumors that my escape was engineered by others, and that I myself am incapacitated or unconscious. As you see, that is not the case. Not only was I able to elude the grasp of my tormentors, I remain in perfect health, as ready to champion your cause now as when I helped you to overthrow our unjust monarchy. Once again, I am ready to lead you, my people, into a glorious future.

"To achieve that future, however, we will all need to show strength. You must begin now to gird your loins for battle, that we may finally, permanently overthrow the exploitive elites who held us down for so long. Soon, I intend to lead you into that battle myself. By necessity, my current location is secret but once my demands are met, secrecy will no longer be necessary."

He pauses to flash a toothy smile at the camera.

"To you Martians who style yourselves leaders, here and on Earth, my demands are simple and few. Complying with them promptly will ensure minimal damage or bloodshed. Refusal will ensure the opposite. I expect some of you will doubt my ability to enforce my demands. To silence those skeptics, I have arranged for a little demonstration to give you a taste—a very small taste—of what will follow if you defy me.

"My demonstration will occur exactly twenty-four hours from the airing of this video. You have until then to meet my demands with no negative repercussions to Nuath whatsoever. If you prefer to wait, you will not find my demonstration pleasant. Should even that fail to convince you to comply with my demands, I am prepared to repeat it, each time on a massively larger scale. Those will be capable of crippling all of Nuath, perhaps permanently."

Faxon punctuates that threat with another broad smile at the camera.

"Believe me, I have no desire to cause such destruction. I hope you will not compel me to do so. To avoid it, you so-called leaders need merely grant these three simple requests:

"First, you will release every supporter of mine who is imprisoned in Nuath.

"Second, you will ensure my safe passage to the Royal Palace in Thiaraway, under a guard composed of those freed supporters.

"Finally, you will arrange for the execution, on Earth, of those last scions of the antiquated, tyrannical Sovereign line, Emileia and Malena.

"The lives of two girls are obviously a negligible price to guarantee the safety of hundreds of thousands. Should Earth's current Martian leadership be unwilling to carry out that last item, I call upon those of you on Earth who have friends and family in harm's way here in Nuath. If you would spare the lives of those loved ones, you will encourage —*strongly* encourage—your self-styled *Echtran* Council to do the right thing.

"Remember, you have twenty-four hours—less, by the time you on Earth hear this—to avoid even minimal repercussions. I trust you will choose the path of wisdom. Never forget, you can't keep a good Mech down! Faxon out."

———————————————————————

6

Action potential

———————————————————————

THE HOLO SCREEN DISAPPEARS. I sit gaping at the empty space above my bed for several long seconds before my mind reengages. Looking down at the omni in my hand, I see that Shim's message was sent nearly two hours ago, which means four hours of Faxon's countdown have already elapsed.

Frantically, I reach out for Rigel's mind. *Are you awake? Please be awake!*

I'm here, I'm here, comes his groggy response. *What's wrong? You sound scared.*

Because I am. I just heard from Shim and…we have a problem. How soon can you get here? Or— I stop to think for a moment— *the O'Garas' house might be better.*

Scrambling out of bed, I peel off my nightgown and start throwing on the first clothes I find. *I need to tell Molly, too. And her parents.*

Tell them what? There's now no trace of sleepiness in Rigel's mental tone. *What happened?*

Faxon's making threats. And demands. I can show you when we meet at Molly's.

I feel a stab of panic from him, from five miles away. *I'll come to you first. If you're in danger, I don't want you leaving the house before I get there.*

I don't think I'm in immediate *danger,* I reassure him—and myself—but *I can wait here if you want. See you soon.*

Breaking off my connection with Rigel, I text a quick message to

Molly asking her not to leave for school before we get there, then rush to the bathroom to finish getting ready for school.

Rigel makes it to my house in record time—no way he stayed anywhere close to the speed limit. I'm outside before he can get out of his car and clamber into the front seat.

"I know you didn't take time to eat," I say before he can start asking questions. "Here."

I hand him one of the homemade granola muffins my Aunt Theresa pressed on me before I left, along with half a bottle of orange juice.

"First can you tell me what's going on?" he demands. "What did Shim tell you that scared you so badly?"

"It'll be easier to show you, but I want to show Molly at the same time. Let's go."

Nodding, he crams half the muffin into his mouth and drives the half block to the O'Garas' house around the corner. I scarf down my own muffin along the way, then chug some orange juice before handing the rest to Rigel. He finishes his muffin and the rest of the juice, then we hurry up to the O'Garas' front porch. Molly opens the door before we can knock.

"What's going on?" She looks at me, then Rigel. "Nothing good, it looks like."

"No, it's not good. Are your parents here? Good. You can all see it at once."

Tristan pulls up to the curb just then and Molly motions him to join us.

"Mum? Dad?" Molly calls out as we all troop into the house. "M's got something she wants to show us."

Mrs. O appears from the kitchen wiping her hands just as Mr. O comes downstairs. Everyone follows me into the living room.

"A message from Shim was waiting for me when I woke up," I tell them. "The good news is, he's conscious and well enough to do some Regent stuff from the hospital. The bad news is... Well, you'll see. I haven't answered Shim yet. Maybe you guys can help me decide what to say."

Pulling out my phone, I unlock the omni features with a retinal scan and play Shim's audio message for them.

"He sent this to me more than two hours ago," I say when it ends. "You'll see why that matters in a minute."

Punching a command into the little holo screen, I set my omni on the coffee table like Mr. O did Tuesday evening. A second later, Faxon's smarmy face appears.

"Greetings, fellow Martians!"

Everyone else gasps, then stays quiet as the rest of the video plays— and for almost a full minute after it ends. I'm the one who finally breaks the stunned silence.

"Like I said, Shim sent this over two hours ago, which means there's now less than twenty hours till Faxon's demonstration, whatever it is."

"He's bluffing. He must be," Mr. O'Gara declares. "He can't possibly be in a position to threaten anyone while still in hiding. He may have a handful of Mechs helping him, but they can't do anything on any significant scale without revealing Faxon's whereabouts. And that bit about an escort composed of his imprisoned supporters? Ridiculous. Escort from where? Notice he didn't mention that. It's clearly a bluff."

"Of course it is," Mrs. O emphatically agrees, though I sense her fear. "No doubt he hopes enough people are still cowed by him to accede to his absurd demands just on the chance he's telling the truth—something he was never known for. Shim is far too level-headed to believe him, I'm sure."

Rigel has my hand in a death-grip, so I'm fully aware of his growing tension before he speaks up. "What about that last demand? If Shim's right that a lot of *Echtrans* will see this, things could get really dangerous for M and Molly even if Faxon *is* bluffing about what he can do in Nuath."

"Rigel's right." Tristan's protective arm around Molly tightens. "He just painted a big target on their backs for anyone here who believes him. Fear can make people do awful things, even if they don't actually support him."

"I'm afraid that *is* true," Mr. O admits. "The Council is likely to receive at least a few outlandish demands before the day is out."

Even as he says that, Mrs. O'Gara's omni pings. Her eyes get wide when she looks at the screen. "Oh, dear," she says. "I'm afraid it's already beginning."

Molly leans over to look, but her mother whisks the omni out of sight.

"We need to keep them safe!" Tristan exclaims. "Should we all hide out here? Or would NuAgra be more secure?"

"Huh? What about school?" Molly asks. "We're already going to be late."

Both boys look at her like she's crazy.

"School?" Rigel says. "You can't go to school! Not when—" He motions toward my omni, now sitting innocently on the table.

As if in response, it pings. I pick it up. "It's from Kyna. Looks like it went to the whole Council?"

Mrs. O pulls her omni back out. "Yes. She's called an emergency meeting at six o'clock, at NuAgra."

I glance at Molly. "Before our broadcast. Good thing we decided to do it live."

"No kidding," she says. "But seriously, what about school? M and Tristan and I have our French midterm and I don't dare skip today's show choir rehearsal. If this thing just aired in Nuath a couple hours ago, we shouldn't be in any actual danger yet. Most people here won't even have seen it, except maybe in Ireland."

"When they do, some will probably panic—and us not showing up at school would worry them even more," I point out. "We should go, if only to prove we're still okay. Sure, the Council might get a few messages calling for our heads, but it's not like Faxon told people to go after us directly."

"That doesn't mean some won't try," Tristan protests. "We know there are crazies out there."

"None living in Jewel," I insist. "Everyone here was re-screened after what happened to Bri and Deb last month. Right?" I look at Mrs. O.

After a moment's hesitation, she nods. "Yes. I helped to reconfirm the loyalty of everyone connected with NuAgra, which I believe includes every *Echtran* living within about twenty miles."

"My dad said a few of the most recent arrivals flunked." Rigel's still worried. "They were supposedly relocated, but still…" The look he gives me is anguished.

"I'll be fine," I tell him. "*We'll* be fine," I emphasize to Tristan. "Well, except for being late to school. Come on. We still have you guys as our Bodyguards, plus Cormac's there. And he and Rigel's dad added lots of extra security to the school, remember?"

Mr. O unexpectedly backs me up. "The Sovereign did make a good point that the girls attending school could be reassuring to our people. They'll likely be safe enough there for today."

That finally convinces Rigel and Tristan to drive us to school. I message Cormac with a brief update from the car, promising to explain more when I get there. Then I notify Shim about tonight's Council meeting and ask him to send as complete an update as possible to both me and Kyna before then.

We reach the school well after the late bell, so we have to stop by the office before we can go to first period. The school secretary frowns when we come in, but Tristan gives her his most charming smile.

"We're really sorry we're so late," he tells her. "Can we get tardy passes for class?"

Her frown disappears, her cheeks going pink. "Of course, Tristan. As you're all such good students, I'm sure your teachers will be understanding."

She writes out Tristan's slip first, then Molly's. I wave them on to class, since I still need to talk to Cormac. I'm trying to come up with a pretext to do that when he steps out of his office.

"Tardy students?" He scowls convincingly at us.

"There was an, uh, emergency," I explain, though of course he knows. "We got here as fast as we could."

"Without breaking any traffic laws, sir," Rigel adds with a perfectly straight face.

Cormac's scowl stays in place. "Into my office, both of you."

He turns on his heel and we meekly follow him into his office. After closing the door, he sketches me a quick bow.

"Your message was rather cryptic, Excellency. What has occurred?"

"This." I pull out my omni and replay Faxon's message for him at minimum volume, so no one outside can possibly hear it.

When it ends, he remains silent for several seconds, then nods. "I'll implement extra security at once. You'll notify me if you see or hear anything suspicious?"

"Of course."

"Very well, I suppose you'd best get to class."

Rigel and I are a solid half hour late to Pre-Cal, which gets us stared at. I hardly notice, I'm so busy silently reassuring Rigel—again.

Cormac will make sure no one comes into the building who doesn't belong here, and you're in nearly all my classes. It'll be fine.

I'm not in your French class. Make sure to check if anyone there feels hostile, okay?

I promise, and when I get there I'm able to confirm to Rigel that I don't sense any threatening vibes before turning my attention to the exam. Fortunately, my facility with languages has also been enhanced by our bond, or I'd probably be writing gibberish instead of French, as distracted as I am.

It's a huge relief when the bell finally rings, so I can escape and check my omni-phone. I didn't dare peek at it while Mme. Broud was prowling the room all through the test.

"Hope you did better than I did," Molly mutters to Tristan and me as we leave the room. "Any more news?"

I glance at my omni screen. Nothing. "Not yet. I thought Kyna might have heard back from Shim, though that would've been pretty quick."

Kira follows us out into the hallway. "You guys look really tense. Has something else happened?" Sean had already left to pick her up when Rigel and I got to the O'Garas' house this morning.

"Faxon's making demands and threats now," I tell her. "We'll try to catch you up over lunch."

Her anxiety instantly spikes, but this obviously isn't the time or place for explanations. "What—? Okay. Talk to you then."

Ever vigilant, Rigel intercepts us on our way to Chemistry. I assure him that I'm perfectly fine, but he doesn't really relax. Neither does Tristan.

When we get to class, the concern I sense from Mr. Abbot, our *Echtran* Chemistry teacher, suggests he's already heard the news. I didn't expect it to make the rounds on Earth *this* quickly! I give him a smile I hope is reassuring, doubly glad Molly and I insisted on coming to school.

"I hear you're in a lot of trouble," Trina gloats as we pass her lab table.

For a second I'm taken aback. How could *she* possibly know…? Then I realize she means being late to school this morning. Her cheerleading buddy Amber helps in the office first period and must have told her we were called into Cormac's office.

"No, only a little," I reply, smiling sweetly. "But thanks for caring."

The look on Trina's face is priceless.

At lunch, we quietly fill in Sean and Kira, though I obviously can't show them Faxon's video. Even so, they're both alarmed.

"Do you think he's bluffing?" Sean asks hopefully.

"Mum and Dad do," Molly tells him. "Guess we'll find out tomorrow."

Kira's gaze darts back and forth between Molly and me. "What kind of demonstration do you think he's planning? And how? Nobody even knows where he's hiding, do they?"

I shake my head. "Shim's hoping they can trace the video source to find him, but he hasn't reported back yet." I've checked my omni several times now, but there've been no more messages from him or from Kyna.

"As long as most people *think* he's bluffing, M and I should be pretty safe," Molly says.

"What about the ones who *don't* think that?" Rigel objects. "My dad says more demands for your heads have been coming in…a lot of them using the exact same wording. That makes him think someone's organizing them, whipping them up. Devyn Kane, maybe?"

Tristan scoots closer to Molly. "Definitely sticking to you like glue for the rest of the day. I can sit in a corner and do homework while you rehearse this afternoon."

She shakes her head in exasperation, though she's smiling. "Sure, if that'll make you feel better. I should be done in plenty of time for that six o'clock meeting," she adds to me.

I glance at Rigel. "I'd like to get to NuAgra earlier, if that works for you?"

He nods—cautiously. *Are you planning to talk with that Mind Healer after all?* he asks silently.

I want to at least see if I can access Faxon's memories, in case it turns out he's not bluffing. Though I really, really hope he is.

We all do. But okay.

.⁺⁺

I message Mind Healer Ava before my next class and she agrees to meet with me after school. After the final bell, Rigel drives me out to NuAgra —though I can tell he still has strong misgivings.

"If she can tell me how to get at buried memories, maybe I can get a start on this project before the Council meeting," I say as we approach NuAgra's front gate. "If it actually works, I can tell them I kinda-sorta have a plan. Just in case."

He's clearly less pleased by that possibility than I am but doesn't argue. Not yet, anyway.

Mind Healer Ava is waiting for us in the big reception hall when we arrive.

"Greetings, Excellency." She bows. "How can I be of assistance?"

Before I can respond, Rigel asks, "Is there a place we can be more private?"

"Of course. Let's go to my office." Ava leads us down one of the hallways off the main area. "This room has extra sound-proofing," she tells us as we go in. "Some of my clients find that conducive to being more open than they might otherwise be. Now, Excellency, what can I do for you?"

"Thank you for seeing me on such short notice," I begin. "Dr. Stuart said you might be able to help me recall events from my earliest childhood, things I can't consciously remember."

She nods, showing none of the surprise I expected. "Quite possibly. Mind Healers are sometimes asked to help people retrieve memories that have been repressed, or for which important details have been forgotten."

"Oh, good," I say without looking at Rigel, knowing he's still not totally on board with this plan. "I'm attempting to chronicle all the events of my life so far, for posterity, but nearly all the records of my earliest years were wiped from the databases while Faxon was in power. If I can somehow remember all the way back to when my parents left Mars with me, I could fill in a lot of blanks."

"I agree, a chronicle is an excellent idea." Though Ava speaks calmly, I pick up both sympathy and distress from her. Because she's heard about Faxon demanding my execution? "You were only a year old when you left Nuath, as I recall."

I steal a quick glance at Rigel, who's sitting expressionless. "Yes, that's what I've been told, though I don't have any *clear* memories from before I was three or so. It's…possible I repressed some of them."

That actually would make sense, considering I lost my birth parents when I was two, then my adoptive parents when I was four. Facts known to most Martians by now.

"Entirely possible," she agrees. "Repressed memories are often inaccessible for good reason. It's a way for the mind to protect itself."

She opens a drawer in a cabinet next to her desk and holds up something that looks like a tiny button. "There is a technique I can teach you which, assisted by this device, should help you to retrieve those memories. If you're *certain* you wish to do so?"

"I'm certain," I assure not just her, but also Rigel—and myself. "Show me what to do."

"Are you really sure you want to do this?" Rigel asks as soon as we leave the Mind Healer's office.

I glance around and note with relief that no one else is within earshot. "Why don't we go to the dining hall and get a snack," I suggest. "It won't be crowded this time of day."

I'm right. Other than a woman off in a corner with a cup of tea or coffee, reading, the big room is empty. We swing by the recombinators for sandwiches, cookies and milk, then go to a table in the exact opposite corner.

"I still think this is a bad idea," Rigel says before taking a bite of anything. "From what we know about Faxon, his memories are bound to be toxic. Who knows what they'll do to you?"

Since coming up with this plan, I've avoided thinking too much about what I might see. But now… Would I witness Faxon murdering my grandparents? Ordering the assassination of my parents? I shudder.

Rigel notices my shudder and catches enough of my thought to understand it. "Seriously, M, why put yourself through that if you don't have to?"

"I should at least try," I tell him after a moment. "After that broadcast of his, a lot of people in Nuath are probably terrified, and as their Sovereign, it's on me to do what I can to reassure them. It's about all I can do from here. And if I'm right about his *fine*, proving it could sway those who only ever supported him for that reason."

He frowns. "I remember how you described experiencing those memories from the Grentl device. You said it was like you were *living* them. Do you really want to *become* Faxon, even temporarily?"

"I…hadn't exactly thought of it that way," I admit.

"Maybe you should, before you commit to this."

I can't deny that bad as it might be to watch Faxon committing heinous acts, experiencing them *as* Faxon would be even worse. I'd absolutely rather *not* do that, but… "Sometimes being Sovereign means doing things I don't want to do. This may be one of them."

For a long moment he doesn't reply. Finally, he manages a semblance of that crooked smile I love. "This is why you're a hero and I'm not. You'd willingly sacrifice yourself for the sake of people you don't even know, while I'd sacrifice all of them just to keep *you* safe. I do admire your stubbornness when it comes to duty—it's one of the things I love about you—but I really, really hate when it puts you at risk."

"I know. But if Faxon's memories can help Shim figure out where in Nuath he'd hide, isn't that worth some risk?"

"*Nothing* is worth risking you, M," he insists. "And not just because it would kill me to lose you. You've become a…a unifying force for our people. If Faxon's escape really does spark some kind of uprising, they'll need that."

I swallow, deeply touched by his faith. His love.

"If there *is* an uprising, knowing everything possible about his background could be the best way to squelch it without bloodshed," I reply gently. "If so, watching some unpleasant memories would be a small price to pay."

Rigel stares at me for a long moment, worry still rolling off him in waves.

"What if it's not a small price?" he finally asks. "You say you have a gut feeling Faxon lied about being a Mech. Well, *I* have a gut feeling—a strong one—that if you go through with this, I could lose you, M. Maybe for good."

7

Guided imagery

"DON'T BE RIDICULOUS," I tell Rigel, startled by his intensity. "You won't lose me. There's no reason unlocking Faxon's memories, assuming it's even possible, should be dangerous. Unpleasant maybe, but not dangerous."

"Maybe not *physically* dangerous," he says, "but you're already under a lot of stress. Delving into that madman's memories could push you over the edge into burnout—or worse."

I reach over and put a hand over his, trying to project calm through my touch. "Right now, I only want to find out if I *can* get at his memories. Until I try, I won't know if Healer Ava's techniques will even help me access my own buried memories, much less Faxon's."

His anxiety doesn't abate. "But supposing they do? Maybe once you start, you won't be able to stop until his entire life experience is in your brain. I'm honestly afraid of what that would do to you."

So am I, if I'm honest with myself, but I don't say so—though of course Rigel knows exactly what I'm feeling.

"How about this?" I ask. "Until we know for sure Faxon's not bluffing, I'll just try to peek at an early memory or two, from before he started building support for a coup. Just to see if I can."

Rigel raises a skeptical eyebrow. "And if he isn't bluffing?"

"Then I'll ask what Shim thinks before I try to access more recent stuff. Remember, this may not work at all. So please, try to relax. And eat something." I push the plate of sandwiches toward him.

60

He keeps looking at me for several long seconds, then exhales gustily. "Okay, fine. But only if I can be right there while you're trying this. Just…in case."

I almost ask him in case of what, but he picks up a sandwich and takes a bite, so I don't. I'm not sure I want to know.

⁘

Half an hour later I'm seated on the comfy sofa in the personal living area of my NuAgra quarters, Rigel by my side. To keep Mrs. O from pitching a fit about us being in here alone together, I told Rigel's dad—who oversees NuAgra's security—he could leave my surveillance cameras on. That definitely beats trying this someplace more public.

"Do you really want to do this before the Council meeting?" Rigel sounds dubious. "It's in barely an hour."

"I know, but if we find out this works, I can tell them I have a plan. Sort of. Plus this means my first attempt *has* to be a short one. I don't see how dipping into Faxon's memories for less than an hour can hurt me."

Rigel seems less sure. "I hope you're right. Can I wake you up if I sense you're getting too upset, like Healer Ava showed me?"

"I guess so, though I plan to start with his childhood memories, so I doubt I'll see anything too bad. Mostly, I just want to get an idea of how well I can control what I access."

With a resigned sigh, he sits back against the sofa cushions. "Go ahead, then."

As instructed, I take out the little button-device Healer Ava gave me and press it behind my left ear. Holding Rigel's hand, partly to reassure him and partly to give myself an extra dose of courage, I close my eyes and begin the deep meditation routine Ava explained to me.

First, I remind myself of my goal—to witness Faxon's earliest significant memory. Then I focus on my breathing while relaxing one muscle group at a time, starting with my toes and working my way up.

When the tension in my scalp finally eases, I visualize a spiral staircase leading down into my subconscious. Once that's clear in my mind's eye, I mentally descend it, counting each stair as I go down. With each step, I picture my destination in more and more detail until I reach the bottom. There, I pause and look around. As Healer Ava suggested, I've envisioned my memory vault as a large library. Shelves and shelves

61

filled with books march away from me, each book containing a different memory from my past.

Moving forward again, I scan the nearest shelf of books. Though the volumes aren't labeled, I sense these, the ones closest to the stairs, are my most recent memories. Older ones will be farther in, with my earliest memories at the very back. Those may be useful at some point, but they're not what I'm after now.

Directly ahead, a long aisle runs between the rows of shelves, beckoning me on. Half walking, half floating, I drift down the aisle. As I go, I glance at the books on either side, trying to guess what's in them. I've progressed less than a quarter of the way when I pause, reaching out to lightly touch the spine of a book on my left.

Instantly, I know it's the memory of the day I met Rigel, the first day of our sophomore year of high school. Tempting as it is to relive it right now, I make myself take a step backward instead, toward slightly more recent memories.

Ah, yes.

Here, on a shelf to my right, are books of memories from my four months in Nuath last spring and summer. And there, just above my head, is the one containing my first encounter with the Grentl communication device. As I reach for it, that book abruptly expands into three thick volumes that I realize must contain the memories extracted from Aerleas, Leontine and Faxon.

Score!

My imaginary fingers tremble slightly as I brush them across the spine of the third, the one I sense is Faxon's—my goal. Before I can lose my nerve, I yank it down and open it. But instead of pages, I find myself facing an archway leading into another whole library. It's clearly much bigger than mine, with book stacks receding into the distance—which I guess makes sense, considering how many more years of memories the Grentl must have pulled from Faxon.

I hesitate, briefly allowing myself to be aware of Rigel's hand encircling mine as we sit together on the sofa. To draw strength from it. Then, squaring my imaginary shoulders, I step through the arch into Faxon's memory library.

If it's arranged like mine, his childhood memories, the ones I want right now, should be near the back, so I hurry down the long central aisle. It takes a while, but when I'm finally nearing the very last shelves, I reach out and grab a book at random.

Steeling myself, I open it and find this one does have pages—though at first they appear to be blank. As soon as I focus, though, shadowy images start to appear, growing clearer and clearer until I'm suddenly sitting in a classroom—an elementary classroom judging by the ages of the students around me. Maybe third grade?

Faxon-me feels sullen, resentful. Glancing down, I see the pants I'm wearing are badly stained and at least two inches too short, noticeably shabbier than my classmates' clothes. At the front of the room, a teacher in an old-fashioned floral print dress is writing with chalk on a blackboard. Though nothing particularly interesting is happening, the level of detail I can perceive is startling.

I spend several moments cataloguing some of those details, then, with an effort, I close the book and the classroom disappears. Back in Faxon's library, I return the book to its shelf with a distinct sense of triumph. Not only did I access a memory, it looks like I can pick and choose which ones I want to look at!

This was all I intended to accomplish in this session, so I head back toward my own library—then pause. I haven't been in this library-within-a-library for very long. Why not take at least one more glimpse into Faxon's past before I leave? Scanning the shelves around me, I notice some books seem more well-worn than others, like they've been handled and read more often.

Theorizing that those might represent more significant memories, I pull out the shabbiest-looking one in the row I'm facing. When I open it, I'm almost immediately immersed in another scene from Faxon's past. This time, I'm in what looks like a small efficiency apartment with a kitchen in one corner. A woman, my—Faxon's—mother, is doing dishes at the sink while I sit nearby on a worn brown sofa watching a black-and-white western show on a small TV perched on a bookcase.

Suddenly the peaceful scene is shattered by loud pounding on the door, accompanied by a male voice shouting. My mother gasps and drops a glass into the sink. As it shatters, I'm engulfed by Faxon's fear, now my own. I hurriedly switch off the TV, then turn to my mother. She's staring, wide-eyed, at the door.

"Let me in, you bitch!" the man outside bellows. The door slams open with a crash. "Did you really think changing the lock could stop me, any more than that stupid restraining order?"

Kicking the door closed behind him, the large, dark-haired man crosses the small room in three strides and grabs my mother by the arm.

"Don't, Frank! Please!" she cries. "Not with—" She glances at Faxon—me and I cringe back against the threadbare sofa cushions.

"What do I care if the kid is here?" the man demands. "No puny, twelve-year-old brat is gonna stop me, either. We can shut the bedroom door if you're feeling shy."

Still pleading, my mother begins to cry as he drags her across the room toward a dark doorway. A rushing, roaring sound fills my ears at the sight and my fear abruptly gives way to fury. Vaulting off the sofa, I move to block their way.

"Leave her alone!" I shout at the man towering over me. He reeks of alcohol. "I'm not letting you hurt her again! Every time you get drunk, you—"

He shuts me up with his fist, a vicious blow that knocks me down. My head hits something sharp as I fall and everything goes dark. As I lose consciousness, I'm dimly aware of him forcing my mother into the bedroom and her heart-rending screams before those fade, too.

When I come to, the awful sounds have stopped but the silence is almost as scary. Sick to my stomach, I roll over onto my hands and knees, then grab the coffee table to help me stand up. The bedroom door is ajar. I stagger over to it and peer fearfully inside.

My mother is on the floor, curled on her side, still softly weeping. Her assailant—my father—is spread-eagled on the bed on his back, snoring. The roaring in my head returns at the sight of him and I'm once more consumed by rage. And hate. And shame, that I wasn't able to protect my mother from him. Again.

I advance into the room, my eyes never leaving the sleeping man's face. He's passed out, in a drunken stupor. I've seen it before, too many times. He won't wake for hours. Or...ever again?

Before I can reconsider, I cross to the bed, grab up a pillow and cover the hated face. My hands now on the back of the pillow, I press harder. And harder. And harder still, when he finally starts to feebly struggle. Climbing partway onto the bed, I use my whole weight to push down on the pillow, holding it in place until he stops struggling. I keep it there for several more minutes, then finally pull the pillow away.

There's no more snoring. No more breathing. My mother is safe from the monster now. For good. The roaring in my ears slowly fades along with the anger that motivated me, replaced by a grim sense of satisfaction.

Then I remember my mother. Scrambling off the bed, I go around to the other side, where she's still lying curled on the floor.

"It's okay, Mom. You don't have to be afraid anymore. Not ever again."

Her face wet with tears, she looks up at me. "What...what do you mean?"

I glance toward the bed. "He's dead. I guess he finally drank himself to death, like you always said he would. Died in his sleep." I reach for her hand. "C'mon, let's get you cleaned up."

⁘

Abruptly, I find myself back in my quarters, sitting next to Rigel on the sofa. "How—? What—?"

"Sorry, M." He puts a protective arm around my shoulders. In his other hand is the little button device I'd stuck behind my ear. "I had to pull you out. You were starting to shake. And the Council meeting's in barely five minutes."

Still trying to reorient myself, I blink at him. "Did...did you see everything I saw?"

Somberly, he nods. "Yeah. Pretty intense. You okay?"

I take a long, shaky breath, then another. "Yes, I think so. Or I will be soon. I should get to the meeting."

"Are you sure?" Worry creases his forehead. "That was some pretty messed up stuff you just experienced."

No kidding. I'd expected a significant childhood memory, but seeing Faxon murder his own father—worse, living it along with him—was a lot more than I'd bargained for. So much for my assumption that an *early* memory would be safe. Not so much.

"Why don't you at least message Kyna, tell her you're going to be late," Rigel suggests, still broadcasting concern for me.

"No, I need to let the Council know I have a plan, even if I don't know yet how much it will help."

I take one more deep, steadying breath and stand up. My legs are still a little wobbly, but Rigel assists me with a firm hand on my elbow.

"I'll walk you to the conference room. If you're really sure."

I nod, pretending more confidence than I feel. "I am. But since you saw everything I saw, maybe you can spend that time writing up some notes about it, while it's still fresh? We can decide later how much to make public. Or not."

"I'd rather stick close to you in case you need…shoring up." He's clearly not fooled by my pretense. "If the Council's okay with it, I can sit in a corner and make those notes during the meeting."

I *am* still shaken by what I just experienced. Having Rigel in the room will help. It always does.

"I'm the Sovereign." I manage a half-smile. "If I want you there, you can be there. And I do. Thanks."

When we reach the Council conference room, I discover a similar discussion going on between Molly and Tristan.

"I know you think you can trust everyone on the Council," he's saying, "but scared people can get a little crazy, do things they normally wouldn't. I need to be where I can protect you, just in case."

Molly opens her mouth to argue, but I speak first.

"It's okay. Tristan can sit in if he wants. I already told Rigel he can, too. Things are kind of weird right now—plus this will save us having to tell them everything later."

Tristan's relief is palpable. I sense a bit from Molly, too, despite her resistance to being overprotected. The four of us enter the room and find the rest of the Council already assembled, Kyna and Nara holographically. At the sight of our boyfriends, several sets of eyebrows go up.

"They're here on my authority, given the unusual circumstances," I inform everyone as the boys move to a couple of chairs against the wall. "Am I right that by now most of you have heard from people calling for Molly's and my execution?"

An uncomfortable silence answers my question. A few even avert their eyes, though I sense discomfort rather than hostility.

"In that case, keeping our personal Bodyguards close at all times seems like a good idea." I take my seat at the head of the table and Molly sits down next to me.

Mrs. O'Gara clears her throat. "At *all* times? Pardon me, Excellencies, but surely you don't expect them to stay with you overnight? Even during a time as stressful as this, appearances do matter."

Molly and I exchange a startled glance. Her cheeks go pink and I feel mine warming, too. We hadn't thought that far ahead!

"Er, only if it seems necessary," I say after an awkward pause. *Awfully tempting, though,* I silently add to Rigel, who doesn't disagree.

Before Mrs. O can say anything else, Kyna speaks up. "I suggest we commence this meeting. I understand it needs to be brief?" She looks to Molly and me.

"Yes, we'll be on the air live in less than two hours and still need to finalize what we're going to say," I tell her.

"And grab some dinner," Molly adds.

"Very well," Kyna says briskly. "As several of you have requested, our first task is to craft a consistent answer to give people who reach out to us. How have you been responding so far?"

Little Nara is the first to reply. "I've made it *very* clear we'll allow no harm whatsoever to come to our Sovereign or to Princess Malena. A few people had the effrontery to argue and I'm afraid I was rather short with them."

"As was I," Teara, Tristan's mother, is equally indignant. "How anyone could *imagine* we'd ever consider such a thing…" She shakes her head angrily.

Malcolm, another Royal, shifts uneasily in his chair. "I, ah, thought it best to delay responding at all until we'd had a chance to discuss things," he admits. "Particularly as his threat is surely a bluff. He can't possibly cause the destruction he threatened while in hiding."

"That depends on where he's hiding," Mr. Stuart says. "I find it deeply concerning that his whereabouts are still unknown. Shim now reports that Faxon's broadcast was routed through several relays before overriding the networks, making it impossible to trace. That, as well as his escape, suggest significant prior planning."

Now Malcolm looks even more uncomfortable. "I, ah, take it none of you are inclined to agree to Faxon's terms even if he's not bluffing?"

"Certainly not." Kyna is emphatic. "Under no circumstances will we capitulate to, or negotiate with, the traitor Faxon. I trust that we are in agreement on that. As to whether he is bluffing…I suppose we'll know by morning. While I believe and hope that is the case, we unfortunately cannot count on it. Should he carry out this 'demonstration' of his, and should it cause significant damage in Nuath, the demands upon us to act will no doubt intensify. It is therefore imperative that we show a united front."

"I'll have someone monitor the 'chain," Mr. Stuart offers, referring to the new, *Echtran*-only internet he set up. "That should give us a better idea of the prevailing mood among *Echtrans* than messages sent by a disgruntled or panicked few."

Kyna nods approvingly. "Thank you, Van. Meanwhile, I will send you all a brief script to use in responding to questions or demands. You may modify the wording if necessary, so long as you keep the meaning —that we will *not* be bullied by Faxon into betraying our principles or our duty."

I sense relief from Rigel and Tristan.

Also from Molly, who now speaks up for the first time. "That's great for M and me, but...what about Nuath? What if Faxon really does cripple it?"

Royal Council member Breann sniffs audibly. "Let's keep in mind that we are the *Echtran* Council." She stresses the word *Echtran*. "Our primary responsibility is therefore to *Echtrans*—those displaced Martians now living on Earth. Nuath now has its own leadership to protect and provide for its people. If Faxon causes any further disruption, *they* are the ones who should deal with it. After all, he poses no real danger to *Echtrans*."

Now I feel a spurt of irritation from Molly.

"Excuse me," she says. "*I'd* like to remind everyone that M is Sovereign to *all* Martians—those on Mars as well as the ones on Earth. She's responsible for the safety and well-being of our people in Nuath just as much as the ones here. We should help her protect them, too."

I decide that's my cue.

"Actually, I may have an idea," I tell them. Hopeful faces turn my way. "Do you recall from my report that the first time I touched the Grentl communication device in Nuath, I was bombarded with memories from everyone else who'd used it? One of those people was Faxon. It's possible his memories can show me where he would hide and any plans he made in case he was overthrown. If so, I can tell Shim how to find and stop him."

Some of the hope turns to skepticism. "Possible?" Breann echoes. "You first encountered that device a year ago. How much do you remember from whatever you saw at the time?"

"Not everything. At least not consciously," I admit. "But I spoke with Mind Healer Ava earlier, and she showed me a way to unearth more details. I tested her technique before coming here and it was...successful." I swallow, not yet ready to describe what I saw. "Successful enough that I'm convinced I can eventually access most of Faxon's memories, up until he was overthrown."

"Eventually?" Mrs. O raises an eyebrow. "Unless Faxon is bluffing, we may have little time before he escalates his threats. Even assuming some specific memory of his will tell us how to stop him, how quickly can you find it?"

I meet her gaze directly, then look around the conference table at the other Council members, compelling their attention.

"As quickly as I need to," I assure them. "If he carries out his threatened demonstration tomorrow, I'll drop everything else and work on this nonstop until I find the answers we need."

8

Negative reinforcement

"I STILL CAN'T BELIEVE you made a promise like that," Rigel grumbles as we sit down to dinner—just as he did silently when I first made it. "Especially after what you saw earlier."

As soon as the Council meeting adjourned, we headed to NuAgra's dining hall with Molly and Tristan. It's fairly crowded now, mostly with singles living at NuAgra and some folks working the evening shift, but we found a relatively private corner table.

Molly picks up her fork, looking back and forth between us. "What did you see? Was it as bad as you expected?"

"It was pretty awful," I admit. "I'd...rather not talk about it over dinner."

"No, that's fine." She shudders. "I didn't know you were planning to dig into Faxon's memories this afternoon."

"I only decided to after I talked with the Mind Healer," I explain. "Rigel had mostly talked me out of it. But with Faxon making threats, I thought I should at least try. It's about the only useful thing I can do from here. If we were in Nuath, Rigel and I could probably find Faxon the same way we found Bri and Deb after they were kidnapped. But since we're stuck on Earth, that's not really an option."

Are you sure? Rigel thinks to me. *Maybe we should at least try.*

I stare at him. *Seriously? Mars is on the opposite side of the sun, literally a thousand times farther away than the moon. Shoot, we haven't even found Devyn Kane yet, right here on Earth!*

No, you're right. I'm grasping at straws, he admits. *I just really hate the idea of—*

"Hey, will you guys stop that?" Molly says. "It's kind of rude, with us sitting right here."

"Sorry." I shoot them both an apologetic look.

Tristan glances at his phone. "You two go live in forty minutes. Maybe you should use this time to figure out what you're going to say?"

That immediately refocuses our attention.

"Most of our audience will have either seen or heard about Faxon's video by now," Molly says, "so we should probably address it straight off."

"Definitely," I agree. "Should we spend the last few minutes taking call-in questions? Or is that asking for trouble?"

She grimaces. "I saw one of the messages Mum got earlier. Hopefully there aren't *too* many people who think the only way to stop Faxon is to show him our heads on pikes, but…there are at least a few. And they're the ones most likely to call in."

"You're probably right. Let's focus on standing strong, and appeal to the basic decency and ethical standards most *Echtrans* pride themselves on. Maybe remind them it's one way we're superior to the *Duchas,* even though I hate playing that card."

"We don't have to bad-mouth the *Duchas,*" Molly points out. "Just say those are values we hope to instill in them, too, over time, if we ourselves don't lose sight of them."

For the next half hour, we alternate fine-tuning our ideas with shoveling delicious food into our mouths. Now that NuAgra is able to stock its recombinators with fresh ingredients from their own greenhouses, it's nearly as good as what we had in the Royal Palace back on Mars.

At ten minutes till eight, I push away my tray and stand up. "We should get to the studio so we have time for a light and sound check before we go live."

"We'll stand guard outside the door," Tristan says, stacking our trays. "Right, Rigel?"

"Yup. But when you're done, I want to talk more about this memory thing you plan to do." *Because I still don't like it,* he adds silently.

Rather than argue when I need to keep my mind on the upcoming broadcast, I just nod. Especially since I'm even less eager to dive into Faxon's memory than I was before my first attempt. I'd rather not think about it at all until I have to.

Ten minutes later, Molly and I are seated on the sofa of our personal set, sleekly furnished in the muted shades of blue and silver Molly picked out. Way better than Gwendolyn Gannett's overstuffed, bright florals. Carleen, the program director, cues the countdown from ten seconds, then the cameras go live.

"Hello, everyone," I greet our audience—roughly fifteen thousand *Echtrans* on Earth, plus the quarter million or so in Nuath who'll see us on delay.

"Most of you are no doubt aware of today's unsettling news," I continue. "In light of that, we're preempting tonight's scheduled interview to speak with you directly. We realize that Faxon's threats this morning, on top of his recent escape, are alarming. We've just met with the *Echtran* Council, and while we won't pretend your alarm is unjustified, we *can* assure you that they, along with Regent Shim's staff in Nuath, are working to minimize any physical or political damage Faxon may attempt to inflict.

"In addition, I'm happy to report that Regent Shim's health has already improved enough that he's able to resume many of his duties, and he's accelerating Nuathan Security's efforts to recapture Faxon before he can become a significant danger. Meanwhile, the Council and I are also making use of resources available to us here on Earth to assist in that task."

I go on to describe some of the measures being taken in Nuath to sweep for hidden explosives and strengthen critical systems. Though I can't mention my ability to access Faxon's memories, I hint at a deeper investigation we believe could neutralize him completely.

"One thing we and the Council must make perfectly clear is that we will *not* allow Faxon to dictate our actions," I conclude. "Centuries of Earth history show that surrendering to a would-be dictator's demands invariably leads to an increasingly repressive regime and an unhappy, downtrodden populace. Faxon proved that yet again when he was in power. We believe our people have the strength, courage and integrity to stand up to a bully, however he may try to frighten us. By doing so, we can set a good example for those around us, to include our *Duchas* neighbors."

I turn to Molly then, and she takes over.

"As you all know," she begins, "I grew up in Nuath during Faxon's time in power, so I totally understand how scared some of you probably are. I vividly remember how he punished those who resisted his political agenda, to include my adopted family, the O'Garas, who suffered personally from his reprisals. Their daughter Elana is still in a Healing facility in Pryderi, recovering from what was done to her. I consider her a sister and absolutely don't want to see anything happen to her, nor to Nuath, my homeland. But the Sovereign is right. Giving in to Faxon, no matter what he threatens or does, would be a huge step backward for all of us.

"Obviously the Sovereign and I have a personal stake in this, since Faxon has directly called for us to be executed. He's always hated Royals, especially the Sovereign line and everything they stand for. But neither Emileia nor I are exactly traditional Royals. She grew up on Earth with no knowledge of Nuath at all, and I grew up thinking I was a member of the Agricultural *fine*. That gives us both the advantage of perspectives no one else in the Sovereign line has ever had. Please. Trust us to do what is best for you. For all of our people."

As she says those final words, I can feel Molly using every bit of her extraordinary Royal "push." Though neither of us expect it to have much, if any, influence over a video feed, we decided over dinner that it couldn't hurt to try.

"I'm receiving regular updates from Shim about the situation in Nuath," I say as the camera comes back to me. "While we of course hope that Faxon's threat is no more than a bluff, Shim is taking every possible precaution in case it's not. I have no doubt that together, our people are far stronger than Faxon ever imagined. That strength will get us through this crisis, after which we'll continue on our path toward the best possible future for all Martians everywhere."

⁘

"You guys were awesome," Tristan declares when Molly and I emerge from the studio at eight-thirty. "That broadcast should go a long way toward calming people…though we'll stay super vigilant till Faxon's back in jail."

I glance at Rigel, who nods. "We watched on the monitor." He nods toward a small screen set in the outer wall of the studio. "Very persuasive. Way to stay on message."

"Thanks," Molly and I say together, then grin at each other—though neither of us is nearly as relaxed as we pretend. If Faxon's promised "demonstration" spooks enough people, things could escalate quickly despite everything we said tonight.

We all head home after that, since it's a school night—though Tristan and Rigel are both more dubious than ever about the safety of us going tomorrow.

"Were you able to make any notes about the stuff I saw in Faxon's memory earlier?" I ask Rigel as he starts the car—before he can try again to discourage me from continuing the memory project.

Though the look he shoots me proves he knows what I'm doing, he nods. "I made a list of the most important stuff you saw. Aside from the whole murdering his abusive father thing, he obviously didn't grow up in Monaru, like he apparently claimed."

"No. Or in Nuath at all."

The details I saw earlier this evening come flooding back. Details I'd pushed from my mind after that horrific final scene, so I could focus on the meeting and our broadcast.

"Both that classroom from my first glimpse, and the apartment he and his mother were living in, were definitely on Earth," I fully realize now. "I'd guess sometime in the sixties, based on what that teacher and his mother were wearing, and the TV he was watching."

"One more thing he lied about," Rigel agrees, "though I'm not sure how we can prove it. Even if we could, I don't see how it'll help Shim's people catch him, or stop him from whatever he's planning."

Unfortunately, Rigel's right about that, too.

"True. I'll need more recent memories for that. If he set up booby-traps or a secret hideout, he probably did it late in his regime, after the Resistance started heating up."

Rigel's worry instantly ramps back up. "You're not thinking of going back in tonight, are you? At least wait until you hear what Shim thinks of this idea of yours."

"I'll message him about it as soon as I get home," I promise. "I should have his answer in the morning. I guess I can wait till then. But if it turns out Faxon isn't bluffing, I'll have to try no matter what Shim says. It's the only useful thing I can do, and I can't do *nothing*."

He doesn't argue, but I still feel resistance coming off him in waves.

I give his arm a little squeeze. "Look, I know you have a bad feeling about me doing this, but with you as my anchor, I should be fine. Please try not to worry so much."

I sense a slight—very slight—lessening of his anxiety. "I'll try. But I really, really hope it turns out Faxon was bluffing or Shim's people catch him overnight, so you won't have to do it at all."

"I hope so, too." And I really, really do. "Meanwhile, let's not borrow trouble, okay?"

That gets a tiny smile from him. "Okay."

As promised, right after I get home I compose a long message to Shim, explaining exactly what I plan to do. Then I set an alarm on my omni-phone to wake me at four. Faxon's promised "demonstration" should occur—or not—around three in the morning and I know Shim will let me know one way or the other as soon as possible.

Not surprisingly, I have a hard time falling asleep. To keep my fears at bay, I use the meditation technique Healer Ava gave me, just to relax. The last thing I want is for Rigel to pick up on my anxiety, since it was hard enough to convince him to go home rather than camp out on my front porch overnight.

I have to work through the relaxation steps twice before my muscles finally loosen up enough that I can drop off. Even then, I toss and turn, waking frequently from nightmares replaying that awful scene from Faxon's youth.

My final dream continues beyond what I experienced during my session this evening, to a confrontation between Faxon and his mother. It's a day or two later, and she clearly doubts his explanation of what occurred that night. She finally goads him into admitting that yes, he smothered his father, only to react to his confession by slapping him, then threatening to call the police.

Turning away, she reaches for an old-style rotary phone but twelve-year-old Faxon grabs her by the arm, yanking her backward.

"I did it to protect you!" he shouts over the roaring in his ears. "You should be grateful! I know you hated him as much as I did, and now he can never hurt you again."

With a cry of pain, she pulls against his grip, then starts sobbing. "What am I going do now?" she wails. "My husband dead and my son a murderer. I never wanted… I never meant…"

"Shh, shh." Faxon puts his arms around her comfortingly, though inside he's still seething with fury at her ingratitude. "No one has to know. Just stick to the story we told the paramedics. Everything will be okay."

I wake abruptly, Faxon's rage and sense of betrayal still pounding through my veins like poison. Rolling over in bed, I gaze around my dark bedroom, reassuring myself that I'm still here. Still me. Not Faxon. As my heart rate begins to slow, I pick up my omni. Nearly four.

No point going back to sleep, even if I wanted to—which I don't. Should I send a message to Shim? It's already past the time Faxon set. Even as I think that, the omni vibrates in my hand and a notification pops up, signaling a voice recording from Shim. Fumbling slightly in my impatience, I open it.

"As promised, Excellency, I'm giving you earliest notice of this morning's events. Though we all hoped otherwise, it appears Faxon was unfortunately not bluffing about his threatened demonstration. Some twenty minutes ago, an explosion at the water reclamation facility in Newlyn caused considerable damage. While the full extent of that damage is still being assessed, the facility will be offline for at least a day or two, possibly more.

"We have the capacity to make up the shortfall temporarily, but if Faxon is able to cripple other such facilities, our water situation could soon become dire. Nor do we dare assume that water reclamation is the only piece of our infrastructure he sabotaged. The news is still filtering out across Nuath, but already I'm getting reports of panic in some villages, exactly as Faxon intended. In light of this event, I recommend you proceed with your admittedly ambitious memory project, in hopes it will allow us to apprehend Faxon more quickly.

"In other news, I have just been informed that the maintenance tunnels beneath the facility from which Faxon escaped were never searched, as Deputy Regent Ewan was apparently unaware of their existence. Not surprising, as most in the Royal *fine* have historically remained rather insulated from the more mundane aspects of Nuath's day to day operations. Rest assured that they will now be thoroughly searched, as I consider it possible, even likely, that Faxon made use of those tunnels in his escape.

"I rather expect we'll hear more from Faxon himself within the hour, taking credit for this morning's explosion and possibly outlining what he means to do next. I will of course immediately forward any such broadcast.

"In the interests of expediency, I am again copying this update to

Kyna. I recommend you both check for messages frequently, in order to keep the *Echtran* Council apprised of developments. Meanwhile, Excellency, please accept my hopes and wishes for your continued health and safety. Shim out."

Because it's not even four-thirty, I don't reach out mentally for Rigel yet. The more sleep he can get, the better shape he'll be in to strengthen me later—and I'm pretty sure I'm going to need all the strengthening I can get.

I replay Shim's message twice to be sure I fully understand it, then climb out of bed and start getting ready for school, keeping my omni at hand so I'll catch any new messages, as Shim suggested.

I get dressed, go to the bathroom and brush my teeth without any more word from Nuath. I'm tempted to use this time to probe more of Faxon's memories now that we know he wasn't bluffing, but I promised Rigel I wouldn't do that without him—plus I left that meditation button in my quarters at NuAgra. So instead, I pull out my Nuathan book-scroll and read back over the few accounts I found of Faxon's final year in power.

At five-thirty I get a quick note from Kyna saying she's now forwarded Shim's message to the rest of the Council. Fifteen minutes later, another audio message from Shim arrives.

"Faxon's expected broadcast aired moments ago on the major feeds." Shim's voice is heavy. "I'd have asked the networks to cut power to limit his reach, but our transparency laws don't allow me to interfere with the sharing of information of general interest to the public—which I'm afraid this is. I'm sorry, Excellency, but his rhetoric is likely to make things even more difficult for you, Princess Malena, and the Council, as well as for me and my staff."

Bracing myself, I click "play" on the attached video and Faxon's smarmy smile again fills the screen.

"As I'm sure you're aware by now, I carried out the promise I made to you yesterday. The water reclamation facility in Newlyn has sustained significant damage. I did hope saner heads would prevail to make that small demonstration unnecessary but alas, that was not the case. Now that you've had a taste of my capabilities, perhaps you will give my modest demands more careful consideration. Otherwise, I will be forced to take stronger measures.

"That water reclamation facility was only the beginning. I also have the ability to disable power generation and distribution, air filtration systems and anti-grav supports, among other things. Each day going forward, I will cripple another, progressively more significant, piece of Nuath's infrastructure until my demands are met. Doubt me at your peril.

"You now know my initial ultimatum was no bluff, nor is the one I have just made. Yesterday I heard some of your network pundits theorizing that I would never destroy Nuath, and thereby myself. They were mistaken. Believe me, I would far rather see Nuath obliterated than submit to a return to prison and the so-called justice dealt out by the corrupt regime created by Royals. Death itself is preferable to that.

"In short, you now have a decision to make. How much are you willing to risk for the sake of two insignificant girls and the continued incarceration of my faithful associates? How many lives will you sacrifice on the altar of vague principle? Consider well and never, ever forget: you can't keep a good Mech down!"

I'm shaking when the video ends—but with fury, not fear. How dare Faxon threaten *my* people after everything I've gone through to protect them?

Last night, I was looking for excuses to avoid going back into Faxon's memories. No more. His smirking, mocking challenge has cemented my determination to do absolutely everything I can to stop him —permanently.

9

Antisocial personality disorder

BY NOW IT'S nearly six-thirty, late enough to reach out to Rigel.

I take a few minutes to calm myself first, channeling my anger into cold purpose, which shouldn't worry Rigel nearly as much as the fear I broadcast to him yesterday.

Are you awake? I send across the miles between us.

Yeah, I've been up for an hour, waiting to hear the latest. You don't sound scared. Was Faxon bluffing after all?

Though I hate to squelch the relief I sense from him, I answer honestly. *Nope, not a bluff. He blew up part of a water reclamation plant and says he'll keep escalating his attacks till he gets what he wants. I should get to work ASAP.*

Now he's the one broadcasting fear. *You mean now? Before school? You said you wouldn't try that again without me, remember?*

This is way more important than school, I point out. *But I guess I should at least bring the others into the loop first—Molly and the Council, I mean. Meet at the O'Garas again?*

Like yesterday, he insists on picking me up first, but otherwise agrees. Next I message Molly, giving her and the O'Garas ample warning to stick around until we get there, then type out a quick message to Shim before going downstairs for a bowl of cereal. Unlike yesterday, Rigel and I both have plenty of time to eat, we're up so early.

When we arrive at the O'Garas' a short while later, I'm mildly surprised by how calm I am, a huge contrast to yesterday morning's panic. Probably because I'm still so pissed at Faxon.

I'm suddenly reminded of last spring, when I was tricked into believing Rigel had deliberately abandoned me in Nuath. The only way I kept myself from dissolving into a useless puddle of despair was by staying angry at Rigel for his apparent betrayal. That anger later turned out to be totally misplaced, but it was *exactly* what I needed to keep me functional while racing against time to save Nuath from the Grentl.

Lesson learned. Stay pissed until the job is done. That should be even easier this time around, since *this* anger is a hundred percent justified!

Everyone is already assembled in the O'Garas' living room when Rigel and I walk in—all four O'Garas, along with Tristan and Kira.

"Sorry to be the bearer of more bad news," I greet them, again setting my omni on the coffee table. "I guess you know by now that Faxon wasn't bluffing about that demonstration. Now he's also upping the ante. He says— well, I'll just let you watch."

I bring up the control panel of my omni and play Shim's intro message, then Faxon's new video. When it ends, I sense horror from everyone in the room. Mr. O is the first to find his voice.

"He must be stopped, and soon," he declares. "Lili told me last night that you have a plan, Excellency?"

"Yes. I'm going to sift through Faxon's memories until I find out how he set all this stuff up, and maybe where he'd be most likely to hide," I confirm. "Shim agreed it's worth trying, so I should probably get started right away. To heck with school."

No surprise, Rigel immediately pushes back. "Won't this afternoon be soon enough? Our Pre-Cal midterm is this morning, then the Chemistry midterm after that. And Tristan and I are supposed to meet with Coach Glazier over lunch. After school, I can drive you out to NuAgra again and you can spend all afternoon on this project...if you still feel like it's the best thing to do."

"Exams aren't nearly as important as keeping Faxon from destroying more of Nuath, maybe even killing people this time." *Not that I believe you're really worried about tests or football,* I add silently. *You're still against me doing this at all, aren't you?*

For a moment he still looks stubborn, though a hint of color creeps up his neck. But then his shoulders drop. "Yeah, I guess you're right."

Now Molly's frowning. "Do you *really* think a few hours will make that much difference?" she asks. "How will you explain missing school? Or did you plan for all of us to skip?"

"No, just me," I tell her. "If we both skip, it could scare people even more than it would have yesterday, once this newest video makes the rounds. I'll wait till Aunt Theresa and Uncle Louie both leave for work, then go back home and get started. Cormac can take care of my excuse for missing school."

"Wait, you want to do this without me?" Rigel exclaims. "No way. You're not doing this alone."

Mrs. O frowns at us. "And I'll not have the two of you alone at Emileia's house all day, unsupervised. Much as I hope her plan can work, there's no guarantee it will—and appearances still matter."

Sean rolls his eyes and I huff out a frustrated breath.

"Fine," I snap. "We'll all go to school and Rigel can take me straight to NuAgra after. Okay?"

Tristan's the only one who doesn't seem happy with that plan, for the same reason as yesterday—he wants Molly wherever she'll be safest. But he doesn't argue, so we all head to school.

Our Pre-Cal midterm goes off without a hitch—I may even have done pretty well on it. Same for the Chemistry midterm, though I sense even more anxiety than yesterday from Mr. Abbot, our *Echtran* teacher. Does that mean he's already heard this morning's news? Not that I can ask in front of a roomful of *Duchas* students.

Molly and I are just finishing lunch an hour later when Rigel and Tristan join us.

"You guys just met with Coach Glazier, didn't you?" asks Bri, the sports nut. "Did he talk about his plans for next season?"

As they answer her questions, I notice Cormac standing near the door leading to the hallway. He's sternly surveying the lunchroom as he sometimes does, every inch the Vice Principal, but I sense something else is up.

Sure enough, Cormac catches my eye and makes a tiny motion with his head, indicating he needs to talk to me. I nudge Molly and nod that way, then silently give Rigel a heads-up as she does the same with Tristan.

The four of us mumble quick apologies to the others at the table, then leave the lunchroom. Cormac is waiting for us just outside the door.

"Excellencies," he says softly, "I'm afraid I have to insist you both relocate to NuAgra immediately. Several credible threats have come in, aimed at the two of you, the school, and various Council members. Despite our extra safety precautions, this building cannot be made secure enough to adequately protect you from multiple determined and potentially armed *Echtrans*."

Molly glances down at her cheerleading uniform, which she had to wear today to support our boys' basketball team ahead of their first playoff game tonight. "Can I at least go home and change first?"

Cormac shakes his head. "Whatever either of you need from home can be brought to you at NuAgra. I recommend you leave the school now and go directly there."

"We should send out a MARSTAR or something saying we've relocated," I tell him, "to keep anybody from attacking the school after we're gone and maybe hurting someone. The last thing I want is for more innocent people to be hurt because of Faxon."

"Yes," Cormac agrees, "that should minimize the potential risk to other students. I will follow you to NuAgra as soon as I reasonably can without raising *Duchas* suspicion."

I nod. "Thanks, Cormac. I'll message Kyna on the way there."

We all head to our lockers to grab our coats and anything else we'll need for the weekend while Cormac goes back to the school office to sign us out.

"We probably should have expected this," I say as the four of us hurry across the parking lot a few minutes later, under Cormac's watchful eye. "At least we got our midterms out of the way first. And this means I can get started on my, um, project sooner rather than later."

Rigel snorts. "Yeah, silver lining. Though I guess the sooner you start, the sooner you can finish."

The boys drive us to NuAgra in record time. Molly avoids eye contact with the woman at the reception desk, clearly embarrassed to walk into the elegant lobby area in her skimpy cheerleading outfit.

"C'mon, let's get to our quarters," she mutters. "Maybe Mum stashed some old clothes of mine here, just in case."

I never thought of doing that, but I don't mind spending the rest of the day in my jeans and sweater. As Sovereign, I usually try to dress a little nicer when I come to NuAgra, but at least I'm presentable. We're just turning into the hallway leading to Molly's and my sumptuous apartments when my omni pings.

"Oh, good. Kyna's already sent out a MARSTAR bulletin," I tell the others, pulling up the holo-screen so we can all read it together.

Quite a few of you have expressed concern for our Sovereign's and Princess's safety in light of current events. You will be pleased to know they are both now safely residing at NuAgra, where they will be as well guarded as is possible anywhere on the planet until all danger has passed. Please check this channel regularly, as the Council will send updates on the situation in Nuath whenever we learn of any significant new developments.

"Why did she tell everyone where you are?" Tristan demands indignantly.

"Because otherwise, someone might have attacked not only the school, but maybe our houses, too," Molly replies. "This will keep people everywhere else safer. Bummer we'll miss tonight's game, though."

I nod, though I'm not as disappointed as Molly is. "Sean will understand. Meanwhile, I'd better put this extra time to good use."

"Guess we should check in with my dad first?" Rigel says.

Molly looks confused. "Huh? Why?"

"Appearances, like your mom is always harping on. The boys aren't supposed to be alone with us in our quarters here," I remind her. "Or hasn't she mentioned that to you?"

She grimaces. "Only about a hundred times. But what does Rigel's dad have to do with it?"

"He's in charge of the security cameras," Rigel explains. "Last night he turned on the ones in M's quarters, in case anyone—like your mom— questions what we're up to in there."

She snorts and shakes her head, then wishes me luck finding what I'm after before continuing on to her apartment.

Rigel's father looks up when we walk into his office. "Ah, Excellency. I just saw the MARSTAR bulletin saying you and Molly will be staying here for the present. A wise decision, as NuAgra is far safer than the high school, or even your homes."

"Cormac and Kyna agree," I tell him. "Anyway, as long as I have to be here, I thought I'd get started on the project I mentioned at last night's meeting. Can you turn my security feed back on?"

"Of course." He's just turning to do that when my omni pings.

I pull it out. "Oh, it's an update from Shim. Looks like Kyna got it, too."

"Maybe they already caught Faxon?" Rigel's mood lightens noticeably at the thought.

So does mine. "Let's find out," I say, clicking to play the voice message.

"Good afternoon, Excellency, Kyna." The heaviness in Shim's voice dashes my fledgling hope. "It appears my suspicion that Faxon might have escaped via the maintenance tunnels was justified. Shortly after beginning our search, we discovered the body of a Maintenance worker at a juncture connecting the Healing facility tunnels to the larger network. He appears to have died by strangulation. It is therefore unlikely that anyone other than Faxon himself knows where he went from there. Unfortunately, those tunnels extend beneath much of Nuath, so by now he could be almost anywhere.

"The deceased worker was someone believed to have assisted in Faxon's escape, as he had not been seen since then. It's possible he was Faxon's only co-conspirator, though we cannot count on that. Though it may strike you as odd, Excellency, that Faxon would kill someone who helped him, that sort of thing is quite in keeping with his history. While Faxon always demanded unswerving loyalty from everyone associated with him, he was never known to reciprocate in kind. Indeed, the years of his tenure were littered with formerly trusted allies whom he later had killed or subjected to mind erasure, often for the smallest of infractions.

"Our search continues, of course. If Faxon is still secreted somewhere within that network of tunnels, our scanning equipment should eventually be able to detect him. That is, unless his hiding place is exceptionally well shielded, as it may well be. In that case, the search will take substantially longer. Your proposed project to explore Faxon's memories may be our best hope of shortening that timeline, which I believe justifies the potential small risk to yourself. Please reassure my grandson that our Mind Healers should be fully capable of mitigating any adverse effects you may suffer from the experience. I will of course notify you both at once of any further developments. Meanwhile, Excellency, I remain your faithful servant. Shim out."

I look at Rigel. "See? He's fine with me doing this. You didn't tell me you contacted him about it yourself."

He shrugs, though with a slightly sheepish smile. "You already think I worry too much. Hearing it from him does help...a little. I guess we may as well get started."

Just a couple minutes later, Rigel and I are again sitting on the couch in my private NuAgra living room. My palms are sweating. Impatient as I've been to continue unearthing Faxon's memories, I can't help dreading what I might see next.

"You don't *have* to do this," Rigel reminds me, picking up on my anxiety and mirroring it with his own. "I'm sure Shim's people—"

"No," I interrupt. "I really do. Even if Shim's people find Faxon fairly quickly, they might not be able to undo whatever he's already put in motion. His memories should help with that, too. I ought to get started."

I open the box holding the tiny electronic button and stick it behind my left ear, then draw a deep breath. As I close my eyes and begin the relaxation exercise, Rigel takes a firm grip on my hand. That skin-to-skin contact bolsters my courage, though it's also a tiny bit distracting.

Either because of that, or because I now know how awful some of Faxon's memories are, it takes me a little longer than yesterday to visualize the staircase leading down to the memory "library." Once I descend them, though, I'm able to quickly find the shelf containing the Grentl device memories. Pulling down Faxon's book, I again open it to reveal the arched entrance to his library.

As I make my way down its center aisle, I notice again how some books are noticeably more worn than others. What I saw last time confirmed my hunch that those contain Faxon's more significant memories.

After locating the book with the upsetting scenes involving Faxon and his parents, I move slowly back the way I just came until I spot the next obviously well-worn book. I doubt I've gone far enough for this memory to be immediately useful to Shim, but if it was important to Faxon, it could be something we should know about. I take it off the shelf, hoping it's just a memory he revisited often and not another horrific one.

Firmly reminding myself that in reality I'm still sitting next to Rigel in my quarters, I open the book and gaze at the shadowy images on the page until they snap into focus. I'm in a classroom again—but one very different from the one I saw yesterday. This classroom is a lot dirtier, the floor littered with scraps of paper, and the boys around me are older. Glancing down at my—Faxon's—hands, they now appear to belong to a young man, not a boy.

As Faxon, I'm seething with fury—and my lip hurts. Even so, I feel a grim satisfaction at having landed more blows than I received before the guards in the hall pulled those other two boys off me. The roaring in my ears is now a near-constant background presence, I'm angry so much of the time.

With the small part of my mind that's still able to observe rather than experience, I try to figure out exactly where Faxon is. I only have time to notice the bars on the classroom's small window before a rough voice calls my name and I'm sucked all the way in.

"You. Frank Jackson. Director wants you. Come with me to the office."

Crap. I'll probably get thrown in solitary for fighting again, even though I wasn't the one who started it…this time. Arguing's never any use, so I get up and follow the burly guard out of the room and down the dim hallway to the main office.

"You're going home," the director, who's more like a warden, tells me when I walk in. "I got a call, something about your mother. Supposedly an emergency, but be back here tomorrow or we'll send the cops after you."

During the train ride that follows, I manage to detach my mind enough to take in more of Faxon's surroundings. I'm almost sure he's on Chicago's El, passing through what looks like a pretty bad part of town. Maybe a useful clue?

Faxon gets off the train and as he walks the few blocks to a rundown apartment building, I let myself sink back into his consciousness. I don't want to risk being thrown out of this memory prematurely. Fully Faxon once more, I again feel simmering anger as I climb three flights of filthy stairs and enter the same shabby apartment I saw in the previous memory.

"Mom?" I call out in what's almost but not quite a man's voice. "Are you here? They told me—"

I break off as a heavy-set woman with gray hair comes out of my mother's bedroom. "Good, you're here. From what that man at the detention hall said, I wasn't sure they'd let you come."

"Who are you?" I demand.

"Mary Griswold, a volunteer with the hospice service. You'd better go in to her. I don't think she has much time left."

Confused by the sympathy in her expression as well as the word "hospice," I push past the woman into the bedroom. My mother is in bed, partly propped up by a couple of pillows. She's changed so much in the three months since I last saw her, I'm briefly shocked out of my irritation at having to come here.

When I was a kid, I thought my mother was the most beautiful woman in the world, an impression that only faded a little as I got older. She was a lot prettier than the other mothers I met at school or in the neighborhood. Younger, too. So young I figured she couldn't have been more than sixteen when she married my much older father.

Now almost all her prettiness is gone, her wasted face deathly pale and her formerly-luxurious brown hair cropped short and obviously unwashed. As I approach, she opens her eyes and gives me a weak smile.

"Frankie. You came. Thank goodness. I—" Her words are cut off by a fit of coughing that clearly leaves her exhausted. When she finally catches her breath, she continues. "Close the door, son. I have something extremely important to tell you…while I still can."

10

Denial

BAFFLED, I—still fully Faxon—shut the bedroom door and lock it, then walk back and lower myself into the straight-backed chair next to my mother's bed.

"What? What do you need to tell me?"

"Something I should have told you much sooner." She sounds apologetic. "It never seemed like the right time, and I wasn't sure it would be safe. But now that I'm... Well, I don't dare delay any longer. You need to know about your heritage. So you can make the best use of it."

"My heritage? If you're going to tell me the guy who abused us all those years wasn't really my father, I'm completely fine with that. More than fine." Some of the guards at juvie hall are sadistic bullies, but I've never hated anyone more than the person I used to call Dad.

Now my mother's smile is sad. "No, I'm afraid he really was your father. It would be hard to deny, you've grown to look so much like him. It's probably difficult for you to imagine, but when he and I first met, and for a few years afterward, he was actually quite charming. Until... he wasn't."

Must have been before I was born, because I sure as hell don't remember him ever being remotely charming. "So what *do* you need to tell me?"

"The truth about myself. And you. I'm afraid it will be rather a lot for you to take in."

"Go on," I say when she hesitates.

Her eyes search my face, then she gives a little nod. "Believe it or not, I was born on Mars. Nearly eighty years ago."

Oh. Great. She's gone nuts. But she looks so fragile, I don't come right out and say so to her face.

"Mars. Okay. Gotta say, nobody would ever guess you're eighty years old. Martians must age a lot slower than humans, huh?"

She doesn't seem to pick up on my sarcasm. "Yes, we do. If I'd taken better care of myself, even here on Earth I would likely live another hundred years. Longer, if I'd remained on Mars, given my bloodline and my family's resources."

"Huh?"

"My family there belongs to the Royal *fine*. When I left, my father was highly placed in the Nuathan legislature. We were exceedingly well off. While there, I lived in…well, dramatically more luxurious surroundings than these." She glances around the squalid little room. "In later years, I frequently regretted leaving."

"Then why did you?" I still don't believe a word of it, but I'm starting to wonder how elaborate this fantasy of hers is.

Her face twists, a tear trickling from the corner of one eye. "I was still in my twenties, just shy of my majority but eagerly looking forward to joining with the young man I loved, when my father arranged a match for me. The man my father wanted me to marry was much higher ranking, second cousin to the Sovereign, but more than two decades older. I refused, then stole away to meet my love, hoping to persuade him to marry me in secret and foil my father's plan. Instead, he turned his back on me rather than risk angering my father or the Sovereign. With no one left on Mars I could trust, I booked a berth on the next ship leaving for Earth, where I could start a new life far from everyone who'd betrayed me."

Wow. More elaborate than I expected. "So I guess you never went back?"

"No, though after a few years I considered it. I'd grown tired of Dun Cloch, the Martian community where I was living. The winters were harsh, even colder than here. I'd made very few friends, partly because I kept my true identity secret. Swallowing my pride, I sent a message to my parents, begging forgiveness and asking to return, but…they rejected me. They'd told everyone on Mars I had died in an accident on Earth. They made it clear they no longer considered me their daughter. I left Dun Cloch shortly afterward and found work here in Chicago, where I eventually met your father. My life improved…for a few years. But soon after you were born, he began to change. I…wish you could have known the man he was at first."

"I don't," I reply harshly. "He must've always been a jerk deep down. Was it after things got bad again that you started concocting this whole backstory? To help you cope?"

She regards me sadly. "I was afraid you wouldn't believe me. But I can prove it."

My eyebrows go up. "You can? How?"

Sitting up a little straighter, she starts to reach toward the nightstand next to the bed, but then falls back against the pillows, coughing.

"I can't…" she gasps, her eyes nearly fluttering closed. But then she rallies a little. "Open the top drawer and reach all the way to the back," she tells me. "You'll find a small cylinder there."

Mystified, I do what she asks. The whole front of the drawer is stuffed with bottles of pills, but fumbling around behind them, I touch what feels like a thick pencil. I pull it out.

"This?"

She nods. "Tap the button on the end."

I do, and the pencil-thing scares the crap out of me by snapping into a stiff rectangle the size of a book, except a lot thinner. I'm so startled I nearly drop the thing.

"What is this?" I demand. "How did it—?"

"Now tap the screen," she instructs.

Nervous now, I do. The whole top of the flat rectangle lights up. There are words all over it, but not English ones.

"I can't— What language is this?" I hear my voice shaking and clear my throat.

"Martian," she says. "Or Nuathan, if you like. Nuath is the name of the underground colony there. If you hold your finger down on the left-hand side of the screen, you can change it to English."

I again follow her directions and see a whole long list of languages—French, Spanish, Italian, Mandarin and more, but with English at the top. I tap that and suddenly I can read what's on the little screen.

"Long, long ago, during the reign of Sovereign Arturo, there was a girl," I read aloud, then look up at my mother. "It's a storybook?"

"That one is," she confirms. "There are several thousand books in there, not all of them fiction—though most are. I always loved stories. But that doesn't matter. Do you believe me now?"

I stare at the impossible device in my hands, then back at my mother. "I...guess so?" I sure can't think of any other explanation for this thing.

"Good. I'm afraid I don't have much time left, but if you do what I suggest, you should be taken care of after I'm gone."

For the first time, it really hits me that she's dying. "Why don't I take you to the hospital, Mom? Maybe it's not as bad as you think. Maybe they can—"

"No." She shakes her head so hard it starts her coughing again. "I did that weeks ago, when the pain started getting worse. There's nothing they can do. In fact, my heart could fail at any moment, so you need to listen to me, Frankie."

Anger wells up in me again. At whatever's killing her, at the doctors who can't help, at my dead father, at...everything. "Okay. I'm listening," I say past the dull roaring in my ears.

"Once I'm gone, you need to make your way to Dun Cloch, in Montana. There's a map in the tablet you're holding. It won't be on any Earth maps. From there, you can take a ship to Nuath. I'm not sure when the next launch window opens, I've lost track, but there's one every couple of years. When you get to Nuath, go to my parents if they're still alive, Maeve and Carrig Galloway. If not, go to my brother Duncan. Beg them to take you in."

"After what they did to you? Forget it."

She sighs. "I realize now that what I did went against every Nuathan tradition. But I was young and foolish and thought I was in love, so I made a choice I've long since regretted. Except for you. You are the one reason I wouldn't change anything, Frankie. If I'd never left, you would never have been born. I'm so sorry I wasn't able to give you a better life, but I feel sure you can still have a bright future on Mars."

"If you say so."

"I do. You can't possibly be blamed for my mistakes, so my family shouldn't hold them against you. Though...if they ask about your father, just say he's dead. Make up whatever story you like. If you can, imply he was also Royal. That should assure their acceptance of you. The important thing is that you not tell them—or anyone—that he was a *Duchas.*"

I blink at her. "A what?"

"An Earth human. Non-Martian. That must *not* be known. Ever. You would never be accepted into Nuathan society, or even by the *Echtrans* in Dun Cloch. Promise me, Frankie."

For a long moment I don't say anything. I sure as hell won't promise to *beg* those people back on Mars for any favors! But when her face starts to crumple again, I relent—a little.

"I promise I'll try to go to that place in Montana," I tell her. "And maybe even Mars. And I won't ever let on who my father was. Good enough?"

She regards me searchingly, like she's trying to decide, then finally says, "Yes. I suppose that's the most I can ask. Even in Dun Cloch I believe you'll have a far better life than you've had here. I wish now I'd taken you there myself. After your father died, I should have—"

"Hey, don't worry about it." I put a hand on her arm. Gently, despite the anger and resentment I'm still feeling. "You did what you thought was best. And I'll be fine. More than fine. I promise."

A smile smooths the worry from her features. "I know you will."

Her eyes drift closed. Seconds later, she stops breathing.

She's dead.

For several long minutes I watch her face, tracing what remains of her former beauty, imprinting it on my memory. Because I intend to make all the people who did this to her pay, one way or another.

Infused with new purpose, I stand up. Still gripping the book-tablet thing she gave me, I stride from the room, then the apartment, ignoring the hovering hospice woman.

If that Dun Cloch place in Montana really exists, I'll find it. That's the first step. Then…I'll figure out the rest from there.

Deep in thought, I'm descending the apartment building stairs down to the street when I feel someone shaking my shoulder. I turn angrily, drawing back my fist to punch the jerk…but no one's there.

Confused, I look around wildly. Then the dingy stairwell around me fades away and I find myself holding a book.

Oh. Right. One of Faxon's memory books. M again, I stare at it for a few seconds, then close it and replace it on the shelf. Still slightly disoriented, I make my way to the archway and into my own library, then to the imaginary stairs that will bring me back to full consciousness.

.⁺₊

"You okay?" Rigel asks as I open my eyes and detach the electronic button from behind my left ear. "Or do you still want to punch me?" He grins, but it looks forced. Mostly, I sense worry and uncertainty from him.

I manage an answering smile. "I'm fine. I think. I will be, anyway. Give me a minute. I guess that was you shaking me?"

He nods. "I didn't want to just yank you out like last time, but you were in a trance for going on two hours. And it looked like you'd gotten all you were going to out of that particular memory."

"Two hours?" It seemed longer…and shorter. "Sorry. That you had to just sit here that whole time, I mean."

"Hey, I'm totally willing to do whatever helps. I am a little stiff, though. You probably are, too."

He's right. Standing, I flex my shoulders and roll my head around, making my neck crackle. Next, I swing my arms a few times, reach up, arching my back, then bend forward to touch my toes. Beside me, Rigel's doing the same.

"We should probably go find the others," I say after a little more stretching. "But first, let's talk about what I…we…just learned about Faxon."

"Good idea," Rigel agrees. "I thought you were going to try for more recent memories? I mean, finding out his mother was Royal and his father was a *Duchas* is pretty huge, but it doesn't get us any closer to stopping what he's doing in Nuath."

Again, he's absolutely right. "I know. But I could tell that particular memory was important to him and wanted to find out why. Now I know. What his mother told him on her deathbed changed him. It's what started him on the path he's followed ever since."

"Yeah." Rigel frowns. "I guess you could say it was his 'inciting incident,' like Ms. Raymond says in Lit class—the thing that sparked his lifelong quest for revenge against both the *Duchas* and Royals. Because of what they did to his mother."

Rigel putting it into words crystalizes the truth of what he's saying. "Talk about generalizing, though," I say after a moment's thought. "Because of what one *Duchas* man did—a man he'd already *murdered*— he launched a vendetta against all Earth humans. And he apparently holds *all* Royals responsible for what one family did to his mother."

"No one ever said Faxon was exactly sane," Rigel reminds me. "So, do you want to write all this down now, or can we go grab a snack first? I didn't really get lunch, so I'm starving."

The mention of something as ordinary as food helps me detach more thoroughly from the disturbing environment of Faxon's mind.

"Yeah, let's find Molly and Tristan and get you something to eat. They'll definitely want to hear what we just found out."

There's no answer when I ring the door chime on Molly's apartment, which is directly across from mine. After waiting a couple of minutes, Rigel and I head for the dining hall and see Molly and Tristan in the big main area, talking with Mr. and Mrs. O'Gara. Molly's holding a small suitcase and her mother has another. They all turn as we approach.

"I packed some overnight things for you both," Mrs. O says, handing her bag to me. "I told your aunt you would be working on a project here over the weekend. Fortunately, she didn't ask for details."

That doesn't surprise me a bit. "Thanks, Mrs. O'Gara. I know Molly will be glad to change out of her cheer uniform. Rigel and I were just making some progress on that, um, project."

"Not alone in your quarters, I hope?" One eyebrow goes up.

I explain about Mr. Stuart keeping the surveillance cameras on, which mollifies her—somewhat.

"Hm. I'll just go speak with him," she says. "Though I suppose it's as well you're not wasting any time. There's no knowing what Faxon may have planned for tomorrow."

As she heads for Mr. Stuart's office, Molly looks at me. "We figured you'd take a break a lot sooner than this." She examines my face. "Was it...intense?"

"Let's go get something to eat and we'll tell you about it," Rigel says.

Mr. O'Gara comes with us to the dining hall, where he invites us to join him at one of the larger tables, where Tristan's mom and Breann are already sitting.

"So, what did you see in Faxon's memories?" Molly prompts as we all sit down. "Last night you didn't want to talk about it."

"This session wasn't as bad, though still kind of unpleasant," I reply, realizing I never told anyone about Faxon murdering his father. "Longer, too. What I learned probably won't help Shim right away, but I discovered some *really* interesting stuff about Faxon."

Everyone's attention is immediately caught.

"Oh? What would that be?" Mr. O'Gara asks.

Before I can answer, Rigel's dad and Mrs. O enter the room and walk over to us. "May we join you? I've just archived the Sovereign's security feed so that it can be reviewed later if anyone deems it necessary." He glances at Mrs. O. "And as requested, it will be monitored in real time going forward."

She looks a little embarrassed. "Thank you, Van. I'm sure you understand, Excellency, why I thought that necessary?"

"Appearances," Molly and I say together, with matching grimaces.

"Yes, Mum, we get it," Molly adds. "But never mind that now. M, tell us what you found out."

Rigel stands up. "Why don't I get us something from the recombinators while you explain, since I already know."

I nod, then take a deep breath and face the others. "The very first time I heard Faxon was supposedly from the Maintenance *fine*, I had a gut feeling that wasn't true. That's what originally gave me the idea of checking out his memories. It turns out I was even more right than I thought."

"You saw something to suggest he belongs to a different *fine*?" Teara asks.

"Way different," I confirm. "And that's not all. I just watched his mother's very last conversation with him before she died—on Earth—when she told him the whole truth about himself. He had no idea before that about Nuath, *Echtrans*, any of it."

There's an audible gasp from nearly everyone at the table.

"How is that possible?" Mr. O'Gara demands. "He always claimed, and everyone believed, that he was born and raised in The Cogs, in Monaru."

"I know. But did he ever offer any proof?" I ask.

He seems as startled by the question as Kira was. "Not that I personally recall, but surely—"

"Kira told me The Cogs has never kept very good records, so it would have been easy for Faxon to create a fake backstory that couldn't be disproven," I point out. "And what he claimed definitely wasn't true. He was born and raised on Earth—in Chicago. At least, that's where he and his mother were living before she died."

They're all still exclaiming over that when Rigel returns with a big plate of sandwiches and two glasses of milk.

I haven't even told them the big news yet, I think to him as he sits down.

I know. I was listening in. You might as well spill the whole thing.

I clear my throat and the others immediately fall silent.

"There's more. Like I said, Faxon grew up thinking he was a *Duchas*

—not that he knew what that was. And his father actually was *Duchas*. Only Faxon's mother was Martian…from the Royal *fine*."

"*What?!*" The word explodes from nearly everybody at the table, followed by, "Impossible!" from several.

Breann shakes her head vigorously. "No. There would be a record. Royal bloodlines have always been meticulously recorded."

"Until Faxon screwed with all the records," I remind her. "He wiped all kinds of things from the databases once he was in charge. They weren't exactly tinker-proof. I mean, the O'Garas flew under the radar as Ags for years so they could head up the Nuathan Resistance, right? Faxon could easily have erased his mother's name and created a fake genealogy for himself."

"Not that he'd have needed to, once he claimed to be from The Cogs," Mr. Stuart admits.

Mr. O is still frowning. "But it doesn't make sense. If Faxon is half Royal and half *Duchas*, why was he so determined to exterminate one and conquer the other?"

"Because he hates them both," I tell him. "His mother's Royal family disowned her when she ran away to Earth rather than submit to an arranged marriage. And his father was a terrible person who abused both Faxon and his mother. From the moment he learned the truth about himself, Faxon's life goal became revenge. On both."

11

Resistance

THERE'S a long moment of silence as they all weigh the logic of my explanation. Finally Mrs. O'Gara, radiating skepticism, turns her searching, lie-detector look on me.

"No offense, Excellency, but how can you be certain these so-called memories are authentic? I'm sure they seem very realistic to you, but without any objective proof, they are—forgive me—all in your head. What you just related sounds more like a scene from a novel than a realistic sequence of events."

"Are you accusing—?" Rigel starts to exclaim, but when I put a hand on his arm, he breaks off.

I look directly into Mrs. O'Gara's eyes. "Everything I've ever absorbed through the Grentl device has proved true. It's how we were able to prevent them from destroying most of Earth's infrastructure last fall, remember? I'm confident that the memories I'm seeing now are just as authentic as those technical specifications were."

"Well," Mrs. O says to the others after a moment, "I can verify that the Sovereign truly does *believe* what she's saying. But that doesn't prove her recollections, or even Faxon's, are accurate. In fact, I don't see how they can be." Then, to me, "Apologies, Excellency, but it all seems so terribly unlikely."

I'm sure it does—to them. I'd planned to tell them about Faxon murdering his father when he was twelve, but suspect that would make them even more skeptical. So I hold off on that. Then Molly comes to my defense.

"Mum, you just confirmed she's telling the truth," she says. "Admit it, you just don't want to believe Faxon is half Royal."

The four Royals at the table flinch visibly.

"It *is* quite a distasteful idea," Teara admits. "But I have no other reason to doubt what the Sovereign has told us. I don't quite see how it will help the current situation in Nuath, however."

"If Faxon begins rebuilding a following, it could become very important," Mr. Stuart says. "I must agree, however, that this rather remarkable news won't help my father locate Faxon or prevent him from wreaking further destruction," he concludes, his expression apologetic.

I honestly can't argue with that—but Rigel does, even though he said the same thing to me earlier.

"I can't believe any of you are doubting her at all." He glares around at the adults. "I hope you'll apologize once we prove it's all true."

His dad frowns at him but he ignores it.

"Well?"

"Of course," Mr. O'Gara says after a moment. "But we're not actually doubting her word, just the reliability of the memories she's retrieving. In Nuath, she only reported getting bits and pieces of memories from the Grentl device because they flashed past so quickly. Nothing approaching the detail we're hearing now. Molly, you're studying Psychology at school. Isn't it true that the human mind often fills in gaps when what we perceive is incomplete?"

Molly darts an alarmed glance at me, then nods with obvious reluctance. "I don't think that's what's going on here, though."

Rigel, who saw and felt exactly what I did back in my quarters, speaks up again. "Don't you think we should at least *try* to find proof of what M, er, the Sovereign learned about Faxon? Like Dad said, it could be really useful if people start swinging his way again."

"That's true," his father agrees. "If nothing else, it would be an important addition to our history databases. Some discreet searches may be able to confirm what we've just been told."

"Shall I ask Kyna to convene the Council so we can put it to a vote?" Mrs. O sounds a bit testy. "Not that this seems like a particularly high-priority item at the moment."

I don't argue with her, either. "No, you're right. The most important thing right now is to stop Faxon from causing any more damage in

Nuath. Though if anyone's curious enough to do a bit of research on their own…?" I glance at Mr. Stuart.

"I'm more than willing," he says, "though I'd have to designate someone else to monitor your security feed when you and Rigel go back to your quarters."

"Maybe Rigel can help you," I suggest, then turn to Rigel. "I definitely appreciated having you there when I was dealing with Faxon's traumatic memories, but now what I'll be looking for shouldn't be nearly as upsetting. I don't think. Probably harder to find, though."

Tristan looks at me curiously. "Why harder?"

"The more significant a memory is—to Faxon, I mean—the easier it's been for me to find," I explain. "But the ones that will be most useful to Shim might not have felt all that important to Faxon at the time, so they could take a lot longer to locate. They'll probably also be pretty boring, so you might as well help your dad," I tell Rigel. "Then no one will need to monitor my security cameras."

Mrs. O'Gara nods approvingly. "The less time the two of you spend in there alone, the less opportunity there will be for gossip about it. Perhaps reserve that for when it truly seems necessary?"

When Rigel starts to protest, I add, "If you're worried, you can tap in now and then. But it seems like a huge waste of your time to just sit there while I sift through what could be years of day-to-day memories."

Some could still mess with your head, he silently cautions me. *Can you avoid those until I can be with you?*

I'll try. I'm sure some of Faxon's later memories *will* be ugly. It's well known he eventually murdered a lot of people, especially Royals. Like my grandparents.

Apparently still unsettled by my revelation about Faxon, Breann abruptly changes the subject. "I'm almost afraid to check my omni, threats and demands have been escalating so much since this morning," she says. "What extra precautions are being taken to keep everyone safe?"

Mr. Stuart outlines the extra security measures he's put in place for NuAgra, as well as what others are doing in Dun Cloch, Bailerealta and other *Echtran* enclaves.

Rigel listens closely as he polishes off the rest of his sandwiches, but my mind is otherwise occupied. I absently nibble on half a sandwich while puzzling over my best strategy to find the memories most likely to help us stop Faxon.

When the last sandwich is gone, I stand up. "Well, I'd better get back to it."

"Already?" Molly frowns at me in concern. "I was going to suggest we check out the fitness center first."

"Yeah, this has been an awfully short break," Rigel agrees.

I blink at them in surprise. "Are you kidding? It's already been a longer break than I should have taken. You heard Faxon's threat. He's going to blow up more and more important stuff until people either give in or Shim stops him. The sooner I find the right memories, the safer everyone will be—including us."

"She's right," Mr. O'Gara agrees. "The whole point of this exercise hinges on the assumption that the Sovereign can find something in Faxon's memory that Nuathan security forces can use to neutralize him. Time is of the essence."

The other adults all nod, including Mr. Stuart.

"Exactly." I turn to Rigel. "You get why I need to keep pushing, don't you?"

Remembering the size of that library, I feel almost panicky. It could take me days or even weeks to locate memories of real use to Shim. How much destruction will Faxon wreak in Nuath in the meantime? Probably a lot.

Though Rigel again glares around at the others, he finally manages a reluctant nod. "I guess so. But I don't like it."

"I don't either," Molly says. "It doesn't seem fair to put this all on M when she's already done so much for Nuath…and Earth."

"I'm putting it on myself," I remind her. "It's not like anyone ever promised being Sovereign would be fair—or easy. Unfortunately, there are certain things no one else can do. Like this."

I stand up and so do several others. Rigel and I accompany his dad to NuAgra's security control center while Molly and Tristan wish me luck before heading to a corner of the atrium to study.

"I've already done all my *school* homework," Molly grumbles, "but now Mum thinks I should use this time to catch up on all the Sovereign stuff I haven't had time to read." Molly's made excuses to avoid that since learning her true heritage.

"Shall we start researching?" Mr. Stuart asks Rigel when we reach his office. "I'd begin on my own, but I'm afraid I don't have enough information to go on."

"Rigel has seen everything I have, so he should be able to give you all the details you need to start looking. And yes," I add in response to Rigel's mental question, "you can tell him what we saw yesterday, too. It might help."

Frowning, Rigel takes my hand. "Are you *sure* you'll be okay alone?"

"I should be fine. Go ahead and keep the cameras on if it'll make you feel better, but these next few hours will probably be more boring than stressful."

Though he doesn't look completely convinced, he just says, "Set a timer to pull you out at regular intervals, okay? Just in case."

"Good idea. I will," I promise, then head to my quarters.

⁛

Despite my brave words to Rigel, I can't help feeling nervous when I sit down alone on the couch in my quarters. But then I remind myself how pissed I am at Faxon and my nervousness gives way to renewed determination.

Faxon absolutely *must* be stopped, and the information necessary to do that *should* be buried in my brain. I just have to find it—and as quickly as possible. Faxon's earlier memories are unlikely to contain anything that can directly help Shim, but if I skip over them completely, I could miss important clues and context. Like...how and when did Faxon become the monster he is now? The better I understand him, the better equipped I'll be to stop him.

After a bit of thought, I decide my best course is to quickly peek at successively later memories until I seem to be getting close to ones that could be directly useful. Then, when I reach the last few years of Faxon's regime, I'll slow down. At that point, I should specifically watch for signs he's getting paranoid about hanging on to power. That's when he'd have been most likely to create both a hideout and the various booby-traps he must have pre-set, to use as leverage if his rule was threatened.

I mentally share my plan with Rigel, who cautiously approves. He reminds me again to set a timer for safety, so I program my omni to ping in thirty minutes. That should keep me from wasting time by getting too deeply sucked into memories Shim can't use.

Finally, my lips set in a determined line, I put the electronic meditation button behind my ear and close my eyes.

"Move forward quickly with *super* brief spot checks, until Faxon starts creating contingency plans," I murmur aloud, to lock in my goal. Then I begin my relaxation breathing.

Mere moments later, I'm walking down those imaginary stairs and reach my memory-library in record time. Either practice is making this easier, or my increased determination is speeding me up. Once there, I go directly to the shelf with the Grentl memory books and yank Faxon's off the shelf. I open it to reveal the entrance to his separate library and walk purposefully through the archway.

Confident that my timer won't let me waste too much time on any one memory, I scan a set of shelves only slightly closer to the present than last time. Spotting another relatively well-worn book, I pluck it off the shelf. This time, I try to hold part of myself back as I open it. All I really need right now is a glimpse of Faxon's mindset and surroundings.

As soon as the images on the page swim into focus, I see he's now in Dun Cloch, the *Echtran* compound in Montana. Once I realize that, I cautiously let myself sink in a little deeper, far enough to tap into his thoughts and emotions.

As usual, Faxon's in a surly mood. He's—I'm—repairing a metal fence, working alongside two other men. Montana sucks almost as much as this job, I'm thinking, but I need the money to buy passage on one of the ships leaving for Mars in a few months.

I might have made it here in time for the last launch window if my mom had told me how well this place is hidden. It took me almost two years to find it, even after figuring out how to open all the stuff in her book-scroll thing. At least there's no way my parole officer can ever track me here.

"If the damned Engineers did a better job designing these things, storms wouldn't knock them down so often," the man next to me grumbles. "Supports weren't sunk nearly deep enough. They never are."

"Yeah, but no use telling them that," the other man says. "Those Science jerks are almost as bad as the Royals—never listen to anything us Mechs say. Someday they'll be sorry."

"You bet they will," I agree. Once I get to Mars, I plan to make sure of it. Somehow.

Getting to Dun Cloch was only my first step. While searching for it, I read enough of the books in my scroll to concoct a convincing backstory for myself. Maintenance seems to be the Martian *fine* farthest removed from Royal, so that's the one I've claimed as mine. Now, after immersing myself in Mech culture, I'm coming up with plenty of other ideas. For later.

With an effort, I wrench myself free of Faxon's mind. Abruptly back in his library, I stick the memory-book back on the shelf. Though it's an interesting factoid that he chose his assumed *fine* while still on Earth, I want to dip into as many more memories as possible before my timer dings.

Moving slowly along the shelves from past to present, I notice two shabby books side by side and can't resist peeking to find out what's significant about the memories inside. That becomes obvious when I open the first one and see Faxon in the act of boarding a space ship that looks like an enormous rock. Guess he earned that passage money he needed. I don't go in deeply enough to hear his thoughts this time—just far enough to sense him struggling to hide his awe, both at the size of the ship and its incredibly advanced tech.

I put that book back and pull out the next, where he's emerging from the ship in Nuath. He's again overcome by wonder, and again doing all he can to hide it. Lightly probing his thoughts, I can tell he's already planning to ditch the identity he created for Dun Cloch, which had him born and raised on Earth, for a different, more useful one.

Though I'd like to stay long enough to learn why, I force myself to close the book because it doesn't really matter…yet.

Two sets of shelves later, I spot another well-worn book. I'm just reaching for it when a soft pinging distracts me. Really? It's already been half an hour? I'm tempted to ignore the timer, but I promised Rigel. Turning away with a sigh, I reluctantly make my way back to my own library, then up the imaginary stairs to full consciousness, where I open my eyes.

Just finished my first thirty-minute stint, I think to Rigel, since I know he'll worry if I don't check in. *No problems so far, and my alarm worked fine. Learned a little, but not much. I can catch you up later. How's the research going?*

Dad and I have hacked into Chicago's police records, but nothing was computerized back in the sixties. Some older stuff was entered into the system later, but there are lots of gaps. Dunno if we'll be able to find what we're after or not. We'll keep trying.

Me, too. I'll take a five minute break, then go back in. I'd like to manage at least a few more stints before dinnertime.

Rigel's worry ramps up a bit. *Be really careful, M, okay? And let me know if you decide you want me there after all.*

I will. Love you!

Getting up, I walk around the room swinging my arms. Then, suddenly thirsty, I go out to the more formal/public area of my quarters and get a glass of water from the recombinator there. After gulping down most of it, I do a few jumping jacks, then go back to my private living room. I settle myself back on the couch and spend the last minute of my self-imposed break deliberately recalling both my anger at Faxon and my goal. Then I reset my timer, close my eyes and start the process again.

This time I only take three deep breaths before the stairs leading down to my library appear. One more breath, and I'm walking through the arched entry to Faxon's library, where I immediately return to the same book I was about to pick up before my break.

In this one, Faxon's standing on the steps of a building in The Cogs, in Monaru—an area I definitely never visited as Sovereign, but that Faxon knows well after three years on Mars. A crowd of several dozen people is gathered on the street below, a far dirtier street than I'd have believed could exist in Nuath.

I again try to hold part of my mind out, to just observe, but this memory sucks me in more deeply than the last two. The crowd is listening raptly as Faxon speaks, their rage nearly matching his…which has now become mine.

"The time will come," I declare, my voice echoing across the dingy alleyway, "when *we'll* be the ones in charge. Nobody has earned that right more than we Mechs have. Who keeps everything in Nuath running?"

"We do!" the crowd yells back.

"Who knows every weld and joint in every *dabhal* building?"

"We do!"

"So who gets every dirty, stinking job when something breaks?"

"We do!"

"But who always has to settle for whatever's left in the markets?"

"We do!"

"And who has the *least* amount of say in Nuath's government?"

"We do!"

"Is that fair?" I demand.

"No!" the crowd screams.

"*Dabhal* right it's not! And I say we're not going to take it much longer! Who's with me?"

"We are!"

"Good. Tell your friends. Spread the word. We have numbers on our side as well as justice. One day soon, those Royals and Scientists will have to recognize the truth *we* already know: you can't keep a good Mech down!"

The crowd roars with approval.

Heart pounding, I wrench my mind free of the scene. Caught between Faxon's savage thirst for vengeance and my own revulsion, I remind myself that what I just saw must have happened nearly forty years ago.

My timer hasn't sounded yet, so after a few calming breaths I move on and pull out the next noticeably worn book I see. Then, steeling myself, I open it.

This memory, maybe five years later, again pulls me right in. I'm now standing on a makeshift stage in front of a massively larger crowd. The speech I'm delivering is similar to all the ones that have come before. Over the past year or so, I've added the depraved *Duchas*, on Earth, to the list of people my followers and I will eventually dominate.

The intensity of the crowd builds until I close with my now-signature line: "You can't keep a good Mech down!"

The crowd explodes, repeating at top volume the familiar chant I've continued to encourage—and have come to love.

Then, "Faxon! Faxon! Faxon!" Men pump their fists skyward and women weep in worshipful adoration.

Caught up in the emotion I've inspired, I'm filled with a fierce joy. I was born for this!

12

Cognitive process

"–SO once he got to Nuath, he ditched the name Frank Jackson and started calling himself Faxon," I tell Rigel, Molly and Tristan as we eat dinner an hour or so later. "Shortly after that, he disappeared into the slums of Monaru, where he started picking up repair work—which he hated—and insinuating himself into the most disaffected subgroups of the Maintenance *fine*."

It's just the four of us at the table this time. The O'Garas left to watch Sean's basketball game, and Rigel's dad went home for dinner with Dr. Stuart, with the understanding that Rigel would be back before bedtime. An understanding Rigel's clearly not happy about.

"So you've been getting, like, snapshots of Faxon's life starting after his mother died?" Molly asks.

"Pretty much," I reply. "I'm trying not to go too deeply into any one memory so I can sample more, faster. Unfortunately I can only hear his actual thoughts if I go all the way in—and some memories are a lot harder to back out of than others."

During my third half-hour session, I sampled my way through a good ten years of Faxon's life, watching his following grow by leaps and bounds. One scene, where Faxon was plotting with his three top henchmen about various ways to sow discord, was particularly compelling. They compared notes on which non-Royals in the capital city of Thiaraway seemed most open to their cause, and which Royals posed the greatest threat.

Leontine will have to go, of course, but the High Chancellor is at least as dangerous to us. A few of the Ministers are getting suspicious, too. Your brother is friendly with Hilagh, right? See if he can arrange a meeting. We need to—

"M?" Rigel's voice is sharp, bringing me abruptly back to the present. "You still with us?"

"Yeah, sorry. Just remembering bits from one of the memories I saw. Faxon co-opted all kinds of people as he built influence. He became a master at playing on their existing fears and resentments, amplifying them. The same tactic Earth dictators have used for centuries. Evil, but…ingenious."

Molly regards me curiously. "Then you're finally seeing some of the stuff he erased from the databases? How many years have you covered so far?"

I think for a moment. "I'd guess maybe twenty years past when his mother died. Which I think was around 1970 or so."

Tristan gives a low whistle. "So he spent two whole decades quietly gathering followers before launching his campaign to take over?"

"At least that long, yeah. And he kept getting better and better at influencing people…and more specific about how he'd exact his so-called revenge once he had enough Nuathans supporting him."

"You still have several years to cover before he was truly in power, then, right?" Molly asks, clearly worried. "Before he started planting all these bombs or whatever he's using now? Sorry—just thinking about friends in Nuath."

Rigel's worry comes through, too, along with anger. "Dad says more and more people here are calling on the Council to give Faxon what he wants. Cowardly jerks. Would it be quicker to skip ahead to his most recent memories, then work backwards?"

"Maybe it would," I admit. "I worried if I skipped too much, I might miss important details that would be useful, but at this rate, it could take me days or weeks to find what Shim needs. Which Nuath can't afford. Coming at it from the other end might save time, especially since I'll have to go a lot slower when I get to the useful stuff."

Starting from the end will also let me skip over the worst of Faxon's purge of Royals. I'd definitely rather not watch that part, with him murdering my grandparents and ordering my own parents' assassinations.

Bonus, Rigel sends silently, picking up on that thought.

"Okay," I say with a rush of relief. "When I go back, I'll concentrate on Faxon's more recent memories." Only now do I realize how much I was dreading some of the scenes still ahead of me. "The important thing is to find out where he set all these explosives, which he can't possibly have done before he was in power. Ditto whatever hidey-hole he's using now. Honestly, I feel stupid now for not doing it that way from the beginning."

Molly objects. "No, not stupid at all! You *have* learned stuff that should absolutely undercut any new support he gets. If you hadn't started at the beginning, you wouldn't know how he originally swayed people to follow him. Or the biggie, that he's half *Duchas* and half Royal."

"Or that he murdered his *Duchas* father," I add without thinking.

Molly and Tristan both look horrified.

"Yeah, sorry, that's the memory I didn't want to talk about last night —the one I saw right before the Council meeting."

"Wow, no wonder you were so rattled!" Molly's sympathy and concern come through clearly. I appreciate both. "How old was Faxon then?"

"Just twelve. From what I saw, his father deserved it, but still…" I shudder.

Molly does, too. "Ugh. If Faxon was that ruthless that young, no wonder he grew up to be such a monster."

My thought exactly. "He and his mother told everyone her husband died in his sleep, so Faxon was never charged. But he must have committed more crimes later, because he was in some kind of juvenile detention facility right before his mother died. It was after she told him the truth that he made his way to Dun Cloch and eventually Mars."

"Sounds like Faxon was a bad seed from the start, then," Tristan remarks.

I nod. "I think even his mother was a little afraid of him." I remember my dream last night. "Though she also loved him. I think he loved her, too—maybe the only person he ever cared about. His whole quest for vengeance on Royals—and *Duchas*—was driven by what both did to her."

We all fall silent for a few moments, then I turn to Rigel. "Did you and your dad get any further with your research?"

He shakes his head. "Not really. There were hundreds of Frank Jacksons in Chicago in the fifties and sixties. It would help if we knew what last name his mother used before she married his father—probably not her real one. That would make it easier to search birth records."

"Faxon must have known it, which means I should be able to find out." I glance at Molly, who's frowning. "But that's not the main priority right now. I need to get info that will help Shim stop Faxon before I do any more digging into his background. Oh, speaking of Shim, I should let him know what I've learned so far, and what I plan to do next."

.˙.

After Rigel and I finish our dinners, we stop by his dad's office. He told us earlier he'd have security staff monitoring the various camera feeds 24/7 while this crisis is going on.

"Hey, Shanna, do you mind turning the feed for the Sovereign's quarters back on?" Rigel asks the woman sitting at the console.

Turning, she spots me and hastily scrambles to her feet. "Excellency!" she exclaims, bowing deeply. "Forgive me, I—"

"Please, it's fine," I quickly assure her. "Thank you, Shanna, for pulling extra duty for all our sakes. I don't know if Van Stuart mentioned it, but the Council has agreed Rigel and I can be alone in my quarters as long as my feed is on and monitored. He's helping me with a project we hope will prevent Faxon from continuing his intimidation tactics."

"Really? Then I wish you both success," she says with another little bow. "My mother is still in Nuath, so I've been very worried about what Faxon might do next."

I give her a sympathetic smile. "I understand. A whole lot of people are worried, but Regent Shim and I are doing everything we can to stop Faxon before he can cause more damage."

When Rigel and I get back to my apartment, I get my omni out to write my update for Shim and see the message light flashing.

"Is that from Grandfather?" Rigel leans over to look at the screen. "I sure hope it's good news."

Unfortunately, it's not.

"Excellency, I'd hoped to have better news for you by now," Shim's recording begins, "but despite an intense, methodical search, Faxon's whereabouts remain a mystery. His hiding place, wherever it is, must be well shielded from all our usual detection devices. That suggests he indeed created a retreat while still in power, most likely against the possibility of a popular uprising against him. We must hope your examination of his memories will turn up the information we need to get past whatever defenses he has in place.

"On a more positive note, I can report that two of the explosives Faxon previously planted have been found and neutralized—one in Thiaraway itself, beneath the *Eodain* legislative chamber, and one in Arregaith's spaceport. Unfortunately, we have no way of knowing how many still remain. Each of the explosives we recovered would almost certainly have resulted in loss of life if detonated. We can only hope that one of those we found and disabled was intended for the next attack. We should know in a few hours.

"I hope your own project is progressing well. Barring a breakthrough at our end, it is perhaps our best hope of locating Faxon and preventing further destruction. The populace here is increasingly on edge, as you might imagine. I expect the same is true for those on Earth with close ties in Nuath. I look forward to hearing what you have learned thus far. As always, I remain your faithful servant."

I exchange a rueful look with Rigel as the recording ends. "I'll tell him what I found out, but I wish I had something more useful to report. Hopefully by this time tomorrow, I will."

Conscious of the security cameras, Rigel gives me a quick, discreet hug. "They've already found and disabled some of Faxon's bombs, so not *everything* depends on you spending hours in his twisted mind. I can tell it's already stressing you out."

Though I can't honestly deny that, I shrug. "The quicker I find what Shim needs, the sooner I can stop being stressed about it. We knew me being Sovereign would have downsides. This one isn't nearly as bad as some we've dealt with. At least we're together."

"For a couple more hours, anyway." Rigel grimaces. "Dad—and especially Mrs. O—were *super* clear I can't stay here overnight, now that Cormac's around. Ditto Tristan, since Molly has Gilda for security. And yes, we did argue," he adds before I can ask.

I sigh. "I suppose as Sovereign I *could* countermand their orders, but I should probably save playing the heavy for something more important. Not that keeping you close isn't important!" I hastily add. "If it weren't for the pushback I'd get, I'd *love* to have you here all night."

A wave of longing sweeps through me...which Rigel picks up and echoes back. Usually, we manage to park and make out for at least a few minutes before and after school, but we haven't had the chance for the past two days. We're both feeling the lack—a lot.

Rigel swallows. "Um, maybe they have a point," he admits. "Because there's definitely nothing *I'd* like more than—" He glances up at the security camera and clears his throat. "So, um, I guess you should finish your message to Shim and get back to those memories, huh? If you're sure you're up to it tonight?"

"I am. I have to be. In fact, since you have to leave soon, I should make the most of having you here to shore me up. I can write my report to Shim once you're gone, since it's already well past midnight there."

Rigel doesn't protest, but I can easily sense his growing resistance to this project. Though I'm as determined as ever to see it through, I'm beginning to understand where Rigel's coming from. The more time I spend inside Faxon's mind and emotions, the ickier it makes me feel, and I'm sure Rigel picks up on that. One more reason to get on with it— and done with it—ASAP.

We don't dare make out with my security cameras on, but I snuggle up to him on the couch as I prepare for my next meditation session. Unfortunately, Rigel feels *so* good close beside me, it's hard to concentrate on what I'm supposed to be doing. I have to spend several extra minutes breathing and meditating to shift my focus away from what I'd *like* to be doing with Rigel, to the stairs I'm supposed to be visualizing.

I'm finally able to see them, but even then it takes me way longer than last time to descend them to my memory library, and then to locate the shelf holding the Grentl device memories. When I do finally get there, I quickly pull down Faxon's book so I can get back into his library.

This time when I go through the archway, I stop in front of the very closest set of shelves. These should hold memories from the very final days of Faxon's reign—the last things he said, did and thought before the Grentl device knocked him out. Much as I want to learn everything I can about Faxon's rise to power, these final books are more likely to help Shim.

Bending down, I grab the very last book on the shelf closest to the library entrance, which I assume will contain the very *last* memory the Grentl pulled out of Faxon. From here, I can work backward.

Opening the book, I sharpen my focus and find myself in a dimly-lit, utilitarian hallway. At once, a huge door slides up into the ceiling, revealing a warehouse space filled with plastic and metal crates.

"My lord," an elderly man beside Faxon is saying—a man my own remaining awareness recognizes as the Engineer Eric Eagan. "I must warn you again that this could be exceedingly dangerous, not just to you but to all Nuath."

"I don't keep you around for advice, old man," Faxon snaps. "Take me to the damned door and open it."

Faxon glowers as Eric shuffles forward to comply. This is the only reason he's allowed this decrepit Engineer to remain in the Palace— one of the few remaining competents on staff. The rest are either bumblers or probable traitors—not that this old man's loyalty is beyond question.

We reach the blank wall with the hidden door and the moment it dissolves, Faxon strides into the chamber containing the Grentl communication device. I've now been sucked in deeply enough to share Faxon's furious resolve to force those damned aliens to share some of their own thoughts.

They must be in cahoots with those blasted Resistance people, I think as Faxon. Why else would they be causing power disruptions, or suck out my memories without giving me anything in return? Angrier than ever, I advance on the device. *This* time I'm going to turn the tables on them. Pry out *their* secrets. Maybe they know something to help me finally dispose of that upstart Royal kid on Earth and weed out any remaining traitors here, so I can grind them to dust.

Gritting my teeth, I grab the two copper projections, just like that first Engineer showed me—the one I had executed for trying to defy me. Again, the prongs sear my hands. The pain is intense but I grimly hold on, willing to suffer a few more scars in return for the information I need.

"Tell me—!" I start to growl, when I feel them pulling at my mind. "No! It's my turn! I'm not letting you—!" But I can't stop them. Scene after scene of everything I've said and done since my last encounter with the device flash by, right up to the present.

When the memory vacuum stops, I grip even tighter, furiously focusing my entire will into forcing *them* to reveal—

The pain in my hands amplifies, searing through me until my head throbs in unimaginable agony. I'm sure it's about to explode when I'm suddenly back on the couch with Rigel, shaking like a leaf and sobbing.

"M! M, are you okay?" he demands, his terror enveloping me like a fog. "I never should have let you—"

"No," I pant, slowly reclaiming my senses. "No, I'm...I'm all right. I think. I…should have realized. Should have known what was about to happen. Should have—"

Rigel pulls me against him, wrapping both arms tightly around me. "So should I. I totally should have pulled you out sooner, before the Grentl could—"

"Not…not your fault." As Rigel's fear for me dissipates, I'm able to absorb enough of his strength to stop my shaking. "It was dumb of me to start with Faxon's *very* last memory. Eric Eagan told me the Grentl shocked him senseless when he tried to use their device again—it's what got him overthrown. If you hadn't pulled me out, I might have been completely incapacitated, too. Then I'd be even *more* useless! Dumb, dumb, dumb."

"You're not dumb." Rigel gives me a little shake. "And you're not useless. Don't say that."

I force a weak laugh. "Thanks, but for someone who's not dumb, I've sure made some bad decisions lately. Like starting with Faxon's early memories, when there was no chance those would help Shim locate him."

"You didn't know if you could access his memories at all until you tried," he reminds me. "It totally made sense to start with something you thought would be innocuous, just to find out. Even if it turned out not so innocuous after all."

He loosens his grip on me and starts stroking my hair comfortingly. "It's like Molly said," he continues. "If you hadn't started with early memories, you wouldn't have learned where Faxon came from and who he really is. You've actually found out a ton in just twenty-four hours!"

"I guess. But the real point of me doing this is to find him and *stop* him before he can do more damage. Who knows what new disaster he'll cause by morning? We could wake up to the news that he's destroyed half of Nuath!"

Rigel frowns, then shakes his head. "No, he won't do that. Not yet. He wants to get Nuath back under his thumb, so I'm sure he'd rather scare people into giving in to his demands than go all scorched earth."

"Even if that's true, the longer I take to stop him, the more stuff he'll blow up. You heard what Shim said about the explosives they found. Next time he probably *will* kill people."

I stop myself from saying aloud that their blood will be on my hands, but Rigel catches my thought and gives me another little shake.

"If he does, that's on Faxon, not you, M. You're doing all you can."

"Am I?" I'm not so sure about that. "Everything I've done so far has just been a distraction from finding the info I really need." I take a deep breath. "Okay. I'm going back in. I'll try for an earlier memory from his final year or so in power."

Rigel's worry spikes again. "Already? You're still awfully shook up."

He's not wrong, so instead of arguing, I slant a look up at him. "I know what'll help."

With a defiant glance at the nearest security camera, I pull Rigel's face to mine for a proper kiss. Sure enough, I instantly feel strength and confidence surging through me, abolishing the last of my nervousness. When I'm tempted—*so* tempted!—to deepen the kiss, I force myself to pull away instead. Stupid cameras.

"There." I'm smiling now. "That should get me through another session or two."

Rigel returns my smile briefly but then his worry surges back, now with an added edge. "What if Mrs. O'Gara looks at tonight's recording? Last time we were caught kissing on camera—"

"It was a disaster," I finish. "I know."

When we gave into the same temptation on our way to Mars, it nearly derailed my Acclamation—which would have meant the end of Nuath. It also led to Rigel having a year of his memory erased, then sent back to Earth without me.

"Things are different now. Now I'm actually Sovereign," I reassure him—and myself. "Mrs. O can disapprove all she wants, but she's not the boss of me. Anyway, it was just a kiss." Kissing Rigel always feels like a whole lot more, though. Almost like I imagine—

He picks up on that thought, too, and shudders with renewed longing. "Okay," he says with an obvious effort. "If you're gonna do this, I guess you should get to it before they make me leave."

Tamping down my own reawakened desire, I nod. "You're right. Okay, here I go."

Closing my eyes, I take a few deep breaths and dive back in.

13

Frustration

KISSING RIGEL definitely strengthened and calmed me, but it's also made it harder to focus on what I'm *supposed* to be doing instead of what I'd *rather* be doing. It takes serious mental effort to shove my frustration away so I can clear my mind.

Firmly, I remind myself of my goal for this session—to dig into the final months of Faxon's reign and excavate any memories of building secret hidey-holes or planting explosives. He could have set everything up well before then, but if I can just catch him *thinking* about it, all the details should be there in his mind.

Unfortunately, I've noticed that when I hold part of my mind back, I'm limited to observing whatever Faxon is doing in the moment. To truly access what he's thinking, what he *knows*, I apparently have to go all the way in and *become* Faxon for the duration of the memory. Much as I hate doing that.

Rigel shifts ever so slightly beside me on the couch and I'm instantly aware of him—and the fact that he doesn't like the idea of me going in that deeply.

It'll be the quickest way to find what I need, I think to him, my focus broken. *We both want this over with as soon as possible, right?*

Right, he sends back. *Sorry. Go ahead.*

I quickly discover that's easier said than done, now that I'm again hyper-aware of Rigel's body right next to mine. *C'mon,* I command myself. *Focus. Visualize the stairway leading down to the library.*

Finally, after several more minutes of breathing and mind-clearing, I imagine myself at the top of the stairs and start descending. Still, every step of the way, I have to repeatedly remind myself to concentrate on my mental goal and not my frustrated physical body. I eventually reach the bottom, but my imaginary feet move slowly, as though wading through thick mud.

As I move forward into my library I feel the thread linking me to reality stretching thinner, but like a rubber band that wants to snap me back—to Rigel. It seems to take forever to reach the shelf holding Faxon's memory-book.

Because I've already taken so much longer than usual to get to this point, I hurriedly yank it down, open it, and step through the arch. I peer down the aisle, trying to gauge how many shelf sections there are per year. Thinking about the memories I've seen so far, I'd guess about three, though years with more significant events might have more books than others.

Reasoning that Faxon's final year in power, when the Resistance was heating up, was probably crammed with emotionally significant moments, I walk past the first three most recent sections and stop in front of the fourth. If I'm right, these books should hold memories from roughly a year before the Grentl incapacitated him.

I scan the shelf in front of me and realize at least a third of these books are worn enough to suggest important memories. With a mental shrug, I pull one out at random and open it.

Like everything else since I began this session, it takes more effort than usual to bring my surroundings into focus. Finally, one of the smaller conference rooms in the Royal Palace materializes around me.

"How has this so-called Resistance not been exterminated yet?" Faxon is demanding, waving a tablet at the man in front of him. "You claimed your enforcers were cracking down on them harder than ever these past two years!"

"Yes, Lord Faxon, they are." The slight, blond-haired man bobs his head obsequiously. "Breaking up that critical Resistance cell early last year really ought to have ended their activities. For a while, we thought it had."

Faxon snorts. "I can't imagine why, when the ringleaders escaped to Earth. The year before last, you insisted making an example of that little farming village that dared to stage a protest would be the final blow needed. It was not."

Though I'm seeing the scene through Faxon's eyes, so far I'm just an observer with no access to his thoughts or emotions. I focus harder.

"Er, no, my lord," the man responds. "At the time, we felt certain the extreme measures we took against Hollydoon for their insubordination would—"

"I'm not interested in your excuses," Faxon snaps. "Brennan informs me your so-called extreme measures instead had the opposite effect. Last year's raid turned up pieces of Resistance recruiting propaganda citing that Hollydoon crackdown as a reason to join them. Who was in charge of that attack?"

The smaller man swallows visibly. "Mercer, sir. He seemed the best—"

"Clearly not," Faxon interrupts. "I want him stripped of rank and given a stint in solitary to think things over. Find someone better to replace him. I need associates I can count on for *accurate* information. People who will carry out my orders properly. Now, get out."

With a sketchy bow, the man scurries from the room while Faxon sits drumming his fingers on the table. I can tell he's seething, but I'm still not in deeply enough to feel his anger myself. I try to sink further into his mind, but can't seem to do it.

"Imbeciles," Faxon mutters to himself. "I'm surrounded by imbeciles." Turning, he punches a button on the vidscreen behind him. "Have Chief of Staff Brennan report to Conference Room Six immediately."

While he waits for Brennan to arrive, I work even harder to tap into Faxon's mind. It's *never* been this difficult before. Usually I have to work to keep part of me out, instead. As the minutes pass and Faxon becomes more and more agitated, I do faintly sense his frustration—or is that my own frustration? I still can't hear any thoughts.

At last the door opens and an imposing man with dark red hair enters. "Yes, Lord Faxon?" He holds himself proudly, a trace of impatience in his tone, clearly secure in his favored position.

For a long moment, Faxon just looks at the man. "I understand the Resistance is growing again," he finally says without preamble. "How is that possible?"

Some of Brennan's assurance fades. "So it's been reported, my lord. We are still working to determine why. As you know, we either control or monitor all communication channels now, and you have successfully sown doubt among the populace about the reliability of those few media outlets that dare to criticize you. Our best guess is that they are sharing information in person rather than electronically, making it more difficult to intercept."

"Then your people need to expose and eliminate those passing that information, along with anyone they've contacted. Dissent is like a cancer. If we don't root it out in its early stages, it will eat away at everything I've built. I won't have my work, my legacy, destroyed by these malefactors."

Brennan looks like he wants to say something, but thinks better—or worse—of it. "Yes, my lord."

"What?" Faxon glares up at him. "If you have something to say, spit it out."

The man shifts his feet uncomfortably. "It, ah, may be time for you to again remind the people of all you've done for them, how much better off they are now than they were under the Sovereigns. These recent harsh crackdowns have led to a lot of grumbling. We need a distraction. One of those rousing speeches you used to deliver might—"

"Yes, yes, I'll give it some thought," Faxon replies irritably. He doesn't like being told what to do. "Do you remember Matthews?" he suddenly asks.

Brennan blinks, his uneasiness more pronounced now. "Your first chief of staff? Yes."

"Good." Faxon holds Brennan's gaze for a long moment. "You may go."

The moment he leaves, Faxon activates the vidscreen again. "Tell my chief of security I want Brennan's movements and communications monitored. I'll expect daily reports. Faxon out."

Slapping both hands down, hard, on the table, Faxon stands. As he strides out of the room, I'm finally—finally!—able to hear his surface thoughts.

Matthews was unflinchingly loyal, too…at first. But over the next five years, his allegiances shifted. I was naive not to notice the signs. If I'd had him executed sooner, that first abortive uprising against me would never have happened.

He turns toward his quarters, still thinking. *Brennan's been my most competent chief of staff yet. Finding someone to replace him who's both competent and loyal won't be easy, there are so few of those left. If he grows any more ambitious, though, I may have no choice.*

Another small movement by Rigel yanks my focus out of the

memory and back to the couch in my quarters. Argh! Why is this so hard right now?

Mentally gritting my teeth, I put the memory-book back on the shelf and pull down another. Again I have to focus for longer than usual before I find myself in a different conference room, in the middle of another meeting. Half a dozen people are present at this one, taking turns reading status reports. It's boring stuff and Faxon doesn't seem all that engaged. I back out.

One more, I tell myself, putting that book back, too. I choose one that's a little more recent and noticeably more worn than the last.

Faxon is standing on a Palace balcony this time, one I stood on myself while giving speeches to convince people to emigrate to Earth. This balcony gives the appearance of being open, but is actually surrounded by near-invisible reactive glass that serves as both shield and occasional vidscreen. Below is a large crowd, some of whom are clearly reporters for the various networks.

"—when the Royals were still in charge?" Faxon is saying, his amplified voice booming across the square below. "They had the best houses, the best food, and plenty of leisure time, while we worked our fingers to the bone for them. Now housing and food are available regardless of *fine*. Scientists don't have any more rights than Mechs now, thanks to me. No other leader could have done that for you!"

Most of the assembled people cheer, some wildly. Faxon smiles. I'm about to pull out of this memory, too, when there's a disturbance near the back of the crowd.

"Where's my son?" a man shouts. "He was forced to join your army of thugs and we haven't seen him since!"

"Your *bullochts* killed my husband just because of something he said," a woman next to him screams.

"When will our village get power back?" a teenaged girl behind them demands. "Nothing's working anymore!"

Faxon's clearly furious, though I'm still not picking up his thoughts or even emotions. He turns to an aide hovering just inside the doorway behind him and yanks the mic button off his collar. "Have those people arrested," he snaps. "And where's my security chief? Everyone down there was supposed to be vetted."

The aide hurries off and a moment later the blond man I saw in a previous memory appears in the doorway.

"How did those hecklers get in?" Faxon demands. "You said you secured the square."

"I...I don't know, my lord. Everyone was scanned and questioned before—"

"Never mind. I want them removed, identified and executed. They're obviously trained actors working for the Resistance, not regular Nuathans. Make sure those reporters know that."

"Y...yes, my lord." Bowing, the man backs away, clearly terrified. And no wonder. He's probably not long for this world either, as pissed as Faxon is.

Turning back to the crowd, Faxon replaces the mic on his tunic and continues his interrupted speech, again extolling the equality everyone enjoys under his leadership. As he starts talking about the abundance they can all expect once the *Duchas* are conquered, Rigel yawns beside me on the couch.

Aware of him again, I suddenly realize how tired I am, too, after getting almost no sleep last night. Maybe that's why I'm having such a hard time getting into Faxon's head?

This memory's not likely to reveal anything I need anyway, so I replace the book on the shelf and go back through the archway to my own library, then up the stairs—a whole lot faster than I came down them.

"You done?" Rigel asks when I open my eyes. Then yawns again.

"For now. I'm tired, you're tired...probably time to call it a night. I just wish I'd found something, anything, that could help Shim."

Rigel wraps an arm around my shoulders. "Hey, you're even more worn out than I am. Give yourself a break. Seriously."

Though I appreciate his support, I feel a spurt of irritation—along with guilt over how unproductive this session was. "You heard him ordering those poor protesters executed. What if taking a break gives Faxon time to kill even more people overnight? Don't I owe them—"

"You can only do so much." Rigel is firm now. "Sovereign or not, you're still just human and need sleep to function. C'mon. Walk me to the door and then get yourself to bed. I'll come back first thing tomorrow."

He's right, as always. "Okay."

Rigel helps me up from the couch. Hand in hand, we leave my private quarters and walk through the outer, more public-facing rooms to the ornate little foyer. We're nearly to the door when I suddenly notice there are no cameras—none—directly in view. I don't say a word, just grab Rigel and pull him against me for a kiss. A *real* kiss. The kind of kiss I've been longing for all day.

After a stunned moment, his arms come around me and he joins in wholeheartedly. Minutes pass before we reluctantly separate.

"Um, wow," he mutters. "I know we both needed that, but won't they—?"

Shaking my head, I look up, then around. He follows my gaze, then grins.

"Ah. That was quick thinking. But I'd better go. If anyone reviews the camera feed, they might notice the delay between us leaving your living room and me leaving your quarters."

"Maybe," I admit with a little shrug. "But it was worth it."

He doesn't disagree. *I just hope they don't put extra rules on us.*

If they try, I'll overrule them. My lack of success is making me cranky, though that kiss did give me another energy boost. "See you in the morning," I say aloud, opening the outer door. "Love you."

"Love you. G'night, M." Even though there are cameras in the corridor, he leans down for a quick, final kiss.

As he walks away, my exhaustion comes crashing back. Yawning, I close the door and turn back to my private rooms, only pausing long enough in the formal area to get a cup of hot chocolate from the recombinator. I'll need it to stay awake long enough to write and send my mostly-useless update to Shim.

⁖

A soft pinging wakes me from a deep, deep sleep. I'm dimly aware of a dream, but the details escape before I can grasp them. Just as well. It wasn't a pleasant dream.

Rolling over, I pluck my omni off the night stand and gasp. It's nearly nine o'clock in the morning! I could swear I set an alarm to go off at five to check on the latest news from Mars.

The incoming message is from Kyna—and sure enough, there's an earlier one waiting, from Shim. I open Shim's first.

"Good morning, Excellency. I do hope you slept well. Rigel messaged last night that you were overtired, so I sent this message non-priority in hopes it would not wake you. I knew, however, that once awake you would want earliest news of Faxon's latest attack on our infrastructure.

"This time, he chose to disable a part of our energy grid that powers the grav/antigrav systems. I admit it took some fast rerouting of power from other areas to shore up Nuath's antigrav roof supports to prevent a partial collapse, but we were able to do so. The initial explosion also caused several injuries, two of them serious.

"Needless to say, our populace is increasingly apprehensive about whatever his next move may be. They would be even more so if they knew that diverting power to the gravitational system has already accelerated the depletion of our energy reserves. We are currently keeping that information confidential, for reasons you will understand when you view Faxon's latest broadcast.

"We've continued our search for other explosives or sabotaged systems, and discovered one more hidden in a large air-scrubbing unit. That explosive has been neutralized, but we have no way of knowing how many more are still live and primed. The maintenance tunnels under the industrial portion of Nuath are being searched as well, though so far without results.

"The information you shared about Faxon was fascinating, though not entirely unexpected, at least by myself. It may prove useful at some point. At present, however, clues to Faxon's whereabouts and future targets will be of more immediate utility.

"Kyna is keeping me apprised of the political atmosphere on Earth, so try not to trouble yourself with that. For now, I recommend you focus exclusively on excavating Faxon's memories. My grandson has again expressed concerns about the toll this project is taking on you, but I'm afraid I must agree with the *Echtran* Council that, given the current situation, some temporary risk to your wellbeing is justified. I continue to believe that after this crisis is resolved, our Healers will be able to restore you to full mental and physical health.

"Faxon's latest recording is attached. I have also forwarded it to Kyna for dissemination to the rest of the Council, to spare you that trouble. I remain your most faithful and devoted servant."

Before watching Faxon's most recent video, which I know will piss me off, I play Kyna's message.

"Excellency, I trust I have waited long enough to allow you the rest I'm told you need," it begins. "By now you will have received Regent Shim's update, as well as Faxon's latest collection of threats and false promises. Rest assured that the Council remains united in its support of you and Princess Malena, despite increasingly vocal demands from a few extremist elements.

"I have scheduled a Council meeting at the usual time tonight, at NuAgra. If you are able, we would appreciate an in-person update on your progress. Though Shim's people were able to partially suppress Faxon's most recent broadcast, it is too much to hope that it will not soon make its way to Earth as the others did. At Shim's suggestion, I have already shared it with the rest of the Council, as they need to be aware of what we are up against. If any had forgotten how diabolically clever Faxon can be, this message will serve as a reminder.

"Wishing you all speed with your project, Excellency, and that you will have good news to share with us this evening. Kyna out."

Now I dread watching Faxon's video more than ever. To put it off for another minute or two, I get up and hit the bathroom, then reach out mentally to Rigel.

Are you up? Hope you got as much sleep as I did!

Got a lot more than the night before, his reply comes instantly. *Woke up nearly an hour ago and just arrived at NuAgra. Have you had breakfast yet?*

A little of my tension eases, knowing he's already here. My rock.

No, I just woke up a few minutes ago. Listened to messages from Shim and Kyna but haven't played Faxon's latest yet. Want to watch it together?

I have a feeling I'll need his strength for that.

Absolutely. I'll wait for you in the dining room.

I throw on the jeans and sweater I wore yesterday rather than rummage through the bag my aunt and Mrs. O packed for me. When I rush out of my quarters, I nearly bump into Cormac, stationed just outside the door.

"Oops, sorry!" I exclaim, barely avoiding a collision. "Um, how's your room here?" I nearly forgot he'd have spent the night in the Bodyguard chamber next to mine.

"Quite comfortable, Excellency, thank you," he responds with a bow.

It probably *is* nicer than the room he's renting over Mrs. Crabtree's garage, across the street from Aunt Theresa and Uncle Louie's house.

"Oh, good, glad to hear it," I say absently as I head to the dining hall. I'm already getting a later start to my day than planned and I'm eager to get my good-morning kiss from Rigel...and to see the traitor Faxon's latest attempt to wrest control of my people away from me.

14

Reinforcing stimulus

WHEN I ENTER the dining hall, Rigel jumps up from the table he's sharing with Molly and Tristan to greet me. His kiss is quick and discreet, but still gives me the boost I crave. Threading my fingers through his, I accompany him back to the table.

"Sorry I slept so late," I tell the others. "I'm surprised your folks aren't already here."

"Oh, they are," Molly says. "Mum, Dad, Rigel's dad and Tristan's mother all had breakfast here, then went off for some kind of Council confab."

Rigel nods. "You only missed them by a few minutes. Speaking of breakfast, I went ahead and got you some scrambled eggs and orange juice from the recombinator." He motions to the plate across from Molly.

"Thanks, but I should watch Faxon's latest before I try to eat anything. From what Kyna said, it's…not good."

Instantly, I sense Molly's and Tristan's heightened anxiety, which only increases my own—and Rigel's.

"All right," he says. "We may as well get it over with."

Setting my omni on the table, I angle the screen away from the few people still eating late breakfasts elsewhere in the big dining hall. I'd rather not panic anyone else yet, though I'm sure they'll hear about it soon enough. I also turn the volume way down before clicking to the video Shim sent.

Faxon's smarmy, smiling face instantly fills the small holo-screen, making my skin crawl. I already hated him for killing my grandparents and parents, but closer acquaintance with his vindictive, self-centered thoughts has made my loathing even stronger.

"Good morning, fellow Martians," he begins. "Did the power fluctuations a short while ago alarm you? They were caused by your so-called leaders scrambling to minimize the results of my second demonstration. I must say, I was rather impressed by their alacrity. Had they not been so quick, a large chunk of Nuath's ceiling would have collapsed, leaving far fewer of you to enjoy this broadcast. Believe it or not, I'm rather relieved they were successful, as I very shortly hope to gather you all under my own, far more robust wings of protection.

"You see, what your illustrious Regent probably won't tell you is that my two small warnings have already slashed Nuath's power supply in half. The next one will halve it yet again. After that, you can look forward to the progressive shutdown of every system not absolutely vital to sustain life, and possibly a few that are. No more transit, water reclamation, simulated daylight or recombinators. The air will soon grow rather stuffy, and I'm sure gravity will need to be reduced significantly, as well. I fear it won't be pleasant.

"How can you escape this fate, you ask? Why, simply by acceding to my modest demands. Once you dispose of your upstart Sovereign and her sister and let me resume control over Nuath, I will quickly restore our power supply to its original levels—and more. Yes, more. In fact, Nuath will become fully sustainable for our people far into the future. No one else will be forced to emigrate to that barbaric hellhole, Earth.

"Under my leadership, Nuath will finally blossom into a truly egalitarian society where no *fine*, no family, will ever go without those things they deserve. I foresee a renaissance, if you will, in healthcare, agriculture, engineering and more, elevating us far beyond anything we ever experienced under the repressive Royals. *My* Nuath will no longer be dependent upon the inferior *Duchas* of Earth for anything. In addition, our *Echtran* brethren who choose to remain on that backward planet can cease skulking and living in shadows, denying their superior nature. I will free them, as well, to finally ascend to the dominant positions a people as superior as ours should occupy.

"What, you may ask, stands in the way of such a beautiful vision? A pair of elitist teenaged girls totally unconcerned with your welfare. Had they truly cared about you, they would have offered themselves up for your sake prior to yesterday's demonstration, rather than cravenly hiding themselves away. Clearly, their loyalties lie only with themselves.

"I feel certain we still have some *true* patriots on Earth, willing to put the good of our entire race above two insignificant remnants of the very *fine* that oppressed us for generations. Your duty is clear. *You* have the power to bring about the glorious Martian future I have just described. I am confident that you won't fail me—or yourselves.

"Until this time tomorrow, I leave you with this final thought: though Mechs have long been regarded as the lowliest of *fines*, I, Faxon, have proven time and again that imposed social status is no barrier to greatness. Indeed, we are *all* Mechs at heart, sharing that same ability to rise above what is expected of us to achieve our true potential. So let my mantra become yours, regardless of your birth *fine:* You can't keep a good Mech down!"

The broadcast ends and we all look at each other.

"Now I understand what Kyna meant about him being diabolically clever," I say, shaking my head. "He's scary good at playing directly to people's biggest hopes and fears. For a second his rhetoric almost made *me* feel like a traitor, just for wanting to stay alive."

I have no doubt that after watching this, at least some of our people will see it that way, too.

"Faxon didn't mention it," I continue after a moment, "but Shim reported his latest explosion caused some serious injuries, though thankfully no deaths."

"Not surprised he left that out." Molly remarks. "It's the same kind of spin we constantly heard when he was in power, always taking credit for anything good and blaming the Royals or the Resistance for anything bad. According to my folks, anyway. I didn't watch the news feeds much."

Molly was only thirteen when the O'Garas were smuggled off Mars after their Resistance cell was exposed...the very cell I heard Faxon talking about last night.

"C'mon, people have to realize he can't really do any of the stuff he just promised," Tristan objects. "Didn't he lie constantly while he was in power? That's what Mother told me."

I frown. "Yes, but from what I've seen in his memories, he actually believed most of what he said, no matter how untrue it was. I'm sure that made him a lot more convincing."

"Do you think he still believes his own lies?" Molly asks.

"It's certainly possible," I admit. "The very fact that he hasn't been found yet proves he has resources no one ever suspected. Some people may think those resources include a way to fix Nuath's power problem—especially if they desperately want to believe that. I've *got* to find something in his memory that Shim can use to stop him. Today."

Rigel pushes my plate toward me. "Not before you've had breakfast. Once you've eaten we'll check in with my dad so you can get back to it…if you really think it's necessary."

"You know it is," I reply, though I obediently pick up my fork. I *am* hungry.

I eat quickly, then stand up the moment I finish. "I'd better not waste any more time. If I don't get what I need by the end of the day, Faxon's almost guaranteed to kill people tomorrow."

Which still will not *be your fault,* Rigel silently insists, also getting to his feet. "Let's go find my dad," he adds out loud.

Mr. Stuart is in the conference room where we have the *Echtran* Council meetings these days, along with Mr. and Mrs. O'Gara and Teara Roark. Not surprisingly, they're still talking about Faxon's latest video.

"—nearly a dozen calls and messages in the past hour. Some have been positively—" Mrs. O breaks off abruptly as we walk in. "Ah, good morning, Excellency. I hope you slept well?" She's clearly a bit flustered, probably because I overheard that last bit.

"Better than I expected, yes," I reply. "I take it people are already freaking out over Faxon's latest?"

Everyone in the room nods.

"I'm afraid so, Excellency," Mr. O'Gara says. "Though of course our Council members continue to assure them that we have a plan that should neutralize Faxon very soon."

Since that last bit is clearly a question, I do my best to answer. "Er, I think so. I was just about to get back to it. Rigel will help again, if that's okay?" I ask Mr. Stuart.

Nodding, he stands up. "I suppose I should reactivate your security cameras."

Mrs. O gets up, too, and follows the three of us out. "Excellency, I'm sure you won't mind if I just take a peek at last night's recording," she says as we reach the security control room. "Then I can reassure anyone who might have…concerns."

Flashing back to what happened on the *Quintessence,* Rigel and I both tense, but I'm careful to keep my alarm—and irritation—from showing.

"Um, sure," I say as casually as possible. "Feel free." Then, to Rigel, "Guess we'd better get started."

How pissed do you think she'll be when she sees us kissing? he thinks to me as we head to my quarters. *And if she notices that gap in the feed at the end?*

My irritation—at Mrs. O, not Rigel—abruptly crowds out my worry. "I don't much care," I declare aloud, though not loudly. "We didn't do anything to be ashamed of."

"No, it's just… No, you're right. C'mon."

Back in my private living room, we again sit side by side on the couch. "I sure hope this will work better now that I've had a decent night's sleep," I comment, sticking the little meditation button behind my ear. "Last night was frustrating." In more ways than one.

Only the knowledge that Rigel's dad—and probably Mrs. O—are watching right now keeps me from again pouncing on Rigel to fortify myself with the kisses I want so badly—which he of course senses immediately.

Thinking like that probably won't help, he remarks silently, his grin tinged with a longing that matches my own.

No, just thinking about it definitely won't. I wish— Okay. Here I go.

Last night, after updating Shim and Kyna, I decided to concentrate next on the most significant-looking memories from Faxon's last few months in power. That's when he should have felt the most threatened, and therefore more likely to create or at least think about contingency plans.

Closing my eyes, I take a deep breath and start my meditation sequence, determined to reach Faxon's memory library way faster than I did last night.

Unfortunately, I discover that's more easily said—or thought—than done. If anything, being better rested makes my body even *more* aware of Rigel's, so close to me on the couch. We're so overdue for a little—

M. His mental "voice" is chiding. *Much as I agree, this isn't what you're supposed to be thinking about right now.*

No, no, you're right. Sorry.

I work harder to clear my mind, methodically thinking through the relaxation steps Healer Ava taught me. Eventually, it works. Mostly. But even after visualizing and descending the stairs to the memory repository, my progress is every bit as slow as last night. Could it be the distraction of having Rigel right next to me that's messing with my focus?

Hoping that's not it, I soldier on until I'm again entering Faxon's library-within-a-library. Scanning the nearest sets of shelves, I see plenty of books that look worn enough to be significant. My targets for today.

I start with one I estimate is about two months later than where I left off last night. Again, it takes more effort than it should to bring the memory into focus.

Faxon's in his quarters, or so I assume. It looks just like the apartment Sean and his dad stayed in while we were at the Palace last summer, except he's added…a throne. It's very similar to the *cathoir* in the main reception hall, where I sat to hear petitions as Sovereign. He apparently created a replica for his own quarters. Delusions of grandeur, much?

"No," Faxon is saying. "I won't schedule elections unless we can positively guarantee the results."

"So you've said, my lord," the man opposite him replies with exasperated-sounding patience. It's Brennan, the same chief of staff I saw last night, so I guess Faxon hasn't executed him yet. "I've spoken with three different Informatics technicians—"

"Loyal ones?" Faxon interrupts.

Brennan lifts a shoulder. "I believe so, yes. They all assured me they can flip twenty-five to thirty percent of the vote after the fact, if necessary. That should be enough."

"*Should* be?" I can tell Faxon is angry, but like last night, I can't *feel* his anger…or hear his actual thoughts. "Not good enough! We need a landslide to put my mandate beyond doubt. Especially with this ridiculous rumor re-energizing that blasted Resistance."

"That's why we need to announce an election," Brennan insists. "We need a distraction, and quickly, before belief that an heir to the last Sovereign might still be alive on Earth can spread beyond the Resistance."

Faxon scowls, drumming the fingers of his right hand on the throne arm. I concentrate, trying again to *feel* what he's doing, not just see it. Instead, I irrelevantly notice that even though this throne has the same dimensions as the real *cathoir*, he's encrusted it with so many gems it's positively gaudy. Why? To imply he's richer and more important than the Sovereigns?

"How did that rumor start?" he demands after a moment. "Have you traced the source? Who leaked it? And why is that dissident media channel still operating?"

"We believe it stemmed from a text-only message from one of our Earth agents who used a less-than-secure channel to report movements he thought suspicious. His message was intercepted by a Palace publicist who theorized rather too openly that those movements might suggest an *Echtran* search for a possible surviving heir. He was dealt with, of course, but the rumor had already begun making the rounds. Fortunately, the media outlets we control, which is most of them, are already deriding the rumor as false."

Faxon slaps both hands down on the arms of the throne and surges to his feet to glare at his lieutenant. "False? It's ridiculous! That so-called Princess perished with her parents. Our assassins confirmed it."

Angry as Faxon clearly is, I still can't tap into his emotions or get a sense of what he knows. I try harder to detach myself from the physical world, where Rigel is only an inch or two away from me, so I can dig deeper.

It doesn't work.

When Brennan pulls out a tablet a moment later and starts going over statistics to persuade Faxon to go along with his suggestion, I give up. Detaching myself from the memory, I rejoin Rigel on the couch with a sigh.

"It's still not working," he says. It's a statement, not a question.

"No. I think…" I hesitate, then blurt out, "I'm sorry, Rigel, but I think you might be the reason."

His head snaps up and I sense his surprise and hurt.

"I don't mean anything you're doing," I hastily clarify. "Just that having you right here next to me makes me want to—" I break off, but my meaning's obvious. "I'd *much* rather focus on you than Faxon. So much I can't seem to get past my distraction." *And frustration,* I silently add.

He frowns. "Thursday night you said having me here helped."

"And it did. Then. But Thursday—" I break off, not sure if the cameras are listening as well as watching. To be safe, I continue my theory telepathically. *It hadn't been as long since we had serious alone time. Maybe if we could sneak off somewhere for an hour or so—*

The wave of longing that sweeps through me at the thought is amplified by Rigel's.

Yeah, I guess I get it, he finally admits. *But I hate the idea of you doing this alone. There could still be some really ugly memories ahead.*

"Tell you what," I say aloud. "Let me try for an hour by myself. If that doesn't help, it's probably something else giving me trouble. But with time so tight, we should find out for sure."

Reluctantly, he nods. "Okay. An hour. I'll go see if my dad's made any progress on finding records from when Faxon was in Chicago."

Like last night, I walk him to the door. And like last night, we take advantage of that small blind spot between cameras for a too-brief but much-needed kiss. I use those few wonderful seconds to absorb as much strength from Rigel as I can before we part with mutual sighs.

"There," I whisper. "That should hold me for an hour."

"Hope so," he whispers back. "Holler if you need me, okay?"

"I will," I promise. *And I'll check in like this after my next try,* I add silently.

With a last tight-lipped, worried smile, he leaves…and I go back to what I'm starting to think of as the dragon's lair.

I settle myself on the couch again, already missing Rigel. Am I being stupid, trying to do this without him? Probably. Most of my other recent decisions have been bad ones. But if there's any chance my theory is right, this experiment should confirm or disprove it. Quickly. I hope.

Though I suspect I've simply lost my ability—or willingness—to immerse myself fully into Faxon's mind, I reactivate the meditation device behind my ear.

Find the memories where Faxon felt most threatened, I tell myself. *How did he plan to wrest back power if he was overthrown? Get that plan!*

With that intention firmly in mind—and without the distraction of Rigel's too-tempting nearness—I close my eyes.

15

Free recall

WITHOUT MUCH HOPE but determined to try anyway, I take a deep breath and begin my usual meditation sequence. To my amazement, the stairs leading down to my memory library appear almost before I think about them. Definitely a great start, though Rigel might not agree.

Thinking of Rigel nearly breaks my focus…but not quite. Reminding myself of my goal, I hurry down the stairs, hoping to make up for lost time. And just like my solo sessions yesterday, I'm almost immediately able to open the arch to Faxon's library. So far, so good!

Wondering if I might now be able to hear whatever Faxon was thinking during the last memory I saw, I go back to the same book as last time.

Again, I see the main room of Faxon's quarters through his eyes, but now I also feel the metal and gemstones of the throne arm as I angrily drum my fingers on it.

"—the media outlets we control, which is most of them, are already deriding the rumor as false," Brennan is saying.

A roaring fills my ears and I propel myself to my feet, outraged. "False? It's ridiculous!" I shout into his face. "That so-called Princess perished with her parents, our assassins confirmed it."

Forceful as my words are, a thread of doubt lingers in the back of my mind—a doubt Brennan puts into words.

"They never actually recovered her body, did they?"

I want to pummel both him and my doubts into submission, but stifle the urge with an effort when Brennan takes a quick step backward.

"The morgue files clearly listed the child as a third drowning victim," I snap. "Nor could a two-year-old possibly have survived that accident, according to my assassins. These malcontents must be getting desperate if they're now pinning their hopes on a girl who's been dead for thirteen years."

"Whether that onetime heiress is alive or not doesn't matter nearly as much as what the people believe," Brennan tells me. "I agree it's extremely unlikely she could have survived, but the mere idea that she might have is dangerous. Announcing an election date should provide enough distraction to quiet the more problematic elements, at least for a time."

Scowling, I sit back down and shake my head. "Not until you can guarantee me an overwhelming win. Most Nuathans love me, but the few who don't are more likely to vote. I can't risk that."

"Suppose we do away with secret ballots?" Brennan suggests. "Tell everyone we can only ensure the vote is fair and tamper-free if votes can be matched to eligible citizens. Say it's simply a security measure to prevent minors and criminals from getting into the system and skewing results."

A slow smile curves my lips. "Hm. Yes. If people know that *I'll* know how they voted, they won't dare support anyone who would oppose me in the legislature. That could work."

With a mental wrench, I pull myself out of the memory at that point, fairly sure Faxon's not feeling threatened enough at the moment to think about contingency plans. What *will* make him do that?

Maybe the news that I really am alive? His invasion plan being ruined? The uprisings that happened after the news started to spread in Nuath?

I study the last two sets of shelves, counting the number of well-worn books before the final one—all holding memories important or traumatic to Faxon. There are over two dozen. Not surprising, considering what I know about his final months in power. Might as well check them out in order—but quickly.

The next scruffy-looking book is only half a shelf ahead of the one I just put back. Too soon to be news of my survival, but—

Immediately on opening it, I find myself in one of the larger conference rooms, surrounded by nine other men. Some I'm confident are unswervingly loyal to me, others I'm less sure of. One of the latter is speaking.

"—unlikely your ships can be completed in time." The thin, sandy-haired man is apologetic but firm. "Our power reserves have fallen alarmingly in recent months, a situation that could panic the populace should they become aware."

"They won't," declares the man on my right—Ciaran, my new chief of staff. "That data has been locked down, restricted to those with a need to know. Lord Faxon, these naysayers don't know what they're talking about. Everything is proceeding on schedule for the planned invasion. All should be ready well before the end of the next launch window."

There's a chorus of agreement from my loyal cadre but some shaking of heads among the few Scientists I've retained on staff against my better judgment. It was Brennan who insisted I needed them but he's gone now. Soon they may be, too.

"The people are quite compliant of late," Philbin, my new security chief, tells me. "Scheduling elections effectively silenced what little was left of the Resistance. No need to actually hold them, as you pointed out, my lord."

That brainstorm was Ciaran's—one reason he took Brennan's place when I decided his ambition was becoming dangerous. I should have replaced him sooner. Scheduling legislative elections without my express authorization was the final straw. Ah, well, he's now enjoying an extended stay with the Mind Healers, having his mind wiped of all state secrets. No need to think about him anymore.

"My lord." It's another one of the Scientists. "I feel obligated to remind you that even if the planned invasion of Earth can proceed on schedule, by then Nuath's power reserves will have been depleted to a point unlikely to sustain life here long enough to evacuate the remaining population."

I glare at the man, whose name I forget. "Then we'll build more ships, get our people to Earth faster. The ones who support me, that is."

He and several other Scientists shake their heads. "That won't help, my lord," insists the sandy-haired geek who spoke before. "The more we build, the more quickly we deplete the reserves. I've run the calculations and there's no possible—"

"Get that man out of here!" I shout, the rushing in my ears deafening as my anger boils over. "All of you doubters, out!"

When the Scientists hesitate, I nod to Philbin, who pulls his weapon from its holster to enforce my command.

"You heard Lord Faxon. Out. Shall I have someone escort them to the Mind Healing facility?" he asks me.

"Yes. We can't risk any of them repeating what they've said here. And postpone those damned elections again," I add to Ciaran as they leave the room, still breathing hard as my fury slowly ebbs. "Make up another excuse. I don't care what it is, anything to keep the people pacified. Once we conquer Earth, everyone will be too grateful to me to care, anyway."

The door closes behind the naysayers and I look to the six ultra-loyalists remaining in the room. "Now. Tell me what else can be done to speed up production of ships and weapons."

Eagerly, they try to out-vie each other in their enthusiasm for my goal of dominating the *Duchas*, vigorously expounding on what a boon it will be for our people. None offer much in the way of concrete suggestions to accelerate our preparations, but their wholehearted support soothes my irritation.

When Faxon finally smiles, I'm able to yank myself out of that particular memory. I've noticed it's easier to do that when his emotions are less intense—which is good, since I'm most likely to discover what I need when he's upset.

I didn't remember to set a timer for this session, but I'm sure it hasn't been half an hour yet. I move to the next significant-looking book, wondering if I—I mean Faxon—can somehow prove those obnoxious Scientists wrong.

The first thing I notice when the scene resolves is that I'm no longer in the Royal Palace. Instead, I'm surrounded by heavy machinery moving big pieces of metal into place in what looks like a half-finished ship of some sort. The site of Faxon's secret military buildup! This *must* mean I'm getting close to my goal.

I dive deeper, only to be instantly swamped by outrage, the roaring in my ears nearly deafening.

"Elgin? He can't have defected! How? Only last week he briefed me on the areas needing more resources to stay on schedule. Who corrupted him?"

"We...we don't know, Lord Faxon." A burly, broad-shouldered man in a greasy tunic bows obsequiously. "None of us suspected. When he didn't report on time this morning, I checked his work station and found it cleaned out, his data erased. He clearly doesn't intend to return. I assure you, if I'd seen the least indication—"

I lash out with a foot while he's still bent in half, sending him sprawling. "I don't want excuses, I want answers! Elgin knows more about this project than anyone. If he goes public with any of it, I'll have a hell of a time playing down how far along our preparations are. Only a fraction of the populace support invasion right now. I need time to get those numbers up before announcing it. I want Elgin found. Now!"

"Yes, Lord Faxon." The burly man, along with two others, scurry out of the enormous workshop, hauling open a heavy door and sprinting upstairs as the door swings shut behind them.

I glare around at the remaining workers. "What are you looking at? You're falling behind—get back to work. With Elgin gone, the rest of you will have to pick up the slack. Any man falling short of his daily production quota will have his rations cut in half."

The men bend back to their tasks as I seethe silently. I was sure Elgin was one I could trust. How could I have been so wrong? Are they *all* against me now? Careful not to let my doubt show, I examine each face in turn, trying to discern what lies beneath.

Ciaran, or someone else in my inner circle, should have picked up on Elgin's wavering loyalty and warned me. What good is a chief of staff who can't spot a problem like that before it's too late? Time to remind him and a few other people that their positions depend on my good will. Which is wearing thin.

"You there," I bark at a man monitoring graviton levels as a propulsion ring is levered into place at the base of the imposing, half-built vessel. "Can you access the status update Elgin was supposed to submit today?"

"Er…I think so, my lord." The man scurries to a different screen and begins punching in codes. "Do you want to look it over here, or shall I have it sent to you?"

I'd intended to have Elgin summarize it, then walk me through an inspection of the ship systems. He had a real knack for explaining the technical jargon. I've never had enough interest in science stuff to learn all the fancy terms, but none of these people need to know that.

"I don't have time now. Send it to my private server on the secure channel." I turn away to hide my uneasiness. "I'll review it later."

Sweeping the enormous room with a last, critical glance, I exit. There's a door to my left leading to the underground tunnel network where a waiting car will whisk me back to the Palace, but I ignore it. Instead, I stride purposefully up the long stairway. Moving helps me think—and I need to plan my next move.

As Faxon's emotions cool down, I'm again able to extricate myself from that particular memory, though with lingering remnants of his anger and frustration. It's too bad Faxon doesn't have my ability to sense people's emotions, or he'd know ahead of time who's likely to betray him. Then he'd be able to—

I break off that thought, appalled. What am I thinking? *Too bad?* It's a very *good* thing he never had an ability like mine, or he might never have been overthrown at all!

I'm so unsettled by that weird, temporary perspective shift that instead of opening another book, I leave Faxon's library entirely and think myself back up the imaginary stairs to my quarters. Once there, I emerge from my meditative state and check my omni. Nearly an hour has passed—oops. Rigel will definitely worry if I don't touch base soon.

When I stand up, I also realize how stiff I am...again. While stretching and swinging my arms around, I reach out mentally to Rigel.

You there?

Of course, he immediately thinks back. *Are you okay? I tried to tap in once or twice, but it was kind of disorienting.*

Considering how chaotic Faxon's emotions are getting, that's not surprising. *I'm fine,* I assure him—and myself. *Has your dad said anything about last night's video feed? You were worried he might.*

No, but I'm not sure he's had a chance to look at it yet, Rigel replies. *No sign of Mrs. O'Gara, so maybe she hasn't, either. Let's hope. So, what more have you found out? Has the memory thing been any easier without me there?*

Startled he even needs to ask, I play down how dramatic the difference was. *Um, yeah, it kind of has. Sorry. Faxon's starting to get more paranoid, but I still have no idea where he's hiding. I must be getting closer, though.*

Want to take a break so we can talk about it?

I glance again at the time—barely eleven o'clock. *How about I spend another hour on this, then meet you for lunch? I'm making decent progress and don't want to lose my momentum.*

Okay, if you're sure. His concern comes through as clearly as his thought. *Just...be careful, okay?*

Careful? I'm just sitting on my couch!

You know what I mean.

I do, but I still think his worry is overblown. *I'm sure I'll be fine, but feel free to tap in every now and then if you want.*

I will. Or I'll try. See you in another hour. Love you, M.

Love you, too!

I continue stretching for another two or three minutes after we break communication, then settle myself back on the couch. Considering how threatened Faxon felt during that last memory, surely he'll either think about or check on his backup plans soon?

Very much hoping I can find what I need by lunchtime, I close my eyes and head back down to the memory library.

.⁺.

"Then, just a couple weeks after that Engineer working on the invasion ships left his post without warning, Faxon discovered his new chief of staff was passing info to the Resistance," I continue before taking another bite of my Caesar salad with shrimp.

Molly and Tristan joined Rigel and me right after we met for lunch, so I'm trying to catch all three of them up at once while we eat.

"But you still haven't figured out where Faxon's holing up?" Molly asks.

"Not yet, but I'm nearly up to when he'll get the news I'm alive, which should either trigger him to create it or double check it, if it already exists. He's already getting paranoid."

Rigel drinks the last of his chocolate milk. "Yeah. Sounds like he was firing people right and left even before the Resistance started ramping up. How many chiefs of staff has he gone through by now?"

"Seven. His first one, Matthews, lasted the longest, five years. Then there were three others who only lasted a couple years each. Brennan was his fifth—you remember him, right, Rigel?"

"The arrogant-looking redheaded one?"

I nod. "Faxon worried he was getting too ambitious, but he was so good at his job he didn't fire him right away. When he finally did, he regretted it later."

I may have been too quick to replace Brennan, I recall Faxon thinking after one of Ciaran's blunders, at a time he was already questioning the man's intelligence. *Brennan may have overstepped his authority, but at least he was loyal. And competent. But that poll, showing nearly a third of Nuathans believed Brennan would be a better leader than me, left me no choice. Then he set an election date before I'd officially approved it, which gave me a perfect excuse to remove him. Still, it's possible I was too—*

"M?" Rigel's touch on my shoulder brings me back to the present. "You zoned out again, like you did yesterday."

"What? Oh. Sorry." I take another quick bite of my salad to reassure him—and myself—that I'm still here in the dining hall. Still me. "Where was I? Oh, right. The guy who replaced Brennan was Ciaran, the one who secretly sold information to the Resistance. Instead of having his memory wiped like Brennan's, Faxon had him publicly beheaded. He… he gave the final order to the executioner himself, then watched." I shudder at the grisly memory.

Molly shudders, too. "Ugh. That's really gross."

I nod. "He was convinced a betrayal like that absolutely required an example to be made." *I can't afford to be seen as soft, with the Resistance growing again. The people need to know—*

"You're doing it again, M." Rigel's voice is sharp with concern.

I blink at him, briefly disoriented as the memory of Faxon's righteous anger fades. "Oops. I didn't—"

Rigel reaches beneath my hair to feel behind my left ear. "You're not still wearing that thing, are you?"

"No, of course not." I pull away, frowning. "I'm not an idiot."

He blinks, clearly startled. "I didn't mean—"

"I put it back in its box when I was done, like always," I inform him, irritated by his lack of trust.

"He's just worried, M," Molly says gently. "We all are. You're pushing yourself awfully hard."

I take a deep breath, letting my momentary resentment drain away. "I know. And I appreciate your concern, I really do. But with so much at stake, I don't have much choice. You all get that, don't you?"

All three of them nod, but I sense their reluctance. Especially Rigel's. His refusal to fully support what I'm doing frustrates me. I have to remind myself again that it's only because he cares about me.

"Anyway," I continue, getting my frustration back under control, "after Ciaran, Faxon promoted his security chief, Philbin, to chief of staff. He didn't trust anyone else enough for the job, so many people had betrayed him by then. When one of his Engineers pointed out a flaw in the accelerated shipbuilding process Faxon ordered, Faxon grabbed Philbin's weapon and killed him on the spot. That's…where I left off."

Again, I feel a tug at my mind as that last memory tries to resurface, but this time I manage to push it away and stay present enough to eat the rest of my salad. The others finish their lunches in silence as well, though I notice Molly shooting worried glances across the table at me.

"Well, I'd better get back to it." I push away my bowl with a sigh, reluctant but also eager to continue scouring Faxon's memories.

Before I can get up, Mrs. O'Gara storms into the dining hall, positively radiating indignation. Mr. Stuart trails worriedly behind her.

Uh-oh, Rigel thinks to me. *Guess they found time to watch last night's camera feed after all.*

But I refuse to cringe. Instead I stand, eyes narrowed, to face her head on.

16

Displacement

"A WORD, Excellency, if you don't mind?"

The edge in Mrs. O's voice confirms Rigel's guess even as it stiffens my resolve not to let her bully me. Though it takes effort, I assume a calm, pleasant expression.

"Of course. I take it you've reviewed my *private* security recording?" My emphasis is slight but unmistakable, causing her to hesitate before continuing.

"Er, yes." She exchanges a glance with Rigel's dad, who looks more embarrassed than mad. "It appears my original reservations about allowing—"

"*Allowing*?" I echo sharply, my assumed calm abruptly vanishing. "Did I miss a Council vote appointing you my overseer?" How *dare* she question my authority?

Mrs. O'Gara takes a half step backward, flushing bright red. "Of...of course not, Excellency! But you must realize that even in a situation such as this, appearances—"

"Appearances? Appearances to whom? Have you scheduled an *Echtran* News Network broadcast of the video feed from my *private* quarters?" I ask Mr. Stuart.

Lips twitching, he shakes his head. "Of course not, Excellency. No one beyond myself and Lili have—or will—view that recording, I assure you."

"I'm glad to hear it. Though now that everyone is well aware we're a couple, I doubt the sight of Rigel and me kissing would upset *most* people." I keep my voice level, reining in my anger at Mrs. O's effrontery with extreme difficulty.

"Er, perhaps not," she stammers, her face still as red as her hair. "Though there was that bit near the end, when you were both out of sight of the cameras…"

I arch an imperious eyebrow. "Do you truly believe I lost my virginity during those two minutes in the hallway?"

Mrs. O isn't the only one who gasps at my words. "I never implied… That is… Of course I don't think—"

"From the first," I interrupt, "you've questioned my judgment, particularly about Rigel. For the better part of a year, you did everything you possibly could to keep us apart. You even voted to have his memory erased!" Why did I allow her to remain on the Council after that? With every word, every memory, my anger builds until I hear a faint echo of the same rushing, roaring sound that always accompanies Faxon's rages. "From the very start, you've—!" I begin shouting, when my attention is diverted.

Whipping around, I catch Molly and Rigel whispering together across the table. "What are *you* two plotting?" I demand.

Before they can answer, Mrs. O sketches a quick bow and scurries off, followed by Mr. Stuart, who shoots a concerned glance at me over his shoulder. Across the table, Tristan is staring at me with his mouth open.

"Well?" I prompt as Molly and Rigel turn to face me, both looking wary. Or guilty?

"M—" Rigel puts a hand on my arm.

I shake him off. "What? What were you two whispering about? Me?"

Molly quickly steps around the table to get right in my face. "Yes. We were. We're really worried about you, M. I won't say Mum didn't deserve that, but you're not acting at all like yourself right now. If you'll stop and think for a second, you'll realize it, too. This Faxon thing is *seriously* messing with your head."

Rigel takes my hand and threads his fingers through mine—firmly. "She's right, M. Please. Stop and think."

The intense emotion he communicates through his touch is harder to ignore than his words. As his love and concern penetrate, I swallow the blistering retort I was about to unleash and look at Molly. Her gray eyes are tear-filled, her primary emotions also love and worry. I force myself to take a deep breath, then another, my fury draining away as quickly as it erupted.

"Oh, geez, guys. I'm sorry. I, uh, guess I did get a little carried away." I glance toward the dining hall door. "I can't believe I went off on your mom like that, Molly. I know she *mostly* means well. Should I go apologize?"

Molly shakes her head. "Not yet. Let her think about what you said first. I think she probably needed to hear it…though maybe not the way you said it." She manages the ghost of a grin.

Rigel wraps an arm around my shoulders. "Yeah, you can worry about that later, after you take a real break from the memory stuff. Get your mind off it completely for a little while."

"Seriously?" I stare at him in disbelief. "After what Faxon did this morning? He could kill half the people in Nuath by tomorrow if I don't stop him. I don't have time for breaks!"

Molly and Rigel exchange another worried glance. "Going crazy won't help you find the right memory," Molly says reasonably.

"I'll never find it at all if I don't keep digging," I insist. "I can tell I'm getting close. Spending another hour doing nothing when I might be just one or two memories away from what Shim needs really *would* drive me crazy."

"Okay, then let's check out the fitness center, like I wanted to do yesterday," Molly urges. "You usually have Taekwondo on Saturdays, right? Maybe a workout or some yoga will help clear your mind."

Rigel instantly agrees. "That's not a bad idea. C'mon, M. You can't spend *all* your time inside your head."

Much as I hate to delay combing through Faxon's final months in power, I reluctantly realize they have a point. Not only am I still achy from sitting so much in one position, it's getting way too easy to accidentally slip back into Faxon's memories—and emotions.

Before, I was counting on Rigel's presence to center me. Since I'm no longer letting him be there with me, maybe concentrating on something else for a little while can at least partially do the same.

"Okay," I finally concede, "but only for an hour or so. I'm *determined* to find something useful in Faxon's memories before tonight's Council meeting."

The four of us head to the next building over. The fitness center is on the ground floor, while the upper ones contain apartments for single and childless NuAgra workers. Priority was given to families for the limited housing in Jewel itself.

This is my first visit to NuAgra's fitness center. The moment I walk in, I'm reminded of the recreation area on the *Quintessence*, the spaceship I took to and from Mars last year. The exercise equipment and game area look almost the same, with a similar padded area for stretching and yoga-type activities. There's even a movie screen at one end of the big room.

Molly also notices the resemblance. "Gee, this looks familiar. Well, except for that." She points and I see an indoor pool in a glassed-in enclosure.

"Oh, wow," Tristan exclaims. "Wish I'd brought my swim trunks. I will tomorrow. What's wrong?" He shoots a concerned look at Molly, who suddenly looks embarrassed.

"Um...I can't swim. It wasn't exactly a thing in Nuath."

He puts an arm around her. "No, I guess it wouldn't be, with water so scarce on Mars. Don't worry, though, we'll teach you."

"Okay. Someday." She doesn't seem particularly enthusiastic about the idea. Then she turns to me. "Let's see if they have any yoga videos, like they did on the ship. That should clear your mind, before you have to go back into Faxon's."

Sure enough, we find a forty-five minute yoga video from the same series we watched on the *Quintessence*. The guys opt to lift weights instead—just like Sean did before.

As I focus on the various yoga poses the instructor demonstrates, I begin to feel more like myself than I have since breakfast. Maybe I really did need this. Like in the previous videos, at the end of the workout we're supposed to lie flat on our backs in "corpse" pose, close our eyes, and empty our minds of all thought. I do as instructed, but on my second deep breath, I suddenly find myself in Faxon's memory library, facing the same set of shelves where I left off.

Though I'm dimly aware this isn't what I'm supposed to be doing right now, I can't resist pulling out a book. As long as I'm here, why not? Maybe it'll turn out to be the exact memory I need, and I won't ever have to experience Faxon's warped mind again. Spurred by that incentive, I open it.

"This doesn't prove anything," I insist as Faxon, working to hide my alarm. "Boyne Morven's been on Earth so long he's starting to jump at shadows."

Philbin, now doing double duty as my security chief and chief of staff, shrugs. "Perhaps so, but you instructed him to follow every lead, no matter how tenuous," he reminds me. "I agree, those internet searches alone weren't cause for concern—any *Duchas* might have made them. But a mere week later, half the *Echtran* Council converged on the same small Earth town where those searches originated. That does seem to justify a closer look. If there's any chance at all she could still be alive—"

"Yes, yes, I know," I snap impatiently. "It could undo all the progress I've made building support for my invasion. But she can't be. It's impossible."

Philbin regards me impassively for a moment, his expression giving nothing away. "Shall I tell Morven to ignore it, then?" he finally asks.

Huffing out an irritated breath, I shake my head. "No. You're right. We need to be sure. Tell him to send someone—undercover—to check things out on the ground."

"That's precisely what I was going to suggest," Philbin says. "Morven reports that Jewel, the *Duchas* town in question, has only one high school. If the girl survived she'd be fifteen now, so would presumably be enrolled. It should not be difficult to discover whether or not one of the students is Martian."

I scowl. "It was Boyne Morven himself who assured me the Princess perished along with her parents in that accident he arranged thirteen years ago. If he was wrong, if a mere baby somehow survived when both parents were confirmed dead, the mistake is his to rectify."

"Indeed." Philbin begins typing into his tablet. "Unlikely as it is she's alive, should Morven or his agent locate her, they'll need to exterminate her as quickly and quietly as possible. News of her existence cannot be allowed to spread beyond Jewel, Indiana. If even a hint of it were to reach Nuath, it could be disastrous to your invasion plan."

"Nonsense," I scoff. "A single Ossian Sphere can easily dominate one small town and dispose of anyone inconvenient who happens to be there. Boyne Morven has six of them at his disposal, enough to subdue the entire *Duchas* population."

"Only if we can send enough trained forces to Earth to supplement the Spheres' effects," Philbin points out. "That's why strong Nuathan support for this plan is so vital. News of the Princess's survival could quickly undermine that support, even revive what's left of the Resistance. Should they stage an actual uprising, your safety could be at risk, in which case you'll need—"

M? M! Come on, snap out of it!

You're scaring us, M. Please!

You can do it, M, come back to us!

Three different voices are suddenly shouting in my head, confusing me. Where am I? What was I doing?

"How—" I start to say, then break off. My chief of staff has disappeared, along with the room where we were talking. "What—?"

"M!" Now I hear a voice with my ears, not just in my head. "Are you still in there? Talk to me!"

I open my eyes and see Rigel's anguished face inches from mine. Behind him, Molly and Tristan are staring down at me, their worry also palpable.

"Why did you pull me out?" I demand, Faxon's frustration amplifying my own.

"You're kidding, right?" Molly asks in amazement. "M, you were out for over ten minutes! We weren't sure you were going to wake up at all."

Rigel and Tristan both nod, their expressions somber.

"It's never been this hard to bring you back before," Rigel tells me, worry still rolling off him in waves. "And you weren't even wearing that button device. I knew this memory thing was dangerous, but—"

"But I was so close!" I exclaim. "They were actually starting to talk about his contingency plan. I've *got* to go back in!"

Sitting up, I look around and realize with a start that we're all still in the fitness center. "Um, maybe not here, though. I'll go back to my quarters first."

"No, M." Rigel's tone allows for no argument—a tone I don't remember him ever using to me before. "You can't. We won't let you. It's too dangerous. You just proved that."

"Won't *let* me?" I echo, aghast. "Don't be ridiculous. You all know the stakes as well as I do."

Molly grabs one of my hands in both of hers. "He's right, M. There has to be another way, one that won't risk losing you completely. You said Shim's people already found some of Faxon's bombs, let them find the rest. He wouldn't want you to end up in a coma or something."

I shake my head fiercely. "No. Shim already said it's worth the risk, that a Mind Healer can fix me after, if necessary. His people could take days or weeks to find all the bombs, if they even can, while Faxon keeps blowing things up and killing people. Isn't saving hundreds, maybe thousands of Nuathan lives worth screwing with my head a little?"

"Not to me." Rigel is emphatic. "*Nothing* is worth losing you, M."

"He's right," Molly agrees. "You've risked your life enough times already, M. Let Shim's people handle this crisis. You've done enough."

I can feel her using "push" on me, which infuriates me even more.

"Stop that!" I snap at her. "How can you say I've done enough when I haven't found *anything* useful yet? Sure, I found out Faxon was born on Earth and is half *Duchas*, but that doesn't get Shim any closer to stopping him. I *have* his memories of planting all those bombs and setting up his hidey-hole. I just need to unlock them. And I'm *so close!*"

"Do you really know that, or do you just hope you are?" Tristan asks in what strikes me as an overly-reasonable voice, like he's trying to convince himself as much as me.

"I really am. I can tell." I glare around at them. "I thought the whole point of this break was to make it easier for me come back at it fresh and finally unearth the information Shim needs."

The three of them exchange glances.

"That was before this happened." Molly's almost as worried as Rigel. "What you're doing is obviously way riskier than we thought."

"There's no risk to my life, just my mind—and even that should be temporary," I insist. "You have friends in Nuath, I've even met some of them. Don't you want me to do whatever I can to save them?"

Now she looks troubled. "I did, but that was before—"

"Nothing's changed, not really." I try to sound as reasonable as Tristan just did. "I'm almost positive I can find what I need before tonight's Council meeting. If I do, Shim's people can nab Faxon before he carries out whatever he's planning next—which could save a *lot* of lives! I appreciate that you all care about me, I do. But you can't let your emotions cloud your judgment about what really matters."

I sense Molly's starting to waver. If I can persuade her, Tristan will probably go along, too. Rigel's not budging, though.

"M, I told you two days ago I was afraid if you did this I could lose you. You're only proving I was right. I know you're the Sovereign and all, but I can't let you continue with this. If I tell Mind Healer Ava what's really going on, I'm sure she'll back me up."

Frustration and anger sweep through me, as intense as anything I've felt as Faxon. A familiar rushing sound fills my ears and I surge to my feet.

"None of you have the right to stop me! Not even you, Rigel. Faxon killed my *family*, remember? The only way I can get even is to *stop* him, once and for all. Which is *exactly* what I'm going to do."

They all look shocked speechless by my outburst. Before they can say anything else, I turn and stride out of the fitness center. Driven by cold fury—mostly at Faxon, but a little at my friends, too—I break into a run and reach my quarters just as Rigel catches up with me.

"M, wait!" He grabs my arm before I can palm open the door. "Please! You're not yourself right now, you know you're not—or you would, if you'd take a moment to think. Let's go talk to the Mind Healer, see if she knows a way to keep you from—"

"No. I'm sorry, Rigel, but I *have* to find out where Faxon's hiding. Now. Before tonight's Council meeting. Lives are at stake." Shaking off his hand, I press my palm to the door and it slides open.

When he reaches for me again, I shake my head and back through the opening, into my quarters.

"I have to do this alone," I tell him. "I'll let you know when I'm done. Until then…leave me alone."

I shut the door, engaging the genetic lock no one else can open, but not before I see the stricken look on Rigel's perfect face. It twists my heart. *I'll make it up to him later*, I promise myself, shoving away a stab of guilt. I don't have time for it right now.

17

Divergent thinking

MOLLY

TRISTAN and I come running up just as Rigel turns away from M's closed door, his expression stunned. Bleak.

"She...she told me to leave her alone." He sounds like he can't believe it. "She shut me out."

"What?" I exclaim. "That's not like M at all."

He shakes his head, looking dazed. "No. It's not. I tried to tell her that, but—" He flaps a hand at her door. "I'm really scared she's going to hurt herself, Molly. You saw how hard it was to pull her out a few minutes ago. In there by herself...what if she can't get out at all?"

"I guess...give her a little time?" I'm actually super scared for M, too, but showing it would only make Rigel more frantic. "If she really is right on the verge of finding Faxon's hiding place, maybe it'll only take her an hour or so to get all the info Shim needs. Then she won't ever have to look into Faxon's memories again."

I got a glimpse of that twisted mind myself while we were all trying to pull M out of her trance. No wonder it's messing her up.

"I hope you're right, but...what if spending all this time in his head damages her mind permanently?" Rigel puts my fear into words. "She might not be our M at all after this."

"Maybe if we all go in there and try again to reason with her?" Tristan suggests.

Rigel slaps a hand against the door control. "We can't. She locked herself in. I tried to convince her to talk to the Mind Healer first but she wouldn't listen. Just—" He swallows. "Told me to leave her alone. But how can I, when she could be hurting herself?"

Tristan frowns. "Do you think your dad can get the door open? He has access to all the security stuff here, right?"

Sudden hope lightens Rigel's expression. "Good idea. Come on."

My mum is already talking with Mr. Stuart when we reach his office.

"—realize she's the Sovereign," she's saying, "but she's also under-age. With no true parental supervision, and no Regent here on Earth to advise her, it falls to those of us closest to her to exert some measure—" She breaks off when we rush in. "Is something wrong?"

"Maybe," I say. "M blew up at all of us, then locked herself in her quarters. We're all really worried about her."

Mum sniffs. "Well. Apparently I'm not the only one she's been rude to. Of course, Shim did warn us this project of hers could temporarily affect her mental stability. He seemed to think it worth the risk."

"But what if it's *not* temporary?" Rigel demands. "When we were in the gym just now, she fell into some kind of memory trance and it took all three of us to wake her up. Someone needs to be with her."

"You, in other words?" Mum raises an eyebrow at him. "I agreed to that yesterday, but that was before—"

I make an impatient noise. "Mum, this isn't about appearances, it's about M's safety. Mr. Stuart, can you open her door so we can at least make sure she's okay? She wasn't acting at all like herself."

Though he looks sympathetic, he shakes his head. "Her lock is genet-ically keyed. It can't be overridden, short of dismantling the door. Unless there's real reason to believe she's in imminent danger, that doesn't seem justified."

"If she's trapped in her mind, she might as well be in a coma," Rigel insists. "Don't you consider that dangerous? Dad, she could starve to death in there!"

"Oh, come now, that's a bit extreme," Mum scoffs. "She had lunch barely an hour ago. Other than being rather testy, she seemed fine then."

"Maybe physically," I allow, "but digging around in Faxon's memory is seriously messing with her mind—and it's getting worse."

Rigel nods emphatically. "A *lot* worse. Yesterday, when she was still letting me keep her grounded, she was mostly okay. But once she started meditating alone we could all see the change in her. She claims she can sift through memories faster that way, but—"

"Faster is exactly what we need," Mum interrupts. "The sooner

Faxon can be captured the better. Our people are getting more and more strident, demanding results. There are reports of increasing unrest in Bailerealta and Dun Cloch and at least one incident bordering on violence in Nuath. If the Sovereign needs solitude for this project of hers to succeed, that's what we should give her."

Mr. Stuart nods. "I'm afraid I must agree. I believe Shim would, too. Did she give any indication how her, ah, research is progressing?"

"She *claimed* she was right on the verge of finding the memory she needs," I admit. "That's why she was so mad when we woke her up in the fitness center."

Tristan adds, "She seemed sure she'd have it before tonight's Council meeting, but—"

"But if she can't wake up on her own," Rigel interrupts, "and you won't let us wake her up, how can she pass on any information she gets? What if she never wakes up at all?"

Mr. Stuart puts a hand on his shoulder. "It's much too soon to assume that will happen," he says soothingly. "She only shut herself in a few minutes ago, didn't she?"

"Yeah, but—"

"Tell you what," his father continues. "If there's no word from her in an hour or two, I'll turn on her security feed, just to confirm she's in no physical danger—though I really shouldn't without her permission."

Rigel glowers. "One hour."

"Fine," his dad agrees. "One hour."

"Meanwhile," Mum says, "you three may as well finish any homework you have. Molly, you should also spend some time on your *other* studies. If there's a chance the Sovereign may truly become incapacitated, you'll need to step up."

All three of us stare at her in horror.

"Temporarily," she hastily adds. "Just until she's herself again."

Rigel clearly wants to keep arguing, but I grab his arm along with Tristan's and pull them away. "C'mon. I'll set a timer for fifty-five minutes. Then we'll come back and see how she's doing."

The next hour feels more like three. After sending M a voice message, Rigel starts pacing. With him so agitated, Tristan and I can't concentrate on homework—and studying my Sovereign stuff seems too much like giving up on M. It's a huge relief to all of us when my timer finally sounds.

Rigel immediately heads to the exit, but Tristan and I are right behind him. Mum is in the big reception hall chatting with Mrs. Roark and the woman at the desk, but breaks off to intercept us.

"You said you would wait an hour," she reminds Rigel with a frown.

"It's been fifty-eight minutes, Mum." I wave my omni-phone at her. "By the time Mr. Stuart can get the cameras on, the hour will be up."

She doesn't answer, just gives a little huff and follows us to his office.

Mr. Stuart is obviously expecting us. "I take it you've had no word from her?" he asks Rigel when we walk in.

"No, and I've tried reaching out both by phone and mentally. Usually I can at least pick up a little of whatever she's seeing or thinking, but all I've been able to get are emotions—mostly angry, chaotic ones. Probably Faxon's."

"Then it sounds as though she's doing what she needs to do," Mum says, like she expects that to be encouraging.

It's not.

"That won't do any good if she can't wake up," I remind her.

"Exactly," Rigel agrees. "Dad?"

Mr. Stuart is already fiddling with the security camera controls. "All right, here's the feed for her private quarters." He points to a screen that just lit up.

We all lean in to look and see M sitting stock still on her couch with her eyes closed.

"Is she at least breathing? Can you tell?" I ask after two or three minutes pass without the slightest sign of movement.

"Of course she is," Mum immediately replies. "She wouldn't still be upright if she weren't."

Even so, Mr. Stuart zooms the picture in until we can all see the very slight rise and fall of her chest.

"There. You see? She's fine," Mum says. "All that worry—"

"She's breathing, but that doesn't mean she's fine," Rigel argues. "Mind Healer Ava told her to only do short stints, like half an hour at a time. Definitely no more than an hour. Go ask her."

Mum frowns. "Healer Ava isn't here, as it's Saturday," she informs him. "Does she even know what the Sovereign is attempting? I thought it was agreed to keep that information quiet until we learn whether it's successful."

"No," Rigel admits with obvious reluctance. "M told her she needed to access her own early memories, for an autobiography. If she'd known what M really planned to do, she probably would have insisted on a lot more precautions. Dad, you *have* to let us go in and wake her up. It's the only way to be sure we even can."

"Absolutely not!" Mum exclaims. "Didn't you say she expects to discover where Faxon is hiding before tonight's Council meeting? Interrupting her now could break her focus and prevent her from doing that."

Before Rigel can snap at Mum, I jump in. "What if *she* can't break her focus? We told you how hard it was to bring her out of her trance or whatever back in the fitness center."

"Let's give her another hour," Mr. Stuart suggests—again. "I'll keep her camera feed on and check it regularly. If she shows any sign of distress, we'll take action."

"Thank you, Van. That seems a fair compromise." Mum smiles at us like that should do away with all our worries. "You lot can go back to the dining hall or wherever you like and come back here in an hour for a status update."

Rigel glares at her. "The Mind Healer recommended short stints," he repeats. "Who knows what two or three uninterrupted hours in Faxon's mind will do to her? She was already acting a little crazy, but she could end up incurably insane! Are you willing to risk that?"

"Son." Mr. Stuart again puts a hand on Rigel's shoulder. "I seriously doubt one more hour will cause her any permanent damage. I promise to keep an eye on her and let you know immediately if I spot a problem. If there's still been no movement at all from her in another hour, I agree it may be time to do something—but not quite yet."

Rigel continues to scowl, clearly not on board with more delay. "Fine," he snaps after a moment. "But if she's still in a trance an hour from now, I'll...I'll break down her door myself!"

Turning on his heel, he strides off toward the dining hall, muttering under his breath. After a startled second, Tristan and I follow.

We go back to the table where we left our books and try to settle down for another wait—though Rigel spends the first ten minutes fuming.

"It's like they don't care about her at all!" he rants. "I really thought Dad did, at least. Sure, I get that what's happening in Nuath is important, but—"

"But nothing's more important to you than M," I finish for him. "I know. But it's not true that they don't care about her. They have to, she's the Sovereign. I guess…I guess it's like M said, this is just one of the risks that go with the job. And Shim did say this shouldn't do anything to her the Mind Healers can't fix."

I don't completely believe what I'm saying, but I put just enough persuasive "push" behind my words to calm Rigel down a little. I doubt it'll last long, but he's at least able to dictate another message to M on his omni without sounding frantic.

I set another timer, but barely half an hour passes before Mum hurries into the dining hall, all smiles. "Good news! The Sovereign did indeed wake up on her own, so your concerns were clearly overblown."

Rigel jumps to his feet. "She's awake? Has she come out yet? Did she find the memory she was looking for?"

Mum's smile takes on a slightly disapproving edge. "She's still in her quarters, but your father said she opened her eyes and moved around a bit, then checked her omni and closed her eyes again. I presume she still needs a few more details."

He stares at Mum for a long moment, brow furrowed, then blurts out, "I don't believe you."

She gasps. "Excuse me? I assure you, young man—"

"You said M checked her omni. I've sent her two messages since she went in there. She wouldn't have gone back into a trance without touching base."

I come over and touch his arm. "Rigel, we know she's not herself right now. It's true under normal circumstances she'd never do that, but with the way she's been acting—"

But he's already heading for the exit. I exchange a quick glance with Tristan, then we both sprint after him, Mum blustering behind us. We catch up with Rigel just as he storms into his dad's office.

"What's going on with M?" he demands. "Mrs. O'Gara claimed she woke up and checked her omni, but I know she was lying. She—"

"Calm down, son," Mr. Stuart says sternly enough to cut off Rigel's tirade. "Lili was telling you the truth. Here. I'll replay that portion of the recording for you."

I crane my neck to look past Rigel and sure enough, a second later the screen shows M waking up and talking to herself for a minute, though we don't hear anything. Then, just like Mum said, she picks up her omni and scrolls the screen—and sets it back down. After that, she rolls her neck and shoulders around a little, then closes her eyes again.

Rigel, I notice, has gone a shade paler. "What's she doing now?" he asks.

Mr. Stuart returns the picture to the present and we see M again sitting totally motionless on her couch, just like before.

"Young man," Mum says from the open doorway behind us, "I believe you owe me an apology."

Rigel wheels around to face her, his face now flushed. "Okay. Fine. You told the truth. But M's obviously *not* okay! If she won't reply to my messages, you *have* to let me go in and check on her."

When both she and his dad refuse, he goes ballistic. "She's nothing but a tool to you, is she?" he bellows. "You don't give a *damn* what happens to her, as long as she keeps working to fix your problem! It's not her fault Faxon escaped, and it won't be her fault if he blows up Nuath, either. Just because she thinks she *might* be able to—!"

"Rigel!" his father snaps.

Mum steps into the office and slams the door shut. "Young man, I think you'd best go home before your outbursts cause speculation among the NuAgra workers." She looks almost as angry as Rigel is. "The Council is already fielding an alarming number of demands to give Faxon what he wants. If Emileia can do what she's promised, we'll be able to pacify everyone with the news that Faxon has been captured and Nuath is safe from any more of his attacks. Meanwhile, the last thing we need is a rumor that the Sovereign is already incapacitated."

"Even if she is?" He looks ready to launch himself at her.

Stepping between them, I pull out the big guns. "Mum, Mr. Stuart, why don't you let me see if my genetic makeup is close enough to M's that I can open her door without breaking in?" I ask reasonably, summoning every bit of my *graell*-enhanced persuasiveness I can without touching Tristan. "If it works, we can go in and talk to her for a few minutes, get a feel for how she's doing mentally, then—"

"How dare you?" Mum gasps, her blue eyes blazing into mine. "How *dare* you use 'push' on your own mother? It seems you can't be trusted any more than Rigel can! Well, I've had enough. Rigel, go home. Now. Someone will let you know when the Sovereign finishes her work. And Molly, consider yourself confined to your quarters until the Council meeting."

I stare at her in disbelief. "You're sending me to my *room*? Seriously?"

"Princess or not, you're still under my authority while a minor," she reminds me sharply. Then, to Mr. Stuart, "I suppose your son can return for the meeting as well, if he's calm enough by then to do so without creating a scene."

Mr. Stuart frowns uncertainly for a moment, then nods. "Rigel, I think you'd better do as she suggests. Go home and cool down, try to get your mind off M for a little while. I promise to let you know the moment she finishes what she's doing."

"What?" Rigel shouts. "Forget it! I'm not leaving her!"

His father raises an eyebrow. "Please don't make me call security on you, son. If you want to be allowed back for the meeting, you need to leave now."

Outraged, Rigel spins around and storms out of the office. Tristan and I are again hard on his heels. Mum and Mr. Stuart come after us.

"You're to go to your room, Missie," Mum reminds me before we reach the outer door. "Tristan, you can either go home as well or wait in the dining hall until tonight's meeting."

I don't think Rigel's in any shape to drive right now, Tristan tells me silently. *Why don't I take him home? We'll both be back in plenty of time for the meeting.*

Much as I don't want Tristan to leave, he's right about Rigel. *Okay, I agree.*

Tristan catches up with Rigel. "Hey, how about I drive us both?" Rigel pauses, still glowering. "Meeting's at seven, right?" Tristan continues. "We'll be back here by six-thirty."

Rigel grudgingly agrees to that.

Leaning down, Tristan gives me a quick kiss, even with Mum right there. "See you then. Love you. Stay safe, okay?"

I swallow. "Okay. You, too. Love you!"

The boys leave and I round on Mum. "You didn't have to do that! Rigel was totally right that someone should check on M in person. What if she gets stuck in Faxon's memories for good? Is catching him by tonight really worth losing our Sovereign?"

"I'm sure it won't come to that." Mum pats me on the arm like I'm twelve. "Though even if it did, we have you, so it isn't as though we'd be without a leader."

I slap her hand away. "Don't say that! Are you *hoping* something happens to M so I have to take over? That's awful!"

"No, no, of course not," she quickly protests, but I catch the flash of guilt in her expression. Because she's never quite forgiven M for rejecting Sean as her Consort? "Now, off to your room with you."

With one last, withering glare at her, I march off to my quarters, hoping against hope that M can finish her project quickly…and that she'll still be M when she's done.

18

Compulsion

AFTER SHUTTING my door in Rigel's face, I head to my living room, still breathing hard. Why can't he understand that I *have* to do this? Why can't Molly?

Sitting down on my couch, I work to compose myself. To forget that stricken look on Rigel's face just now and Molly's shock when I snapped at her—twice. Or how much I felt like Faxon when I got mad at them a few minutes ago, right down to that rushing sound he always hears when he's angry. Am I becoming the very person I hate most?

It's a terrifying, revolting thought, but I have to keep going. Shim himself admitted I have a better chance of finding Faxon quickly than he does, and Faxon *must* be stopped!

With renewed determination, I pluck the meditation button out of its box and stick it behind my ear. I'm obviously able to reach a trance state without it now, but with the *Echtran* Council meeting in less than five hours, I need all the help I can get.

Closing my eyes, I take a deep breath—and instantly find myself back in Faxon's library without any of the time-wasting, intermediate stuff. Excellent.

Without hesitation, I grab the same memory-book I was yanked out of twenty minutes ago so I can learn the rest of Philbin's plan to keep Faxon safe.

"Should they stage an actual uprising, your safety could be at risk," I again hear him saying when I open the book, "in which case you'll need to move to a secure location."

I was right! The secret hideout! Eager for more details, I sink all the way into Faxon's mind.

"Why would the people riot against me?" As Faxon, I'm incredulous. "They love me! You saw the most recent poll."

"The opinion polls have become less reliable now that responses are no longer anonymous," Philbin reminds me. "Barely a quarter voted in the last one. That makes it difficult to accurately gauge public opinion."

I snort my derision. "It can't have changed that much. With the so-called Resistance all but dead, it can't possibly pose enough of a threat to justify me going into hiding. How would that look? But if it makes you feel better, tell Morven to have an Ossian Sphere prepared for use in Jewel, on the off chance his research turns something up. That's more than enough firepower to ensure no rumor of a surviving Princess ever leaves that town."

Philbin nods resignedly. "Very well, my lord. I'll send the message to Morven now. We should have his response in an hour or so. While we wait, I'd like to discuss ways to recruit more people into your enforcement units. The most recent media appeals don't seem to be working and more conscriptions could turn sentiment against you. Perhaps increasing the incentives we're offering…"

As they go off on that tangent and Faxon's earlier alarm subsides, I'm able to wrench myself out of the memory. I feel even guiltier now for lambasting Rigel and the others for pulling me out of this memory. Guess I wasn't quite as close as I thought.

Still…the secure location Philbin mentioned *has* to be where Faxon is right now. But did it already exist, or is it yet to be built? I still don't know. I move on to the next worn-looking book, only a few ahead of the last one—so maybe a week or two later?

I get sucked in more quickly than I mean to and find myself again in the huge, underground ship-building compound I visited before. The moment I become Faxon, I realize he's in a rare *good* mood this time.

"That's excellent news," I gloat. "I should have guessed Elgin was trying to sabotage the project, his reports were always so pessimistic. You've now corrected the problems?"

"Yes, my lord." It's the same burly Mech I knocked down when Elgin first deserted. "Construction of the first two ships is now back on schedule and the others will be on track within weeks. We should still be able to commence the invasion before the next launch window closes." The man goes on to explain their progress in more detail.

This memory obviously won't give me what I need, so I back out—though it's surprisingly difficult to separate myself from Faxon, even though his emotions aren't all that engaged. When I finally manage to close the book, I shove it back in place and scan the final set of shelves in frustration.

The memory Rigel and the others interrupted would've been around the start of September—that's when members of the *Echtran* Council came to Jewel to do that blood test to prove I was heir to the last Sovereign. Faxon's secret retreat *had* to be in place before the Grentl zapped him senseless three months later…which means there *must* be memories of him creating that hideout or at least thinking about it somewhere in front of me.

Unfortunately, practically all the books on these last few shelves are well-worn enough to be important. I don't dare skip any, but I've simply *got* to get through them faster!

Setting my ultimate goal firmly in my mind, I open the next likely book, determined to keep enough of my consciousness free that I can easily get out as soon as I see what the memory is.

Opening this book reveals Faxon back in his quarters, facing what appears to be a hologram of Boyne Morven, the man who tried to kill me a year and a half ago.

"—enough research to learn there is indeed an *Echtran* family living in Jewel," the holographic Morven is saying. "The Stuarts. Van Stuart is son to Shim, current leader of the *Echtran* Council, which explains that visit three weeks ago. Van and his wife have a boy attending the high school there. He likely made those internet searches we discovered, so there's still no reason to believe Leontine's granddaughter somehow survived. As I've assured you repeatedly, there's no possible way she could have.

"However, because your security chief was so insistent, I'm sending my best, most loyal agent to Jewel to check things out in person, though it wasn't easy to get rid of a high school teacher on short notice without raising suspicion. My agent will take that teacher's place in a classroom the Stuart boy attends daily. It should be easy to discover whether the kid is friends with an *Echtran* girl. If not, I hope we can consider this matter closed, my lord. Then I can continue my preparations for your arrival on Earth next summer."

The recording ends and Philbin, who played it from his omni, smiles. "Morven's reasoning seems sound, my lord—though I'm reluctant to rule out the possibility that the Stuart family moved to Jewel in the first place because of those rumors about the Princess. Having his agent infiltrate the high school as a final precaution is wise."

Faxon snorts. "Wise? Overkill, I'd say, and it's distracting Morven from his main mission. I knew this was a wild goose chase from the start."

Though Philbin seems momentarily confused by that Earth expression, he shakes his head. "We need to be absolutely sure before the invasion plans progress much further—especially as we're getting more pushback about it than expected."

"Yes, yes, I suppose we can hold off publicizing the full plan until we receive final confirmation from Earth," Faxon reluctantly concedes.

"I'm glad you agree. Here's the timetable I propose, once we have that confirmation." Philbin pulls out his tablet.

Fascinating as it is to watch events I remember so well from my enemy's perspective, I pull out of the memory before I can sink in too deeply. In fact, I withdraw all the way back to my living room, where I can think more clearly, though I chafe at the delay.

"Okay, let's see," I mutter to myself. "It was the tag end of September when Smith showed up at Jewel High..."

I'd nearly convinced Rigel it was safe to end our pretend breakup by then, so Smith's arrival was a real gut punch. Instead of getting back together, I had to watch Rigel double down on fake-dating Trina, including that kiss that nearly destroyed me. Though it *did* throw Smith off for a couple of weeks.

I doubt Faxon had much reason to think about a secret hideout again before the second week of October. That's when I overheard Smith talking on the phone to Morven about an invasion plan and decided revealing myself was the quickest way to stop them—though I had to get right in Smith's face to do it.

Yes. The memory of Faxon getting *that* news is the one I should try to find next.

Before closing my eyes again, I glance at my omni to check the time. Yikes! How have I already been at this for an hour and a half? I also have two messages from Rigel waiting. I don't dare open them, afraid they'll distract me too much. Though by now he must be frantic, I even resist reaching out to him telepathically. I absolutely can't afford to get sucked into another argument right now, especially a mental one.

Promising myself again that I'll make it up to him later, I roll my stiff neck and shoulders a few times, then go back in…only to find myself in the memory I just left. Not what I wanted!

With an effort, I pull back out. The next well-worn book is too soon, but I peek into it anyway, only enough to tell that Faxon's happy. He's just received Morven's confirmation that I'm *not* in Jewel—which of course has Faxon, Philbin and three other people in the room with him positively jubilant. Nope, no point sinking all the way into that memory.

Maybe this one? I open the next promising volume.

Faxon's in the same small conference room as in the last memory, surrounded by the same men, but his mood is wildly different. "How?" he demands, clearly livid.

Ah, I think as myself, then settle into his mind. It's a seething mess.

"Just days ago Morven's agent concluded the girl is definitely *not* in Jewel, and now he says she *is*? What changed?"

Philbin glances around at the other three men—they all look stunned, too. "Morven claims the girl intentionally revealed herself to his agent. He doesn't know why, nor how she escaped his detection earlier."

"*Why* hardly matters." I slap my palm down on the table, making everyone jump. "Not if she really is the heir. Does he have *proof* of that?"

"You heard his message, my lord. He…sounded quite certain. She absolutely must be terminated before word of her existence can spread beyond the Stuart family and the *Echtran* Council. I assume they kept her identity secret to protect her, but foolishly left her quite vulnerable in that small *Duchas* town. When they discover she's revealed herself, they'll likely move her to a more secure location. Morven needs to act quickly."

I regard Philbin through narrowed eyes, trying to gauge whether he really believes what he's telling me. Twice now, he's expressed reservations about my invasion plan. Could this be a ruse to make me rethink it?

"Agreed," I say after a moment. "Whether she's really the heir or not, she must be eliminated. I won't let one stupid little girl get in my way when I'm so close to success. If his agent fails, tell Morven to do it himself."

As Philbin starts typing into his tablet, I think of something else.

"One more thing. These men—" I motion around the table— "are now a security risk. I want them disposed of as well." Ignoring stammered protests from the shocked men, I stride from the room.

My—Faxon's—emotions become less chaotic now that he's dealt with the problem. Briefly aware of myself as M, I'm sickened by the casual ruthlessness I just witnessed. Those men gave no indication they were disloyal—but apparently even Philbin is suspect now.

I consider reaching out to Rigel before continuing, just to center myself a little. But before I can decide whether the benefit would be worth the delay, I'm suddenly sucked back into Faxon's twisted mind.

"Are you *sure* you haven't heard anything more from Morven?" he—I—demand of Philbin. "It's been two days!" We're in my private quarters, where we can't be overheard.

"I'm afraid not, my lord. He last messaged that his agent was captured before killing the Princess, so Morven himself was leaving for Jewel within the hour to finish the job."

I glower at my second-in-command. "So much for his best agent. But Morven has Ossian Spheres and at least two dozen *Echtrans* under his control. Together, they should make short work of the girl."

"I agree, though by now he's had more than enough time to travel to Jewel and carry out the mission." Philbin is visibly nervous as he glances again at his omni. "I expected word from him hours ago."

"I'm sure there's a reasonable explanation." I refuse to panic, though the lack of news makes me uneasy, too. "If Morven *were* captured or killed, how would we get word? Is there someone you trust enough to ask?"

Philbin begins scrolling through his contacts. "I don't dare message anyone whose loyalty is less than rock solid. That could risk spreading word of the heir's existence further, if she indeed survived. Safer to simply ask a mutual acquaintance or two about Morven's whereabouts."

"Do it. We *must* learn what happened…but be careful with your wording. Say nothing that could lend credence to those rumors about the Princess, not with my invasion preparations at such a critical juncture."

"Agreed, my lord. I'll send inquiries to two different longtime friends living on Earth. If there's any, ah, news circulating there that we need to be aware of, one of them will let me know."

Better than nothing, but I'm both frustrated and unnerved by Morven's continued silence. "I'm scheduled to meet with the energy team in twenty minutes to look over their figures. I should go. Varying my routine could fuel speculation here in Nuath."

By the time he leaves his quarters, Faxon's emotions are calm enough that I'm finally able to completely withdraw from his thoughts. I close the book I'm holding—one I didn't even consciously open—and reach for the next. Faxon should get word of Morven's failure any time now, and that's *bound* to make him think about his contingency plan!

I'm just about to open the next worn book when I realize I need to pee. Eager as I am to continue, I know I'll concentrate better without that distraction, so I think myself back to consciousness.

The first thing I do when I open my eyes is check my omni again. There are now *four* messages waiting from Rigel and two from Molly— but it's also after five o'clock. Less than two hours to find what I need. I'll have to make it up to both of them later.

I try to ease my stiff neck and shoulders on the way to the bathroom, doing my best not to panic at how short my time is getting. On the way back, I gulp down some water—my throat's really dry.

After what feels like ten minutes but my omni says was only three, I sit down and close my eyes again…and instantly find myself where I left off last time, completely bypassing both my imaginary library and Faxon's. I'm really getting good at this! Still, knowing now how hard it can be to get out of Faxon's head, I try not to go in *too* deeply yet. Not until I reach something useful.

Keeping as much of myself back as I can, I manage to just skim his consciousness as he goes to that energy meeting, then two more meetings. Acutely aware of time passing in the present, I'm relieved when Faxon finally returns to his quarters. Philbin is waiting near the door, his expression grave.

"You have news?" Faxon asks as he ushers his confederate inside, away from prying ears and eyes.

Philbin, noticeably paler than normal, nods. "I'm afraid so, my lord. One of my friends has responded and…it isn't good."

As the dread Faxon tried to ignore during those meetings surges back, I let myself sink into his mind. "What?" I demand, now fully Faxon. "What does he say happened?"

"Not only did the Princess survive, Morven was captured, along with most of his followers. And that's not even the worst." Philbin looks positively sick as well as scared. "A few hours ago, the *Echtran* Council sent a MARSTAR bulletin to all *Echtrans* on Earth, officially announcing that the Princess has been found alive and her lineage officially verified."

Fear and fury rise up in my throat, nearly choking me. "How could Morven fail?" I rasp. "His Ossian Spheres should have made him invincible!"

"My friend forwarded me the bulletin—you can read it yourself. It gives few details, simply stating that the Princess was successfully defended by a small force led by Shim Stuart and his family, and that Morven is now in custody. I'm...I'm afraid we'll have to call off the invasion."

"No!" Grabbing an ornate vase from a nearby shelf, I hurl it against the wall to smash into a thousand shards, making Philbin flinch. "I've spent *years* planning this! Morven *assured* us—"

With a visible effort, Philbin pulls himself together to become businesslike. "Morven's assurances matter little now, my lord. The *Duchas* outnumber us twenty thousand to one. Without those Ossian Spheres to subject them to our will, invasion would be suicide."

I glare at him as the truth of his words sinks in. "What do you propose?" I grind out through tightly clenched teeth.

"Earth conquest may no longer be viable, but you still have uncontested control of Nuath, my lord," he replies. "We must do everything possible to keep news of the Princess and Morven's defeat from spreading here. I recommend shutting down all communication channels—the entire *grechain*—and disabling every system capable of receiving signals from Earth. At least until we know more."

Focusing on logistics helps to keep panic from clouding my reason. I give a terse nod. "Do it. Immediately."

"I can do it more quickly from here, my lord, if you're willing to give me access to your control console."

I hesitate, then nod again. "Very well. Just a moment." Angling my body to shield what I'm doing from Philbin's view, I punch my secure series of codes into the nearest vidscreen. "There. Do what you need to do."

He swiftly disables channel after channel of the Nuathan network, making sure none are left operational, then double checks them all.

"All communications are locked down, my lord," Philbin informs me after several minutes, "though I fear this may only delay the inevitable. It's imperative now that we prepare a fail-safe to keep you in power should the worst happen and public sentiment turn against you. I recommend a secure retreat, from which you can remotely control—"

I wave a dismissive hand, my mind already on other things. "Very well, very well, work up some plans and I'll take a look. Meanwhile, we need to learn what happened to Morven's Ossian Spheres. Were they *all* captured or destroyed? Did he even bring them to Jewel?"

Philbin regards me dubiously. "I don't know. The MARSTAR bulletin didn't mention them at all. Getting additional news from Earth will be difficult, with all incoming comm traffic shut down, but I'll do my best to learn more. With your permission, my lord?" At my impatient nod, he bows and leaves.

If Morven only brought one Sphere with him, our allies should still control the rest, I tell myself. *If so, my invasion can still proceed on schedule.* Pacing my living room, I feel more and more certain that must be true. Increasingly hopeful that I can yet achieve my long-held dream of Earth domination, I smile.

And I, as M, abruptly become aware of myself again—along with a panic nearly as intense as Faxon's was a few minutes ago. Apparently his secret hideout doesn't even *exist* yet, which means I'm still days or even weeks from my goal!

I try to withdraw from this memory back to Faxon's library, so I can check later books, but nothing happens. I'm still stuck in Faxon's living room as he mentally tweaks his invasion plan to account for the unwelcome news of the Princess's—my—survival.

"It must be possible," he mutters, still pacing. "I'll *make* it possible!"

Again I try to escape, thinking with all my might about my own memory library and the imaginary stairs leading up to my quarters. Again, I fail.

Crap.

Rigel was right.

I'm trapped. Lost.

Maybe for good.

19

Explicit memory

STILL LINKED to Faxon's mind as he continues pacing and strategizing, I struggle to control the frightened desperation I feel as M. As my capacity to think clearly returns, I realize I'm simultaneously aware of both Faxon's thoughts and my own.

Before, I had to essentially become him to hear his actual thoughts, and once I pulled back, they went silent. So this is new. And maybe useful?

Now that I can reason again, I figure I might as well make the most of being stuck here. I'll worry about getting out once I find what I need. But how? Can I locate Faxon's remaining significant memories without scanning the books in his library?

His library and mine are just mental constructs, I remind myself. A way to organize memories, mine and Faxon's, that are actually all in my head. Surely it should be possible to keep moving forward through Faxon's memories from inside one? Worth a try.

Hanging onto my own consciousness while still immersed in Faxon's past, I refocus on my goal to find the exact details Shim needs to locate and stop him.

Where's your secret hideout, Faxon? I demand, even though a memory can't possibly hear me. *Where will you go when your plans come crashing down? What's your fail-safe?*

Of course he doesn't react. *I still have a few dozen remaining allies on Earth,* he's thinking, completely hung up on salvaging his invasion.

The hideout! Think about the hideout! I silently shout. There *must* be a way I can direct these memories without a bunch of imaginary books. They're *all* somewhere in my mind.

Move faster! I command, trying to force Faxon past this useless scene. Suddenly, almost like he heard me, his pacing speeds up and we're both being dragged ahead in time, like a film on fast-forward. Memories of that evening, that night, and the whole next day flash past, faster and faster. It's exhilarating…and terrifying.

Two more days pass, or so I guess, though we're now moving at such blurring speed I can't tell for sure. *Your hideout!* I think again. We move even faster for a moment, then abruptly slow.

"Destroyed? All of them? Are you sure?" I feel Faxon's outrage and crushing disappointment along with my own relief that we finally stopped. We're back in his quarters, though it's now days later.

Philbin nods. "I'm afraid so. I briefly disabled our communications block so that my Earth contact could get a message through to me. He'd spoken with a member of Morven's group who escaped from Jewel. The man claimed the Sphere Morven brought along was destroyed during the battle and several of his comrades captured. The *Echtran* Council then forced them to reveal where the other Spheres were located."

"Is that all?" Faxon snarls. His dream of invasion in ashes, he can barely restrain himself from taking out his fury on Philbin, by far his most trusted remaining ally.

"I'm…afraid not, my lord. It appears news of that battle and the Princess's survival had already reached Nuath by the time we cut communication with Earth. Now, despite the blocks still in place here, that news is beginning to spread. Earlier today, there was a small attempt at an uprising. Quickly put down, of course. All participants are now in custody."

With a convulsive movement, Faxon kicks over the nearest chair. "*Dabhal* and damnation! In custody? Have them all executed—at once!"

"Of course. I'll see to it myself," Philbin assures him. "However, if that abortive uprising is any indication of how this news may reinvigorate the Resistance, we must work swiftly to strengthen your grip on Nuath. We can begin by publicly broadcasting those executions, after which I'll stage military training exercises throughout the colony to remind everyone of how our forces quashed insubordination in the past. In addition, we should begin construction at once on the secure retreat I mentioned earlier. That will ensure your physical safety while allowing you to maintain complete control over all of Nuath."

Philbin shares his plan for a small but secure fortress, undetectable by any normal means, from which Faxon can communicate with the people and exact any necessary retribution. I listen carefully as he describes the features he recommends for the very hideout I need to locate—once it's actually built. Time to fast-forward again.

Concentrating fiercely, I try hard to envision the retreat Philbin is still talking about. His voice speeds up, then fades out and once more Faxon and I are hurtling through the next few days. At least, that's what it feels like, though when we stop, we're again—or still?—in Faxon's quarters. I get the impression he rarely leaves them now. Like before, Philbin is the only other person present.

"—growing unrest despite the military exercises I ordered," Philbin is saying. "I fear the next uprising may be far more widespread—and dangerous."

"To me?" Faxon asks incredulously. "Surely they can't breach the Palace itself."

"Not easily," Philbin agrees, "but the Palace is too big to be made completely secure. There is also a growing risk of betrayal from within, loyalties are now shifting so quickly."

Are Philbin's loyalties shifting? Faxon wonders. He's tempted to ask him outright, but doesn't dare risk alienating one of the only people he trusts. "That two millisecond power glitch yesterday," he says instead. "Do we know yet how the Resistance caused it?"

"No. We're not even certain they did, though it seems the most likely explanation. The Engineer who reported it is still being questioned. Meanwhile, I'd like to show you the schematics for your secure retreat."

I pay close attention as both Faxon and myself as Philbin pulls the blueprint up on his tablet.

"The living area will be here." He points. "Small, but well appointed. Adjacent will be a control room, from which you'll be able to access most major systems and broadcast securely to virtually every public feed. Complete secrecy during construction is vital, though it will slow progress. Workers will need to be isolated from day one and their memories erased when the structure is complete."

I should have let Philbin start work on this sooner, Faxon thinks. *What if there's not time to finish it before— No! These recent uprisings are anomalies.*

Once we root out those responsible, my position will be stronger than ever. I'll make sure of it. Still…

"Where will it be located?" he asks. "And what about supplies?"

"The quickest option is to retrofit an existing storage area along the underground route to your shipbuilding facility," Philbin replies. "That will take far less time than building from scratch. I've already identified one less than a mile from the Palace that should serve the purpose. As for supplies, we'll have the recombinator stocked for at least a month to be safe, though I don't anticipate you ever needing to stay there for more than a few days at a time."

The thought of *ever* needing to hide like a hunted animal galls Faxon, but he'd rather be safe than sorry. "Fine. Get it built as quickly as possible, but be careful while choosing your work crew. I don't want to risk sabotage, or word of this leaking out before they can be sequestered."

Okay, Faxon, let's see the finished product, I command our mutual memory. *Show me your first visit to it.*

It only takes me a moment of intense focus before we're again whipping forward. I'm definitely getting better at this! I just hope it's not too late.

This time, I'm able to catch occasional glimpses along the way, along with flashes of Faxon's mental state. Enough to tell the Resistance is now growing by leaps and bounds. I also briefly witness the scene where Faxon tortures the location of the Grentl device from an Engineer, then has the man killed. Quickly as it passes, it sickens me.

The dizzying speed continues for a long time, through what I estimate are two or three more weeks, before we finally slow to a stop again.

I feel a surge of triumph as I realize we're actually inside the secret hideout!

Probing Faxon's mind, I discover his paranoia is now beyond extreme. There was a major popular uprising two days ago that couldn't be completely quelled. Since then, more and more members of Faxon's security force have been deserting. Other previously-trusted allies keep changing sides as well, each one creating new vulnerabilities. Faxon is increasingly suspicious of Philbin, too, but there's no one else he can fully depend on.

"You said the living area would be well appointed," Faxon complains as our surroundings solidify. "I suppose it will do for a true emergency, but I'd hate to spend more than a day or two here."

Looking around through his eyes, I try to absorb every detail I can, though his extreme agitation makes it hard to concentrate.

"If we have time, my lord, I'll have more amenities installed," Philbin apologetically assures him—from a safe distance.

I don't blame him. Faxon's recent memories show he's lashed out physically several times over the past few weeks.

"Did you use the specs from that secret room I found in the Palace, as I suggested?" Faxon asks.

"Some of them," Philbin replies. "We don't have the technology those aliens used to change the molecular structure of the entrance to make it dissolve like that. Nor have we had time to create a similar genetic sensor calibrated specifically to you, my lord. But the shielding is similar, which should make these chambers undetectable by even our most sensitive scanning equipment."

Faxon glowers at those caveats. "I thought I would be the only one able to get inside?"

"Quite so, my lord. The door can only be opened by combining a numeric code with a spoken command, though at the moment there's a temporary, secondary code in place that bypasses the voice command, to allow workers access for the final modifications we're making."

After sweeping the cramped living space with a critical glance, Faxon —and I—step through to the control room behind it. "What, exactly, can I do from here?"

"This setup allows you to record broadcasts." Philbin points to a small camera and screen. "While this terminal will let you monitor most critical systems. You'll be able to remotely redirect portions of the power grid from here, and send electronic signals to receivers we can put in place throughout Nuath. I suggest presetting explosives in strategic loca-tions designed for maximum intimidation effect. Those can be used to forcefully remind the populace of the consequences of rebellion. You'd be able to trigger them all from here, in whatever order or intensity you choose."

"Excellent," Faxon says with a slow smile I share. "Start setting those explosives right away. Lots of them. The people need to know that if they cross me, it won't end well for them."

Abruptly aware I'm again identifying a little too closely with Faxon, I pull back my focus so I can think as myself. If that latest uprising was the one the O'Garas were celebrating before Thanksgiving that year,

Faxon will only be in power for a couple more weeks. From this point on, I need to proceed more slowly—if I can.

Tomorrow. What happens tomorrow? My demand works better than I expect. We speed up briefly, then stop, long enough for me to glean from Faxon's mind what he's experienced since yesterday. Encouraged, I repeat the same command over and over, spending just enough time in each memory for me to catch up.

As the days pass, I frequently catch Faxon thinking about his hideout, and about the extra explosives he's having Philbin plant for him. I know I'm on the right track when those include the bomb he used last night and the one Shim's people found beneath the Legislature.

Faxon repeatedly has Philbin change the hideout's numerical entry code, then finally tells him to delete the supplemental one for workers, as construction is finished. What I still need, though—what Shim will need, besides the exact location of the hideout—is the *final* code Faxon settles on. I suppose it's possible he changed it again after his escape, but so far only Philbin has done it. Faxon's not super techy, so maybe he doesn't know how.

I can hope.

By now, only days remain before the Grentl will zap Faxon senseless. Every final detail *has* to be in place before that, so I must be getting very, very close.

Sure enough, pushing forward one more day finally lands me on the memory I've been chasing from the start—but I can tell immediately it will be an ugly one.

"You're sure, my lord?" Philbin is asking resignedly. He and Faxon are back inside the hideout. "I do have other duties, you know, and changing your code every other day interferes with me carrying them out."

"Yes, yes, you've whined about that before," Faxon snaps. "This will be the last time. I guarantee it." Because he doesn't intend to give Philbin a chance to tell anyone else what it is.

Swallowing my revulsion at what Faxon's planning, I watch carefully as Philbin laboriously keys in the thirteen-digit code, committing it to memory.

"Same voice command as before?" Philbin asks when he's through.

"No, I'll update that as well. Enable recording."

Philbin does so.

Faxon speaks clearly into the microphone. "Faxon, supreme and final ruler of Nuath, has need of his private retreat in order to safeguard his person and enforce his will upon the populace." He steps away from the mic with a smile. "A bit more secure than the last one, wouldn't you say?"

Philbin nods, though he looks wary. "Extremely secure, my lord, though rather a lot to remember verbatim."

"Let me worry about that." Faxon's still smiling.

Together, the two men walk back through the living area to the outer door. "May I now return to my duties, my lord?" Philbin asks.

"No, not quite yet," Faxon replies. "There's one last service I require from you. Your eternal silence." On those final words, he whips an ampule from his pocket and jabs it into his confederate's arm.

Philbin's eyes widen for a split second before he collapses in place. Faxon waits a moment, then bends down to check that both breathing and heart have stopped. He nods in satisfaction. Now, absolutely no one on Mars other than himself can find or enter this place. The memories of every worker who ever saw it have been wiped, except the few heard grumbling, who were simply killed. The only task left is taking Philbin back to his quarters so that he can be discovered there, dead of an apparent massive heart attack.

The part of me that's still M recoils in horror as Faxon drags his last trusted ally through the door and into a waiting hovercar just outside.

"Seal entrance," Faxon says. The door to his hideout slides shut and disappears, indistinguishable from the surrounding pinkish-gray rock of the tunnel.

He then climbs behind the controls of the hovercar and pilots it through a maze of narrow, interconnecting tunnels. With an effort, I suppress my disgust so I can carefully note every turn until we reach the wider conduit running directly between the Palace and the underground shipbuilding facility.

Certain now that I have everything I need, I try—hard—to wrench my mind away from Faxon's. I still can't do it.

Helplessly, I watch Faxon turn left and drive to a small parking area below the main one under the Palace. Once there, he hauls Philbin's dead body onto a mag-lev platform. I try to blot out the awful scene, desperate now to get back to my apartment, to my body.

Rigel? I frantically send. *Are you there?* Maybe if I can connect with him, he can pull me out like before.

But if he responds, I can't hear him.

I have no idea how much time has passed in the present—way too much, I'm sure. Has the Council meeting started? Is it even still Saturday? I *have* to get out! It's the only way I can share everything I've learned with Shim!

As Faxon guides his grisly cargo into an elevator, I desperately try to imagine myself back in my NuAgra living room, hoping with all my might it will materialize around me. It doesn't. I can't even sense my physical body, which must be painfully stiff by now. And hungry.

Is it possible there's more I need to discover? Maybe Faxon *did* change the code again? I may as well find out, since I'm unable to escape.

Tomorrow. What happens tomorrow? I demand, trying hard to ignore the sight of Faxon maneuvering Philbin's corpse through the Palace to his quarters. To my relief, it works.

Over the next two days I experience Faxon describing how he "found" his chief of staff dead when he failed to appear as scheduled. Then ordering several more memory wipes and an execution—all people he suspects of disloyalty, though without any actual proof.

Another uprising occurs and is put down. That does get Faxon thinking about his fail-safe again, but only to reassure himself it'll be there if he needs it.

The day after that, I find myself back in a room I recognize all too well, where Faxon again advances on the Grentl device, determined to force information out of it.

With a stab of panic, I realize I'm about to relive his very last memory —and this time Rigel can't help me when I get zapped along with Faxon. When he again grabs the device's two prongs, all I can do is brace myself.

Helpless, I re-experience the initial searing pain, the Grentl absorbing Faxon's most recent memories, Faxon's futile attempt to reverse the process, then the far more excruciating pain that builds to an agonizing climax…until everything goes dark.

20

Separation anxiety

RIGEL

"WE SHOULD GO," Tristan urges when I hang back in NuAgra's parking lot to look back. "You don't want them to call security, do you? It's just for a few hours—I promise we'll be back well before tonight's meeting."

I scowl at him. "It feels all wrong to just leave her! Who knows what spending all this time in Faxon's memories will do to her—and nobody else even seems to care!"

"I care," Tristan assures me. "Molly cares. A lot. Trust me. But you heard your dad. If we don't leave now, they might not let us come back at all—and neither of us want that. Right?"

"No, but—" I break off, pissed at Tristan now, too, for being so damned reasonable. "Fine. Let's go. But I want to be back here at six."

He nods. "Six. You got it. C'mon."

I get into Tristan's little black Porsche, parked a few spaces away from my car. Unfortunately, he's right that I shouldn't be driving right now. I'm so furious at Mrs. O and my dad, I can barely see straight. I won't be able to help M at all if I get into a wreck.

No one's home when we get to my house. My mom's probably doing rounds at the hospital.

"You want to come in?" I ask, hoping he'll say no, so I can fume in peace.

"Sure," Tristan says with a shrug. "Got anything to eat?"

I know he's trying to distract me, but I play along. What else can I do?

"Let's see what's in the fridge."

We're both picking at bowls of ice cream and a bag of chips—neither of us has much appetite—when my mom comes in from the garage.

"Your father called me," she explains. "He, ah, thought I should come home and check on you, so I arranged for Dr. Wills to finish my rounds for me. Are you all right?"

I snort. "No, but what difference does it make? If I can't help M, or even *see* her, I might as well waste time here as at NuAgra." I don't mention it wasn't my choice, but I'm sure Dad told her what happened.

Her expression is sympathetic, but she knows me well enough not to risk setting me off again by spouting something that's supposed to be soothing. Instead, she turns to Tristan.

"It's good to see you, Tristan. How is Molly holding up?"

"Surprisingly well," he tells her, "but we both agree with Rigel they should check on M with more than cameras."

Now Mom looks troubled. "My husband explained the situation to me. He and Lili O'Gara seem certain she's in no real danger. I hope they're right. It does sound as though the surest way to keep both girls safe is to stop Faxon as soon as possible—which is what M is trying to do."

I slam my fist down on the bag of chips, crushing most of them. "Why is it on her? Why is *everything* always on her? She can hide it from most people, but I know how stressed she was even before this. I'm afraid this'll push her over the edge into a real mental breakdown. Or worse!"

Mom puts a hand on my arm with that calming thing she does. "I agree, far too much has been expected of a girl her age, but it was her own decision to explore Faxon's memories. Shim and the Council seem to think it's Nuath's best chance to avoid further destruction and political upheaval, and perhaps they're right. We all must hope she can find what she needs to without incurring any permanent damage."

"Yeah. Let's hope." But by now I don't have much of that left.

The next two hours creep by. I let Tristan load some complicated new online role-playing game on my computer and try to learn it. Anything to take my mind off what M might be doing to herself. I'm usually a whiz at games like this, but I can't focus. It takes me three iterations before I can outscore Tristan.

Between rounds, I fire off a couple more messages to M and try over and over to get through to her mentally. I do catch an occasional glimpse of what she's seeing in Faxon's memories, but never enough to make sense of it. Nothing of M's own thoughts at all.

At four I call Dad to check on her, but he just promises—again—to let me know the moment there's any change. Finally, a few minutes after five, my phone rings.

"Is she awake?" I demand, not even bothering to say hi.

"Not now," Dad says, "but she was briefly. A few minutes ago, she stood up and stretched, then went into the bathroom. Then she drank some water before sitting back down and closing her eyes again. I assume she hasn't yet found what she's looking for, but she appeared physically fine. I knew you'd want to know."

Not quite what I hoped, but at least she's not in a coma. "Thanks, Dad." I hang up and share the news with Tristan.

"That's good, though, right? It proves she *can* wake herself up. Did your dad say anything about Molly?"

"Um, no, but I didn't think to ask. Sorry."

He's obviously worried too, what with threats against our girls flying around. I start to turn back to the game, then stand up instead.

"You know what? Screw this. It's almost five-thirty. Let's go back to NuAgra."

I half expect pushback from Tristan, but don't get it. "Yeah, let's go. Even if they make us sit in the dining hall, we'll be in a better position to protect them than we are here."

"We're leaving!" I yell up the stairs before opening the front door.

Mom comes hurrying down. "You have news?"

"Not much—Dad can give you the latest, but I need to see what's going on for myself."

She frowns at me, gauging my mood, then nods. "Very well. Just... keep your temper, so you're not sent away again."

"Right. Bye, Mom."

It seems to take longer than usual to reach NuAgra, even with Tristan going well over the speed limit. He's nearly as eager to get back as I am. Finally, we turn onto the two lane country road that leads to the front gate...and see flashing lights up ahead, still more than a mile this side of NuAgra.

"What's that about?" Tristan mutters.

"Let's find out."

It's nearly dark, so it's another half mile before we can tell it's a police car, lights flashing, and what looks like a roadblock being set up. As we get close, I can also see two police officers and a man I recognize as a NuAgra security guard. All three wave at us to stop.

Tristan puts down his window. "What's going on?"

"Chemical spill," one of the cops replies. "You'll have to take another route to wherever you're going."

Tristan and I exchange a glance.

"Um, we're going to NuAgra. This is the only way to get there," I say across Tristan. "They're expecting us."

"Sorry," the officer says. "We can't—"

He breaks off as the NuAgra guy walks up. "It's okay, Jacobs," the *Echtran* security guard says. "Their parents work there. You can let them through."

The police officer shrugs, though he looks dubious. "If you say so. Watch out for that spill," he adds to Tristan, who nods and drives on.

"What do you think's really going on?" I wonder aloud. "Bet it's not really a spill."

"Extra security?" Tristan guesses. "They've been getting all those threats and demands…" He speeds up. "Yeah," he says a minute later. "There's definitely something happening up ahead."

I squint through the windshield and see a good-sized crowd milling around on the road in front of the NuAgra gate, only visible at this distance because the area's well lit by spotlights.

"What the hell?" I exclaim. "Are they trying to force their way in?"

Tristan floors it, but then has to slam on the brakes when several people jump right out in front of us. "Hey! Get out of the way!" he yells out his window.

I put my window down and yell at them to move, too. Instead, they spread out, blocking the whole road so Tristan can't go around them, then start walking toward us.

"You have your weapon?" I ask. Tristan nods. "Good. Me, too. If they want a fight, let's give it to them."

We both jump out, our energy weapons at the ready.

Just then, one of them calls out, "Zell was right! It's them. Somebody message the Leader we've got the Royal brats' boy toys."

"Boy toys?" Tristan repeats with an incredulous laugh. "Seriously?"

I don't laugh. I aim my weapon. "Royal *brats*?" These are obviously some of the jerks calling for M's execution. In other words, murderers. "You'll never—"

Before I can finish, they rush us. I stun the nearest one and Tristan stuns another, but then the other five are on us. The guy up front, the biggest guy in the group, smiles—a nasty smile I want to punch off his face. Screw stunning.

But as I draw back a fist, I'm suddenly enveloped in a choking cloud of gas and everything goes black.

21

Consciousness

WHERE AM I? When *am I?*

Slowly, slowly, my darkness gives way to something else. Books. I'm lying on the floor, looking at a shelf full of books.

The memory library! I'm out! Well, partway out.

Shoving to my feet, I hurry through the archway into my own library, then look for the stairs leading back to reality. They're not there.

"No!" I shout. At least my mind does. I still have no sense of my physical body. I may have finally escaped Faxon's mind, but I'm clearly still trapped in my own.

Rigel? Rigel, please answer me! I frantically think to him, over and over, but he doesn't reply. Can't he hear me? Or am I only imagining sending thoughts to him, without actually doing it? How can I even know?

Panic clouds my reason and I stare around wildly, trying to *force* that imaginary spiral staircase to appear. It doesn't. All I see are rows and rows of memory books. Maybe one of those can help me?

Desperate to reconnect with Rigel after the way I treated him, I head deeper into the library. After so many awful Faxon memories, I'm starving for a happy one—and most of mine involve Rigel.

I pause at a shelf roughly a year or two before the present and start running my fingers over the book spines, getting a sense of what's inside each one. When I find the earliest one involving Rigel, I snatch it off the shelf and open it.

Immediately, I'm reliving my very first sight of Rigel, when he walked into Homeroom the first day of our sophomore year. The way his voice made my whole body tingle, before he ever even looked at me. Pushing ahead like I did in Faxon's memories, I skip to lunch that same day, when Rigel unexpectedly introduced himself to me. Then our first touch the following day, when the electrical jolt that created our bond freaked us both out and he ran off. Then, finally, wonderfully, the very first time he kissed me.

Rigel? I send again, as hard as I can, trying to reach across the years from that magical moment to now. *Rigel, where are you?*

Amazingly, this time I receive an answer!

M? I hear my name faintly. Then, stronger, *M, is that you? Are you still in there?*

The voice isn't Rigel's, though. It's Molly's.

Molly? I think back, confused but relieved to hear *anyone* at this point. Unless I'm imagining this, too? *Where are you?*

Yes! I now sense her relief, too, nearly as strong as my own. *Yes, it's me! I'm here in your quarters. Can you open your eyes?*

I try, really try, but I still can't even feel my body, much less control it.

Pull off that button thing behind my ear, I suggest. *Maybe that will help.*

Okay, done.

I try again and slowly become aware of sensations—hands gripping my arm so tightly it's almost painful, but also wonderful. A moment later I'm able to force open my eyes. I gaze around, half-incredulous, at the living room I used to think was way too formal to belong to me, but now feels like the home I was desperate to return to. Finally, I focus on Molly's worried face.

"I'm out!" I rasp, my throat even drier than last time. I swallow. "I'm...I'm really out," I repeat more clearly. "Molly, thank you, thank you! But...how did you get in here?"

"I'm your twin, remember? Maybe not identical, but my DNA's apparently close enough to yours to open your genetic lock—not that anyone would let me try earlier. I've been *so* scared about you, M!"

I? Not we?

"Where's Rigel?" I ask.

She frowns. "That's something else that scares me. He and Tristan were supposed to be back in time for the Council meeting but they haven't shown up."

"The Council meeting!" The deadline I set for myself! "What time is it? What *day* is it? I feel like I was stuck in there forever."

"It's still Saturday, but the meeting started half an hour ago. When they told me you still weren't awake, I pitched a fit, demanded they send someone in after you. The Council yammered a while and finally put it to a vote...but voted four to three *not* to interrupt you. I was so pissed I stormed out, saying I was going back to my quarters, except I came here instead and convinced Cormac to let me try your door. And it worked! Did you ever find—?"

At that, everything floods back. "Yes! I know where Faxon is. I need to tell Shim right away." I jump up, then nearly collapse.

Molly grabs me in time to keep me from falling. "Are you okay?"

"Yeah, my legs are just asleep from sitting in one position so long. But let's get to the meeting. I need to tell everyone—especially Shim— what I learned."

With her support, I limp through the living room to the outer door. "You said Rigel and Tristan were supposed to be back. Why did they leave?"

"Mum." Her voice reflects the disgust I sense from her. "Rigel got frantic when you stayed in that trance so long and he couldn't contact you. He made a scene and Mum got pissed. Then I tried to use 'push' on her and she got even more pissed. She sent Rigel home and me to my quarters until the meeting. Rigel was so upset, I asked Tristan to drive him."

My Bodyguard Cormac is waiting outside when we leave my quarters. He looks relieved to see us.

"Thanks for humoring me," Molly tells him. "It worked, see?"

He nods, smiling, then follows at a distance as we hurry toward the Council conference room.

"Anyway, once she let me come out," Molly continues, "I found out the boys weren't back yet—and Tristan's not answering my messages."

Her worry is contagious.

"Oh! Rigel sent me a bunch of messages earlier," I suddenly remember. "Maybe one says where they are."

Pausing outside the meeting room, I play his four messages, one after the other.

"M, please don't shut me out! We're all worried about you. Please, please touch base soon."

"It's been an hour now, and I'm getting more and more worried. I know you feel like you have to do this today, but you're risking your mental health. Please reply!"

"Mrs. O is pissed I keep insisting someone check on you. She's making me leave NuAgra. Tristan's driving me—I probably am too crazy with worry to drive myself. We'll both be back in time for the meeting, though!"

Then finally, "M, it's been almost four hours. Why aren't you answering? I've been trying to reach your mind all day, plus sending all these messages. Please, please answer me if you can, one way or the other."

"He sent the last one nearly two hours ago," I say anxiously. "When I couldn't escape after finding what I needed, I did try to reach out to him telepathically, hoping he could help, but he didn't answer. Let me try again, now that I'm out."

Rigel? I send as loudly and clearly as I can. *Can you hear me now? I'm out, I'm done, I found Faxon's hideout!*

I "listen" for all I'm worth but seconds pass, then a full minute, with no reply.

"Well?" Molly finally asks.

I shake my head, my worry ramping up several notches. "Nothing. There's no way he's too far away to hear me, so he must either be asleep or unconscious." I refuse to mention the only other possibility.

Even so, Molly's face goes white. "He and Tristan can't both be asleep! What if—?"

Before she can finish, the conference room door hisses open.

"Ah!" Mrs. O'Gara exclaims. "I was about to go after you, Molly. Why didn't you tell me the Sovereign had come out of her quarters?" Then, to me, "Did…you find the information you were seeking, Excellency?" She's noticeably more deferential than she was at lunch—probably because of the way I blew up at her. "Molly kept insisting we interrupt you, but—"

"If she hadn't, I'd still be trapped inside my mind." I walk past her into the room where the rest of the Council is assembled. "Everyone, I know where Faxon is. I have to tell Shim right away, and then we need to—"

I'm interrupted by excited exclamations, most of the Council members surging to their feet.

"You discovered his hiding place?" Kyna's holographic image stands up, too. "You're sure?"

"Yes, yes, I'm sure," I impatiently confirm, my earlier triumph nearly forgotten in my worry for Rigel. "I'll dictate my message to Shim right now and you can all hear it, too. Then we need to find Rigel and Tristan!"

Reactions range from relieved to confused, but I ignore them all, pulling up Shim's contact in my omni.

"Shim, I know it's after midnight there, but I finally found Faxon's hideout, in one of those underground tunnels you've been searching. It's holographically disguised and has special shielding to prevent detection, but I can tell you exactly where it is and how to get in."

I go on to describe the precise location of the hideout, along with the alphanumeric access code and verbal command for entry. "It may be keyed to Faxon's voice, so try to cobble it together from recordings, if you can. Tell your people to be careful when they go in—Faxon is probably armed."

I hit send, then turn to the Council, some of whom quickly close mouths that had fallen open. "Now. Has anyone heard from Rigel or Tristan since they left NuAgra this afternoon?"

Tristan's mom shakes her head. "I'm afraid not, Excellency. When Molly, er, Princess Malena expressed concern a short while ago, I did try calling Tristan, but he didn't answer."

"My wife told me both boys left our house roughly two hours ago, shortly after I last spoke with Rigel." Mr. Stuart is equally worried. "She said they were intending to come straight here, but they never arrived."

Mrs. O'Gara makes an impatient motion. "They likely stopped for something to eat before the meeting and lost track of time. I'm sure they're both fine."

"Seriously, Mum?" Molly exclaims, aghast. "They're obviously *not* fine, or they'd answer our calls and texts. You wouldn't let me interrupt M earlier because you said frustrated people kept calling the Council, either demanding our heads, or desperate for proof we're actually doing something. Now they're even demonstrating. What if they took out their frustration on Tristan and Rigel? They were safe here!"

"Demonstrating?" I echo, even more scared now. "Where? Desperate people are dangerous."

Mr. Stuart points his omni at a wall and a vidscreen appears. "Here, among other places," he says. "They began gathering outside the gate about an hour after the boys left. As their numbers grew, we set up roadblocks in both directions to prevent more *Echtrans* from joining—and to keep any *Duchas* motorists from seeing or hearing things they shouldn't."

The vidscreen shows the scene outside—a mob of several people dozen outside NuAgra's front gate, waving signs and chanting. Listening closely, I hear, "Bring them out! Bring them out!" Some of the signs say the same, while others read, *DO something!*

"They're demanding Molly and I go out to them?"

"We assume so," Malcolm says. "Though they must know how ridiculous that demand is. They weren't this unruly when Breann and I arrived, around five o'clock, so we didn't think they posed a threat."

Tristan's mother frowns. "Perhaps not to the Sovereign or Princess, given how well-protected NuAgra is, but the boys are another matter. Lili, I do wish you'd consulted the rest of us before sending them away."

Mrs. O looks nettled. "Both young men are trained Bodyguards. They should be able to handle themselves."

"Apparently not," I retort, "or they'd be here by now! For all we know—" I break off when every Council member's omni pings at once.

As they pull out their devices, Teara Roark sucks in a horrified breath and Mr. Stuart curses aloud. I sense the most extreme emotion from those two, but everyone else is also alarmed.

"What?" Molly and I demand together, grabbing our own omnis. Whatever the message is, we didn't get it—probably because our numbers aren't available to most *Echtrans*, like the Council's are.

It's Breann who answers, her voice shaky. "A ransom note. How dare they!"

"I'm…I'm sure it's a bluff," Mrs. O says, though she's also visibly shaken. "They can't possibly—"

With an exasperated huff, Molly lunges over and snatches her mother's omni out of her hand, then holds it so I can see the screen, too.

We will no longer sit idly by to watch our homeland destroyed and our loved ones endangered, it reads. *Tell the Sovereign and her sister to be outside the gates by nine o'clock tonight if they ever want to see Rigel Stuart and Tristan Roark alive again. If they don't care enough about Nuath to do the right thing, perhaps saving their boyfriends' lives will motivate them. Tell them to come out alone, or both boys are as good as dead.*

Attached to the message is a picture of Rigel and Tristan, bound, gagged and apparently unconscious. Molly and I stare at each other in horror.

"They wouldn't really kill them, would they?" she gasps.

I want to say no, but… "Fear can make people do terrible things,

things they normally wouldn't." I saw multiple examples in Faxon's past.

Molly springs to her feet. "Then let's go. It's only an hour till their deadline."

I jump up and we both head for the door while the Council sits stunned. Then they all start shouting at once.

"Stop!"

"Don't be ridiculous!"

"You saw that mob out there!"

I whirl to face them. "And mobs can be deadly! Those people have Rigel and Tristan and we're *not* going to let them be killed!"

"I'm sure it won't come to that," Mrs. O exclaims. "We'll simply tell them Faxon's capture is imminent and I'm certain they'll let them go."

"You don't know that," I snap. "We can't prove it, so why won't they think we're just making it up, to buy time? Shim hasn't even received my message yet, much less caught Faxon. But tell them, if you think it'll help."

Breann looks at her omni and blinks. "My message is gone. Do any of you still have it?"

They all check and shake their heads. It's disappeared off Mrs. O's omni, too.

Molly hands it back to her mother. "Now the only way to reply is to go out there. C'mon, M."

"No! Don't let them!" Even as a hologram, Nara's distress is clear. "Can you make an announcement they'll hear outside the gates? Or send a MARSTAR bulletin?"

Mr. Stuart looks dubious. "I'm certainly willing, if the Council agrees. But what should we say? That we hope and believe Faxon will be in custody within hours? We can't honestly claim more than that, at the moment."

"No." Kyna's tone allows for no argument. "We mustn't get ahead of ourselves. If we put out such a statement and it proves false, it will further erode trust in this Council. Forgive me, Excellency, but all we truly have at this moment is your conviction that the information you sent to Shim will result in Faxon's capture. If the Sovereign is wrong, if Faxon is hiding somewhere other than the location she observed in a memory from more than a year ago, we may be no closer to capturing him than before. Not until we receive confirmation from Shim that

Faxon is in custody, can we truthfully relay that information to our people."

"But that will take hours!" I protest.

"Way past nine o'clock," Molly agrees. "We can't wait that long!"

Kyna's hologram regards me sadly. "I'm sorry, Excellency, Princess, but I can't condone a premature official announcement in hopes of swaying terrorists. Surely you can see that?"

"Then we're going out there," Molly declares. "M and I will figure out *some* way to keep both the boys and ourselves from being killed. It's not like we want to die, either."

I nod. "What she said. I promise we'll do everything possible to get us all out of this alive, but we can't do it from in here."

Teara leans forward. "Excellencies, believe me, I would do almost anything to save my son's life, but we can't possibly risk both of you. You're too important to our people, to our future." She has tears in her eyes but I can tell she means what she says.

"I agree." Mr. Stuart's voice is also thick with emotion. "I know Rigel would never want you to sacrifice or even risk yourself for his sake, Excellency. He'd never forgive me if I allowed it."

"Allowed?" I round on him, suddenly as furious as when Mrs. O used that word to me at lunchtime. "I'm not asking for anyone's permission! *I'm* the Sovereign and I say Molly and I are going to rescue Rigel and Tristan. *None* of you have the authority to stop us."

Everyone is startled to silence, even Molly.

Kyna is the first to find her voice. "Excellency, your safety—"

"Is my concern," I snap. "Molly, are you ready?"

"No, *not* only your concern," Kyna loudly contradicts me. "Van?"

Nodding, Mr. Stuart touches a control on his omni. "I'm sorry, Excellency, but I've sealed the door. We need to discuss this. I propose sending out a trained negotiator while a security squad secures the entire area. I'm sure between them they can—"

"What? No!" My fury mounts higher. "You saw their message. If a bunch of security guys go out there instead of us, they might kill Rigel and Tristan outright. I *insist*, as your Sovereign—!"

M, wait! Molly's voice says in my head. Glancing at her in confusion, I see her hand on my arm. *I have an idea. Just play along, okay?*

"Mr. Stuart, do you really think your negotiator can save them? Or at least buy some time until we hear Faxon's been caught?" she pleads convincingly.

His relief is clear. "Yes, Molly, that's exactly what I'm hoping." Then, to me, "I understand you want to rush to Rigel's rescue, but I beg you to please let us handle this. I have no more desire for my son to be killed than you do."

"That does sound safer," Molly reluctantly admits. "If the two of us go out alone, they might kill us and both our guys, too."

I'm about to argue that Molly's way more persuasive than any negotiator could be, but she tightens her grip on my arm. *Say you agree! Trust me!*

Reining in my anger, I force myself to nod. "Maybe she's right. Do you really think you can get them back safely?"

"I really do," Mr. Stuart assures me. "Thank you, Excellency."

Still keeping hold of my arm, Molly takes a step toward the door. "While you work out your plan, can I take M to get something to eat? She never got dinner."

Mr. Stuart looks to Kyna, who nods.

"Of course," she says. "I'm sure you'll be able to view the situation more calmly after a meal, Excellency. We'll start working out the logistics immediately and will present our rescue plan when you return. That should set both of your minds more at ease."

I doubt that, but Molly thanks everyone effusively and propels me out the now-open door.

"Why did you agree?" I demand as soon as it closes behind us. "This sounds like a surefire way to get both boys killed. It makes way more sense for *us*—"

"Yes it does, but we don't have a plan yet," she quietly reminds me. "Anyway, you really do need to eat something and…chill a little. You sounded like you were channeling Faxon again just now."

Even as she says it, I realize she's right—on both counts. "Yeah, maybe I was. But the clock is ticking and they want to discuss things to death."

"Let's go to your quarters. You can eat and we can plan without any interruptions."

We head that way, Cormac again following a respectful distance behind. As soon as Molly and I are back in my apartment, I reengage the genetic lock.

"It's already five past eight," I anxiously point out. "Less than an hour—"

"I know," Molly interrupts. "We'll hurry, but not before I feed you something." She goes to my recombinator and punches in an order. "Would Cormac help us get outside the fence if you ordered him to?"

"Not if he believes it'll put me at risk. Which I'm sure he would. Plus Kyna may have already thought of that."

Molly hands me a tuna sandwich and a glass of milk. "Then I'll call Sean." She pulls out her phone. "Maybe he can help."

A moment later, I hear Sean's voice. "Molly? What's going on?"

"Can you come to NuAgra right away? M and I need you to break us out while the Council's busy talking."

"Huh?"

Motioning me to start eating, she explains the situation to Sean while I stuff my face. When she finishes, there's a brief silence at the other end before he replies.

"Mol, maybe the Council's right," he says cautiously. "I'm sure those kidnappers would jump at a chance to kill you and M, since that's one of Faxon's demands. This could play right into their hands. It would be dumb to—"

"We can't just sit here and wait, Sean!" Molly flares. "Could you, if it were Kira?"

I hear his intake of breath. "No. I couldn't. Okay. I'll pick her up and head straight there. Most people don't know what we can do, especially all together. Maybe that'll help. But how will you get outside? The Council's not going to let you just waltz out the front door."

"We'll come up with something," Molly assures him. "Just...hurry. Please!"

$$\frac{\qquad}{22}$$

Survival advantage

MOLLY STICKS her omni in her back pocket and turns to me. "Are you done eating?"

Gulping down my last bite of sandwich, I nod. "What do you think? Go out through the greenhouses? Or can you schmooze your way past the guards at the front door?"

She grimaces. "Without Tristan? Probably not. Especially if the Council's got someone watching in case we try that. I think we'll have better luck sneaking out the back."

"Then let's go." I'm already heading for the door.

As soon as it opens, we hit our first snag—Cormac, again standing guard right outside.

"Excellencies." He bows. "Shall I escort you back to the Council chamber?"

"Um, no," I reply. "We were going to… going to…"

"Check out the selection in Greenhouse Three and put in an order to restock our recombinators," Molly quickly supplies. "We're both nearly out of fresh produce—guess no one knew ahead of time we'd be spending so much time at NuAgra. The Council's not expecting us back for half an hour, so this seems like a good time."

Though he looks dubious, he doesn't question her story—but does insist on coming along.

"With the unrest outside, the Council has asked Gilda and me to keep a twenty-four hour watch," he explains when I frown at that precaution. "Her shift will begin at midnight."

"Oh, um, okay." I pretend a calm I definitely don't feel. "Thanks." Hoping this new telepathy thing with Molly still works, I brush my hand against hers. *Now what?*

Give me a sec, she thinks back.

I relax slightly. If anyone can figure out a way to ditch Cormac, Molly can.

Sure enough, as the three of us enter the moist warmth of Greenhouse Three, Molly grabs my hand. *Idea! Follow my lead,* she says silently, then lets go to clutch her stomach.

"Urgh, I think that burrito I had for dinner is starting to disagree with me. I need to hit the bathroom. Now." She hurries toward a door near the back wall.

After a startled second, I turn to Cormac. "I'd better go with her, make sure she's okay. If she's not, if we need you to get a Healer, I'll let you know." I rush after Molly before he can reply.

She's waiting just inside the bathroom.

"What's the plan?" I whisper. "Climb out a window?"

Molly shakes her head. "I don't think there is one," she whispers back. "But look." She points past sinks and stalls to another door. "I used to come to the greenhouses sometimes to practice when I still thought I was an Ag, and remembered they all share bathrooms."

We push open the other door—into Greenhouse Two. No one else is in sight, so we race for the rear exit. Moments later we're outside, looking across acres of tilled research fields. And shivering.

"I forgot it would be freezing out here," Molly says, "but bringing coats obviously wasn't an option. Luckily we can use our our climate control apps."

We both activate that cool feature in our omnis and we're immediately as warm as we were indoors.

"This way," Molly says then, moving off to the right.

As quickly as we can without tripping over furrows, we head for NuAgra's perimeter fence.

"There are surveillance cameras all over the place," I remind her. "How soon will Sean get here?"

"I'll ask—and tell him where to meet us."

Slowing down slightly, she pulls out her omni. "Hey, Sean, how close are you? Okay, good. Keep watching for any sign of Tristan's car between there and here. We're outside now, in the fields behind the greenhouses. Meet us at the fence, a couple hundred yards before you reach the gate. See you soon. They're about five minutes away," she tells me.

We both speed up again. "So, how cool is it that you and I can do the telepathy thing without our boyfriends now?" Molly comments after a moment.

"Very cool. Not to mention useful." *Can you hear me when we're not touching?* I add silently.

She doesn't answer.

"Guess you didn't hear that?" I say aloud. "We must have to touch for it to work."

"Still might come in handy when we face the bad guys." She shoots me a quick grin.

We continue scurrying across the fields at an oblique angle toward the twelve-foot chain-link fence stretching off into the distance. We've nearly reached it when I hear shouting off to our right.

"Uh-oh. Are they already after us?"

Molly glances in the direction of the voices, then shakes her head. "I think it's just those protesters in front of the gates. Maybe that'll be enough distraction nobody will notice us."

"But that might." I point up at the nearest camera, slowly rotating atop a fence pole, between coils of razor wire.

"Do you think together we can zap it?" Molly asks.

"Worth a try."

Linking hands, we point at the camera. The electrical surge we produce isn't anywhere near as strong as we can do with our boyfriends, but the camera stops rotating.

"Well, we did *something*," I say, "but just in case..."

We edge closer to the fence to stay out of its line of sight.

"C'mon, Sean. Hurry up!" Molly mutters under her breath.

Almost like he heard her, Sean's blue Toyota appears a second later. He spots us waving and pulls onto the shoulder, and he and Kira jump out. She immediately notices the camera and before I can suggest it, they zap it properly.

Sean steps forward. "We could have used Molly back there at the roadblock," he says. "They're telling *Duchas* there's a chemical spill. Wasn't sure they'd let us through until Kira thought to ask if they'd seen two boys in a black Porsche."

"And?" Molly and I demand together.

"They did," Kira tells us. "They said they came through about an hour and a half ago, just as they were setting up the roadblock."

I suck in a breath. "They must have grabbed them right outside the gate!"

"But they can't have taken them far, if there are roadblocks," Molly points out. "Can you guys get us the rest of the way out of here? Maybe we can catch them by surprise."

"We could try climbing…" I dubiously eye the razor wire.

Kira shakes her head. "Our way will be quicker. And safer. It's electrified. Hold still."

The two of them link hands again, then Molly starts to rise off the ground. After a startled moment, she grins. "Awesome. Now I know what it feels like to fly."

Sean and Kira levitate her up and over the fence, then turn their attention to me. It's a weird sensation, being invisibly lifted through the air. I'm almost eye-level with the razor wire coils when an alarm sounds behind me and white light suddenly bathes the fields we just crossed.

"Crap!" I exclaim. "Cormac must have found out we ditched him. Hurry!"

Their concentration briefly broken, Sean and Kira nearly drop me onto the razor wire. But after a sickening lurch, I again rise smoothly, up and over the fence. The moment I'm on the ground, we all scramble into Sean's car.

"So, what's the plan?" he asks.

Molly and I exchange glances. "Um, this was mostly it," she admits, "but Tristan and Rigel have to be somewhere close. We need to find them. Then rescue them. Somehow."

"M, can't you ask Rigel telepathically where he is?" Kira asks.

"I've been trying to contact him for the last hour," I tell her. "He's not answering. In the picture the kidnappers sent with their ransom note, they both looked unconscious." I still refuse to think about the alternative—especially since my very last words to Rigel were *leave me alone*.

Sean puts the car in gear. "I'll get us closer to that crowd…but not *too* close."

Headlights off, the Toyota creeps forward, but stops well before reaching the brightly lit area in front of the gate. It's twenty minutes to nine.

"Let's go on foot from here," Sean suggests. "It'll be quieter."

We all climb out, careful not to slam the doors. Sean puts a finger to his lips.

"Too bad invisibility isn't anybody's superpower," Molly whispers, getting a quiet—but slightly hysterical—chuckle from all of us.

As we stealthily approach the raucous crowd, I try again to contact Rigel. *Are you there? Please, Rigel, please, please answer me if you can!*

I "listen" hard for several heartbeats, then pick up what might be a fleeting impression of his mind. No words, just a sense of confusion that *feels* like Rigel…but before I can even try to locate him, it's gone.

Rigel? Rigel? But now there's nothing. Am I so desperate to believe he's alive that I imagined it?

Frustration and disappointment overwhelm me. A roaring sound fills my ears, along with a sudden, murderous urge to rush the mob and kill every last person keeping Rigel from me. I walk faster, a low growl escaping my throat.

Molly catches up and grabs my arm. *What are you doing?* she silently asks. Sean and Kira are both staring at me.

I stop, abruptly myself again, and belatedly realize I have no weapon. Do the kidnappers? *Are we crazy to be out here unarmed?* I think to Molly.

Maybe. Can you sense anything from the bad guys?

The crowd is farther away than I can normally gauge emotions without Rigel's help, but I try anyway. Like with the camera, Molly's touch helps some, boosting my range just enough that I can now sense anger, fear, desperation…and at least two "bad guy" vibes. Faxon supporters?

I mentally relay my impressions to Molly.

What about Tristan and Rigel? Can you tell if they're up ahead? she asks.

Not if they're unconscious. But let me try something else.

Clinging to Molly's hand, I gradually widen my scan. Not a lot, nowhere near as much as when Rigel and I located Gordon Nolan two towns away. Even so, a moment later I detect another "bad guy" vibe somewhere behind us, nastier than the ones up ahead. I whirl around to face the way we just came.

"What?" Sean whispers.

"There are more of them back there," I whisper, pointing. "At least one, maybe more. Do you see anyone?"

We all peer back down the road but it's deserted, dimly lit by the searchlights now sweeping the NuAgra fields—looking for Molly and me.

I probe harder. "I think they're farther back than where you picked us up."

"Maybe that's where they're holding your guys," Sean says. "Let's take the car. It'll be quicker and maybe safer. We don't want to get caught in the open between whoever you're sensing and that mob up ahead."

We hurry back to the car, painfully aware of passing time. As Sean makes a U-turn in the middle of the road, Kira watches the crowd at the gate, in case any of them come after us. "I don't think they've spotted us yet," she says.

"How far?" Sean asks as we pass the place they levitated us over the fence.

Grabbing Molly's hand, I re-focus. "Maybe a couple hundred more yards? Oh, probably at that abandoned gas station!" It's where Bri and Deb did their 'stakeout' last month, climbing up on the roof to watch the NuAgra gate with binoculars.

Sean accelerates and a few seconds later we reach a rutted gravel drive, barely visible in the dark. He turns in, but stops well before we reach the building. "This gravel's noisy. If we go much farther by car, they'll hear us."

Getting back out, we make our cautious way on foot down the weed-choked lane. Ahead, a dark rectangle looms against the night sky—the old gas station. Now I can sense those two *Echtrans* I felt before even without Molly's help. One has a vibe even ickier than Lennox, the Dun Cloch ex-governor who nearly murdered Rigel.

Then, suddenly, I again sense Rigel himself—strongly enough this time to get a lock on his location. I reach over and touch Molly's arm.

The boys are here! Just up ahead!

Tristan and Rigel both? she thinks back.

I hadn't specifically tried to sense Tristan before, but when I concentrate harder I pick up a tiny hint of his consciousness, too. I nod.

Molly taps her brother on the shoulder. He and Kira turn and I point, silently mouthing, *They're here!*

When Kira pulls out a weapon, I suddenly remember she's also a trained Bodyguard—Sean's. Heartened, I pick up the pace, listening for all I'm worth. Soon I hear voices ahead.

"Well?" a woman's voice demands. "Have they figured out what all those lights and sirens are about? Are they finally sending out the Royal brats?"

"Zell says there's no sign of them yet." The man's voice makes my skin crawl—definitely the person giving off that intensely negative vibe. "All the activity is behind the buildings. Maybe they're assembling a strike force to try to take us all out at once, not that it'll do these two any good." There's a pause, then I hear, "What now, Zell? Yeah? Probably a delaying tactic. It's two minutes to nine."

"What did he say? What's happening?" The woman feels distinctly nervous.

The man just feels angry—and determined. "No sign of the girls but some guy is approaching the gate. Probably some slick negotiator but we're not cutting any deals. They either give up those girls or—" He makes a nasty, squelching sound.

Beside me, Molly lets out a faint gasp. She's obviously hearing all this, too.

We round the corner of the building and see over a dozen RVs and campers parked behind it, along with a few cars. The protesters must have assembled here before heading to NuAgra. One at a time, I scan the larger vehicles, searching for the boys' vibes.

"There," I whisper, pointing at a dilapidated-looking trailer attached to a pickup truck, off to our right.

Silently, the four of us make our way toward the trailer, still listening hard. We're maybe thirty yards away when the man inside barks out a laugh.

"Are you kidding? How gullible do they think we are? Of course they'd claim they have Faxon cornered once they know we have hostages. It's a load of crap. Faxon's way too slick to be caught by those idiots. It's a stalling tactic, like I said. Well, I'm done with their games. Time to let them know we mean business."

"What are you going to do?" The woman feels scared now. "These boys are our only bargaining chip. You can't—"

The man lets out a disgusted sound. "Don't tell me what I can't do! Wait outside if you don't have the stomach for it. It's past nine. That so-called *Echtran* Council might not keep their promises, but I'm sure as hell keeping mine."

"But—" She breaks off with a sharp cry, and a second later comes stumbling out of the trailer holding her face.

I start running at it flat out, terrified the kidnapper will kill Rigel before I can stop him. The other three are hard on my heels, the time for stealth past. The woman hears, then sees us. Her eyes widen. She turns back to the trailer to shout something, but I send her sprawling with a sweep of my arm, cutting her off mid-word. Using my momentum to vault up the trailer stairs, I burst through the flimsy door.

A beefy, bearded man turns at my entrance, the silver *Echtran* weapon he'd been aiming into the far corner swinging up and around to point at my chest. I'm so enraged by the sight of my Rigel, bound and gagged on the floor, I barely notice. With a strangled cry, I launch myself at the villain responsible.

His shot goes wide as I crash into him and then I'm on top of him, pummeling his head with both fists. "How dare you touch him!" I scream into his face. "You're nothing! You're scum!"

Half-blinded by fury and nearly deafened by the roaring in my ears, I'm only dimly aware of Molly darting past me to the boys on the trailer floor. Then I hear her exclaim, "They're alive! M, they're both still alive!"

Though the kidnapper's no longer moving, I aim one last, vicious punch at his nose before scrambling off him to join her.

"Rigel?" I cup my hands—both bloodied—around his precious face. "Rigel, can you hear me?"

His eyes flutter open. *M?* comes his thought. He's still gagged. *How —? Where—?*

Weeping with relief, I fumble to remove the dirty cloth tied over his mouth. "I'm here. You're safe. Oh, Rigel, I'm so sorry I—"

"M? Molly?" comes Sean's voice from behind me. "Everything okay in here?"

"More than okay," I tell him, smiling down at Rigel. "We got here in time—barely." I press my forehead against Rigel's for a grateful second, then continue working on the gag.

The trailer door creaks and Sean comes in. "So they're both all right? That's— Whoa, what did you do to this guy?"

Tearing my eyes away from the wonderful face I was afraid I'd never see again, I glance over my shoulder. A faint groan comes from the man on the floor, but he's not moving.

"He was just about to kill them," I tell Sean. "I stopped him."

"I guess you did." Sean leans down and picks up the weapon the kidnapper dropped and sticks it in his pocket. "Kira stunned that woman outside, but we should probably get out of here before anyone else shows up."

I look over at Molly. "Is Tristan awake?" She nods, looking as relieved as I am. "Sean's right. Let's get them untied so they can walk. Is there something we can use to cut these zip ties?"

Sean rummages around in the trailer's tiny kitchen. "Ah!" he exclaims, tossing a pair of scissors to Molly, then handing me a knife.

Finally getting Rigel's gag off, I make quick work of the plastic ties around his wrists and the bigger ones around his ankles.

"Can you sit up?" I ask him.

"Um." He tries and fails.

I slip an arm under his shoulders and help him to a sitting position. "It'll be a lot easier if you can stand up. I'm not sure I can carry you."

"Yeah, sorry," he croaks. "Still kinda groggy. They gassed us with something."

Ducking down, I get my shoulder under Rigel's right arm. "C'mon, I'll help you up." Then I hear voices in the distance. "Crap. We need to get out of this trailer—we're sitting ducks here."

Beside me, Molly's struggling to get Tristan to his feet, too. "Sean, can you help us?"

He comes over and grabs Rigel's left arm and Tristan's right, while Molly and I support our guys from their other sides. Like some weird five-legged race, we all shuffle to the door of the trailer. Sean kicks it open and we see Kira tying up the woman I knocked down on the way in, now unconscious.

"She already had a phone in her hand when I stunned her," she tells us. "Sorry, I should've been quicker. I messaged NuAgra security and told them where we are."

The shouts from the road are louder now. The crowd of protesters must be coming this way.

"We should get back to the car before that mob gets here," Molly says. "I don't think Tristan and Rigel are up to fighting just yet."

At that, I feel Rigel straighten a bit, taking more of his weight on his own legs. "I'm feeling better, now M's here," he says. "How about you, Tristan?"

"Same, but definitely nowhere near full strength yet," Tristan replies. "It's okay, Molly, I can walk now if you steady me."

Kira joins us, taking over from Sean on Tristan's other side so he can help more with Rigel. "Let's move," she says.

That allows us to speed up, but we're still at least fifty feet from

Sean's car when the first few demonstrators turn down the driveway and see us.

"It's them!" a man up front shouts back. "The Sovereign and the Princess! They've got the hostages!"

A roar breaks out behind him, then the sound of pounding feet. We push ourselves faster, but not fast enough. In moments, the leaders are between us and the car, with dozens more blocking the lane behind them.

My relief at finding Rigel alive is swallowed up by fear as I realize we're outnumbered nearly ten to one—with two of us barely able to stand.

We may all die yet.

23

Mob mentality

"WHERE ARE THOSE SECURITY GUYS?" Sean yells, fumbling in his pocket for the *Echtran* weapon he picked up in the trailer.

I hear an energy blast next to me and the man closest to us goes down.

"Do you know how to use that?" Kira asks Sean as she stuns another one.

"I do." Tristan snatches the weapon out of Sean's hand and brings down another—but now the mob is nearly on us.

Two more shots and two more fall, but the rest are still coming, faster than Kira and Tristan can fire. In seconds we'll be overwhelmed.

Let's see how many we can take out, I think frantically to Rigel.

Right, he sends back. *Try a wide spread.*

Together, we send out a diffuse electrical blast that encompasses the next wave of attackers, nearly a dozen of them. Most go down, but three are already scrambling back to their feet as more surge past them. Crap. To be effective, we'll have to stun them one at a time.

Then Molly steps forward, still clinging to Tristan's left arm. "Stop!" she shouts at the crowd, using her bond-enhanced "push."

Most of those within hearing screech to a halt.

"You don't really want to do this," she loudly continues. "They were telling you the truth back at the gate—Regent Shim knows where Faxon is and he should be arrested within a few hours. Killing us would make you just as bad as he is!"

The three Rigel and I failed to incapacitate pause to listen, but several others resume their advance. Meanwhile, those farther back continue pressing forward. Like our electrical ability, Molly's apparently works best at close range, on just a few people at a time—and we still have dozens to deal with!

I narrow my focus to a single man, one who's clearly not stopping. "Again!" I say aloud to Rigel.

Okay, but let's not be murderers either, okay? he thinks with a concerned glance at my face.

Even though I pull back—with an effort—our bolt easily takes the guy down in his tracks. Meanwhile, Kira and Tristan stun two more.

The mob is finally slowing, after seeing so many of their comrades fall. More cautious now, they start fanning out to surround us, though not in any kind of disciplined order.

Molly desperately continues exhorting those within earshot to calm down. A few more seem to, but others are still surging forward from the rear. Rigel and I take another one down, again careful to only stun.

"Good shot, Kira!" Tristan exclaims as she brings down another. "We just need to hold them off until—"

He breaks off with a grunt and Molly screams.

Looking back, I see Tristan face down, Molly on her knees beside him. Then I see the man from the trailer behind them, holding yet another energy weapon. Though his face is still covered with blood, he's grinning.

"One down, five to go!" he shouts triumphantly. "Don't you know you can't keep a good Mech down? Let's finish this!" He turns the weapon on Rigel.

That roaring sound again fills my head, along with the rage I felt back in the trailer—identical to Faxon's rage when yet another insider betrayed him. I tighten my grip on Rigel's hand.

Clearly sensing my intent, he silently shouts, *No! Just stun him!*

Instead, I unleash a blinding lightning bolt straight at the man's chest. He flies backward, sizzling as he goes, then lands, still smoking, twenty feet away.

"M!"

M!

Molly's shout and Rigel's horrified thought barely penetrate as I wheel around to face the encroaching crowd on my right. Still blinded

by unreasoning fury, I point at the woman closest to me, fiercely grati‐
fied by the sudden terror on her face.

"No!" Rigel yells out loud, wrenching his hand from mine. "M, stop!
You just—! We can't—!"

I lunge for his hand but he snatches it away. "He deserved it!" I
scream. "He tried to kill you! They *all* deserve to die!"

"M, don't!" Molly cries. "Tristan is still alive, look. *Please* don't kill
anyone else!"

Forcing my gaze away from the terrified woman in front of me, I
glance down and see Tristan beginning to stir, Molly's tear-streaked face
pleading up at me.

"But they—" I start to protest, anger still surging through me.

Not all of them, M, Rigel silently insists. *Most are just scared for their
families in Nuath.*

An unexpected wave of calm hits me…from Molly? "Please, M," she
entreats. "You're not a murderer. Don't let them turn you into one."

Augmented by her persuasion, the calm penetrates, abruptly
defusing my rage. Momentarily confused, I look back at the man I just
electrocuted—murdered—without Rigel's consent. What have I done?

What's left of the mob hangs back, cowed by Kira, holding both her
weapon and Tristan's…and by what they just saw me do. As the woman
I nearly killed slowly backs away, I start to shake.

Cautiously stepping back to my side, Rigel wraps an arm around my
shoulders. *It's okay. You're okay now. Help is on the way.*

I gaze helplessly up at him, then hear sirens, quickly growing louder.
A second later, two motorcycles screech around the corner ahead, red
lights flashing.

"Everyone sit down and put your hands up!" an amplified voice
commands. As the protesters hastily comply, a dozen more armed men
on foot come into view.

"Looks like the cavalry finally arrived." Sean's voice is faint with
relief. "Better late than never, I guess." He sends a wary look my way.

And no wonder. If Molly and Rigel hadn't stopped me, several more
people would almost certainly be dead now. I've turned into a monster.

No! Rigel tells me sternly. *You're not the monster, Faxon is! You just need
help kicking him out of your head, that's all.*

Swallowing, I nod. *Let's get back to NuAgra.*

⁘

At least two dozen protesters are still conscious, but NuAgra's security detail seems to have them under control as the six of us make our way past the seated crowd. No one tries to stop us, though a couple of security folks bow to Molly and me as we pass.

"Did any of them see—?" I start to ask, but Rigel shakes his head.

No, he sends silently. *They all got here after. But…I think you have to tell the Council, M.*

Again I nod, still numb with shock at what I did back there.

Before it even occurs to me to wonder how we'll all fit into Sean's little Toyota, Mr. Stuart's car pulls up behind it and he jumps out.

"Are you all—? Oh, thank God!" he exclaims, hurrying forward to hug Rigel. "When we learned the Sovereign and the Princess had also disappeared, we feared the worst. How did you—?"

"Let's all get back to NuAgra before we explain, okay, Dad?" Rigel breaks in, tightening his arm around me. "We're all kind of shook up. Especially M."

His father shoots a curious look at me but doesn't ask any more questions. "All right. Sean, are you fit to drive? Good. You four get in Sean's car and I'll take Rigel and the Sovereign in mine. I need to touch base with the security chief, then we can all go back. The Council is still assembled and I know they'll want to hear everything you can share."

I barely hear him, still careening between self-loathing and relief at having Rigel back safe. Much as I need to, when he and I get into the back seat of his dad's car, I'm afraid to touch him, knowing now what I'm capable of.

⁘

Preoccupied as I am, I'm totally unprepared for the emotional scene that erupts when we enter the Council conference room several minutes later.

Amid cheers and excited exclamations, Teara Roark leaps from her chair to wrap her arms around Tristan. Mrs. O'Gara also rushes to gather Molly into a hug, then looks confusedly at Sean.

"How—? Why—?" But then she pulls him into a hug, too.

Mr. O, who must have joined the group while we were gone, embraces both of his children the moment his wife releases them.

Then the questions begin in earnest, every Council member

demanding at once to know what happened. I stare at them mutely until Kyna calls them to order, her amplified voice cutting through the chaos.

"Everyone, please be seated," her hologram booms through the room. "It's late, and we have quite a lot to discuss."

Rigel gives my hand a quick squeeze, then goes to the chair by the wall where he sat for Thursday night's meeting. I nearly ask him to sit next to me instead, then remember—again—what I did. What I made Rigel do.

Molly clings to Tristan for a moment, then kisses him in front of everyone before reluctantly letting him go to join Rigel. It makes me realize Rigel and I haven't kissed at all since the rescue and battle. Will he ever want to kiss me again? I won't blame him if he doesn't.

"Now," Kyna continues at normal volume after a moment. "I suggest we take things in order. Excellency, Princess, I should first like to know where you disappeared to, and how. Poor Cormac was beside himself with worry and remorse at what he considered a dereliction of his duty."

He's in the room, too, I suddenly notice, standing silently against the far wall. His expression is stoic, as always, but I can sense his distress and guilt—though it's nothing compared to mine.

"Cormac didn't do anything wrong," I blurt out, my first words since arriving.

"M's right," Molly agrees. "We intentionally gave him the slip. Sorry, Cormac, but with the clock ticking, we didn't know what else to do."

I nod, more than willing to let Molly do the talking—which she seems to realize.

"We only pretended to be okay with it when you wouldn't let us go after Tristan and Rigel," she explains to the Council. "I called Sean and convinced him to help break us out, then we—okay, I—tricked Cormac when we got to the greenhouses. He couldn't have known what we were going to do. Even M didn't know until we did it. But," she adds hastily at her mother's gathering frown, "it's a really good thing we did, because Tristan and Rigel would both be dead now if we hadn't."

"How can you know that?" Breann demands. Our negotiator—"

"Wouldn't have stopped them killing the boys," Molly insists. She goes on to describe the conversation we overheard before we burst into the trailer. "Someone did tell him about the negotiator claiming Faxon would be caught soon, but he didn't believe it. He was an actual, hard-core Faxon supporter, not one of the regular protesters. If you didn't turn us over to the mob, he was absolutely going to kill Tristan and Rigel at a minute past nine. We stopped him just barely in time. He totally would have killed us, too, if he'd had a chance."

A visible shudder goes around the room.

"What I don't understand," Malcolm says, "is how the six of you fended off that entire group when they attacked you. No offense, Excellencies, but you are all just teens."

"Bonded teens," Teara reminds him. "I'm sure that conferred some advantages."

"It definitely helped," says Sean, who's sitting with Kira next to Rigel and Tristan. "And Kira was amazing—her Bodyguard training really paid off. She slowed the mob down a lot, stunning people right and left. So did Tristan. M and Rigel stunned a few, too, and Molly talked some of them down. Even so, things were getting awfully dicey before—" He glances over at me, then away. "I mean, it's really good the NuAgra security people showed up when they did," he awkwardly concludes.

"But how did the Sovereign and Princess escape the grounds?" Malcolm asks. "They can't have gone out the front gate, it was being monitored."

"No, we went over the fence," Molly admits. "Sean and Kira…helped."

Mrs. O looks sharply at Sean. "Helped? You were actually able to—?"

"Levitate them over, yeah," he admits. "I know you'll say we shouldn't have, that we put M and Molly at risk, but like Molly said, if we hadn't, Rigel and Tristan would be dead."

"I still think—"

She breaks off when Mr. Stuart's omni pings. As he reads through the message, his eyebrows go up.

"What is it, Van?" Kyna asks.

"A report from the security detail," he says. "They've taken all the protesters into custody, and those who were stunned are reviving, to include a woman near the trailer Molly described. One man, however, is dead. Apparently by electrocution." He looks questioningly at Rigel, then me.

I swallow. "That…was my fault." I force out the words, the enormity of my crime inescapable. "He—"

"He shot Tristan and was about to shoot Rigel," Molly breaks in when I hesitate. "It was the same man who almost killed them in the trailer. M was only—"

"No," I interrupt. "Don't cover for me, Molly. I went overboard and I know it." I turn to Mr. Stuart. "It wasn't Rigel's fault. At all." It's vitally important that he and everyone else know that. "He only meant for us to stun the guy but I was too angry to listen."

Everyone falls silent for a long moment, staring at me with varying degrees of shock and horror. I writhe inwardly, knowing I deserve their judgment. There's no excuse for what I did. None.

"That's...unfortunate," Mr. Stuart finally says. "The man likely would have been a valuable source of information. He matches the description of a known Faxon supporter, wanted for various crimes back on Mars. He disappeared from Dun Cloch immediately after his Orientation last summer, before he could be tied to those crimes. I suspect he's been one of the chief agitators on Earth ever since, stirring up dissension against this Council and the Sovereign."

Kira speaks up for the first time. "From what we overheard, he was the one directing that mob."

"I see." Kyna seems to have regained her usual composure. "Had he been captured, he almost certainly would have been subjected to the *tabula rasa*, once his memories were extracted. Some might say he received a more merciful end than he deserved."

In my unreasoning fury, I totally ignored the fact that Martian law doesn't include a death penalty. Their ultimate punishment, for even the most heinous of crimes, is a complete memory wipe. While it's true many of them consider that a fate worse than death, the decision wasn't mine to make.

"I lost control. I'm sorry." I cringe at the lameness of my apology. "I know it doesn't excuse what I did, but spending all that time in Faxon's memories messed me up way more than I expected—or realized. I'm going to ask Mind Healer Ava if she can somehow help me *permanently* separate myself from his mind. It's...not a place I want to visit again."

"Understandable," Teara murmurs, her eyes wide with sympathy.

Nara's hologram nods her agreement, tears in her eyes. Breann, Malcolm and Mrs. O, however, continue to regard me uneasily—then Malcolm voices what I'm sure they're all thinking.

"Until that can be done, for everyone's safety I suggest the Sovereign and Rigel Stuart keep their distance from each other. Should she lose control again, she'll be able to cause far less damage without access to that aspect of their bond."

There's a murmur of agreement—even from Kyna and Mr. Stuart.

"No!" Rigel jumps to his feet. "She needs me to ground her. Don't you?" he asks me.

"Yes," I confirm aloud. *But they're also right*, I add silently. *I couldn't have killed that man without—*

I was caught off-guard, Rigel interrupts my thought. *I didn't realize until too late what you intended to do.* Then, to the others, "The *last* thing you should do right now is separate her from the people who care most about her."

Torn, I remain silent. As much as I long for Rigel's emotional support, I'm terrified I could use him to kill again, if I fly into another Faxon-induced rage.

You won't, Rigel thinks firmly. *I won't let you.*

When he used those words to me before, back in the fitness center, they made me furious. Now I desperately want to believe them...but don't dare.

"Maybe..." I send a silent apology to Rigel. "Maybe it would be safer if we can't touch each other." He sucks in an outraged breath. "Just for a little while," I assure him. "Just until I can be evaluated and treated by a Mind Healer." I fervently hope that's possible.

"We can discuss those details later," Kyna says before Rigel can argue again. "Right now, we need to decide what to tell our people, and what to do with the people in custody. Did any protesters escape our security force?"

"I'm told not," Mr. Stuart replies. "Some may have left early on in the demonstration, but not once the mob became violent. We had roadblocks in place by then and would have seen them."

Kyna nods approvingly. "In that case, I recommend they be held in a secure area at NuAgra until they can be discreetly transported to Dun Cloch for questioning and possible charges. With luck, that sole fatality won't prevent us from gleaning valuable information from the others."

I flinch at the word *fatality*. My fault. All those people saw what I did.

Molly touches my arm. *It was self defense*, she insists silently. *For all you knew, he'd just killed Tristan and was about to kill Rigel.*

True, that *is* what I thought. But I still could have just stunned him. If only I'd been able to control my temper, to stop and think—

A pinging from both my omni and Kyna's interrupts me before I can sink back into a morass of regret and self-loathing. Swallowing, I pull it out. "It's a holo message. From Shim."

"You'll need to play it, Excellency, as I'm not physically there," Kyna tells me.

Nodding, I touch the display button and a small but lifelike image of Rigel's grandfather appears in the middle of the big conference table. At once I'm struck by how tired he looks—and how old.

"Excellency, members of the *Echtran* Council," he says with a slight bow, "I am extremely relieved to report that the former dictator Faxon is again in custody. We have also now disabled all remaining pre-set explosives. The information Sovereign Emileia relayed to me was unerringly accurate, allowing our security force to locate and access Faxon's hiding place without further delay. Judging by their report, he was extremely surprised by their entrance, as he clearly considered his bunker invulnerable. Indeed, without the Sovereign's help, it would likely have taken us weeks to find it, given how well hidden and well shielded it was. Yet again, Excellency, all of Nuath owes you a very great debt of gratitude. Your efforts almost certainly prevented thousands, perhaps tens of thousands of casualties.

"I'm told that Faxon's bunker also contained extensive data banks. They will take some time to analyze, but we hope to retrieve—" Pausing, he looks off to the side. "Yes, yes, very well. Thank you."

Shim faces the camera again. "The Healers insist I return to my bed. I'll send a more thorough report tomorrow, but I knew you would be eager to share the news of Faxon's capture with our people on Earth. Many have been understandably anxious for their friends and family in Nuath and this information should relieve them greatly. Until tomorrow, Excellency, I remain your faithful and *very* grateful servant."

With a final, deeper bow, his image disappears.

After a moment of silence, the room explodes with cheers.

"It's over!"

"Excellency, you did it!"

"Oh, thank heavens!"

Kyna's holographic image turns to me with a smile. "We again have great cause to be thankful to you, Excellency. I admit I had my doubts about this unorthodox solution when you proposed it, but your idea paid off handsomely, despite the risks. In light of that, I'm sure we can all agree to consider your earlier, ah, lapse an unfortunate accident."

"Accident?" I repeat, incredulous. "But I—"

Molly clutches my hand at the same time Rigel thinks to me, *You heard what Grandfather said. You saved thousands of Nuathan lives!*

Yes! Molly silently agrees, clearly having heard him. *Innocent lives. What's one criminal, who deserved to die anyway, compared to that? If the Council is willing to drop it, let them!*

"Thank you," I finally continue. "I...I guess nothing else needs to be decided tonight."

Even though everyone here knows as well as I do that I'm a murderer.

24

Debriefing

"YES, I believe anything else can wait until tomorrow," Kyna agrees. "I suggest we adjourn now. I'll write up a MARSTAR Bulletin based on Regent Shim's report immediately, so it can go out tonight. This has been an exceedingly long and stressful day for all of us, but particularly for you, Excellency," she continues. "We'll reconvene tomorrow, after you— and we—have all had time to rest and recover. Regent Shim will likely have further updates for us by then, as well. Shall we say two o'clock?"

There's an enthusiastic chorus of agreement by the Council. I seriously doubt *I'll* be "recovered" by tomorrow afternoon, but I don't dampen the jubilant mood of the others by saying so.

"Very well, I'll notify Regent Shim about the time. We stand adjourned. I wish you all an excellent night's sleep." Kyna bows deeply to me, right fist over heart, then her holo image winks out.

A collective sigh goes around the table.

"Well. We can finally relax." Breann yawns. "I have every intention of making Kyna's parting wish come true. This has been an extremely stressful week."

Everyone else gets to their feet, their parting chatter upbeat, though Breann and Malcolm both shoot dubious looks at me on their way out of the room. Nara takes a moment to murmur a few words of sympathy and encouragement to me, then she, too, disappears with a final bow.

"Sean, you should take Kira home," Mrs. O says as the rest of us go out to the main entrance hall. "I'm sure her parents are worried about her by now. Tomorrow, we'll talk about the part you two played in tonight's events," she adds ominously.

They nod and leave, both looking slightly nervous.

Mrs. O then turns to Molly and me. "Late as it is, most people won't hear the good news until tomorrow, so I believe you girls had better stay here again tonight."

"I have to agree," Mr. Stuart says. "Even with the enhanced security systems we installed at your homes last fall, neither is as safe as NuAgra."

I can't imagine going home could possibly be any riskier than what we went through tonight, but I'm still too consumed by guilt to argue. At least I can't hurt anyone else from inside my quarters here.

"Rigel, why don't we head home?" his father says then. "Your mother is eager to see you, so she can satisfy herself you've taken no lasting damage from this ordeal. She can check out Tristan as well, if you'd like," he adds to Tristan's mother.

"Thank you. I'd appreciate that." Teara and Mr. Stuart move toward the front doors.

Rigel and Tristan hang back and Molly rushes into Tristan's arms. "I wish you didn't have to leave. I came so close to losing you tonight —twice!"

He gathers her in for a hug. "I'll come back first thing tomorrow, I promise." Leaning down, he gives her a lingering kiss that his mother and hers both pretend not to see.

Rigel, meanwhile, gazes at me so longingly I take a step toward him —but Mrs. O clears her throat.

"Excellency, didn't you agree—?"

I stop. "Sorry." My apology is mostly to Rigel. "You're right, I did. I love you, Rigel. I'll…see you soon, okay?"

"After she's spoken with our Mind Healer," Mrs. O'Gara clarifies. "Correct?" That last is to me.

Swallowing, I reluctantly nod. "Yes," I whisper, the anguish on Rigel's face tearing at my heart. "That would probably be safest. I'll message her tonight and ask if she can see me tomorrow, even though it's a Sunday."

Because until she can certify me safe, I add silently to Rigel, *I won't quite trust myself around other people—especially if you're close by. Not after what happened tonight.*

It only happened because you spent all that time in Faxon's head, Rigel reminds me. *You won't ever have to do that again now he's been caught, right?*

I sure hope not. Maybe after a good night's sleep I'll be myself again and the Mind Healer can attest to it.

"Rigel? Are you ready?" his dad calls before he can reply. He's waiting by the front doors with Tristan and his mom.

"I love you," I repeat urgently to Rigel. "Always."

He swallows visibly. "Ditto. I'll be back first thing tomorrow, too. Just in case." With one last, longing look, he turns and follows the others out.

"You girls should get to bed," Mrs. O says then. "Especially you, Excellency. Like everyone else, I'm very grateful for what you accomplished today, but you must be dead on your feet."

I know it's just a figure of speech, but it reminds me yet again that someone really *is* dead. Because of me. Because I lost control.

"Off you go, then." She shoos us toward our quarters. "The more sleep you can get, the better."

I'm sure she's right, but when I reach my quarters, I don't hurry to bed. First I send a quick message to Mind Healer Ava, asking for another meeting at her earliest convenience. Then I take my time washing my face and brushing my teeth, reluctant to face whatever dreams might be lurking. It's past midnight when I finally crawl under the covers.

Are you still awake? I send to Rigel. *Did your mom give you a clean bill of health?*

Yes and yes, he replies. *Are you okay?*

I take a moment before answering. *Not sure. You were right that digging into Faxon's memories was way riskier than I thought. I never had a chance to tell you tonight, but I really did get trapped in there. I might still be, if Molly hadn't been able to pull me out. I'm kind of afraid to go to sleep after that...but talking to you helps.*

I'll talk as long as you need me to, he promises, *but you have to be tired, after the day you've had.*

Not as tired as I am scared I'll get sucked back into Faxon's head as soon as I drift off, I tell him, even as I feel tendrils of sleep tugging at my mind.

I'll try to check in on you a few times during the night, okay? And you can totally reach out to me if you need to. I'll be here. But along with his assurance, I sense his exhaustion.

For his sake, I pretend more calm than I feel. *You need sleep at least as much as I do, after what you went through. I'll only wake you up if I have to. Tired as I am, maybe I won't dream at all. I can hope. I love you, Rigel.*

Love you, M.

I wait a few minutes, then lightly touch his mind. As I expect, he's already sound asleep.

My turn.

I turn off my light and close my eyes, only to be met by a vivid replay of what happened earlier—what I did. I try to force my mind to focus on other things, like how much I love Rigel and how grateful I am he's okay, but the awful vision keeps recurring. And recurring.

Desperate to make it stop, I turn my light back on and pick up my battered copy of *Jane Eyre*. Gradually, the familiar story relaxes me. I'm just reading the part where Jane repudiates Mr. Rochester's love and runs away when my eyes finally drift closed.

✦

The brown-haired man gasps in pain. "Please, my lord, I can't! I was sworn to secrecy by Sovereign Aerleas herself. I'd rather die than violate—"

Roaring fills my ears at the name. "And your family? Your children? Will you sacrifice them to your ridiculous oath? They'll all be killed, painfully, if you don't tell me where that room is and how to get into it," I coldly inform the Engineer. "Do you want their blood on your hands, too?"

The man stares up at me in horror. "My…my family? You wouldn't—!"

I smile. I have him now. "I assure you, I will. Which shall it be?"

The Engineer crumples in on himself. "All right! All right! The room is…"

The scene fades.

I'm in my new, fully secure hideout. "I require one last service from you. Your eternal silence." I pull the ampule of poison from my pocket and thrust it against Philbin's arm. His eyes go wide—he clearly didn't expect this. Good. As he falls to the floor, I smile grimly. No one can touch me now.

Again the scene shifts and changes.

It's night and I'm outdoors, facing an angry mob. "You can't keep a good Mech down!" a voice shouts from behind me. I turn to see a bloody-faced man holding an energy weapon. The rushing sound returns and I prove him wrong with a deadly lightning bolt to the chest.

The roaring in my ears continues as I turn back toward the mob closing in on me. Baring my teeth, I shoot a bolt at the woman nearest me. Almost before she hits the ground, smoking, I fire off several more lightning bolts. People start dropping left and right, just as I intend. They all deserve to die for what they tried to do!

I turn to scorch another but Molly jumps in front of me. "M! Stop!"

The roaring in my head intensifies and I blast Molly, too. Like the first man, she flies backward, sizzling, to hit the ground several yards away. Dead.

For a moment it's eerily quiet. Then, before I can register what just happened, Tristan screams, "NO!" and races past, knocking me aside. The roaring sound returns, louder than ever. I fry him before he reaches Molly's side.

As I see Sean and Kira running toward me, I'm suddenly aware of Rigel, trying to pull his hand out of mine—but I'm too strong, my grip viselike. Before he can stop me, I electrocute Sean, then Kira. They go down as easily as the others.

The roaring finally begins to fade…and I find myself in the school cafeteria. Trina is sauntering toward me, smirking.

"Guess everyone was right about you, Marsha," she says in her bitchiest voice. You really are—"

The sudden rushing in my ears drowns out her words and I silence her with a bolt to the face that makes her head explode. Everyone in the cafeteria screams in terror but I don't care. Idiot Duchas.

"M! What have you done?" I turn to see Rigel staring at me, horrified. "This has to stop."

"Don't look at me like that, Rigel," I plead in the sudden silence. "Trina deserved it. You know she did. You…you still love me, don't you?"

Instead of love, his hazel eyes register disgust. "I'm sorry, M." He lifts the hand I'm not holding and points a weapon at my chest.

The roaring surges back and I react before he can fire, needing no weapon but myself. Rigel falls to my feet in a smoking heap. The sound in my head abruptly stops and I stare down at him, appalled.

"Rigel! No!" I cry aloud, waking myself. I lie there, disoriented, then realize I'm still in my bed, in my NuAgra bedroom. It was just a dream.

Relief washes through me, only to be swamped by revulsion as every detail of that dream comes rushing back. Reliving Faxon's worst memories and my own atrocity at the end of this evening's battle was awful enough. This was much, much worse.

I not only murdered all the people I care most about, I enjoyed doing it! Except Rigel. Again, I see him looking at me with disgust, then lying dead at my feet, gone beyond recall. I start to shake. I really am a monster!

No. It was a dream, I insist to myself. *Just a dream.* None of it happened. I didn't *really* kill Rigel or Molly or any of the others. Not even Trina.

Yet?

My gorge rises and I vault out of bed and race to the bathroom, just in time to throw up in the toilet. I kneel there until I'm sure I'm done, then shakily get to my feet. Going to the sink, I rinse out my mouth, then brush my teeth again.

When I get back to the bedroom, I check the time—nearly six. I obviously did get a few hours of sleep before that horrible dream. That's good, because there's no way on Earth I'm going back to sleep now. Or maybe ever.

I tentatively reach out for Rigel's mind, needing reassurance that he really does still love me—but he's deeply asleep. Though I can't bring myself to wake him, I feel an irrational sense of loss. That revolted look on his face…his dead body on the cafeteria floor…

I know it's stupid, that it didn't really happen. I also know that if I tried, I *could* wake him up now—but I won't. Not just so he can tell me something I already know. Instead, I head back to the bathroom for a shower. Maybe it can wash away the memory of the worst nightmare I've ever had.

Standing in the stream of hot water a few minutes later, though, I start to cry. Because there's only one way to guarantee I can never, *ever* do what I did in that dream.

.⁺⁺

I spend a solid half hour in the shower, grateful for the plentiful water on Earth. By the time I towel off and get dressed I've stopped crying, though I still feel shattered.

A light touch of Rigel's mind shows him still sound asleep, so I check my omni—almost seven. There's nothing more from Shim yet, but I have a reply from Mind Healer Ava.

I'm at your disposal, of course, Excellency. If you can give me an idea of what you'd like to discuss, I'll have a better idea of how soon we should meet and how much time to set aside.

Hm. How to let her know it's urgent, without sharing too much information in writing? I think for a moment, then type my reply.

I'd like to talk about what my memory exploration revealed. I also want to get your assessment of my current mental state, as I have some concerns.

About five minutes later, she messages back.

Excellency, I'm attaching the PPE, our standard psychological profile exam, which will provide a fairly comprehensive evaluation of your present state of mind, including any areas of particular concern that should be addressed. Please do your best to give thorough, honest answers, as the questions will become progressively more personalized based on your responses. The full test may take up to an hour to complete, but should ideally be completed in one sitting. I also recommend installing the app I've linked, which will allow your omni to record your physical reactions as you work through the test.

You may of course do this at your convenience, whenever your schedule allows. When you have a chance to complete it, send it back to me and we'll go from there.

There seems no point in delaying, especially since Rigel's still asleep. Maybe once Healer Ava looks over my results, she can suggest a way to keep me from hurting people that's less drastic than staying completely away from Rigel. I hope so.

I get a cup of strong Irish Breakfast Tea from my recombinator, then settle myself on the couch and install her app. I register the app with my thumbprint, then open the psych test itself on my omni's holo screen— the same test I took nearly a year ago at the Council's request, before my trip to Mars. They wanted to make sure I was mentally stable enough to stand for Acclamation…and deal with the Grentl. I passed that test just fine, but somehow doubt I'll do as well on this one.

Taking a fortifying sip of tea, I dive in.

The first three screens contain a series of yes/no and multiple-choice questions, requiring more and more thought as I go on. A few make me distinctly uncomfortable, but I do my best to answer them honestly, keeping my thumb on the omni's sensor so it can record my reactions.

After that are a few essay questions I don't remember seeing before. I'm asked to list any traumatic incidents I recall, then describe how I feel about them now. This takes a long time, I experienced so many inside Faxon's memories—not to mention what happened last night. I spend nearly an hour dictating answers before I feel like I've covered them all.

Next, I'm presented with a bunch of hypothetical situations, some of them potentially upsetting. For each, I have to select my most likely initial physical and mental response. These are even harder to answer truthfully. Still, I do my best, fully aware that my choices for several of those scenarios aren't anywhere close to what most people would consider normal.

Finally, the test circles back to more questions like the early ones, but rephrased—I assume to double check I really meant what I said. Nearly two hours after beginning the test I'm finished. Quickly, before I can change my mind, I send the completed test back to Mind Healer Ava.

Feeling drained, I let out my breath and lean back against the sofa cushions. It's Sunday, so she probably won't even look at it today, but I hope she'll at least get to it early-ish tomorrow. I head to the recombinator for another cup of tea and maybe some breakfast. Before I even reach it, she messages me.

Excellency, I've just glanced over the bullet point summary of your evaluation so far, but I believe we should meet as soon as possible. I realize it's the weekend, but is there any chance at all you can see me sometime today?

I immediately message back with, *Yes! The earlier the better.*

A moment later, my omni pings again. *I can be at NuAgra in forty-five minutes, if that will work for you, Excellency?*

Yes, that's perfect, I reply, relieved. *Thank you!*

I'd rather not see anyone else until I've met with her, so I go ahead and get breakfast from my personal recombinator. I'm finishing a bowl of yogurt with plenty of fruit, along with my second cup of tea, when Rigel mentally reaches out to me.

Good morning! he sends. *Are you awake? How did you sleep?*

Pretty well for most of the night, I report—truthfully. *I hope you got plenty of sleep?*

Yep! In fact, I just woke up. If you haven't had breakfast, I can head to NuAgra now so we can have it together.

Actually, I've arranged to meet with Mind Healer Ava in just a few minutes. Much as I long to see him, I don't dare postpone this appointment. *Why don't you go ahead and have breakfast at home and we'll get together after?*

I sense his sudden concern, but all he asks is, *Are you sure?*

Yeah, I'd like to take care of this as soon as possible. My head's still a little messed up but hopefully she can help me get it on straight again, so we won't have to stay apart after all. I consider telling him about my awful dream, but can't bring myself to do it. *I love you!* I say instead, sending a burst of emotion along with my thought.

He hesitates just long enough to scare me, then responds, *I love you, too, M. More than life itself. I'll be at NuAgra by the time you finish with the Healer and you can tell me everything she said, okay?*

Okay. Love you! I repeat, just to hear him say it again.

He repeats it with no hesitation this time, which helps me breathe a little easier as I finish my last few bites of yogurt. I down the rest of my tea, then rack the dishes in the sterilizing cabinet next to the recombinator.

Going back to my bedroom, I put on a fresh pair of pants, nicer than the jeans I wore for two days, and a pretty blouse. A glance in the mirror as I brush my hair assures me I don't *look* like a monster.

I hope Mind Healer Ava can help me feel less like one inside.

25

Informed consent

IT'S ONLY BEEN forty minutes, not forty-five, when I tap tentatively on Mind Healer Ava's office door.

"Come in."

Relieved I won't have to wait, I enter.

Healer Ava looks up from the tablet on her desk. The sudden spike of anxiety I sense from her as I walk in isn't reassuring.

"Ah, Excellency, good morning. If you'll have a seat?"

Swallowing, I close the door behind me and sit down in the comfortable chair across from her. "I assume you saw something in my test results that made you think we should meet right away?"

If anything, her discomfort increases. "I'm afraid so. Though I must say, I'm at a loss to understand how these results could differ so dramatically from those you produced just a year ago."

She glances at the tablet in her hand, then at me. "You also didn't exhibit any of the irregularities I'd have expected to see, based on these results, when we met a few days ago. I can't imagine how any of the early childhood memories you intended to explore could have been traumatic enough to account for these scores."

I hesitate, then blurt out the truth. "I'm afraid I wasn't completely honest with you before. The memories I was after weren't really from my own childhood…and I'm sure they're the reason for those scary test results. You can have this back, by the way. I'm done with it." I set the little box containing the button device on her desk.

She frowns at it. "I…don't understand, Excellency."

"You will, once I explain everything. Er, we're not being recorded are we? I know everything I say here is confidential, but what I'm about to tell you needs to be extra private. In fact, some of it is highly classified."

Her brows go up in surprise. "I normally do record sessions to assist in my notes, though of course I erase the recordings afterward. However, in this case—" She touches a spot on her tablet. "I've disabled recording. You also have my word that anything you tell me will be held in the strictest confidence."

"Thank you. By now you've probably seen the MARSTAR Bulletin that went out last night, about Faxon being caught?"

Looking even more startled, she nods.

"That only happened because of the memories I was able to retrieve using your methods…and that." I point to the little box.

She still looks mystified, so I go on to tell her about my first experience with the Grentl device last spring, and how it bombarded me with the memories of my predecessors—including Faxon's.

When I finish, she's noticeably shaken. "Well. Yes. I can see why that information would be classified, Excellency." She falls silent for a moment, digesting what I told her, then manages a tiny smile. "Please. Continue."

"Because all those memories came at me so quickly, afterward I could only remember tiny flashes of them, just bits and pieces. Then, with so much else going on, I mostly forgot about them—until this past week. When Faxon escaped and the Nuathan authorities couldn't find him, it occurred to me that those memories might be useful. If I'd really absorbed *all* of Faxon's memories, they would have to include any secret hideouts he created while in power." Despite her promise of strict confidentiality, I don't mention my Scepter. "I asked for your help so I could dig into Faxon's memories. Not mine."

She stares at me. "And…that's how he was finally found and captured?" she asks in amazement.

"Yes, though finding what I needed took longer than I hoped it would. Thursday evening I used your methods to make sure I really could access Faxon's memories. Then I spent most of Friday and all of Saturday exploring them until I finally found the info Regent Shim needed to catch him. At first I took breaks, like you suggested, but Faxon was already blowing things up in Nuath. I knew the longer I took, the more damage he'd cause, so I started doing longer and longer stretches at once. Yesterday afternoon, I spent nearly five hours straight inside his memories."

"Five hours?" she gasps.

I nod. "With so many lives at stake in Nuath, it seemed worth the risk. Even Regent Shim agreed." Rigel didn't, but there's no point telling her that. "And it *did* pay off. Faxon can't hurt anyone else now."

"Yes, I was extremely relieved to receive the news of Faxon's capture, as I have a sister, a niece and a nephew in Nuath. I…have cause to be very grateful to you, Excellency. Though had I known you meant to attempt such a thing, I'm sure I would have advised against it." She glances down at her tablet. "Based on these results, the experience took a substantial mental toll on you."

That doesn't surprise me. "Reliving so much of Faxon's past was… awful," I confess. "He was pretty messed up even as a kid, then got crazier and crazier as he grew up. All the horrific things he did…" I shudder. "I couldn't just watch, either. I had to experience them *as* Faxon, as though I myself did those terrible things and felt all those ugly emotions. It definitely affected my own mental state. And the more time I spent in his head, the worse it got. Regent Shim and I both knew ahead of time that was a risk, but he seemed sure a Mind Healer could, um, fix me afterward, if necessary. Can you?" I plead.

Healer Ava sits back in her chair. I sense sympathy but also a lot of worry. "I'll absolutely try, Excellency, though I'm afraid neither my training nor my experience included anything like this." She pauses, frowning, then continues, her emotions now tinged with fear. "I must tell you that this morning's evaluation indicates extreme mental instability, bordering on psychosis. Under normal circumstances, results like these would demand immediate admission to a Mind Healing facility, voluntary or not."

"You mean I should be…committed?" I didn't expect *that*! "So I really am crazy?"

She attempts a smile but fails. "That's not a term we use, Excellency. What symptoms are you experiencing?"

"Anger, mostly," I tell her. "Out of all proportion to the cause. Yesterday, I blew up at people, including my friends, and said some really hurtful things. Even to Rigel. Then last night—" I break off, swamped again by self-loathing.

"Yes?" she prompts. "Did you physically hurt someone?"

"Worse. I…I killed someone."

Her eyes widen. "Intentionally?"

Swallowing, I nod, then relate the events of last night, starting with the mob at the gate and the ransom note, neither of which were mentioned in the MARSTAR Bulletin. When I describe how I beat the head kidnapper bloody, then used Rigel to electrocute him, I can sense Healer Ava's shock and horror, though she does an admirable job of hiding it.

"The Council seems to think he deserved it," I conclude, "but even so…" I trail off.

"From what you say, it does sound as though what you did was justified." Her voice is gentle, remarkably free of judgment.

I shake my head. "No. I could have—should have—stopped him without killing him. But I was too furious. Totally out of control. He was dead before I could even stop and think. Then I very nearly killed someone else, a woman who wasn't even armed. Rigel and my friends stopped me in time, but it was close. It was…it was like Faxon was right there in my head, making me act like he would. There must be some way to keep him from doing that. To keep me from…from channeling him. Ever again. I don't want to hurt anyone else."

"Hm. Perhaps…" she begins uncertainly.

I interrupt with an idea that's just occurred to me. "I know Mind Healers can erase memories, even put extra blocks on particularly traumatic ones. Could something like that work?"

She looks dubious. "We have equipment in Dun Cloch capable of that, but given what you've told me, I don't know if it would be useful in this case. Our instruments aren't precise enough to erase specific hours or minutes of memory. Even pinpointing a single day is difficult. We'd likely need to erase your entire experience with the alien device you described. Even then, you would still possess these more recent memories of delving into Faxon's past, unless those were erased as well. As Sovereign—"

"I can't afford to lose all of that," I finish with a sigh. "You're right. But I also can't afford to fly into murderous rages at the slightest provocation, like Faxon did."

"Agreed. For the safety of all concerned, I strongly recommend you remain at NuAgra until your condition can be treated. With your permission, I can seek the advice of our top Mind Healers on both Earth and Mars on how to proceed, though I suppose they would require security clearances. Meanwhile, your responsibilities as Sovereign would need to be delegated to others. Your test results suggest extreme stress, which I suspect you've been suffering even prior to these recent events."

I can't deny that. Rigel's been saying the same thing for months, but—

"Wait. Let me make sure I understand. You think I should step down as Sovereign? Abdicate?" A distant but ominous rumbling begins in the back of my mind.

"Only temporarily," she assures me. "You could name your sister, Princess Malena, as Acting Sovereign, and the Council could—"

The rumbling gets louder. "Molly's not ready for that!" I exclaim. "And I'm not *about* to give that kind of power to the Council when some of those Royals—!"

Breaking off, I jump to my feet. "Forget it. I'm done here."

"Excellency! Please!" She stands, too, reaching a hand toward me. It appears empty, but I slap it away, hard.

"Don't touch me!" The rumbling becomes a roar. I turn toward the door, then whirl back around to advance on her instead. "Did the Council Royals put you up to this?" I demand.

Open mouthed, Healer Ava backs away shaking her head.

"It's exactly the sort of thing Lili O'Gara would do," I continue, still advancing. I look around for some weapon. "For months, she's been angling for Molly to assume more power."

The Healer's eyes go wide with fear, vividly reminding me of the woman I nearly killed last night. That fear brings me back to myself. As Faxon, I'd gloat over it, but as M, I'm appalled.

"I'm sorry," I gasp, abruptly sitting back down. "I'm so sorry. I should never— That's exactly—"

She cautiously sits, too, her fear ebbing…slowly. "Exactly the sort of thing you described, and want to prevent in future," she finishes for me.

"Yes," I whisper. I'm scared, too—by how close I just came to hurting her. If I'd had a weapon… "You were right. I have no business being around people right now. I'm not safe." Especially if Rigel's within reach. "I'll do what you said, ask Molly to be Acting Sovereign and delegate as much authority as possible to her and to Council leader Kyna. I trust them both completely."

"I think you're making the right decision, Excellency." She's clearly relieved, though I still sense concern. "I suppose the Council will need to be notified, as will your sister."

I nod. "There's a Council meeting at two o'clock this afternoon, so I can tell them then. They'll have to vote on Molly becoming Acting Sovereign. Would you be willing to help me explain why all this is necessary? I know it's Sunday, but—"

"Yes, Excellency, I'm more than willing to attend."

"Thanks. I'll give Molly a head-up in advance, so she doesn't feel blindsided." I also need to tell Rigel, who won't like this plan at all. I doubt Molly will, either…though I'm sure Mrs. O will be thrilled. "I should probably also make sure Kyna's okay taking over some of my duties."

She looks back down at her tablet. "Before the meeting, I'll write up a summary of your results and my recommendations. I'll also begin putting together a preliminary treatment program for you, Excellency. A combination of time-tested anger management techniques and the therapy we use for victims of post-traumatic stress should prove useful."

Hope I'm almost afraid to feel blossoms in my chest. "Do you think that can work? This…Faxon-psychosis won't be permanent?"

To my relief, she smiles. "I seriously doubt it will be permanent, Excellency. As the precipitating trauma only occurred over the past few days and concluded barely twelve hours ago, the effects are bound to fade in time."

My relief drains away. "How much time?"

"I really can't say. My colleagues may suggest approaches I haven't considered, once I'm authorized to contact them, but I doubt any course of treatment will be a quick fix."

"Meanwhile, I could still hurt people." It's a statement, not a question. "Unless I'm locked up." Away from Rigel.

⁙

It's nearly eleven o'clock when I finally leave Healer Ava's office, after continuing to talk with her a while longer.

Though she strenuously objected to the term "locked up," she didn't argue when I offered to be more or less confined to my quarters here at NuAgra. Which will amount to the same thing, if not as scary as the locked, padded cell with bars on the windows I first imagined.

I just finished with the Mind Healer, I send to Rigel after I step into the hallway. *Are you here yet?*

Got here over an hour ago, hanging out in the cafeteria with Molly and Tris-

tan. How did your meeting go? I…didn't think I should listen in. Is she willing to tell the Council you're okay now?

The meeting went all right, I hedge. *I'll come join you and we can talk about it. I also need to apologize to all of you for how I acted yesterday afternoon. I'm so, so sorry I shut you out like that, Rigel!*

It's okay, he assures me. *You weren't yourself.*

Despite his words, I pick up an echo of the pain I caused him by rejecting his help and telling him to leave me alone. I hurt him badly— and Molly told me how frantic he was.

Anyway, he continues after a moment, *you more than made up for it later by saving my life, remember? See you in a minute.*

I stop by my quarters to brush my hair again and put on a touch of lip gloss, shoring up my resolve to stand firm when I tell the others what I've agreed to do. Already, I'm dreading their reactions—especially Rigel's and Molly's.

The first test of my resolve comes the moment I enter NuAgra's dining hall. Rigel hurries forward to greet me and my heart turns over at the sight of the gorgeous face I love so much—and came so close to losing forever.

"Good morning," he says, smiling. "I missed you." He reaches for me, as eager for a much-needed kiss as I am.

Summoning every bit of my will, I put up both palms before he can touch me. His arms drop and the instant hurt I sense from him makes me want to throw myself into them—but I can't.

"There's some stuff I need to tell you," I force myself to say instead. "Molly, too."

Rigel closes his eyes and swallows, then turns to head back to the corner table where Molly and Tristan are sitting. "So. I guess your meeting with the Mind Healer didn't actually go so well after all?" he asks without looking at me.

"I… She does think she can help. Eventually. Meanwhile—"

"M!" Molly interrupts, jumping up from the table. "How did it go? Until Rigel got here, I figured you were just sleeping late—I sure did! But then he told us you were meeting with the Mind Healer. Did she help?" While talking, she drags me to a chair. "Oh, and have you had breakfast? No more skipping meals, okay?"

Despite my anxiety and depression, her enthusiasm almost makes me smile. Almost. "It's okay, I ate in my room," I assure her, sitting down. "And Healer Ava thinks she *will* be able to help, but…she warned me it'll probably take a while." I glance at Rigel, who frowns, then goes to sit on the opposite side of the table.

Molly looks back and forth between us. "And meanwhile you still have to stay away from Rigel? That sucks! No wonder you both look so unhappy. I take it you're not on board with this plan?" she asks Rigel.

"No. But apparently the Healer agrees with M that it's the only way to keep her from hurting people."

Except Rigel. And me. Am I being unfair to him? To myself? Or do I want to believe that so I don't have to go through with this?

"Rigel's one of your Bodyguards," Tristan points out. "How can he protect you if he has to stay away from you? Not to mention you'll probably both get sick."

"Exactly!" Rigel shoots him a grateful glance. "Plus I've almost always been able to calm you down when you get upset. I want to help, M," he adds softly, reaching across the table. "Please let me."

I put my hands in my lap and immediately feel his hurt—again. It makes me long to give in, but then I remember that awful dream and my flagging resolve stiffens.

"Healer Ava will try to track down some antidote for us," I say. Rigel flinches, but I try not to let it distract me. "Because yes, she does agree you and I need to keep our distance until we're sure I won't channel Faxon again and hurt people—or worse. Like...I did last night. Or even lash out at people verbally, like I did to all of you yesterday. I'm *so* sorry about that. I know you were only trying to help."

"You weren't yourself," Molly says, just like Rigel did when I silently apologized to him a few minutes ago. "We all realized that. We weren't mad, just worried."

Tristan and Rigel nod their agreement, though Rigel still looks tense. I hurt him most of all...and I'm still doing it.

"I'm still really sorry about the things I said to you," I insist. "Especially since you guys turned out to be right. Shutting everyone out and continuing all alone was every bit as dangerous as you warned me. As dangerous as Rigel predicted."

"But you were right, too, M," Molly says matter-of-factly. "You found Faxon before he could blow anything else up and kill people—probably lots of people. Maybe locking yourself in your quarters really was the only way to do that, risky as it was."

I hadn't thought of it that way. "Maybe it was," I admit. "Isolating myself definitely helped me go through his memories faster, which I needed to do. But if you hadn't pulled me out, I might still be trapped inside my mind."

"And Rigel and Tristan would probably be dead," Molly adds with a shudder. "I'm *so* glad I was able to get through to you!"

"Yeah, about that," Tristan says. "Apparently you two can now communicate telepathically with each other? That's pretty cool." He's clearly trying to lighten the mood.

Rigel stares at him, then at Molly and me. "You can? When did that happen?"

"Oh, I told Tristan but I guess you wouldn't know." Molly explains how she was able to open my door when the Council refused to do it, and then reach out to me mentally when I was frantic to escape my memory-trance.

"Sorry I didn't tell you last night," I say to Rigel. "It only works when we're touching, but it came in really useful even after Molly pulled me out."

Molly nods. "I doubt we could have snuck out to rescue you two without it. And hey, maybe it'll keep improving like our *graell* telepathy has, so we can eventually do it long-distance!"

"Maybe." Momentarily distracted, I nearly smile—then remember what I came here to do. "I, ah, need to tell you the rest of what Mind Healer Ava and I talked about this morning. What we decided. You're… probably not going to like it."

26

Overcompensation

MY WORDS immediately refocus everyone's attention.

"I already don't like it." Rigel frowns. "Are you saying there's something even worse than us not being allowed to touch for who knows how long?"

I nod. "While going so deeply into Faxon's mind for that long did help me find him faster, it also messed with my head way worse than I expected—as I proved last night. That's why we need to stay apart until the Mind Healers can fix me."

Molly looks skeptical. "Last night you were pretty extremely provoked. I can't imagine you'll hurt anyone again, now that you won't be digging into Faxon's twisted mind anymore. Torturing yourself—and Rigel—just as a precaution seems like a huge overreaction."

"No," I tell her. "It's not. I got mad again this morning, while I was talking with Healer Ava—so mad it scared her. It scared me, too, because for a minute there, I really *did* want to hurt her. Fortunately, her desk was between us, so I couldn't reach her before I snapped out of it. But if you'd been there," I say to Rigel, "I might have killed her, too."

For a long moment, I think I've finally convinced him.

Then he shakes his head. "I don't buy it. I can tap into your emotions, remember? If you start getting really angry, I won't let you touch me. But otherwise I can be there to help, to calm you down before it ever reaches that stage. Doesn't that make the most sense?"

Much as I wish I could agree with him, I can't. "No. Not right now. I'm too unpredictable. Too dangerous."

"But—" Molly begins.

I stop her with a frown. "Just listen. Please. I know you guys and some people on the Council want to play down what I did last night, out of gratitude or whatever, but it's not safe. *I'm* not safe. Healer Ava agrees."

I hesitate for a second, then tell them about the psych test I took and what it revealed.

They all look stunned.

"*Psychosis?* Did she really say that?" Molly demands indignantly.

"Bordering on, but yeah," I confirm. "She was…pretty freaked out by my results. Basically said that if I weren't the Sovereign, she'd have to have me committed."

Rigel stares at me in disbelief. "Committed?" he repeats. "That's crazy!"

"No, *I'm* crazy. Unstable, anyway. And the last thing our people need is an unstable Sovereign, especially after this past week. Healer Ava is going to do her best to fix me. But in the meantime, along with avoiding Rigel, she wants me to step back from my duties."

Molly sucks in a breath. "But—"

I continue inexorably, cutting off her protest. "That's why I've agreed to step down as Sovereign and stay confined here at NuAgra until further notice."

All three of them stare at me in shock. "Step *down?*" Molly repeats. "You don't mean—?"

"Yes." I look her directly in the eye. "Until the Mind Healers are sure I'm…safe again, I plan to abdicate and name you Acting—"

"No!" she interrupts. "No, no, no, don't even *say* that!" Her eyes are now wide and scared. "*Definitely* don't say it, or even hint at it, in front of my mum! She's already got me studying extra Sovereign stuff, 'just in case.' I do *not* want her to think I might *really* have to take over!"

She's so rattled, I turn to Tristan. "I think Molly would be up to it, don't you? Way more than I was at the start."

He puts up both hands. "Don't drag me into the middle of this! I'm sure Molly's up to whatever will be required of her, but I can't believe such a huge step is necessary."

I glance over at Rigel, whose shock is fading. "Neither do I," he agrees, though I can tell his feelings are mixed. He *has* been begging me to delegate more, and there's no denying that our path as a couple would be massively easier if I weren't Sovereign…

True, he thinks to me, *but not like this. This is going way too far.*

Is it?

"It should only be temporary," I say aloud. "Healer Ava believes I'm suffering from post-traumatic stress disorder, or something similar. She thinks the after-effects of what I experienced will fade over time, especially with techniques she'll show me to help me control my emotions better."

"And in the meantime, she wants to lock you up?" Rigel's own emotions are still chaotic. "That's awfully extreme."

"Not as extreme as what I did last night. Rigel, I *killed* a man! And forced *you* to be an accessory to murder!" Shame and self-loathing assail me again. "How can you even stand to look at me?"

"No." He shakes his head fiercely. "It wasn't murder, even the Council said so. It was self-defense, to keep *him* from murdering me and Tristan—and you and Molly."

Much as I want to believe that, I know better. "I—we—could have just stunned him. Like you wanted to. Like you *told* me to, but I ignored you. What if somebody at school, like Trina, makes me mad while I'm holding your hand and I electrocute *her,* right in the cafeteria? Last night…" I swallow. "I dreamed I did exactly that. Then you—" I break off, unable to continue, but he plucks the terrible images from my mind.

"It was just a dream, M," he tells me firmly. "You didn't really kill Trina." *And I would* never *try to kill you, even if you did,* he adds silently.

"Not yet." I take a shaky breath. "But until I somehow get Faxon out of my brain, I can't know *what* I'm capable of. It's like he…he takes over when I get angry, and I just react without thinking."

Molly's still broadcasting distress and denial. "What about school?" she demands. "You can't just drop out."

And what about us? Rigel asks silently. *You swore I wouldn't lose you, but now you want to lock yourself away from me?*

The anguish I feel from him makes me want to cry. I feel like a monster for doing this to him…but not as horrible a monster as I'd be if my dream became reality.

Swallowing, I answer Molly instead of Rigel. "Aunt Theresa can tell the school I'm sick." I probably will be, after a day or two without Rigel. "I *can't* risk losing my temper there like I did last night."

"I still think you're *way* overreacting," she insists. "Why can't you just—?"

With my emotions already frayed, their continued resistance pushes me closer to the edge. When I hear the beginnings of that low rumble, I jump to my feet so quickly I knock my chair over.

"Can't you see I'm trying to do what's best for *everyone*—including all of you?" I'm hit by that scene from my dream where I killed Molly. My sister. "You *saw* what I did last night! Do you *want* me to kill more people?"

"Of course not!" Molly protests, aghast.

Rigel again reaches a hand toward me. "You won't, M. You know I've always been able to—"

"Things are different now," I insist, backing away. "Don't you get it? *I'm* different now. It's like none of you even—" I bite back my next hurtful words and turn away. "I'm going to go catch up on homework. I'll see you all at the meeting." Leaving them to gape at my back, I storm off to my quarters.

Once locked in, I stand in my entryway for a full minute, waiting for my heart to stop pounding, my breathing to slow—and the Faxon-anger roaring in my ears to quiet.

Slowly, it does…but as my anger fades, guilt crowds in to take its place. I'm obviously not safe around people yet, not even people I love. Will I ever be? Right now, I only seem able to hurt them—with words if not actions.

Remembering the anguish in Rigel's eyes—the anguish I caused him *again*—I start to cry. Yesterday I felt so terrible for telling him to leave me alone, I couldn't *wait* to apologize as soon as I completed my mission. Being Rigel, he forgave me. Of course.

Then I turned right around and shut him out again!

"I'm so sorry, Rigel," I sob, then send the same words to him mentally. *The last thing I ever want to do is hurt you, but I keep doing it over and over.*

There's a long pause before he replies. When he does, I can tell he's working hard to hide how upset he is. *It's not your fault, M. That whole Faxon thing messed up your head way worse than even I expected. You're only overreacting because you're not thinking straight right now. If you need time to figure things out, take it. When you're ready, I'll still be here for you.*

Gratitude wars with guilt that's stronger than ever. I totally do *not* deserve him. *Thank you. I love you, Rigel. You really are my rock.*

I try. I love you, too, M. And…we'll get through this, like we do everything. Together.

Swallowing back more tears, I send one last burst of love and gratitude his way. Then I break our mental link before my tortured thoughts can upset him even more.

From the earliest days of our relationship, people have tried to keep Rigel and me apart. First to throw off Faxon's people when they were after me, then because stupid Martian tradition decreed I was supposed to pair with Sean. Allister and Lennox nearly *murdered* Rigel to keep him away from me, then Mr. O and others erased his memory for the same reason. Each and every time, we fought the odds and came out stronger. Together.

But now *I'm* the one keeping us apart. What's wrong with me?

The easy answer is Faxon.

Except…this is by no means the first time Rigel's been hurt because of me. No, every single time Rigel has been in danger, every time he's nearly died, it's been because of me. Me! I really must be a monster to keep hurting the very person I love most in the world.

More depressed than I can ever remember, I pick up my Calculus textbook.

✦

For an hour, I try to distract myself with math, French and some accumulated Sovereign stuff, but then my stomach growls. It's well past noon. Lunchtime.

Should I just eat in my room again? After my latest outburst, I'm both afraid and embarrassed to face the others. I do need to apologize to Molly and Tristan, though. Again. Doing it by text feels cowardly and lame, but—

M? comes Rigel's tentative thought just then. *You feel up to having lunch with us? You seem…pretty calm right now.*

Yeah, okay. If I follow through on my plan, I may not see him again for a long time. Surely I can risk one last meal together, as long as we don't touch? *Be there in a minute.*

Hoping I'm not being stupid, I wash my face, brush my hair, and head back to the dining hall. It's a lot more crowded now, but no one's too close to the corner table where Molly and Tristan are still sitting.

"Have you guys been here since I left?" I take my same seat next to Molly.

"No, we just got back." She eyes me warily—and no wonder. "We all spent half an hour in the fitness center, then Rigel stopped by his dad's office. He said you reached out to him and apologized? Does that mean you're…feeling better?"

I force a tiny laugh. "For the moment. I need to apologize to you guys, too, for going off on you again. I should have left the second I started getting pissed."

Molly shrugs. "Hey, you were in control enough to leave before you totally lost it. That's progress, right?"

Is it? I'd sure like to believe that. "Let's see how lunch and the Council meeting go before we get our hopes up. Your father's still getting anger management treatment in Denver, isn't he, Tristan? Is it helping? That's one of the things Healer Ava wants to try."

"Yeah, it actually seems to be helping a lot, though it's too soon to know if the change will be permanent," Tristan replies. "He's come to visit a few times since he started and he's definitely a lot more pleasant to be around than he used to be." He falls silent for a second and I sense his conflicted feelings. "Mother and I both hope it will last, though we're almost afraid to," he adds wistfully.

"I get that. I hope it will, too." I'm sure I'm not the only one who's noticed how much happier and more confident Teara seems without Connor around to bully her. "It's…encouraging that his treatment's already working so well." *After four months*, I think but don't say.

Tristan leans forward. "I can guess what you're thinking, M, but your anger issue is nothing like my father's. He's had a nasty temper for as long as I can remember. You only started losing your temper this weekend—a side-effect of that Faxon-memory thing you had to do. That should make yours a whole lot quicker and easier to treat."

Molly nods. I feel her sympathy and concern for me.

"Thanks," I tell them both. "I guess time will tell."

Rigel enters the dining hall then and my heart lifts in spite of myself at the sight of him. His dad comes in just behind him but goes to a different table, where three other Council members are already sitting.

"Hey," Rigel greets me—us—with a smile that looks only slightly forced. He also goes to the same chair as before, across from Tristan.

I smile back, though I still feel guilty for what I'm putting him through.

Molly stands up before I can apologize again. "Let's get lunch. The Council meeting's in just over an hour."

We all follow her to the recombinators, though Rigel's careful to keep a good two arm lengths away from me. Even so, his *brath* feels more magnetic than usual. Maybe because we haven't touched since last night —or kissed for more than a day? Suddenly twitchy, I have to fight an urge to move closer to him.

"Have you heard any more from Shim yet?" Molly asks when we sit back down with our food.

Grateful for a safe topic, I shake my head. "No, but Kyna messaged to say he promised her a more complete update in time for the meeting."

"I guess Faxon is still entitled to a trial before they do a mind wipe?" Tristan says.

"Yes, unfortunately," I reply. "First they'll do a memory extraction— which should confirm everything I learned about his origins."

"That's what my dad said," Rigel tells us. "He quit doing research on Chicago once Faxon was caught. It shouldn't be necessary now."

Once we've finished our meals, Rigel goes to get us all ice cream. Just as he hands me my favorite mint chocolate chip, my omni pings.

"Shim's report?" Molly guesses as I pull it out.

It is. "I may as well play it now. Looks like everyone else is." I nod at the table where the whole Council is now sitting, omnis open.

Setting mine on the table, I start the message and Shim appears on the holo screen.

"Excellency, members of the *Echtran* Council, I'm pleased to report that we discovered substantially more information in Faxon's databases than anyone expected, with more still to be analyzed. As a result, the attached report is quite lengthy. You may not have time to read it all before your meeting, so I'll briefly summarize what we've found so far.

"We now have complete schematics for the battle ships Faxon was constructing, which will greatly speed the work of retrofitting them for transport. This should allow emigration to proceed far more quickly, beginning with the next launch window. In addition, it appears Faxon had at least one power cell taken offline for study, which partially accounts for the dramatic drop in Nuathan energy reserves during his tenure. If our Engineers can restore its functionality, Nuath's viable exis- tence could be extended by several extra decades, particularly if combined with increased emigration. That would give our researchers substantially more time to find a permanent solution to Nuath's energy crisis.

"Though I hesitate to say this, Faxon's escape—and recapture, thanks to our Sovereign—could well prove a blessing in disguise for Nuath. As we continue to gather more information over the coming days and weeks, you can expect further updates. Again, I must commend you, Excellency, for your courage in subjecting yourself to Faxon's memories despite knowing the risks. Your willingness to sacrifice for our people has once again proven how fortunate we are to have you as our Sovereign."

With a parting bow, Shim concludes his video message.

The attached report is over fifty pages long.

"I guess we should at least try to skim this before the meeting?" Molly says.

I forward it to Rigel's omni and Molly shares hers with Tristan, then we all spend the next fifteen minutes clicking through Shim's report, most of which appears to be good news.

"This is cool," Tristan comments at one point. "From the records they found, there might have been *two* power cells taken offline, though they've only located the one so far. If they could get both up and running, that would take most of the pressure off needing people to emigrate."

"It would," I agree. In which case all the time I spent last summer convincing people to move to Earth, when I was desperate to get back to Rigel, might not have been necessary after all. The thought makes me a little grouchy.

The final section of the report details a few of Faxon's atrocities that were previously unknown—though not to me. I skip that entirely since once was more than enough.

"Ew," Molly says when she reaches that part. "I knew he was evil, but...ew."

Shortly before two, I stand up. "I want to stop by Mind Healer Ava's office before the meeting," I explain when the others look up in surprise. Earlier, I stormed out before telling them she'd be attending the meeting to help justify my decision. "I'll see you all there."

"Tell her how you controlled your temper enough to leave instead of blowing up this morning," Molly eagerly suggests. "And how you've been totally fine since coming back for lunch. When she sees you're already getting so much better, she'll probably realize you don't need to step down after all. Or stay away from Rigel, either."

I doubt that, but her optimism is so contagious, I can't help hoping she's right. My spirits are lighter than they've been all day when I knock on Healer Ava's office door. She opens it at once.

"Ah, thank you for stopping by ahead of the Council meeting, Excellency." She motions me inside, then closes the door. "I wanted to tell you privately that I've run your test results—anonymized, of course—through our most sophisticated diagnostic tools. I'm now doubly glad you've voluntarily chosen to remain here at NuAgra for the present, as all three analyses agree that the patient in question should absolutely be kept confined and under strict observation."

My brief hope pops like a bubble. "That's...disappointing." Huge understatement! "I guess we'd better go tell the Council."

27

Persuasion

EVERYONE IS ALREADY SEATED when we reach the Council chamber, including Kyna's and Nara's holograms. Rigel and Tristan are over by the wall again, in the same chairs as before. I motion Healer Ava to another chair near them before taking my usual seat next to Molly.

"Mind Healer Ava is here at my request," I say in response to everyone's curious glances.

Mrs. O sniffs. "To tell us you need not keep your distance from Rigel Stuart, I assume?"

The disapproving glance she sends his way immediately makes me bristle. I force myself to stay calm…then Malcolm speaks up.

"I suppose we can take the Mind Healer's recommendation into account, but I believe this Council should be the final authority on that."

"Final authority?" That ominous rumbling I hoped never to hear again sounds faintly in my ears.

His smile is patronizing. "Only last night you admitted to a lack of judgment, Excellency, did you not? Speaking of which, I see no reason for those teenaged Bodyguards to be present now that the danger to you and Princess Malena is past."

The rumbling gets louder. "Don't you *dare—*" I begin, my voice rising, when Molly stops me with a hand on my arm.

Don't, she silently cautions me. *They'll see it as proof they're right.* Along with her caution, I feel calm flowing from her, like I thought I did last night when I was so out of control. Almost before I'm sure it's real, Rigel adds his own calming vibes from across the room.

Listen to her, he sends silently. *It's one thing for you to decide we should stay apart right now, but let's not give the Council a reason to mandate it!*

With their combined help, I bring my anger back under control. Only then do I realize it's a good thing Rigel's *not* sitting next to me. For a second I was nearly pissed enough to fry Malcolm where he sits. I don't even want to think what the consequences for *that* would be!

In the awkward silence that follows my near-outburst, Kyna clears her throat noisily.

"Shall we get started? I'm sure everyone is eager to enjoy the remainder of the weekend, now that this recent crisis is happily over. I assume we've all seen Regent Shim's latest message and at least glanced over his report?"

Everyone nods, the tense moment past.

"Yes, wonderful news," Nara exclaims.

Others enthusiastically echo her words. Several also repeat Shim's thanks to me for the role I played in turning potential tragedy into unexpectedly positive news for Nuath.

I manage a tight smile, still shaken by how close I came to losing control just now, even if no one but Molly and Rigel noticed. Faxon's effect on me obviously hasn't faded as much as I hoped. Maybe I should make my announcement now?

But as soon as everyone quiets, Kyna turns to Rigel's dad. "Van, you have a security update?"

"Yes," he replies. "We've reinforced the recently-identified weak spots in NuAgra's security." He glances at Molly and me. "A discreet but thorough sweep of the surrounding area confirms that the agitators have dispersed. The online chatter from the radical groups we've been monitoring has largely died down, as well. A few cells will still bear watching, but none are within several hundred miles of Jewel."

Kyna nods approvingly. "Then it should be safe for our Sovereign and Princess to return to their homes and resume their normal routines?"

"I don't see why not." Mr. Stuart smiles over at us. "There appear to be no remaining threats in or near Jewel."

"Not true," I contradict him. "One significant threat does remain. Me."

A startled murmur goes around the table. "What do you mean, Excellency?" Kyna asks.

"I mean it should be safe for Molly to go home, but not me. Not yet. Regent Shim and I knew spending so much time in Faxon's memories might affect my mind, but the effect was worse than either of us expected. This morning, Mind Healer Ava had me repeat the psychological profile test I took last year before going to Mars. The results were… disturbing. She doesn't feel I'm mentally stable enough right now to go home or to school."

My words are greeted by a stunned silence. Kyna is the first to find her voice.

"What exactly are you proposing, Excellency?" she asks me.

"Healer Ava and I both believe I should temporarily step down as Sovereign and remain confined here at NuAgra until she and her colleagues can declare me cured of my…Faxon psychosis. I realize I haven't yet appointed an Earth Regent, so I hereby name my sister, Princess Malena, Acting Sovereign."

Beside me, Molly gasps in protest. "M, no! I thought you—!"

The rest of her sentence is drowned out by every Council member shouting at once.

"What?"

"Impossible!"

"Excellency, there are certain procedures—"

"You can't mean—?"

Fighting desperately to keep my emotions under control, I push to my feet and hold up a hand. They fall silent and I turn to Healer Ava.

"Mind Healer, will you please share your findings with the Council?"

"Er, yes." She stands up, too, and swallows nervously. "As the Sovereign indicated, the psychological profile she completed this morning indicates extreme mental instability. Because her behavior is likely to be very unpredictable just now, I recommended the, ah, steps the Sovereign wishes to take. Particularly given the events of last night, which she described to me, I don't believe she can safely resume her normal activities until her condition can be stabilized. The Sovereign has authorized me to share a summary of her test results and my proposed treatment plan with any of you who would like to see it."

"Yes I would, thank you," Kyna says, her initial shock fading. "But while I don't doubt your expertise or judgment, Healer, I'm afraid your recommendation isn't at all practical. Our people, both here and especially in Nuath, are only now beginning to recover from an extremely stressful week. Many are still anxious about our Sovereign and her sister after Faxon's demands, and calls by some to give in to them. It is absolutely vital they be reassured that both are alive and unharmed, as rumors to the contrary have already begun circulating. The surest way to refute those rumors is to allow both girls to return to their homes and to school. What *specific* risk do you believe that poses?"

Healer Ava hesitates. "I'm sure Princess Malena can attend school as usual without any risk at all. The Sovereign, however, could pose a danger to others in such a setting. I would prefer she begin receiving treatment immediately. Today, if possible."

"Suppose she and Rigel Stuart agree to stay several feet apart at all times?" Kyna suggests. "I am right, am I not, that physical contact is still required for the two of you to generate the enormous electrical charges of which you are capable?" she asks me.

"Yes," I reply, glancing over at Rigel.

I don't like it, he thinks to me, *but if the alternative is you being locked up, I'll go along with it.*

That still sounds risky to me. "I don't know—"

"You were fine at lunch," Molly interrupts to remind me. "You didn't get mad once. And even when you got a little upset before that, you didn't try to do anything violent. Honestly," she insists, now to everyone, "I think she's already getting better." She's so earnest, even I'm tempted to believe her—until I remember that's Molly's special power.

Now Healer Ava looks uncertain. "I suppose it's possible that because the onset of the Sovereign's condition was so rapid, her recovery could be equally rapid. Still, until that can be verified—"

"How about this for a compromise?" Molly's voice now holds a hint of desperation—and a whole lot of "push"—though I doubt anyone else can hear it. "Suppose she goes home and to school, but still comes to NuAgra every day for counseling and treatment? Somebody can drive her here after school, then back home. It would prove she's okay to any *Echtrans* who are worried, and the *Duchas* won't get suspicious about her not being at school. It should also keep her and Rigel from getting sick, which they will if they're nowhere near each other. And she won't have to abdicate, even temporarily. It's perfect!" She looks hopefully around the room.

I'm tempted to call her out for using "push"…but I don't. Her solution does sound a whole lot less unpleasant than being locked away for who knows how long. But it also assumes I really can hold it together at school. Can I?

You can. Rigel's mental tone is confident. *I'll help. So will Molly.*

I will, Molly silently agrees, her hand still on my arm. *Trust us!*

I do trust them. I'm just not sure I can trust myself.

But already, Healer Ava is nodding. So is every member of the Council...except Mrs. O, who's frowning suspiciously at Molly.

"Will that be acceptable, Mind Healer?" Kyna asks when no one voices an objection.

"I suppose so," Ava replies, "as long as certain precautions are taken. She should be continuously monitored. We have devices that can do so both remotely and discreetly. I'll keep an eye on her readings, and if any raise serious concerns, we can reevaluate."

Rather to my surprise, everyone seems okay with that—especially Rigel and Molly.

Kyna turns to me. "Excellency? Are you comfortable with the compromise Princess Malena proposes? If you can attend school for even a week, it will go a long way toward reassuring our people after the recent threats you and your sister received."

Comfortable? Not really. But— "As long as Mind Healer Ava feels it's safe, I guess it does seem like the best option for now," I reply. "I agree that our people will recover more quickly from what they just went through if they believe things are already back to normal." Whether it's true or not.

"Very well, then." Kyna smiles. "That's settled. Any further updates we receive from Regent Shim can be shared with the rest of the Council electronically, along with any new developments here. Let us all hope nothing of note will arise to require another meeting ahead of our usually scheduled one next weekend. Adjourned."

Molly jumps up, grinning. "C'mon," she whispers to me. "Let's get out of here." She motions to Tristan and he and Rigel follow us from the conference room while the Council members are still chatting.

"That was a great idea, Molly," Tristan says once we're far enough from the doorway to talk without being overheard. "Did you just think of it on the spot?"

She nods, still radiating relief. "I had to do *something*. Sorry, M, but I really can't believe you need to be locked up 24/7 and I *totally* don't want to be Acting Sovereign. Isn't this way better? You and Rigel didn't even have to promise to stay apart."

"Hey, that's right!" Now Rigel's grinning, too. "Good timing, Molly."

I look back and forth between them, incredulous. "Just because I didn't yell and throw things at lunch, you guys act like I'm all better. I'm not. You saw how close I came to blowing up at Malcolm before Molly stopped me."

"But we did stop you," Molly reminds me. "We can do the same thing at school. Seriously, M, I think you're doing a lot better already. You'll believe it, too, once you make it through a couple of normal school days without wanting to kill anyone. Shoot, I don't know if even I can do that. I want to kill Trina at almost every cheer practice!"

That forces a small smile from me. "Not *quite* the same as actually doing it." I turn to Rigel then. "Even though we didn't have to promise, I still think you should stay out of my reach until I'm sure I can control my temper. It's the only way to be *sure* I can't fry anybody—like Trina—if she makes me mad."

He suddenly looks—and feels—a lot less cheerful. "But—"

"Excellency?" Mrs. O'Gara interrupts. "Kyna suggested I take you home, but Mind Healer Ava would like to meet with you again first. I'll wait for you in the dining hall." She turns to Molly. "You can ride back with us if you don't mind waiting a bit."

"No, that's okay. Tristan will drive me," Molly's quick to reply. "I'll see you at home later on. And M, I'll see you at school tomorrow." They hurry off.

I have no trouble sensing what she and Tristan are thinking about. They're nearly as overdue as we are for some serious making out. I try—hard—not to be jealous that they'll have a chance to catch up in just a few minutes. Unlike us.

I'll be jealous enough for both of us, okay?

At Rigel's thought I experience a wave of longing so strong it makes me swallow. When Mrs. O heads to the dining hall, I impulsively say to him, "Why don't you come with me to Healer Ava's office? I'd like you to hear what she has to say."

"Sure. It's not like I'm in any hurry to leave you."

Together—but not together enough—we go to see the Mind Healer.

⁘

"Thank you for coming so promptly, Excellency," Healer Ava greets me when I show up at her office for the third time today. "Please come in."

I glance at Rigel. "Is it all right if he sits in for this? I mean, I'll tell him everything you say anyway, so he might as well."

Though a slight frown forms between her perfect brows, she nods. "That is completely up to you, Excellency."

Shutting the door behind us, I sit down across from her desk. Rigel moves to the couch a few feet away.

Healer Ava relaxes slightly. "As you requested, I forwarded your test results to Regent Shim. Also to Council leader Kyna, as she asked. Do you truly intend to go home today and return to school tomorrow?" Now that she's away from Molly's influence, she seems to be having second thoughts.

"That's what you and the *Echtran* Council agreed to," I remind her.

"Yes. Your sister did seem quite sure that you're already making progress. I'll do what I can to speed it along. In the meantime—" She picks something up from her desk and holds it out to me— "I would like you to wear this."

I take what looks like a simple copper bracelet, but with tiny, rounded crystals embedded along half of the inside surface. "What is it?"

"A monitoring device. We use them to track various health metrics when a patient's condition doesn't require hospitalization but still merits ongoing observation. I had this one calibrated to continuously measure your heart rate, blood pressure, adrenal levels, and neural activity, among other things. It's programmed to alert me should any critical metric spike into a danger zone."

"Sort of an early warning system?" I slip the bracelet onto my left wrist and it automatically resizes itself for a perfect fit.

She gives me a slight smile. "You could say that. Shall we go over the treatment program I have in mind? The sooner you begin it, the more quickly you should be able to put this current difficulty behind you."

"I'll start today," I assure her—and Rigel.

He sits quietly while Healer Ava carefully explains the various mental exercises she believes will be most useful for me.

"Though your specific situation is unique, these time-proven methods should help you control your emotions while at home and at school. You, ah, don't happen to have access to any weapons at home, do you?"

"Weapons?" I think for a second. "My uncle has a hunting rifle, but he keeps it locked up…and I have no idea how to use it."

She nods. "Good. Though I seem to recall you are also trained in martial arts?"

"I have a red belt in taekwondo," I admit. "I guess that *could* make me dangerous." Especially since thanks to my Martian strength and reflexes—and my bond with Rigel—I can out-spar most black belts. "But probably not deadly?"

Healer Ava raises an eyebrow. "Let's hope not. At school, however, there's a larger concern." She looks over at Rigel. "This morning, you and I agreed that the surest way to prevent another devastating electrical attack would be for the two of you to avoid touching while you are still undergoing treatment. Are you both still willing to abide by that?"

I nod, though I sense some resistance from Rigel. "It won't be easy, but…yes." *Right?* I think to him.

Reluctantly, he nods, too. "If you think that's the only way she can safely go to school?"

"I'm afraid I do, yes," she confirms, dashing our last hopes. "I also recommend you delegate as many of your responsibilities as possible, as we discussed, even though it appears you won't be stepping down entirely."

"Yes, I just need to figure out exactly what I can hand off, and to whom," I agree. Out of the corner of my eye, I see Rigel shift slightly on the couch. "I'll talk to Kyna about it this week."

Healer Ava nods her approval and stands up. "Excellent. In that case, I believe we're done for now. I'll see you again tomorrow after school. I've cleared my afternoon schedule from three o'clock on, as I assume you'd like to keep this as low key as possible."

"I would, yes. I'll arrange to come here straight from school." I get to my feet. "Thank you so much, Healer Ava. For everything."

"It is my honor, Excellency." Right fist over heart, she bows deeply.

Though I feel totally undeserving of her regard right now, I just incline my head the proper degree and leave her office, Rigel following a few steps behind me.

"So," he says when we're alone in the hallway. "Sounds like she finally convinced you to do what I've been saying for months—delegate."

I shoot him an apologetic glance. "I should have listened to you. She thinks stress probably made this worse, and reducing stress will help me get over it sooner."

"Then at least one good thing will come out of this."

"Other than saving thousands of Nuathan lives?" I ask, brows raised.

He shrugs. "That, too. But *you're* what I care most about, M. Always. I'm in favor of anything that will get you over this Faxon mind-mess quicker. Because not touching is going to suck."

He's not wrong.

Just then I see Mrs. O'Gara coming toward us. "Ah, I was just coming to see if you were finished, Excellency. Are you ready to go?" She darts a frowning glance at Rigel.

"I guess so," I reply heavily. "See you at school tomorrow," I tell Rigel, a lump in my throat, then silently add, *I'll do absolutely everything I can to get better quickly, I promise. I love you!*

He just nods back, but says silently, *I know you will. I love you, too—no matter what.*

For now, that will have to be enough.

28

Approach-avoidance conflict

AN ICY DRIZZLE is falling when the O'Garas drop me off at home fifteen minutes later. The damp chill and lowering gray sky match my mood perfectly. Even though I know I'll see him tomorrow, my goodbye to Rigel felt like the hardest yet.

"Ah, good, you're back," Aunt Theresa greets me when I walk in. She seems oddly relieved to see me. "Did you finish whatever business you had to attend to out at NuAgra over the weekend?"

Sometimes her lack of curiosity about anything Mars-related is a blessing. "Mostly. There are still a few loose ends to tie up, so I'll be going back out there most afternoons."

For a moment I think she's going to ask for details, but she doesn't. "Oh, good," she says—absently, though her words accompanied by a surprising amount of anxiety. Was she actually worried about me? Surely not.

"Aunt Theresa, is something wrong?" I ask her.

She regards me uncertainly. "I'm…not sure. Yesterday—"

"A camera crew came to the house," Uncle Louie tells me, rousing himself from the NBA game he was watching. "I thought it would be cool to talk with them, maybe get on TV, but Theresa—"

"I turned them away," my aunt finishes for him. "They were clearly, ah, *your* people, claiming they wanted to interview us. About you. But when Lili O'Gara came by Friday to get your overnight bag, she cautioned us to avoid talking to strangers while you were gone. Something about politics."

My uncle rolls his eyes. "I'm sure they just—"

"No, you did the right thing," I tell my aunt firmly. "I definitely would have been told if a legit film crew were coming here."

I'm willing to bet that "crew" planned to use my *Duchas* guardians as leverage—before they later lucked into Rigel and Tristan instead. What would have happened if Mrs. O hadn't been foresighted enough to warn them—or if Uncle Louie had answered the door? He could have gotten them both killed!

I hear the beginnings of that awful, distant rumbling and turn away before I can lash out at Uncle Louie for being so dense. "I'm going to go unpack," I say abruptly, heading for the stairs.

Once safely in my room, I take several deep, calming breaths, reminding myself it wasn't really Uncle Louie's fault. Neither he nor my aunt had any clue what was at stake. They also have no idea how dangerous I am right now. I'd rather keep it that way.

Are you all right? Rigel's sudden thought startles me.

I think so…now. How did you know—?

Thought it might be a good idea to do occasional spot checks. See how you're holding up.

I feel a spurt of irritation. *You mean spying on me?*

What? No! But when I tried to reach out a couple minutes ago, you felt too angry to hear me.

Oh. *Yeah, sorry, I probably was,* I admit. *I just found out those guys who grabbed you and Tristan yesterday came here first.* I repeat what my aunt and uncle told me.

Wow. That could have been really bad, he agrees. *We should thank Mrs. O. But you're okay now?*

At the moment. But it's scary how suddenly that Faxon-rage can hit me. I'm going to try a few of those calming exercises Healer Ava gave me.

Good idea. Reach out if you need to. I'll be here.

Again, my gratitude is tainted by guilt. I *so* don't deserve him! *I will,* I reply after a moment. *Thanks. I love you!*

I sit down at my desk and pull up the anger management techniques Healer Ava shared to my omni, even though I'm no longer angry. She said the more I practice them, the more easily I'll remember them when I am.

I start with twenty minutes of deep breathing and progressive muscle relaxation, though I skip the recommended meditation. I do *not* want to risk getting sucked back into Faxon's memories!

Next I read through and dutifully repeat a long list of positive affirmations aloud. I don't believe any of them right now, but supposedly they can still help. Physical exercise is also recommended, so after that I get up and do two dozen jumping jacks followed by a dozen pushups to burn off excess adrenaline.

I'm debating whether to shower or move on to other suggestions when my omni pings. It's a message from Shim, but sent only to me, not to Kyna or the Council.

My Dear Excellency, I've now been fully briefed about the events of Saturday night, as well as your current mental condition, something you and I both knew was a possible risk. I'm sorry to learn those concerns were justified, but remain confident that the unpleasant psychological effects will dissipate with time and treatment. I very much agree with Mind Healer Ava that eliminating as many sources of stress as possible will speed your recovery. Kyna can advise you as to which duties you can safely and easily delegate, and to whom. Perhaps Princess Malena can be of assistance there as well. Your heroism in undertaking this effort cannot be overstated, my dear Emileia. I know circumstances have often forced you to shoulder the burdens of your position alone, but pray do not hesitate to accept any help now offered. We cannot afford to lose our Sovereign.

Wishing you a speedy return to full health, I remain your faithful servant.

Smiling, I type a quick thanks and send it, comforted to have Shim fully in my corner, even if he can't do much more to help from millions of miles away.

By the time I go downstairs to help Aunt Theresa make dinner, I feel more like my normal self than I have since Friday, a breakthrough I share privately with Rigel. My improved mood lasts through dinner, but as bedtime approaches I start getting jittery, remembering last night's awful dreams. Will tonight's be as bad? Worse?

The whole time I'm getting ready for bed, I become progressively more nervous. To stall, I rearrange my nightstand drawer, my bookshelves and the top of my dresser. When I finally get into bed, I reach out to Rigel. As usual. And instantly picking up on my anxiety, he comes through for me again.

I don't blame you after last night, but you'll be okay, he assures me, then continues sending soothing thoughts and vibes until I'm drowsy enough to sleep. *Don't be afraid to wake me up in the night if you have bad dreams again*, he reminds me as I drift off.

Beyond grateful to have such an incredible, supportive guy in my life, I drowsily agree before sinking into sleep.

.⁺✦

Like last night, I'm tired enough that I sleep soundly and dreamlessly for several hours…until jerking awake, heart pounding with horror, sometime after four. Again, it takes me a minute to remember with relief where I am—in my own bedroom at home, in my own bed. *Not* the high school cafeteria, where I took out Trina and her whole posse with lightning bolts, with Rigel nowhere in sight. Not until my heart slows do I realize that's not even possible.

Still, I feel compelled to make absolutely sure. I get my old phone out of my nightstand, place it at the foot of my bed, and try to fry it from a few feet away. Sure enough, nothing happens. But…I'm not angry right now.

I deliberately summon the rage I felt when I saw that kidnapper about to shoot Rigel, then try again to fry my phone.

Still nothing.

Doubly relieved, I let my rage drain away, pushing away the vision of what followed it last night. Putting the phone away, I lie back down and actually manage to go back to sleep…without bothering Rigel.

Unfortunately, when my alarm goes off a couple hours later, it jerks me out of another, nastier dream about Faxon torturing my grandfather, Leontine, ahead of his scheduled execution. It takes some effort to shove the ugly scene from my mind, glad now I woke up when I did.

When I go down to breakfast, I still feel tired and grumpy. Also a little achy—probably a symptom of Rigel-deprivation. When I see Healer Ava this afternoon, I'll ask if she's tracked down that antidote yet.

Yesterday's freezing drizzle is now mixed with sleet when Molly and Tristan pick me up. I'd almost think my mood was affecting the weather if I didn't know how typical this is for early March in Indiana. On the way to school, I make the mistake of admitting how crappy I feel.

"Well, duh." Molly glances back at me. "You knew that would happen if you and Rigel stay apart too long. He's probably starting to feel yucky, too."

"Probably." Guilt assails me again. "At least I'm not locked up at NuAgra for the duration, thanks to you. That would be even worse." But safer? "This way we can at least see each other."

She shrugs. "True." I sense sympathy, but also impatience. "That should help. A little."

I manage to hide my irritation at her attitude until we reach the school parking lot. Once there, I get out first and hurry off, so Molly and Tristan can have a few minutes alone—that same precious slice of time I loved spending with Rigel.

It's sleeting harder now, so I run the last few steps to the building. I reach Pre-Cal early enough to mentally run back through some of Healer Ava's exercises. If nothing else, it keeps me from completely retreating into my thoughts, which are increasingly unpleasant.

Good morning, I missed you, Rigel thinks to me when he walks into the classroom. Even from across the room, his *brath* energizes me. Some of my achyness subsides, too. *Am I allowed to sit at my usual desk?* he asks then.

Instead of the more-or-less-cheery greeting I was about to send back, I frown. *Um, maybe not? If I happen to get pissed at something the teacher says—*

He gives an audible, disgusted snort. *Aren't you taking this a little far?*

If so, I refuse to admit it while he's so dismissive. *I killed a man the night before last, remember? I'd rather not take any chances.*

Fine. His irritation comes through loud and clear as he goes to an empty desk two rows over. Staying apart is making us both grumpy.

Molly and Tristan come in a moment later and look at us in surprise. Taking her usual seat next to me, on the opposite side from where Rigel normally sits, Molly whispers, "Are you *really* sure this is necessary?"

My glare makes her draw back.

"Don't you start, too," I hiss, then turn away. Don't any of them get it? They *saw* what I did Saturday night!

My mood continues to deteriorate over the next forty-five minutes. When the teacher calls on me, it's all I can do not to snap at him. Being in the same room as Rigel but unable to touch feels almost worse than being completely apart.

As we all leave the room after the bell, Rigel briefly gets close enough that his *brath* surrounds me. Instinctively, I sway toward him, then remember with a jolt why I can't and step away.

He notices—of course. *Sorry,* he silently apologizes. *I wasn't thinking.*

Neither was I. An overwhelming longing sweeps through me to reach out and take his hand—but I swiftly suppress it. *I'm sorry, too.*

French class is a little less frustrating without Rigel in the room. But Molly, Tristan and Kira are, and even though they don't say anything, I can feel them judging me. I avoid eye contact.

Chemistry is the worst. Rigel and I share a lab table, making it impossible to maintain a truly safe distance. His *brath* is magnetic, like it's trying to drag me closer to him. I respond by scooting my stool several more inches away and refusing to look at him.

He reaches out telepathically but I stubbornly block him, telling myself I've already heard all his arguments and don't need to hear them again. I rush off to Lit class when the bell rings—not that it does any good, since Rigel's in there, too.

Halfway through fourth period, I feel my first twinge of nausea— another symptom of Rigel-withdrawal. Ugh. He immediately senses it.

Let me help! he sends urgently from three desks away. *I'm not feeling so great, either.*

Guilt assails me, stronger than ever. I *deserve* to feel awful after what I did, but Rigel doesn't. Instead of replying, I slam my mental shields back up to keep him out of my head.

When the bell rings, I again try to escape quickly, but Rigel's closer to the door than I am. He reaches for me as I pass him, his eyes pleading. Though the temptation to let him touch me is overwhelming, I fiercely suppress it and jerk back before his fingers can brush mine. Out of the corner of my eye, I see Trina watching…and smirking.

A few minutes later, in the lunch line, I hear her obnoxious, nasal voice somewhere behind me.

"Whatever she's mad about, Rigel, I'm *sure* it's not your fault. But maybe this fight can have a silver lining, if you know what I mean? If Marsha's no longer interested, there are plenty of other, better girls who are. Like me. Now you have a chance to trade up."

Glancing back, I see Trina leaning in close to simper up at *my boyfriend*, both hands wrapped around his upper arm. Rage sweeps through me. I imagine blowing up Trina's head with a lightning bolt, like in that dream—only with Faxon's fierce relish instead of my own horror. I take a menacing step toward her, my tray forgotten.

Sensing my sudden fury, Rigel gives me a warning frown. In my current mood it feels like a betrayal, like he's choosing her over me.

Taking another step forward, I reach for his hand—but he pulls it away, shaking his head.

Just in time, the calm Rigel's frantically sending me penetrates and reason returns. But for how long?

Clinging to my temporary grip on sanity, I abandon my tray and flee the cafeteria without a backward look.

.•.

I spend the rest of lunch in the media center, keeping my mental blocks firmly in place as I go back over all Healer Ava's mental exercises. I practice the ones I can discreetly do in public, like deep breathing and muscle relaxation. Then I write out all the affirmations, which I still don't believe.

Anger is a choice. My emotions are mine to control. I am able to stop and think before reacting. I am capable of turning angry feelings into a learning experience. Stuff like that.

When the bell rings, I consider ditching the rest of the school day, then decide that's cowardly. Trina's not in fifth period Government, so that should be relatively safe. I hope.

Most my other friends are, so I get some curious looks when I walk in. Molly knows better than to ask why I ran off earlier, but my *Duchas* friends aren't so reticent.

"Hey, M, you okay?" Bri asks when I pass her and Deb. "What was the deal in the lunch line?"

"I, uh, remembered something really important I forgot to do," I lie. "Something I can't talk about here." I look around significantly at our non-Martian classmates.

They immediately take my implied meaning. "Oh! Right," Deb says. "No worries." Apparently satisfied, they start working on their joint project.

Rigel and I should be finishing ours, too, but he knows better than to suggest it. Instead, he mumbles something about research and retreats into his textbook. I do the same. If he's reaching out to me silently, I don't hear him. Maybe he's given up by now. I don't blame him. I wish I could block out my own thoughts, too.

Trina *is* in my sixth period Econ, but I sit as far from her as possible and avoid looking her way, afraid one of her smirks might set me off again. Rigel's in Weight Training this hour. I feel his occasional light touch on my mind, probably to gauge my mood, but he doesn't try "talking" to me.

Last period is Publications, but fortunately Angela, our editor, sends Rigel to the computer to troubleshoot the website, and me to the long layout table on the opposite side of the room, making it easy to avoid each other.

Missing lunch has made me surlier than ever, so I barely speak to Mr. O when he drives me to NuAgra that afternoon, though I do remember to thank him. Healer Ava was right. Going to school was a bad idea.

I stop by my quarters for a peanut butter sandwich and some milk before going to see her, but only manage to force down a couple bites, I'm feeling so queasy now.

"Good afternoon, Excellency," she greets me when I arrive. "I hope your first day back went…well?"

I close the door behind me and sit facing her desk. "I didn't hurt anyone, if that's what you mean."

She seems unsure whether my comment deserves a smile or not. "Did, ah, anything else untoward happen at home yesterday, or today during school?" she asks then. "Your monitor did pick up a few spikes in adrenaline and heart rate, though nothing *quite* severe enough to indicate a true emergency."

"I, um, got a little angry at my uncle when I first got home, but I went upstairs before doing anything about it, and it only took me a few minutes to calm back down. But at school today I got pretty mad at a cheerleader who's never liked me." That's putting it mildly! "I *wanted* to hurt her but I just…left in a hurry again."

Now Healer Ava does smile. "Then it sounds as though your sister was right about your progress. Until you're able to control your anger completely, leaving when you're upset is a much healthier way to respond than lashing out. Are you finding the techniques I gave you helpful?"

"Some. Going off by myself and taking deep breaths seems to help the most." I don't tell her how stupid I think the affirmations are.

She asks more questions I answer as honestly as I can, including whether I'm still keeping my distance from Rigel.

"Yes, but it's hard on both of us. We're already not feeling great, which definitely isn't helping my mood."

She surprises me by smiling. "Then you'll be pleased to know Healer Morag sent some of the antidote you mentioned along with her grandson when he returned from Nuath. The Healers in Bailerealta are having it shipped here. It should arrive tomorrow."

"Oh. That's really good." *It won't fix my main problem, but if it keeps Rigel from getting sicker, I'll at least feel less guilty.*

To tide me over, she prescribes me some nutritional supplements to compensate for my lack of appetite, then talks me through a few more calming exercises.

After an hour, I get up to go. "Thanks again," I say, though I don't feel any better than when I got here. Maybe worse. "I'll come back tomorrow."

"I look forward to it, Excellency. I should have the antidote for you and your young man by then." She bows as I leave.

Mr. O'Gara mentioned when he dropped me off that Mr. Stuart would be driving me home, so I go outside to meet him…only to see Rigel's car waiting at the curb! My initial surge of elation quickly gives way to panic—and then I realize it's Rigel's dad behind the wheel, not Rigel.

He puts down the passenger window. "Ready to go home, Excellency?"

Swallowing back a rebuke for scaring me like that, I force a smile. "Yes. Thanks, Mr. Stuart."

"Rigel suggested I take his car, as it has more security features," he explains as I get in.

I press my lips together, grateful but guiltier than ever. Rigel's still trying to take care of me, even while I keep pushing him away. Though his dad speaks pleasantly, when I focus, I sense some suppressed resentment. He probably also thinks I'm overreacting by staying away from Rigel…and making his son suffer.

"Healer Ava's having some of the antidote Rigel's grandmother made in Nuath sent here," I blurt out. "It's supposed to get here tomorrow."

Mr. Stuart's brows go up. "That's good to hear. I assumed Morag hadn't sent any back with Rigel, as she seemed certain a single dose would provide permanent results."

"It mostly did, until he and I re-bonded last fall. Along with restoring Rigel's erased memories, that must have undone the antidote. We both felt pretty yucky when we had to be apart this past Thanksgiving."

"Yes, I remember. When I get home, I'll share the good news with Rigel and his mother. She's been worried."

Yet another reason to feel guilty.

I make myself eat a cookie and a little more milk when I get home, then attempt some homework at the kitchen table.

Aunt Theresa gets home fifteen minutes later. "Marsha, did you remember to put the laundry in the dryer?" she asks before even saying hello. Normally that doesn't bother me, I'm so used to it.

Today, I stand up and glare at her. "Do you think I'm your servant?" I demand. "Maybe you've forgotten, but I happen to be Sovereign of every single Martian on Earth *and* on Mars, a quarter of a million people."

Gaping, she takes a hasty step backward. "I...I... Never mind," she stammers. "I'm sorry. I'll do it myself."

Her expression reminds me of how various underlings looked when Faxon lashed out. Which makes me realize I sounded exactly like him just now.

"Sorry," I mutter, though I'm not. I'm still pissed. Not safe.

Hastily gathering up my books, I hurry up to my room, lock the door, then just stand there, breathing hard.

What's *wrong* with me? Those stupid exercises are supposed to be helping, but I feel like I'm getting worse. Twice today—when Trina came on to Rigel at lunch, and just now downstairs—I felt more like Faxon than myself. Am I turning into a soulless monster, too?

I throw down my books to do jumping jacks until my heart is pounding and I'm gasping for breath. Then I force out all the pushups my arms will let me, determined to exhaust myself. It doesn't take long, with my energy reserves so low from avoiding Rigel.

After that, I go to the bathroom for a glass of water and a quick shower, then put a sign on my bedroom door asking Aunt Theresa to leave my dinner outside it. Safest if I don't try to interact with anyone else today.

M? Rigel's mental "voice" is tentative. *Are you willing to talk to me yet?*

A wave of longing sweeps through me to hear his voice for real, to touch him. Kiss him. I suppress it. *Maybe in a bit,* I reply after a moment. *I'm going to try to take a nap.*

Yeah, good idea. I'm pretty tired, too. We'll talk later, okay?

I don't answer. Though I hadn't actually planned on a nap, it suddenly seems like a good idea—if I can avoid any more awful dreams.

29

Belief perseverance
RIGEL

WHEN M DOESN'T ANSWER me, I start to reach for her mind again—and then back off. I'm pretty sure she made up that bit about a nap just to shut me up, but at least she let me in for a minute. First time since this morning.

She's beyond messed up right now, but nothing I can say or do from this distance will help. It's obvious to me what will, but she'll shut me back out if I suggest it again. Damn Faxon, anyway. It's *his* fault I feel like crap, not M's.

I try to do some homework, but I'm too worried about her to concentrate. On top of Faxon screwing with her mind, she's got to feel every bit as gross as I do.

After a few minutes, I can't resist testing her mood again. To my surprise, she really is asleep. Guess she wasn't lying about that nap after all. I yawn. I may as well take one, too. I wasn't kidding about being tired.

I wake to a gentle tapping on my door.

"Yeah?" I mumble.

"Dinner's ready, Rigel." It's my mom. "If you feel like joining us?"

Staying apart from M makes me grouchy, but I've tried not to take it out on my parents. Even so, they have to know I'm not feeling my best.

"Yeah, okay. Be down in a minute." I hit the bathroom, then go downstairs. Mom and Dad are already seated at the kitchen table.

"Good news, Rigel," Dad says as I join them. "The Healers in Bailerealta had some of the antidote serum you and M were given in Nuath last summer and they've agreed to send it to Jewel. It should arrive sometime tomorrow."

This is a gut punch I wasn't expecting. "Who told you that? M?"

"Yes, when I drove her home from NuAgra this afternoon. The Mind Healer inquired about the antidote at M's request. They both must feel the two of you should avoid touching for a while longer."

"How much longer?" I demand. "Did she say?"

Dad shakes his head, his expression sympathetic. "I'm sorry. I realize this isn't easy for either of you, son, but the antidote should at least alleviate the physical side effects."

I stare at him, struggling with a feeling of betrayal. Why would M tell my dad about this but not me? Not that she's telling me much of anything these days.

"Well, forget it. I'm not taking any stupid antidote. M can if she wants, but—" I break off.

"Rigel," Mom says gently. "I'm sure M doesn't want you to get sick any more than she wants to get sick herself. If she and Mind Healer Ava both agree it's safest—"

"Right, it's not like I should get a say." I shove to my feet. "I'm not hungry after all. Maybe I'll have a snack or something later." I'll have to at least pretend to eat sometime, or mom might try to sneak that stupid antidote into me when it gets here. Not that I'll let her.

Back upstairs, I pace my room. There must be *some* way I can make M see reason! Why can't she understand our bond has a better chance of curing her than anything a Mind Healer can do? Probably because she's not thinking straight right now.

Hoping she's awake again by now, too, I cautiously reach out to her. *Hey,* I send long distance. *Did you get a good nap?*

Half to my surprise, she answers. *I don't know about good, but I got a nap. How about you?*

Yeah, I slept some, too. Are you feeling a little better now?

I think so. For the moment. Thanks, by the way, for not letting me electrocute Trina at lunch. I really did want to for a minute.

I could tell. But you didn't. Remember I said I wouldn't let you do anything like that again? I won't. I could probably keep you from getting angry at all if you'd just let me—

Don't, Rigel, she interrupts. *Don't start again. I can't risk it. I won't.*

But—

Before I can finish my thought, she blocks me, her mental shields going up so she can't hear me—and I can't hear her.

"Dammit!" I say aloud. How can I help her if she won't even listen to me?

In desperation, I call Molly.

"Rigel?" she answers in surprise. "What's up?"

"What do you think? M. She keeps shutting me out and I don't know what to do."

Molly hesitates a sec before saying, "Neither do I. She won't talk to me, either. I've tried, but every time I even hint she should rethink this separation thing, she bites my head off. Making her angry again doesn't seem like the best plan."

"She's angry most of the time anyway," I admit. "She was ready to throttle Trina in the lunch line today—or worse—until I warned her off. You convinced the Council she's getting better and I wanted to believe it, too. But she's not. I think she's getting worse—and she knows it. It's making her even more determined to stay away from me. She's...she's having some of that antidote my grandmother made in Nuath brought here to Jewel."

I hear a gasp from Molly's end. "Does that mean she's planning to let them lock her up after all?"

"I don't know *what* she's planning. She won't talk to me. In fact, she can hardly think rationally at all now. I know I can help, but—"

"She keeps shutting you out. I know. I'm sorry. I feel awful for both of you. And for me, too, especially if M appoints me Acting Sovereign after all. Ugh. My mum… One of us *has* to get through to her, Rigel! I'll try again tomorrow."

"Thanks, Molly." I doubt she'll have any more luck than I have, but I'll take all the help I can get. Except that antidote. Going that route would feel like giving up on M—something I'll never, ever do.

30

Learned helplessness

I WAKE up the next morning more tired than when I went to bed. Even though I napped for over two hours, then went back to bed for another ten, I feel like I hardly slept at all. I definitely dreamed, though, because I distinctly remember two more unpleasant scenes from Faxon's past, and yet another awful replay of Saturday night.

Rigel attempted our usual bedtime "chat" but I cut him off. Now I feel guilty and stupid for doing that. Maybe it would have helped? It did the night before. Or maybe not. Whenever he suggests abandoning my plan, I feel worse about what I'm doing to him. To us. And the guiltier I feel, the angrier I get. At myself. And at Faxon, whose twisted mind did this to me and keeps doing it.

Sitting up, I check my omni like I always do first thing and find another private message from Shim.

Excellency, my grandson reached out to me last night to tell me the situation from his perspective. Much as he might wish me to, I don't feel qualified to countermand anything a trained Mind Healer recommends, and I told him as much. I do, however, feel comfortable advising you to never underestimate the power of the bond you share with Rigel. I feel certain that power is far greater than anyone, to include the two of you, yet realizes. Also know, my dear Emileia, that I will support you in whatever you do.

Always your faithful servant, Shim

Frowning, I read through the brief message twice more. The power of our bond? That's what I used to murder a man. Is Shim suggesting I might do even worse things if I'm not careful? I'm sure he's right.

That certainty is reinforced while I'm getting ready for school. The wire hanger holding the blouse I plan to wear tangles with the next one —which is enough to infuriate me. Instead of carefully separating them, like I usually would, I scream, yank both off the rod and fling them on the floor. Even then, I have trouble getting them apart. By the time I do, I'm flushed and breathing heavily, struggling—again—to get my temper back under control.

I've always felt off-kilter whenever I'm away from Rigel a little too long, making me clumsier and more irritable than usual. Now, though, it seems like the tiniest mishap is enough to turn that unsettled feeling into anger, even fury, without warning.

By the time I go downstairs, I'm more than half tempted to skip school entirely. Surely the safest thing would be to tell Aunt Theresa— and everyone else—I don't feel well and just stay home. But for how long? For good? Drop out of school completely? I want to believe I can eventually be cured, but—

"Ah, good, you're up early." Aunt Theresa bustles into the kitchen. "Do you think you can eat breakfast rather quickly? Molly called a few minutes ago to ask if I can drop you at school today, as she's tied up."

The look she gives me is both wary and curious. She's probably worried I'll blow up again, and she knows Rigel normally drives me— but I don't try to explain.

"Oh. Sure. I was only going to have some orange juice and a piece of toast anyway." I manage a few sips of juice and three or four bites of toast, then declare myself ready.

Aunt Theresa continues darting questioning looks my way during the drive, but I ignore her. I'm working too hard to stay myself, stay in the present, to worry about anything else.

When we pull up to the school, I see Molly, Tristan, Sean and Kira waiting out front, despite the still-crappy weather. Watching me. Safety in numbers? I thank my aunt for the ride and walk over to them.

"What's this? An intervention?"

Though I try to say it lightly, nobody smiles.

"Sort of, I guess?" Molly admits when no one else answers me. "We all remember how awful it felt to be apart this past Thanksgiving and want to spare you and Rigel from going through that again. None of us believe staying apart like this is still necessary. Not now."

Their concern is touching, but I shake my head. "No, it really is. You don't know—" I break off.

"Then tell us," Molly prompts, her eyes wide and concerned. "Please, M. We're your friends."

I hesitate for a long moment, then give in. "Okay. I may not be digging into Faxon's memories on purpose now, but I can't stop dreaming about them. He's still here, in my head. Every time I get the least bit upset, I start feeling the things he'd feel and want to do the things he'd do. So far I've avoided getting violent again, but I still lash out with words. To you. To my aunt. Even to Rigel. As long as he's out of my reach, I can't do much worse than that. Otherwise…"

"You really think you'd hurt someone?" Sean looks skeptical.

"Maybe? Yesterday in the lunch line, I sure wanted to hurt Trina. I honestly think I would have, if Rigel had been right next to me."

Molly huffs out an impatient breath. "Come on, M. Not saying Trina didn't deserve it—I saw how she was playing up to Rigel—but I can't believe you'd *ever* use deadly force unless you were directly threatened."

"I'm not sure that's true. In some of the dreams I've had…" Though I hadn't planned to, I describe my horrible dream from Saturday night, where I killed them all. On purpose. "I know it was just a dream," I conclude, "but I really am afraid if I lose control and have Rigel with me, I might kill someone before he could stop me. Maybe even someone I care about. I can't risk it. I *won't* risk it."

They all fall silent for a moment, then Kira asks, "Isn't the Mind Healer giving you something to help?"

"Just a bunch of mental exercises and affirmations. I asked about drugs, but she says the ones that work on *Duchas* are mostly ineffective on *Echtrans* because we're resistant to most drugs. I *have* been using the exercises she gave me, but they're not helping yet. In fact, I'm getting worse," I continue miserably. "Yesterday I got pissed at my aunt for something she does all the time and it was like Faxon was talking with my voice. The antidote is supposed to arrive in Jewel today, to keep Rigel from getting any sicker. Which is good, because I think Healer Ava was right to begin with. I should be committed."

Molly puts an arm around my shoulders. "No. You're strong enough to beat this, M, I know you are. We'll help all we can. Rigel can help even more, if you'll let him."

Abruptly annoyed, I step away from her. "I told you, I *can't*. You've seen how much electricity our bond can generate, how powerful it is." Shim's caution echoes in my mind. "It's just too dangerous."

"But—" The warning bell rings, cutting off whatever Molly was going to say.

Just as well. Before my irritation can turn into anger, I turn away from her worried face. "Come on. We'd better get to class."

Today's even worse than yesterday, in every sense. In Pre-Cal, the urge to give in and touch Rigel is stronger than ever—and having to resist it makes me grouchier and grouchier. So does blocking him when he tries again…and again…to reach out to me. I hated it when he did that to me last year, so I know how much he must hate it now.

Will it make him hate *me?* I'm still haunted by the way he looked at me at the end of that first awful dream…

Toward the end of second period French, I give in to the temptation to eavesdrop on Rigel and Trina, both in Spanish class just two rooms away.

As I suspected, Trina's taking advantage. "If Marsha keeps giving you the brush-off," I hear her whispering—in his *ear?*— "you really need to move on."

"It's not like that," he replies. "We're just taking a little…break, that's all."

Trina sniffs audibly. "I don't blame you, anyone would need breaks from a brat like that. If you're smart, and I *know* you are, you'll make this break a permanent one."

He doesn't answer and a moment later the bell rings.

Seething—again—I walk with Molly to Chemistry, where I see Trina and Rigel entering the classroom just ahead of us. There's a sound of distant thunder, getting closer. Clenching my jaw, I walk faster—until Molly grabs my arm.

M! You can't *let Trina get to you,* she silently insists. *You know she'd love to get you in trouble.*

I nod and slow down, but the low rumbling doesn't stop. I'm still steaming when I walk into the room—and come face to face with a smirking Trina.

"I always knew you're not as smart as you pretend, Marsha, but I guess you're even dumber than I thought. Looks like your little snit was *just* the nudge Rigel needed to realize how much better he can do than a loser orphan nobody like you."

"A nobody?" I echo, lifting my chin so I can look down my nose at her. "For your information, I'm the exact *opposite* of a nobody! You're just a stupid cheerleader at a podunk school, but I'm—"

Molly jumps between us before I can finish. "Shut up, Trina, before your ridiculous ego gets you in trouble. You think you're the queen of the school but half the time people are laughing at you behind your back —even your so-called friends. Trust me, I've heard them. Plenty of times."

Trina's smirk becomes a glare—at Molly. "And who do you think *you* are?" she demands. "Another nobody, that's who. The only reason you're popular at all is because I took pity on you and let you on the cheer squad. Obviously a mistake."

Molly laughs. "Well you can take your pity and shove it, Trina, because I'm done. Find yourself another flyer. C'mon, M."

Grabbing my arm again, Molly steers me to my lab table, where Rigel looks nearly as dumbfounded as everyone else in the room.

"That was quick thinking, Molly," he says in the sub-whisper no *Duchas* can possibly hear, then turns a concerned glance on me. "You okay now?"

I shake my head, appalled at how close I came to telling Trina and everyone in the room that I'm the Martian Sovereign. Not that anyone would have believed me, but still…

"No. Definitely not okay," I force out through clenched teeth. "I'll be lucky if I make it through the day without throttling her."

"M." His voice is gentle now, and I can sense both him and Molly trying to soothe me. "It's obvious staying apart is making you worse instead of better. As soon as you're calm again, you *have* to let me—"

Even though he knows better than to reach for me right now, I jump away from him, sending my lab stool clattering. "No! I can't! You don't know—"

"Then tell me," he murmurs, righting my stool. *Please,* he adds silently as the room quiets down.

But I can't find the words to explain what I'm feeling—like I could fly apart into a million dangerous shards of rage at any moment, hurting anyone in my path. And that's just me by myself. The lightning bolts we can generate together would make it a thousand times worse.

Frustrated by my inability to communicate that, I pull my stool to the far end of the lab table and slam my mental shields into place. Again.

Then I spend the whole period naming my triggers and reciting affirmations in my head. All the stuff that's *supposed* to help me control my temper. Rigel picks up the slack on the Chem lab I should be helping with. Of course. Which makes me feel even guiltier.

All through Lit class I still feel like a powder keg, ready to explode if Trina so much as looks my way. Sensing my mood, Rigel ignores her completely, even when she talks directly to him. I still want to blast her into dust.

I consider skipping lunch again, but because that made me even grumpier yesterday, I go to the cafeteria for water and a fruit cup I can take to the media center. Up ahead in the line, Rigel is keeping a safe distance from Trina. Safer for her, that is.

Afraid she'll set me off again anyway, I try not to look at her—which is why I don't notice her stopping just past the cashier to wait for me.

"So, Marsha, what were you about to say to me at the start of Chemistry? Something about how very *important* you are?" she snarks.

That low rumbling begins again and I have to fight a strong urge to knock her stupid tray out of her hands. "Nothing you'd understand, Trina. Get out of my way."

I start to go around her, but she moves to block my path.

"No, I really want to know. Because the only thing that ever made you even the tiniest bit important in your whole pathetic life was hooking up with the star quarterback. Now you're stupid enough to throw even *that* away. I may only be head cheerleader of a podunk school, but you're nothing. Lower than dirt. Even your own *parents* didn't want you."

They're all words I've heard from her before. Words I can usually let roll off my back. Not today.

The low rumbling erupts into a roar and I lash out the way Faxon attacked anyone who questioned his authority—physically as well as verbally. Furious, I lunge forward and both her tray and mine crash to the ground.

"You're the pathetic one, you stupid *Duchas*!" I scream, aiming a vicious knife-hand strike at her throat. "You have no idea—!"

"No!" Molly seizes my arm from behind in time to prevent what could have been a killing blow. "M, you can't!"

Trina backs away, her eyes wide. "She's crazy! Totally nuts! Keep her away from me!"

Her sudden fear elates me. I try to pull out of Molly's grasp, but

Tristan steps up, taking a firm grip on my left arm while Molly keeps hold of my right. They both flood me with calm thoughts. My rumbling increases for an instant, then gradually starts to subside. As the red fog of rage clears from my vision, I see Rigel hurrying toward us.

"Don't!" Molly cries before he can touch me. "It's not safe yet." She tugs on my arm. "C'mon, M," she says quietly, still projecting calm with that new talent of hers. "Tristan and I will take you to the school nurse. You're obviously not feeling well." That last bit is loud enough for others to hear.

I continue to resist for an instant, still determined to make Trina *finally* pay for all her nastiness over the years. But then the combined calm from Molly, Tristan and now Rigel penetrates and I go limp. "Okay," I whisper. "Let's go."

Though I'm no longer resisting, Molly and Tristan keep holding onto me even after we leave the lunchroom.

"You okay now?" Molly asks as we near the front office. "I'm…I'm really sorry I didn't believe you this morning. You weren't kidding about how badly the whole Faxon thing affected you—way more than I realized. I guess maybe my compromise wasn't such a great idea after all."

Just then my pocket vibrates. "It's my omni," I tell them. "Can I—?"

After a second, Tristan reluctantly loosens his hold so I can pull it out. It's a message from Healer Ava.

Excellency, it's imperative that you return to NuAgra immediately! Your mental state is deteriorating rapidly, based on the readings I just received from your monitor. You are simply not safe to be around other people right now, particularly Duchas. *If I don't hear from you within the next few minutes, I'm afraid I'll be forced to send a security detail after you.*

Wordlessly, I show Molly the screen.

She frowns while reading it, then looks at me. "Do you think she's right?"

"Yes." I swallow. "I think she is. If you hadn't stopped me, I might have killed Trina right there in the cafeteria. If Rigel had touched me, I absolutely would have. I'm sure of it. They need to lock me away until I'm cured. If that's even possible."

I imagine spending the rest of my life in a padded cell—thanks to Faxon. He'd love that, if he knew.

When we get to the front office, Molly takes me to Cormac instead of the school nurse. Fortunately, he's there, his door open. He looks up in surprise as we enter and Tristan closes the door behind us.

"Excellencies." He stands and bows. "Is there something I can do for you?"

I'm about to ask if he can drive me to NuAgra, but Molly speaks up first.

"M just had an, er, incident with Trina Squires in the cafeteria. We thought we should tell you before anyone else does. All she really did was knock Trina's tray out of her hands, but I'm sure Trina will describe it differently, to make M look as bad as possible."

He raises his eyebrows. "I see. Excellency?"

I nod. "She made me mad and I, um, kind of lost control. Mind Healer Ava—"

Molly jumps in again before I can finish. "Mind Healer Ava just messaged she'd like to see M as soon as possible. If you'll give Tristan and me a pass, we can drive her to NuAgra as soon as we check in with our fifth period teacher."

Cormac shoots a concerned glance at me, but nods. "Very well. I'll go to the cafeteria now to see if any students are willing to give statements about what happened. I'm sure it can be minimized to avoid drawing undue attention."

"Will you be okay here for a few minutes?" Molly asks me as soon as he's gone.

"I...I think so." I sit down in the chair across from Cormac's desk. "I'll message Healer Ava to expect me within half an hour. But make sure Trina stays away from the office while I'm here, okay?"

"We will," Molly promises. "And we'll tell Ms. Kowalski and everyone else you're sick, okay?"

I nod again. "Thanks. And tell Rigel...tell him I'm sorry. See you soon."

With last, worried looks over their shoulders, Molly and Tristan leave, closing the door behind them.

After two minutes of deep breathing, I message Healer Ava, then reach out mentally to Rigel.

Did Molly and Tristan tell you what the Mind Healer said? I ask.

Yeah, they did, he instantly replies. *But you're not really going to let her lock you up, are you?*

I think I have to. Before I really do kill someone else. That taekwondo move I tried to use on Trina could have, even without your help. I'm not safe around people. At all.

There's a pause before he responds. *For how long? And where?*

I don't know, I admit. *For as long as the Healers think it's necessary. Maybe Dun Cloch? They have real holding cells there, and more Mind Healers than NuAgra does. I'm sorry, Rigel. So sorry. For everything.*

31

Commitment

I SPEND the next ten minutes alternating between despair and self-recrimination, with occasional spurts of anger. Mostly at Faxon, the main one at fault for all this, but also at Trina. And at my friends and even Rigel, who stubbornly refused to understand until I nearly killed again.

I also worry, a lot, about what will happen if the Mind Healers insist on removing me to Dun Cloch for days, weeks, even months. That antidote is supposedly on its way here, but what if we're now immune to it? We did both get sick over Thanksgiving.

If it doesn't work, Rigel will keep getting sicker and sicker, which is totally unfair to him. So will I, but at least I deserve it. But whether it works or not, I have to let them lock me up. It's the only way to guarantee I can't hurt anyone else.

Except Rigel.

That thought torments me more than all the others.

Cormac opens the door. "Excellency, your sister and Tristan Roark are here to drive you to NuAgra, if you're ready."

Sighing, I stand. "I'm ready. Thanks, Cormac."

Molly and Tristan are waiting for me in the outer office, wearing twin expressions of wary concern.

I half expected Rigel to be with them, but he's not. I should be relieved, but I feel a stab of disappointment. What if we can't see each other again for days? Weeks? Longer? I thought he'd at least want to say goodbye in person before I'm locked away from him.

"How are you doing?" Molly asks as I join them. "Better?"

"Better than at lunch." I don't feel an urge to explode at this exact moment, anyway. "Let's go."

When we step outside, the icy drizzle has finally stopped, but it's still overcast. I sense high levels of nervousness from both Molly and Tristan as we cross the parking lot. They have good reason, I've been acting so irrationally. But I hate that even my closest friends are afraid of me now.

"Would you guys feel more comfortable letting a NuAgra security detail take me out there?" I ask when we reach Tristan's Porsche. "I'll totally understand if you do."

Molly flashes me a startled glance. "What? No! Of course not. We're driving you, just like we promised. Right, Tristan?"

He nods, but a look passes between them that makes me wonder if they did consider backing out. Only because I'm fairly sure I can hold it together for the fifteen-minute drive to NuAgra, I get into the back seat without arguing.

"What is Trina saying?" I ask after a few minutes, when their silence starts getting to me. "Have you heard? Is she threatening to press charges?"

Tristan chuckles. "She apparently made some noises like that at first. But when Cormac and others pointed out that her damages only amounted to a spilled lunch and a well-deserved scare, she realized how dumb that was."

"Not to mention the flak she's already getting from the rest of the cheer squad for me quitting," Molly adds. "They don't have another decent flyer."

Another wave of guilt hits me. "Don't quit just because of me, Molly. Especially since I probably won't be back at school anytime soon."

"It's not just because of you. Trina's been getting on my last nerve for months now," she assures me. I wish I could believe her.

The closer we get to NuAgra, the more depressed I feel. I'm messing up the lives of the two people I care most about in the world, not to mention my own. Molly will eventually be fine as Acting Sovereign, but I'm less sure about Rigel. He hasn't tried to reach me telepathically since I told him I was sorry and I don't dare reach out to him now. What more can I say, besides *I'm sorry*?

We're almost to NuAgra when Tristan suddenly slows and turns left —into the gravel drive where we faced that mob Saturday night. Where *I*—

"What are you doing?" I exclaim.

"Keeping a promise," he replies, his tension evident in the set of his shoulders.

We round the corner of the old gas station and I see the field where all the protesters' vehicles were parked that night. It's empty now except for a single car. Rigel's. As we pull to a stop, he gets out.

"What is this?" My voice is panicky now. "Some crazy plot you all cooked up to make me return to the scene of the crime? Don't you realize how dangerous this is?"

"Only if Tristan and I stick around," Molly says. "We promised Rigel that before handing you over to the Mind Healers, we'd give him a chance to talk to you. Alone. That way the only risk is to him. He swears he's more than ready to take that risk."

Molly opens her car door and pushes her seat forward for me. At the same time, Rigel starts walking toward us, a grim, determined smile on his face. The face I was afraid I'd never see again. How many times have I had that exact same fear? Way too many. Even so—

"This is a bad idea," I insist, now feeling betrayed as well as panicky. "You need to take me to NuAgra, Tristan. Now."

"Nope." There's no wavering in his tone. "If you don't want to risk hurting Molly and me, you should get out of the car." Rigel's nearly reached us. "Like now," Tristan adds.

I still hesitate.

"M?" At the panic in Molly's voice, I vividly recall electrocuting her, then Tristan in my horrible dream, in this very place. Terrified that vision could become reality, I scramble out.

"I'm out. Now go!"

Rigel pauses while Tristan turns the car around.

"Let us know how it goes," Molly calls out the window as they head back to the road.

Swallowing, I turn to face Rigel. "Why are you doing this?" I whisper. "You're the very *last* person I want to hurt."

His smile goes crooked, twisting my heart along with it. "I know. And you won't—definitely no more than you've already been hurting me—hurting both of us—these past few days. I love you, M. Don't you love me?"

"Of course!" I exclaim. "You know I do. That's why—"

"Then prove it." He takes two quick steps forward, bringing him within arm's reach. "You were always willing to fight for our love in the past, no matter who was threatening it. Why won't you do it now?"

I frown, confused. "Who do I fight? Myself? The monster Faxon has turned me into? How do I do that?"

"M." Another step and now his hands are on my shoulders, sending strength and vitality surging through me. Through both of us.

I shudder with relief, even as part of my mind is screaming this is wrong. Dangerous. But is that *my* mind? Or Faxon's? I don't know anymore.

"M," he repeats. "Our love, our bond, saved the whole world last fall, don't you remember? Why would you think it's not strong enough to save you now?"

"I...I..." I shake my head and try to back away. "That was before I turned into a monster."

Instead of releasing me, he pulls me closer. "You're not a monster, M, you're a hero. Faxon is the monster. You stopped him from killing thousands of people. Tens of thousands. Thanks to you, he'll never have power or influence again. The only bit left is the hold he still has on your mind. It's time to strip him of *that* power, too."

I stare helplessly up at Rigel. "How? Healer Ava says my mental state is still deteriorating, even though I've been doing everything she told me to."

"Hey." He gives my shoulders a little shake. "The Mind Healers also told you the year they erased from my memory was gone forever, remember? They were wrong. Because of our bond. Don't underestimate what it can do."

Shim's message this morning said the same thing. I assumed he meant the damage our bond could cause. But maybe he meant—?

"Saturday night, when I told you I wouldn't let you hurt anyone, you believed me," Rigel reminds me. "You trusted me. Trust me now, M."

My heart pounding crazily, I nod. "I do trust you, Rigel. Always."

"Good." He smiles, then lowers his lips to mine. The kiss, our first kiss in days, vibrates through me, touching every cell in my body. As Rigel deepens the kiss, I cling to him, gratefully absorbing the healing our bond imparts—not only to my body, but also my mind. All the confusion and anger melts away, leaving clarity in its wake.

Yes! he exults silently, his mouth still on mine. *I can feel you coming back to yourself, becoming my M again. Let's banish Faxon back to oblivion, where he belongs.*

As we continue kissing, my memories of Faxon's horrific deeds start to fade until they're more like dreams barely recalled than atrocities I experienced. Committed. Instead, I start remembering wonderful moments from my own life—all involving Rigel. All the close calls we've had that ended happily. And how very much we love each other.

Several ecstatic minutes later, he lifts his head to gaze at me. "Thank you," he says. "For letting me help."

"You mean finally?" A shaky laugh escapes me. "You did more than help, you just performed a miracle! Thank you, Rigel. For not giving up on me even when I did."

"I'll never give up on you, M. And don't you ever give up on us. Okay?"

I smile the first real smile I've managed in days. "I won't," I promise. Just then, the sun comes out, warming us both. I turn my smile up to it for a grateful moment before looking at Rigel again. "So…now what?"

He wraps an arm around my shoulders. "Mind Healer Ava is expecting you, right? I guess we should go see her. See if she thinks you're still a danger to anyone. Because I don't."

"Neither do I. Not now." My mind is finally my own again. Thanks to Rigel. "But I guess we should see if her tests agree."

Hand in hand, we turn toward Rigel's car. Together. Just as we should be.

⁘

As Rigel drives the rest of the way to NuAgra, I send a quick message to Molly with the good news. In the parking lot, we indulge in a few more delicious kisses before getting out. With each one, I feel myself growing stronger. More mentally sound.

Even so, I can't help feeling a teensy bit nervous when I knock on Healer Ava's door a few minutes later. What if she doesn't believe me?

"Come," she calls.

The door opens and I'm startled to see two burly security guards flanking her desk. She seems similarly startled to see Rigel with me.

"Excellency!" She rises, her alarm evident. "I thought we agreed—"

"I know," I interrupt. "We were wrong. Staying away from Rigel was the exact *worst* thing I could have done. If I'd been thinking more clearly, I'd have known that, but I wasn't. Now I am."

Her brows draw down in a frown. "The readings from your wrist monitor—"

"Were accurate at the time, I'm sure," I finish. "I really was a danger to others. I'd just proven it, in fact. I don't think I am now, though. What does my monitor say?"

Dubiously, she checks her omni—then her brows go up. "Completely normal levels, both physically and mentally. I don't see how that's possible, less than an hour after those earlier readings."

I smile up at Rigel. "No, you probably don't, but I do. Impossible as it might seem to you, I'm perfectly okay now. Is there a test I can take to prove it?"

Though she still looks uncomfortable, she nods. "Repeating the one you took Sunday morning will give us the most comprehensive results. I'll send it to your omni now—though I must warn you against expecting any significant change so soon."

"Thanks. I consider myself warned. I'll take the test as soon as I get home and send it back to you the moment I finish. If you still think it's necessary after analyzing the results, I promise to come back so you can lock me up."

"Very well, Excellency. The new test should be on your omni now. We'll talk again after you return it to me."

I thank her again and leave her office, still hand in hand with Rigel.

We take our time getting home, stopping along the way for another lengthy makeout session. We still have a lot of catching up to do. Every kiss makes me feel that much stronger and healthier in mind and body. How on Earth did I ever think staying apart could be a *good* thing?

Even with that wonderfully rejuvenating delay, I'm home a solid hour early, so I go upstairs and take my followup psych test while I have the house to myself. It's not nearly as upsetting or draining this time.

Still, I'm surprised when Healer Ava messages me a mere twenty minutes after I send it back to her.

Excellency, I'm very happy to report that the results of your most recent test confirm what you told me earlier, as do your continued normal wrist monitor readings. Though I told the Echtran Council it was conceivable your mental health could rebound as rapidly as it deteriorated, I confess I considered it extremely unlikely. I would like you to continue wearing the monitor for at least another week just to be certain, but clearly there are more aspects to a graell bond than the published research has indicated. When your duties allow, I would welcome an opportunity to discuss it with you.

Speaking of those duties, I still feel it would be very beneficial for you to delegate as many as you can. This latest test, while well within normal parameters, indicates a higher level of stress than is usually seen someone your age. You've proven yourself more than capable as Sovereign to our people, but it seems unreasonable to expect you to shoulder the full burdens of your position before you've completed your formal education. I hope you'll strongly consider taking my advice in this area.

I already promised Rigel I'd do exactly that, so I compose a message to Kyna on the spot, asking if she'll consider acting as temporary Regent while still continuing as head of the *Echtran* Council. There's another idea I want to float past Molly, but I'll wait till tomorrow to do that.

After that, I record a video message for Shim. I figure my good news will be more believable if he can see and hear me when I share it. At the end, I thank him for his reminder about my bond with Rigel. As always, he was right.

Aunt Theresa gets home just as I finish. I run downstairs to cheerily greet her before throwing in a load of laundry without being told.

✦

The next morning Rigel picks me up for school, greeting me with our usual good morning kiss. It feels more right than ever, making me appreciate "normal" in a way I never have before.

Molly, Tristan, Sean and Kira are again waiting outside the school when we arrive, but unlike yesterday, they're all smiles.

"Molly told us your good news," Kira says when we join them. "We're all super relieved. We were so worried about you."

"I'll try really hard not to say, 'I told you so,'" Molly adds with a grin. "But...I told you so."

Her smugness at being right doesn't dampen my mood, it just makes me laugh. "You did. So did Rigel. I really wish I'd listened sooner, but better late than...*too* late."

I shudder to think how close I came to letting myself be locked away from Rigel for who knows how long. My mental state would almost certainly have kept going downhill no matter what the Healers did. The only *real* cure for me was Rigel. I smile up at him gratefully—again.

First and second period are only remarkable by how massively better

I feel than this time yesterday. Even so, I experience a twinge of nervousness as I approach Chemistry class. This will be my first time facing Trina since yesterday's incident. The first true test of my miraculous recovery.

Sure enough, she confronts me the second I walk in.

"Seriously? I can't *believe* they let you come back to school, Marsha, after you attacked me *again* yesterday! How many times does it take to prove you're a menace? At least you didn't break my nose this time. The only reason I didn't press charges is because I was sure they'd finally suspend you."

"You still can if you'd like," I reply with a smile. To my immense relief, I don't hear even the faintest trace of Faxon-rumbling.

Her eyes narrow as she takes in Rigel's and my clasped hands. "Aren't you afraid to be this close to someone so obviously *unbalanced*, Rigel? She could turn on you next—you saw what she did yesterday. She's dangerous. Totally unpredictable."

"Not to me." The look he gives me melts my heart—again. "She knows that now, too."

Trina huffs out a snort, then turns to Molly, who's just come in behind us. "Hey, Molly, sorry about what I said to you yesterday." Her voice is now syrupy sweet. "I didn't mean it, you know, I was just mad at Marsha. You'll stay on the cheer squad, won't you?"

Molly regards her speculatively for a moment, then smiles. "Maybe. On one condition. You need to apologize to M, too."

Trina's blue eyes go wide. "To— No way! She tried to *hit* me at lunch yesterday, you saw it!"

"Because you kept taunting her, even when she tried to ignore you," Molly calmly reminds her. "What you said to her was way nastier than what you said to me."

"Only because it's true!" Trina spits out. "She's a disgusting little nobody and always has been. Why can't *anyone* else see that? Sorry, Molly, much as we need our flyer back, that's a price I can't pay." Whirling, she stomps off.

Molly turns to look at me with a trace of concern. "You okay?" she whispers.

Grinning, I nod. "Totally fine. Thanks to Rigel—and you. Neither of you ever gave up on me. But don't you want to cheer for Sean during the playoffs? She gave you a perfect opening to come back."

"I can cheer for him just fine from the bleachers," Molly replies with a shrug. "Better, with no stupid cheer routines to focus on instead of the game."

I regard her uncertainly, but my emotion-sensing ability confirms she means it. "In that case...since you won't have cheer practice, can you come by my house after school? There's something I'd like to talk about —privately."

"Sure, but what—?"

The teacher calls the class to order then, cutting her off. I just smile.

To keep Molly from questioning me over lunch, I suggest to Rigel we eat alone in the courtyard, since the sun's still shining today. He readily agrees.

Molly's waiting on my front porch when Rigel drops me off that afternoon. If she and Tristan cut their after-school parking time short— unlike us—she must be *really* curious to hear what I have to say. I hope that's a good sign.

She follows me inside and sits at the kitchen table while I pour us both glasses of milk and set out a plate of my aunt's cookies.

Molly picks up a cookie, then laughs. "I just realized this has been the lead-in to almost every important conversation you and I have had. Is this another one?"

"Maybe?" I reply. "That depends on you."

She frowns. "What do you mean?"

I hesitate, trying to gauge her mood. Still more curious than anything else. "How much Sovereign stuff has your mother made you learn so far?"

Now alarm creeps in. "Not as much as she'd like, but a bunch. Why? You're not still—"

"Thinking of asking you to take over? No." She relaxes, so I continue. "But Rigel—and Healer Ava, and Shim—are right that all my duties have been stressing me out. They think one reason Faxon affected me so badly was that my mind was already stretched so thin. I've promised them to hand off as much as I can. Kyna's agreed to take over most of the admin stuff as soon as she finishes her current research project, but I'd really like it if you could help out, too."

She regards me suspiciously. "How? With what?"

"I thought we could figure that out together. Now that you won't be busy every day after school, I could sort of...mentor you? Instead of cheer practice, you can watch me do the Sovereign stuff I've been doing every day and decide which things you're willing to help with or think you might be good at. If we can eventually start sharing the load, I could almost have a life again—more than lately, anyway."

Molly sits back in her chair, relieved but thoughtful. "So sort of on-the-job training? Mum'll be ecstatic if I tell her—which I guess I'll have to." She grimaces.

"Okay, the one sour note might be making her happy." I can't suppress a grin.

She grins back. "I guess I can live with that, if you really think I can help you out."

"I really do. Thanks, Molly. I promise not to push."

"*Not* worried about that, trust me," she says with a chuckle. "You've insisted on taking on way too much, for way too long. I'll do my best to make you less of a control freak, a little at a time."

I jump up and give her a hug. "Thank you! I'm *so* lucky to have you as a sister. This will make Rigel really happy, too."

It does. That evening we go on our first real date in forever, my duties have kept me so busy lately. He's taking me to The Rib House, Jewel's only "fancy" restaurant, so I save my news about Kyna and Molly to tell him over dinner.

"Finally!" he exclaims after I explain. "I just wish we hadn't had to practically lose each other to make you see how necessary this is."

We spend the rest of the meal happily discussing all the things we want to do together once I have more free time in my schedule. Then, on the drive home, we stop at the arboretum for yet another excellent makeout session. Rigel uses the climate-control app on his omni so the cold won't cut it short, since we still have some catching up to do.

"Mm," he finally says after a good twenty minutes of kissing. "Think we can plan on more evenings like this one in the future?"

"Absolutely," I murmur, leaning against him. "The worst thing about being Sovereign has been all the time it's kept us from spending together. If everything works out the way I hope with Kyna and Molly, maybe we can go back to how things were in the beginning, when I was just a Princess."

Smiling, he shakes his head. "No, you've grown way beyond the person you were then. So have I. Now our future will be even bigger and brighter than we ever could have imagined back then."

"You're right," I agree with all my heart. "It will. We'll make sure of it. Together."

Together, he agrees, lowering his lips to mine for another kiss. *Always.*

About the Author

New York Times and USA Today bestselling author Brenda Hiatt writes novels of sparkling romantic adventure spanning Regency England, Americana, contemporary teen science fiction and more. Which ever you pick up, you'll find excitement, romance and, always, an uplifting happy ending. In addition to writing, Brenda is passionate about embracing life to the fullest. She enjoys scuba diving (she has over 60 dives to her credit), Taekwondo (where she's currently working toward her 4th degree black belt), hiking, traveling…and reading, of course!

For a free Starstruck short story and the earliest news about Brenda Hiatt's books, subscribe to her newsletter at: brendahiatt.com/subscribe

Connect with Brenda at:
brendahiatt.com

www.ingramcontent.com/pod-product-compliance
Lightning Source LLC
Chambersburg PA
CBHW051254210726
48287CB00002B/496